THE
TRANQUILLITY
ALTERNATIVE

ALLEN STEELE

ACE BOOKS, NEW YORK

This Ace Book contains the complete text of the original hardcover edition. It has been completely reset in a typeface designed for easy reading, and was printed from new film.

Excerpt from *Across the Space Frontier* by Cornelius Ryan, copyright © 1952 by Crowell-Collier Publishing Company, 1980 renewed by Viking Penguin Inc. Used by permission of Viking Penguin, a division of Penguin Books USA Inc.

Excerpt from *You Will Go to the Moon* by Mae and Ira Freeman, copyright © 1959 by Mae Freeman and Ira Freeman. Reprinted by permission of Random House, Inc.

THE TRANQUILLITY ALTERNATIVE

An Ace Book / published by arrangement with the author

PRINTING HISTORY
Ace hardcover edition / March 1996
Ace mass-market edition / April 1997

All rights reserved.
Copyright © 1996 by Allen M. Steele.
Cover art by Bob Eggleton
This book may not be reproduced in whole or in part, by mimeograph or any other means, without permission. For information address: The Berkley Publishing Group. 200 Madison Avenue, New York, NY 10016.

The Putnam Book World Wide Web site address is
http://www.berkley.com/berkley
Make sure to check out *PB Plug*, the science fiction/fantasy newsletter, at http//:www.pbplug.com

ISBN: 0-441-00433-4

ACE®
Ace Books are published by The Berkley Publishing Group, 200 Madison Avenue, New York, NY 10016.
ACE and the "A" design are trademarks belonging to Charter Communications, Inc.

PRINTED IN THE UNITED STATES OF AMERICA

10 9 8 7 6 5 4 3 2 1

IN MEMORY OF DOT HILL

The space station, with all its potentialities for exploration of the universe, for all kinds of scientific progress, for the preservation of peace or for the destruction of civilization, can be built. When the decision has been reached and the funds have been appropriated, the rest is only a matter of time. Many factors make the station inevitable—not the least the insatiable curiosity that has sent man across the oceans and finally into the air. Perhaps the military reasons for building such a station are in the long run the least significant, but in the existing state of the world they are the most urgent. Unless a space station is established with the aim of preserving peace, it may be created as an unparalleled agent of destruction—or there may not be time to build at all.

Under the impetus of their considerations, perhaps the space station will become a reality, not a generation hence, but in—say—1963.

—**Wernher von Braun**
Across the Space Frontier (1952)

If we had a base on the moon, either the Soviets must launch an overwhelming nuclear attack toward the moon from Russia two to two-and-a-half days prior to attacking the continental U.S., or Russia could attack the continental U.S. first, only and inevitably to receive from the moon some 48 hours later sure and massive destruction.

—**Brig. General Homer A. Boushey**,
director of advanced technology, USAF
(as quoted by *Aviation Week*;
September 29, 1958)

"My fellow Americans . . .

"Early this morning, a giant rocket was launched from a secret military installation in Germany. Unlike the V-2 missiles and buzz bombs which have been previously launched by the Axis against France and Great Britain, this rocket was a manned space plane, piloted by a single human being. This space plane, which is known to have been code-named the *Amerika Bomber,* was believed to have been carrying an eighty-ton incendiary bomb, which the Nazis intended to drop from high altitude above Earth's atmosphere into the New York City metropolitan area.

"This sneak attack on American soil, the most scurrilous assault against a civilian population since the beginning of this war, was unsuccessful. It was foiled because our allies in Europe became aware of Nazi Germany's efforts to develop such a weapon, and they warned us that an attack from outer space was forthcoming, thus allowing our own scientists to develop a countermeasure.

"At 5:35 A.M. Pacific War Time on the West Coast, another space plane, this one built by the United States Army Air Force, was launched from a secret location in the southwestern United States. I can now tell you that this manned spacefaring vessel was christened the *Lucky Linda,* and its single pilot was a young U.S. Navy captain named Rudy Sloman. In a feat of great daring, Captain Sloman flew his craft above Earth's atmosphere, whereupon he intercepted the *Amerika Bomber* above the Gulf of Mexico and destroyed the invading space plane before it could complete its foul mission.

"Captain Sloman then piloted the *Lucky Linda* through fiery reentry in American skies and successfully landed his craft at Lakehurst, New Jersey, not far from the city he saved. Because of Captain Sloman's heroism and the great efforts of the scientists and engineers who designed and built his craft, the United States of America has nothing to fear from Adolf Hitler and his Nazi war machine.

"I realize that many of you may be incredulous at this news, and that much of it sounds like the stuff of newspaper comic strips. Yet I assure you, as your President, that these events have occurred just as I have spoken of them. The first American has braved the airless reaches of outer space, and surely there will be more to follow.

"This is a great victory for our nation, a great day which will be remembered throughout history, and a great step into the future for the human race.

"May God bless us, and thank you."

ONE

Satellite Beach, Florida, is a small town on Cape Canaveral, located on Route A1A at the doorstep of Patrick Air Force Base. Once a tiny fishing village whose original name is long forgotten, it received its more glorious nomenclature with the beginning of the Space Age and the arrival of the Air Force. Even so, it's still little more than a wide spot in the road: a handful of residential neighborhoods and retiree trailer camps, some strip malls, the inevitable fast-food restaurants. One has to drive north to Cocoa Beach or south to Melbourne before finding much more on the highway than a line of motels built for visiting servicemen.

The night was cool—64 degrees, chilly by Floridian standards even at this time of year—but compared to the harsh Massachusetts winter he left behind two days ago, the man in Room 176 of the Satellite Beach Holiday Inn thinks it's a balmy summer evening. He had wanted to leave his motel room door open to allow in the sea breeze and the dull sound of the Atlantic surf from across the highway, but the plain-clothes security escort the company had assigned to him wouldn't hear of it. *Just normal precautions,* the private dick whom he had taken to thinking of as Mister Mom had said as he gently closed the door. *I'd rather keep it shut, sir, if you don't mind . . .*

Yes, he minded. In fact, he minded just about everything

right now. This motel, purposely selected because it was out
of the way and unlikely to be found by reporters covering
tomorrow's launch. Having Mister Mom for a roommate on
his last night on Earth for the next ten days, when he'd just
as soon be left alone until morning. And the job itself—Jesus,
why hadn't the Germans picked someone else instead of him?
Someone who really wanted to go to the Moon?

But if anyone had asked what the single most irritating
thing in his life was right now, the one thing that irked him
the most in a universe seemingly determined to make life
insufferable, he would have replied that his pizza was late.

It had been almost a half-hour now since Mister Mom—
whose real name, almost forgotten by now in his disdain, was
Mike Momphrey—had used his cellular phone to call some
no-name pizzeria just down A1A and place an order for a 12-
inch pizza. A half-hour ago, for Christ's sake . . . in Boston,
it would have been delivered ten minutes ago, and not just
because it came from Domino's. It was this kind of lousy
service that drove him straight up the wall. No wonder the
country was going down the toilet; twenty miles from the
place where rockets are launched into space, and you can't
get pizza delivered before it's cold.

Of course, he realized upon further reflection, if the country
wasn't heading down the tubes, he wouldn't be killing time
before he boarded a ferry rocket almost as old as he was.
Pizza and the American space program: they were much the
same thing these days, when you stopped to think about it. . . .

He didn't want to think about it. He tried to shut it out of
his head as he hunched over his Tandy/IBM, set up on a table
at the far end of the room and wired into the room phone's
dataport. Meanwhile, his jacket off and cast aside to expose
the black leather shoulder-holster strapped across his shirt,
Mister Mom lay on the single bed near the door watching the
ATS Evening News on TV. The volume was turned down low,
but the man at the computer could still hear the anchorman's
droning voice . . .

*American forces in Sarajevo reported heavy casualties to-
day due to mortar assaults upon the city airport. Five Ma-
rines were killed and six were wounded when a convoy was
attacked at dawn. U.S. Navy warplanes from the U.S.S.* Kitty

Hawk bombed suspected Serbian strongholds in the hills west of the city and claimed to have inflicted considerable damage, according to Pentagon spokesmen, but . . .

Nothing new. This foul little undeclared war had been going on for almost four years now, and the nightly body count had long since assumed the innocuousness of football scores. He shook his head as he concentrated on keeping up his end of the real-time conversation. About ten minutes ago he had signed onto Le Matrix, and his girlfriend was on-line right now. Her cyberspace presence was the only thing keeping him from going completely apeshit.

R U nervous? Mr. Grid had just asked. Her question appeared as a short line of type next to her screen name.

Fuck, yes, I'm nervous! he typed. Using obscenities was a TOS offense on Le Matrix, but they were in a private room where no one else could hear them, and Mr. Grid had long since become used to his salty language. **Wouldn't you be?**

In Los Angeles, entertainer and civil rights activist Michael Jackson led two thousand marchers through the city's South Central neighborhood, in a peaceful demonstration against alleged assaults against black residents by L.A. police officers. At the same time, across town in Hollywood, Jackson's common-law wife Brooke Shields held a press conference in front of the Dorothy Chandler Pavilion, in which she turned down last week's Oscar nomination for Best Actress as a protest against what she called American apartheid . . .

Why nervous? I'd LOVE to go to the Moon!:) she responds.

He scowls. He hates it when she uses smiley-faces. How many times has he told her that he considers cute on-screen emoticons to be the last resort of the illiterate? Sure, she's trying to cheer him up, but still . . .

A spokesman for Bob Dole told reporters today that the former President saw no wrongdoing in recent disclosures that he had accepted sizable contributions from European-owned companies during his 1992 reelection campaign. Mr. Dole, present in Wichita this morning for the dedication ceremonies of his presidential library, refused to answer questions from reporters . . .

Good, he types. **Then you can go . . . I'll stay here.**

Mr. Grid's response: **LOL! U sure are cranky tonight. What's your problem?**

Pizza is late, Thor200 replies, his fingers flying across the keyboard. **Ordered it 30 mins. ago. Getting pissed off.**

Pepperoni/olives/extra cheese?

He sighs, smiling despite himself. She knows him all too well. Sometimes he wonders, if he were to ever walk into a room where she was sitting, whether she would recognize him immediately. How many visual clues has he revealed about himself during the last eighteen months of their relationship? His age? His wire-rim glasses? The slight paunch around his middle, due in part to an addiction to one particular kind of pizza?

How did you possibly guess? he says.

King Charles arrived today in Washington, D.C., where he was warmly greeted at the White House by President Clinton. While the two men sat down to discuss the proposed Anglo-American Free Trade Agreement, Hillary Rodham Clinton escorted Princess Diana on a tour of the Library of Congress, where the Magna Carta is currently on display . . .

There's many things I know about you, m'lord. All your particular likes and dislikes.

He raises an eyebrow. Indeed, she does; although they might not recognize one another if they were in the same room together, he was aware of precisely how she would respond in the darkened bedroom of his ancestral manor, beneath silk sheets with a fire crackling in the hearth nearby. He knows the touch of her hands, the taste of her lips, the athletic muscles of her body . . .

A TV commercial interrupts this train of thought: a harried housewife with a throbbing headache, screaming for fast fast relief. He glances at Mister Mom; the security man intently watches this bit of Madison Avenue insipidity, apparently checking out the actress's boobs. To each his own, even if it's banal beyond belief. . . .

Another time, Countess, he types reluctantly. **When I conclude my business tomorrow eve, mayhap the Duke can come visit milady's chalet.**

A short pause, then another line appears on the screen: **The Countess would be most honored by his presence. Perhaps**

his visit to the far north provinces will prove ... inspirational.

He smiles and is about to reply in kind when there's a knock upon the door. Finally! He immediately scoots back his chair, then remembers his manners. BRB ... **pizza man's here.**

"I'll get it," Mister Mom says, already on his feet and walking toward the door, pulling on his jacket to hide the shoulder holster. "Who's there?" he calls out, his hand on the doorknob.

A muffled reply comes from the other side of the door. The security man slides the window curtain aside an inch to peer outside; satisfied, he unlatches the lock and opens the door. The college-age kid standing on the walkway outside the room cradles a red thermal pizza bag in his arms; in the parking lot behind him is an old Honda Civic, its hazard lights flashing against the darkness.

The kid glances at the order slip taped to the top of the bag. "Mr. Smith? Large cheese pizza, pepperoni and olives?"

"That's it, yeah." Mister Mom digs his left hand into his jacket pocket, pulls out a small roll of bills.

"That'll be ten-seventy-five, sir." The delivery boy reaches into the bag and carefully withdraws a brown cardboard box; as Mike peels off a ten and three ones and holds it out to him, the kid simultaneously thrusts the box into his hands.

A line of type appears on the screen: **Pizza? Mmmm ... cut me a slice, will you?**

Caught off-guard, Mister Mom tries to balance the box and at the same time keep the money from falling to the floor. "Oh, and I've got a coupon here, too," the kid says as his right hand disappears into the bag. The security man is still attempting to juggle pizza and cash when the kid pulls his hand out of the bag once more.

It is a weird sound—*thufft! thufft!* like tiny fists punching through a thick pillow—that makes him look up from the computer screen, just in time to see his bodyguard stagger back from the door. For an instant he thinks Mister Mom has simply tripped over something, but then the cardboard box slips out of his hands and topples to the floor, pizza spilling sloppily across the burnt-orange carpet as Mike Momphrey

falls against the dresser, his hands clutching at a large red
stain spreading across his chest, colliding with a heavy brass
table lamp and knocking it over as he . . .

He doesn't get to see the rest. In the next instant, two men
rush through the door before he has more than a fleeting impulse to run into the bathroom and lock the door. The men
have wool ski masks pulled over their faces: this is the only
impression he has of them before they tackle him and crush
him facedown against the floor, knocking the breath out of
his lungs.

He gasps, unable to shout, as he feels the carpet burn
against his face. His arms are savagely yanked behind his
back; his glasses are dislodged, leaving his vision blurred and
obscured.

He hears a thin plastic rip; then a length of duct tape is
wrapped tightly around his wrists, lashing them together. Before he can scream for help, gloved hands wrench his jaws
open and a wadded linen napkin is shoved into his mouth.

In blind panic now, tears streaming down his face, he begins to flail his legs in an absurd attempt to crawl to safety.
For an instant he remembers, in a crystalline moment of
panic-induced recollection, the time Eddie Patterson beat him
up in the playground back in third grade for calling him some
stupid name—if only because this moment of utter physical
helplessness so closely resembles that one . . . except that
when Eddie Patterson whaled the daylights out of him, two
dozen kids had been standing around, screaming their lungs
out until the teachers arrived to pull Eddie off him.

This assault, on the other hand, is totally silent. No one
says anything; everything being done to him is as methodical
as it is violent. Under other circumstances, he might have
actually admired their professionalism and efficiency. The
only voice he hears is that of the TV news anchor, resuming
his teleprompted monologue now that the commercials . . .

*Final countdown is underway at the Kennedy Space Center
in Florida for what may be the last manned American mission
to the Moon. Roxanne Leiterman reports from Cape Canaveral . . .*

Someone kneels against his back, pinning him to the floor.
He feels a hand tear open his right shirt sleeve. Twisting his

head around, he catches a glimpse of the delivery kid kicking aside the remains of the pizza as he eases the door shut behind him, being careful not to slam it. Efficient . . .

Last-minute preparations are being made for the launch of the NASA space ferry Constellation. *A routine monthly flight to the Wheel, like so many others that have gone before it, except that it will begin the closure of a significant chapter in space history . . .*

He feels an instant of wet coolness against his bare biceps, then a sharp pain as the tip of a syringe needle stabs into his arm. He shouts against the cloth lozenge stuck in his mouth and almost gags.

Four days from now, the U.S.S. Conestoga, *the last remaining moonship in the American space fleet, will depart from Space Station One to . . .*

"Turn it off," someone says.

The TV is switched off. He begins to feel lightheaded, almost giddy. In another moment, he doesn't care very much, for his universe is full of masked men with guns, and the only person who could have possibly helped him is wrapped up in bloody bedsheets and being hauled out the door.

No tip for the pizza kid, no sir . . .

One of his assailants bends down to gently lift his head from the carpet and shine a penlight in his eyes. "He's down for the count," he says, his voice muffled by the ski mask.

"Get that thing out of his mouth before he suffocates," someone else says. The cloth is tugged out of his jaws, leaving his mouth dry and sore. He tries to speak, but the words just can't make their way from his brain to his tongue.

"Water," he manages to whisper after a few moments of considerable mental effort. His request is ignored.

"All clear on the street."

"Okay, let's get him out of here before——"

"Problem." This voice comes from somewhere above him. "He's got someone on-line right now . . . they're waiting for an answer."

"Shit." A long pause. "Okay, no problem. The new guy can take care of it. He's coming in right now. Get the bag over his head."

Mr. Grid, he thinks, although thinking is very hard to do

just now. The Countess is waiting for him. Strangely enough, this is a comforting notion; she appears in his mind's eye as a pale goddess surrounded by a nimbus of soft light, her arms reaching out to hold him against her bosom, casting aside all evil and making the bad men go away.

Someone kneels beside him, lifts his head once again. In the last instant before a loose cotton bag closes around his face, he sees the motel room open once more . . .

And he watches himself walk into the room.

Then all is darkness and thick silence, and he falls asleep.

He waited until the team was gone, then quickly checked the room. They had done a good job, all things considered; the snatch had taken less than three minutes, and aside from the table lamp and the trampled remains of the pizza, there were no apparent signs of struggle. No bloodstain on the carpet; that was important. The murdered bodyguard had been wrapped up in bedsheets and spirited away before he could make too much of a mess.

A second man walked into the motel room. He had been standing outside, lingering in the shadows until the snatch team was gone and he was certain that the area was secure. He held the dead man's wallet in his left hand; all he had to do was to substitute his carefully prepared identification card and driver's license for the ones contained in the billfold.

The delivery boy from the pizza place down A1A had already called in sick from a nearby pay phone. He was so sick, in fact, that his vital signs had all flatlined, but that shouldn't bother the gators who would soon be discovering his corpse in an Indian River orange grove.

No one else had seen or heard anything.

The only loose end was a line of type on the screen of a laptop computer.

Hey, what's taking so long?

He walked over to the table and gazed down at the computer.

U **pig . . . you're leaving nothing for me!!**

"Clean up that stuff," he said, snapping his fingers and pointing to the table lamp and the ruined pizza. "Put some fresh sheets on the bed, too."

He sat down at the table, hesitated for a moment, then typed on the keyboard: **Sorry about that. The kid wanted a tip and the pizza was cold.**

He hit ENTER and waited for a reply. Behind him, the security man's substitute was setting the lamp upright and cleaning up the remains of the pizza. He had carefully studied his quarry for several months now, watching hours of surveillance videotape in order to imitate his mannerisms, listening to covertly recorded phone conversations to learn his verbal style. It hadn't been easy for his organization to unearth the on-line relationship between Thor200 and Mr. Grid, yet countless time spent on Le Matrix had finally put that missing piece in its proper place.

LOL! That figures! Did you cut me a slice?

He thought for a moment; then his fingers dashed across the keyboard: **^^^ Here you go. Watch out, it's sort of drippy.**

A short pause, then: **Mmmm! (Crunch.) Just the way I like it!**

He typed: **I have to go now . . . gotta eat and catch a few winks.**

OK . . . see you tomorrow night!

He sucked in his breath as he read this unexpected response. Mr. Grid was expecting to hear from him again within the next twenty-four hours, presumably from the Wheel; whoever this dink was, he was unlikely to accept no for an answer. Yet he had no other choice except to reply.

Okay . . . May be late, but I'll see you tomorrow night. Goodnite.

Nite . . . have a safe flight.:)

Mr. Grid's logon disappeared from the top of the screen a moment later, leaving him alone in the private conversation room. He backed out of Le Matrix, closing cyberspace windows until he reached the opening screen, then signed off the service.

He took a deep breath as he settled back in the chair. The bogus security man was busy remaking the second bed with spare linen he had found in the closet. "Everything okay?" he asked, looking up from tucking in the corners.

"Everything's cool." The doppelganger glanced at his reflection in the wall mirror above the bureau, once again admiring the results of the extensive plastic surgery he had undergone for this role. He was a perfect twin to the man who had just been abducted; tomorrow morning, no one would know the difference when he arrived at Merritt Island to take his place aboard the *Constellation.*

There was only one small detail remaining. He pulled a pocket phone from his jacket and laid it on the table next to the laptop computer. Then he tapped at the keyboard, entering the computer's hard disk, searching the files until he located an encrypted subdirectory.

Now he only had to wait.

"Turn on the tube, man," he said, practicing his new voice. "Maybe we can find a *Star Trek* rerun or something."

Transcript of closed hearings before the Armed Services Committee, United States Senate; June 15, 1950, Washington, D.C. Declassified by White House executive order; October 1, 1993.

From the testimony of General Omar Bliss, U.S. Army Air Force and former director of Operation Blue Horizon, and Dr. Wernher von Braun, Technical Director, U.S. Army Guided Missiles Development Group, Huntsville, Alabama.

Sen. Clayton J. Ewing (D., IA): The chair recognizes Senator Nixon.

Sen. Richard M. Nixon (R., CA): Thank you, Senator. General Bliss, Dr. von Braun, thank you for taking time away from your busy schedules to be with us here today . . .

Dr. von Braun: You're welcome, sir.

Gen. Bliss: The pleasure is all ours, Senator. We're glad you invited us.

Sen. Nixon: I'm certain that you gentlemen, along with your colleagues at the Huntsville facility, are aware of the great interest in manned space flight that has been generated recently within this country. I've read a book that was published last year . . . um, *The Conquest of Space,* by Willy Ley and Chesley Bonestell, which I understand was something of a bestseller . . . and my children have been bothering me to take them to see a new motion picture which has just opened. I think it's called *The Race to the Moon.* . . .

Dr. von Braun: It is called *Destination Moon,* Senator. With all due respect.

Sen. Nixon: Uh, yes, that's what I meant . . . Anyway, these forms of, ah, popular entertainment, along with the wartime success of Operation Blue Horizon under General Bliss's command, has led many people to believe that we could send men to the Moon within the next few years. On the other hand, there are just as many people who claim that putting men on the Moon is highly unlikely. This includes President Truman, who has called it . . . and I quote from yesterday's *Washington*

Star . . . "that crazy Buck Rogers stuff." So I ask you gentlemen, which is it?

Gen. Bliss: Senator Nixon, when our military space program got started nine years ago under the late Dr. Robert H. Goddard, a number of people here in Washington who were cleared for Blue Horizon believed that it was impossible to put a manned payload into orbit at all. Dr. von Braun met similar skepticism from certain officials of the German High Command. Less than three years later, skeptics on both sides were proven wrong when the *Amerika Bomber* and the *Lucky Linda* were launched on the same day.

Now, I won't pretend to claim that we could send men straight to the Moon, using present-day technology. Both the book and the motion picture you mentioned presuppose the existence of atomic-powered rockets, and we simply do not have those yet. But even at our current stage of astronautical know-how, we do believe it is possible to build a fleet of large, three-stage manned rockets, which in turn could be used to build a permanent orbital platform—a space station, if you will—which would enable us to construct vessels to take men to the Moon at some point in the not-so-distant future. The position paper given to the members of this Committee gives the details of our proposal.

Sen. Nixon: I've only had a chance to skim your report, General, and it's quite impressive. So is the estimation of the costs involved. Ten billion dollars is a considerable amount of money.

Dr. von Braun: This is only an approximation, Mr. Senator, but it includes costs for building three ferry rockets and the space station. It's also a long-range program spread over the next ten years, with completion of the space station—the Space Wheel, we call it—scheduled for 1960. This means that outlays for each fiscal year would average only one billion dollars.

Sen. Ewing: Thank you, Dr. von Braun. The chair recognizes Senator McCarthy.

Sen. Joseph R. McCarthy (R., WI): Talking about flying to the Moon is just fine and dandy, gentlemen, but I'm much more alarmed by new developments in Russia. Just three weeks ago the Communists announced that they had launched their first satellite—a Sputnik, they call it—into outer space. This seems to me to be much more critical than putting some people on the Moon, as laudable a goal as that may be. Dr. von Braun, can you tell us whether this Sputnik poses a possible threat to the security of the United States of America?

Dr. von Braun: The satellite the Soviet Union has launched does not, in itself, pose an imminent threat, Mr. Senator. The satellite contains little more than a shortwave radio transmitter. However, it does demonstrate the potential ability of the Soviet Union to place larger satellites, or even manned spacecraft of their own, in orbit above Earth.

Sen. McCarthy: And in your opinion, Dr. von Braun, could one of these . . . um, satellites . . . carry an atomic bomb?

Dr. von Braun: Yes, Mr. Senator, it is possible that it could do so. Former members of my rocketry group at Peenemunde are now working for the Soviet government in Russia, and I can attest to their technical expertise in these matters.

Sen. McCarthy: Then what good does it do for the United States to spend ten billion of the American taxpayers' money to build rocketships or a giant wagon wheel in outer space? The logic escapes me, Dr. von Braun.

Gen. Bliss: Senator, if you'll permit me to explain . . . One of the major purposes of the proposed space station would be to conduct high-altitude military surveillance. As you can read in the position paper, the space station would be placed in an equatorial orbit 1,075 miles above Earth, where it would complete a full orbit once every two hours. Although we feel it's unwise to position the station so that it could pass directly over the Soviet Union and the Iron Curtain countries, this means that station personnel could easily monitor naval activity in the southern Atlantic and Pacific oceans, as well as ground activity in China, the Philippines, and the Indonesian subcontinent.

Sen. McCarthy: So you believe we can use this space wheel of yours to keep tabs on what the Communists are doing in Southeast Asia?

Gen. Bliss: Yes, sir, I believe we can. Additionally, an orbital telescope aboard the space station, similar to ones presently being used at ground-based observatories for astronomical research, could be deployed for spying on Russian military activities. We believe that space telescopes like this could detect the presence of heavy-armor convoys, or even be refined enough to see their air bases.

Dr. von Braun: But this would not be the only purpose of the Space Wheel, Mr. Senator. It could also be used as a . . . uh, a stepping-stone, if you will, to the exploration of the Moon. In twenty-five years, perhaps less, we could use it for the construction of ships for a lunar expedition. In time we could even use the Wheel for the purpose of sending men to the planet Mars. . . .

Sen. McCarthy: That's fine and dandy for kiddie movies, Dr. von Braun, but right now this Committee is far more interested in the military uses of outer space. And for the record, I'd like to know whether your fellow Germans at the Army's Huntsville facility have been checked for possible ties to the international Communist conspiracy.

Gen. Bliss: I assure you, sir, the backgrounds of my men have been thoroughly examined by the FBI, as part of their admission to this country under Operation Paperclip. . . .

Sen. McCarthy: I want positive proof of this, General Bliss.

Gen. Bliss: And I'll be more than happy to provide it, Senator. For the record, though, I'd like to repeat something I said over a year ago to the House Committee on Science and Technology: Military advantage has always rested on taking the high ground, and space is the new high ground. America must take this hill, lest it risk losing its freedom.

Sen. Nixon: I quite agree, General. . . .

TWO

The house was almost forty years old, and nothing about it seemed atypical of Florida beachside cottages built in the fifties. Made of weatherbeaten pine whose boards had warped and been replaced and repainted many times, it was a two-story red split-level with a garage and a storage area on the ground floor and two bedrooms, a den, and a small walk-in kitchen on the second floor. A TV antenna rose from the slanted flat roof; sliding glass doors led to a wide porch elevated on stilts above a crushed-seashell driveway. The house was isolated from the rest of the island by low marshlands, and the white sands and dunes of the vacant beach lay only a few yards away from the back door.

There was nothing unusual about the house except for its location on Merritt Island, near the southern perimeter of the Robert F. Kennedy Space Center. Within sight of the porch were the old ICBM test pads, now either dismantled or used primarily for sounding rockets; gantry towers for *Hercules*- and *Titan*-class cargo rockets rose from the coastline a little farther north, while farthermost in the distance, near the giant white cube of the Vehicle Assembly Building, were the twin Atlas-C launch complexes.

Once, during the fifties and sixties, there had been dozens of houses like this one, built by the Army Corps of Engineers to house military and civilian personnel who had worked countless millions of man-hours building those launch pads. When the space program started winding down in the seventies and the U.S. Space Force was phased out and gradually replaced by NASA, almost all of those cottages were destroyed, most by bulldozers or the occasional hurricane, a few by prototype Tomahawk cruise missiles during offshore Navy tests. Only this lone house was allowed to remain standing, for although no one had lived here year-round in quite some time, it had earned a small place in history, eloquently summarized by its name. It was called, very simply, the Beach House, and it was the last place on Earth where many astronauts stayed the night before they left home for outer space.

The traditional pre-launch barbecue had been held out on the porch earlier that evening; as usual, it drew a small group of invited guests—senior pad technicians, launch controllers, the mission director, and so forth—and for a little while it almost seemed to Gene Parnell as if the good old days had returned. Virtually everyone at the barbecue was an old China hand from way back when the space program was young and the new frontier was there for the taking; they all had tall stories to tell, and they loved to party.

Yet as the sun set and the last few beers were cracked open, a full moon began to rise above the gentle Atlantic surf and it seemed to Parnell that everyone was reminded of just how much had been lost already, and how much more would be lost tomorrow. The jovial atmosphere became sullen and morose and, finally, just a little ugly when Joe Clark and Keith Baldini, two firing-room techs who had worked alongside each other at Launch Control since the Project Luna days, got into a political argument which soon disintegrated into a shouting match that got dangerously close to being settled with fists until the mission director separated the two men and told them to go home. They weren't drunk—they were too professional to get ripped the night before a launch—only angry at the Moon and what their old dreams had bought them, and their demoralization was quietly shared by many there.

At any rate, the fight effectively ended the party. Everyone left shortly after that, stopping by to shake hands with Parnell and give Judith a quick hug before climbing into their Jeeps or sports cars or family vans and blowing the hell out of there, because the Beach House harbored just one too many ghosts for anyone to hang around the place for very long.

This left Gene and Judy alone in the place for the night. In days past, they might have been joined by another astronaut and his or her spouse; they would have shared the Beach House, sleeping in the separate bedrooms until a few hours before dawn when someone drove out to fetch the crewmates and bring them to Operations and Checkout for breakfast, the final mission briefing, suit-up, and walk-out. But Jay Lewitt, the *Conestoga*'s flight engineer, was the only other crew member who had made an appearance, and he and Lisa had left long before the party had broken up. Cristine Ryer didn't come at all, though, and the absence of the mission pilot was noted by Judy as they cleaned up the paper plates and empty beer cans left on the porch.

"She's not a big favorite around here, is she?" Judy was in the kitchen, scraping gummy baked beans and gnawed pork ribs into a compost can before tossing the plates into the recycling bin. "I mean, nobody seemed particularly upset when she didn't show up."

"What, honey?" Gene Parnell pretended not to hear by dumping an armful of Bud Light cans in another recycling bin near the sink. How everything had changed; he remembered when, during another Beach House party many years ago, the pilot of Eagle Four had provided entertainment by lining up empty beer cans on the porch railing and inviting everyone to pick them off with his favorite Smith & Wesson deer rifle. That type of thing didn't happen anymore, now that NASA had been dragged, kicking and screaming, into the era of environmental consciousness. . . . "I didn't quite hear you."

"You heard me." Judy dropped the last plate into the bin and turned to the sink to wash her hands. "No one likes Ryer, and I don't think she likes them either, but nobody wants to tell me why."

"That's because no one likes Cris," he said, hoping that would get her off the subject.

"Don't play stupid with me. . . ."

"I'm not playing stupid, babe," he insisted, lying for all

he was worth. "Cris just isn't . . . I dunno, she just isn't much of a team player. She follows her own drummer and people know it. That's all."

Judy didn't say anything for a few minutes. She picked up a box of detergent and carefully poured a handful of powder into the dishwasher, which was filled with pots and skillets. Watching her, Parnell was suddenly struck by how much older she now seemed, how gray her hair had become. In the thirty-four years they had been married, he had never really perceived his wife as anything except the sexy college girl he'd met shortly after graduating from Annapolis. But that was 1961 and this was 1995; their daughter Helen was now older than Judy had been when they walked beneath the crossed swords of a Navy honor guard on their way out of the wedding chapel. Judith was no crone, but neither was she the lithe Wellesley student he had met at a long-forgotten mixer.

Without realizing he was doing so, he found himself contemplating his reflection in the louvered glass of the kitchen window. Yeah, he had grown old, too. Despite a lifelong regimen of jogging two or three miles each morning before breakfast, there was a small pillow beneath his T-shirt where his waist had once been. His crew cut was salt and pepper, and the short beard he had cultivated years ago was now as white as beach sand. He made the pillow disappear for a moment by sucking in his gut, but nothing could be done about the crow's-feet that appeared at the corners of his eyes when he did so. The last time he looked in a mirror, he saw Cary Grant; now George C. Scott was staring back at him.

"I've heard things about her," Judy said as she latched the dishwasher door and pushed the button; the ancient Maytag grumbled like a freight train leaving a siding. "I've heard she's . . . ah, one of the boys. Is that true?"

It took Parnell a moment to realize that she was still talking about Cristine Ryer. He shrugged as he turned away from the window. There was still some beer left in the fridge; he had had only two this evening and, what the hell, he wasn't the guy doing the flying tomorrow morning. "Been listening to the grapevine again, haven't we?" he said as he pulled out a can. "Want one?"

"Sure." Judy caught the Budweiser he tossed her; even at fifty-four, she was still quick on her feet. Leave it to all those tennis games with other NASA wives to keep her body sound and her hearing sharp. "And don't try changing the subject."

"I'm not." He leaned against a counter as he popped open a can for himself. "I'm just avoiding it, that's all."

"Gene . . ."

"Look, babe . . ." He sighed. "Remember Tommy Sidwell? The guy who rescued twelve men aboard the Wheel when that blowout happened in . . . what was it, '66? The press made him into a hero back then. Cover of *Newsweek,* lunch at the White House with Nixon, the whole bit. Then some asshole from the *Chicago Tribune* discovered that he had a boyfriend and put it all over the front pages."

Judy nodded, her face somber. "I remember."

Gene nodded. "I knew Tom . . . and, yeah, I knew he was queer. So did a lot of other guys who worked with him. It didn't change things for us, because he was a good astronaut and . . . well, when you're up there, that's all that really counts. But after the press blew his cover and Carson started with the jokes, the Space Force threw him out so fast he didn't have time to empty his locker."

Judith didn't say anything. She recalled Tommy Sidwell; once on the short-list for Luna One, reduced within a year to making cameo appearances on *Laugh-In*. He had died of acute alcoholism ten years ago, his obituary a footnote in the same newspapers that had brought him low. "So you don't ask questions like that," Gene went on, "because it's nobody's business what people do when they're not on active duty. What Cris does on her own time—"

"Is her own business," Judith finished, nodding her head. "I understand."

Parnell stared down at his beer. There was more to Cristine Ryer's situation than Judith could have possibly picked up from the tennis court backscatter . . . but this was none of his business, even if Ryer was scheduled to be his left-seater a few days from now. It was all NASA internal politics, anyway, and he didn't want to ruin his last night on Earth for a while by talking about it.

He took a deep breath. "Hey, what do you say we go down

to the beach for a while? Catch a little moontan?''

Judy made a face. "Aw, Gene, c'mon . . . I hate it when you want to . . ."

"Just for a walk. Leave the blanket behind." She had resisted making love on the beach ever since the second night after they moved into their house on Captiva Island, just a few years ago. Despite the romantic allure of that interlude in the Gulf Coast dunes, she had been itching for days afterward. "C'mon, babe," he said, stepping closer to her. "My intentions are strictly honorable . . ."

"I bet." She grinned as she pushed him aside and headed for the porch door. "If I get another rash, I'll send my gynecologist to beat you up."

"Deal." Gene glanced through the open door of the master bedroom as he followed her toward the porch. The den chandelier cast a ray of light across the sagging mattress on the king-size bed, and he smiled to himself.

He hadn't made any promises about what he might do later.

In many ways, it was a night like many other nights: moonlight rippling upon the low tide, casting silver highlights on the waves as they crashed onto the beach; the distant lights of freighters and passenger cruisers, the smell of salt air and brine and seaweed and, just a few miles up the shoreline, the rocket itself, temporarily captured within angled searchlight beams, a tiny silver-blue dart poised on its fins.

None of this was unfamiliar to Parnell. In fact, it was almost akin to *déjà vu,* although the last time he had gone up was for a short visit to the Wheel in connection with his duties as the Flight Director of the American half of Project Ares. That had been back in '74; three months later he had resigned from active flight status, and in the twenty-one years since, he had reported to work at an office which wasn't inside a pressure compartment. Sometimes he had actually relished the fact that he didn't have to subconsciously worry about the source of every breath he took, or that the food on his plate was what he wanted to eat today and not part of a rigorous menu, or that he could take a shower every morning or flush a commode as often as he wanted without having to fret about water conservation.

Sometimes . . . but not always. Walking along the beach, shells crunching beneath the soles of his moccasins, cold ocean surf occasionally washing up around his ankles, he looked up to study the familiar winter constellations—Virgo rising from the east, Leo almost directly overhead, a thin ring around the Moon which almost touched Mars, hinting at rain showers later tonight—and yet his gaze kept returning to the distant rocket.

It had been a long time. Maybe just a little too long.

"Penny for your thoughts?" Judy asked.

He shrugged. "A nickel will buy you my life story."

"Heard it already. Been around for most of it." They had been silent since they left the Beach House, walking side by side along the dark shore. "Scared about tomorrow?"

"Uh-uh. Not about tomorrow." Nor was there any reason for him to be scared. The *Constellation* was a reliable old workhorse; it had made at least three or four dozen orbital missions in its lifetime, and Atlas-C's dated back to 1967. It wasn't like the Atlas-B's, whose third-stage nuclear engines had frightened the piss out of everyone who had ever ridden in them, until they were finally decommissioned in '65 following not-unjustified protests by Barry Commoner and Common Cause. And it sure as hell wasn't the *Discovery,* but then again the *Discovery* had been permanently grounded by White House directive after her sister-ship, the *Challenger,* had exploded shortly after liftoff. That was back in '86; since then no one had even suggested using solid-rocket boosters for man-rated spacecraft.

The Atlas-C ferries, though, had been built to last. Although they were now somewhat obsolete, no one had ever been killed riding one of them. Better safe than sorry: so went the general consensus. On the other hand, the Atlas-C represented the last time anyone within NASA had seriously proposed trying anything new at all. . . .

"Not worried about tomorrow, huh? Well, I suppose that's good." Judy took a deep breath as she folded her arms across her chest. "Got a letter from Gene Jr. yesterday. He says he broke up with his old girlfriend but now has a new one."

"Uh-huh," Parnell said. He was still gazing at the distant launch pad. "What's her name?"

"Her name's Spike," Judith said calmly. "She's the lead singer with an L.A. band called The Doggy Position. Gene says she's got some interesting tattoos . . . oh, and he says he wants to quit his job and open a porn shop in Hollywood. Isn't that nice?"

"Well, yeah, I guess he . . . what?"

Judy punched him in the arm. "Sucker!"

"Jesus, honey . . ." He rubbed at his biceps where she smacked him. Their younger child had been a constant source of worry to them since the age of fifteen, but after being expelled from two private schools, dropping out of one college, being busted for selling marijuana at another, hitchhiking across the country behind a Moby Grape concert tour as a self-proclaimed Grape Nut, and finally cleaning up his act to settle down in Los Angeles and manage a retro-sixties boutique, there was little the kid could do anymore that would surprise Gene. Except maybe this . . . "You're not serious, are you?"

"No, I'm not serious. He's still got his job and Veronica, even though I still think she's a little slut." Judy laughed a little as she nuzzled up against him and gave his arm a small kiss. "Just wanted to make sure you're still with me."

"Umm . . . yeah." He put his arm around her, and regretted his earlier thoughts about her as an old lady. Middle-aged or not, Judy Parnell the astronaut wife was the same woman as Judy Lindstrom the Ivy League debutante. Same wicked sense of humor. "So long as you're not serious about the porn shop."

"Just kidding. I promise." Her laughter died and she was quiet for a moment. "You're worried about the mission, aren't you? Don't bullshit me, sailor . . . something's eating you up inside."

It always came down to this: the eleventh-hour attack of nerves. The crossing of the Rubicon, so they say, except he had been down to this particular river before. In '62, when he had received his orders to join the F-4 Phantom wing aboard the *Enterprise* during Vietnam; in '65, after he had been recruited into the USSF and been posted aboard the Wheel for extended astronaut training; in '69, when he went to the Moon as mission commander of Luna Two; in '72, when he returned to the Moon as commander of Tranquillity Base. All those times, he had accepted his duty to his country, leaving his wife and kids behind. And every time, he had taken a last stroll on the beach with Judy. . . .

Until 1973, that is, when they asked him if he wanted to go to Mars and he said no. By then he was sick of space; all he wanted to do was stay home to raise a family, play a few holes of golf, and go to sleep every night next to his wife instead of simply talking to her once a week on a secure downlink. He turned down Mars and was given an office job in return, and since then, with the exception of one quick trip to the Wheel to shake hands with some Russian cosmonauts in the spirit of McGovern-era detente, the only time he sat in a pilot's seat was in the nine-year-old single-engine Beechcraft Debonair he used for commuting twice a week from Fort Meyers to the Cape.

And now, closing in on his sixties, here he was again. Same beach. Same wife. Same Atlas-C. Same goddamn Moon . . .

"Late for the sky," he murmured.

Judy looked at him sharply. "What did you say?"

"Old song," he said quietly. "From Helen's record collection . . . Jackson Browne, I think. I kind of liked it, so I taped it and put it in the car. Used to listen to it now and then." He tried to recall the lyrics, but couldn't summon them up: "Nah, nah, nah nah nah . . . late for the sky, tah dah, dah dah dah . . ."

Judy giggled and he cast her a stern look. "I'm sorry, hon," she said, "but if that's as hip as you can get . . ."

"Would you rather I started singing . . . uh, the Sex Pistols? Hip enough?"

She smiled sweetly at him. "Dear, they broke up ten years ago. Johnny Rotten does Toyota commercials now."

"Oh, that's who he is? Okay, so I'm hopeless. Gimme a break." He took his arm from her shoulders and tucked his hands in his pockets. "The point is, I don't know if I'm really cut out for this anymore."

Judy slid her hand into the crook of his left arm. "C'mon, Gene. You aced the physicals and you did fine during retraining. You told me yourself that flying the simulators was a breeze. *Conestoga*'s the same ship you've commed before, and nobody's asking you to do much more than ride the old heap. What's the problem?''

The problem was that he was being sent up as a living relic of the glory days, not unlike the *Constellation* or the *Conestoga*. A little older, not quite as obsolete, yet nonetheless sent aloft as a last-gasp public relations stunt for a federal agency that had lost its sense of purpose along with stable funding from Capitol Hill. His first flight assignment in more than two decades was to carve the epitaph for the American space program, and the only items that had been omitted from the crew's personal manifest were a hammer and a chisel.

The rocky plains of *Mare Tranquillitatis* would be the tombstone for a dream that had died hard.

He glanced away from the launch pad. His eyes traveled across the ocean waters until, reluctantly, he found himself gazing up at the trapper's moon. The old whoreson himself, the Man in the Moon, was leering down at him from across a quarter of a million miles of vacuum: *Hey, buddy, I'm waiting for you . . . c'mon back and we'll trip the light fantastic, one last time.*

"No problem," he murmured, lowering his head. "Just thinking aloud, that's all.''

Judy seemed to want to say something, but she remained quiet. Instead, she tugged against Gene's arm to turn him around. "Okay, sailor," she purred. "Time to go to bed. If I let you stay up much longer, you'll miss your wake-up call.''

Turning around, Gene allowed his wife to begin dragging him back toward the Beach House. He glanced at his watch—manufactured in Japan, he reflected, but wasn't everything these days?—and noted that it was nearly nine o'clock. He was due at the O&C Building at three-thirty A.M. sharp. "Christ, I'm still wide-awake.''

"You won't be after I get through with you," Judy said. She let her hand slip from his arm and briefly caress his buttocks, and Parnell grinned despite himself. Some rituals were still as valid today as they had been twenty years ago.

Sometime in the middle of the night, he awoke from an unremembered dream to hear rain pattering on the roof. He stared at the ceiling for nearly an hour, thinking of nothing except how he would miss this simple, commonplace sound, before he fell asleep in his wife's arms once again.

From The New York Times; *April 11, 1956*

U.S. LAUNCHES GIANT PASSENGER ROCKET; SUCCESSFUL MAIDEN FLIGHT ORBITS EARTH AS WHITE HOUSE ANNOUNCES NEW SPACE FORCE

By Joel Brodsky

(Special to The New York Times*)*

MERRITT ISLAND, Fla., April 10—Rising on a column of smoke and flame amid a thunderous roar which drowned out the excited shouts of onlookers, the U.S.S. *Constitution* was launched this morning from the U.S. Air Force Proving Grounds at Cape Canaveral, carrying six men on a test mission into Earth orbit.

Six hours later, after circling the planet twelve times at a record altitude of 185 miles, the giant rocket's winged third stage successfully landed like a jet aircraft on a runway only a few miles from the launch pad.

When it lifted off from Cape Canaveral at 8:16 A.M. EST, the *Constitution* was an enormous three-stage rocket, 265 feet tall and weighing 7,000 tons—the height of a 24-story office building and the approximate weight of a light cruiser. It was propelled into the sky by 14,000 tons of liquid fuel, and less than a minute after ignition it broke the sound barrier as it hurtled over the Atlantic on its way to orbit above the equator.

The rocket's first and second stages, discarded by the *Constitution* during its fiery ascent, automatically parachuted into the Atlantic Ocean, where they were recovered by U.S. Navy vessels.

During the flight, the rocket's six-member crew radioed brief reports to receiving stations around the world, telling anxious listeners that they were safe and that their condition was fine. Captain Charles B. Yeager, the mission commander and pilot, then guided his craft through the critical retrofire and reentry maneuvers through Earth's atmosphere, whereupon the third-stage glider gracefully touched down on a specially constructed runway on the north end of Merritt Island.

"We feel just great," Captain Yeager told reporters shortly after he and his teammates emerged from their craft. "It was a nice, smooth ride all the way."

Other members of the crew were Commander Edw. A. Graham, Jr., co-pilot; Lt. Casey Hamilton, flight engineer; Lt. Kenneth A. Moore, flight mechanic; Sgt. Richard Dunning, mission specialist; and Dr. Walter Kahn, flight surgeon.

One hour after the *Constitution* touched down in Florida, the White House formally announced its intent to ask Congress to approve a plan to split off the Air Force's space program into a separate military branch, which would be called the United States Space Force. In a brief statement to the press, President Eisenhower claimed that the mission's success had proved that the technological capability exists to pursue "a vigorous and ambitious program for the conquest of outer space."

"I have no further doubts now that this country has the ability to build a manned space station," Mr. Eisenhower said. "Because such a station will be vital to our national security, I believe that this administration, along with Congress, should approve the proposed Pentagon plan to establish a U.S. Space Force as the principal government agency behind this noble effort."

Mr. Eisenhower said that he will ask Congress to approve his bill to build a fleet of five "ferry rockets" like the *Constitution* over the next four years and outlay $10 billion over the next seven years for the construction of a wheel-shaped station that would become operational by 1963. The House and Senate had approved a similar plan in 1953, but the President had vetoed the earlier proposal, saying then that the technology for advanced space missions had not yet been proven.

No official statement has yet been released by Premier Bulganin or other Kremlin officials in the Union of Soviet Socialist Republics. The United Nations ambassador, Sergei Titov, was quick to remind reporters that the U.S.S.R. sent an unmanned probe to the Moon almost four years ago. He also pointed out that the *Constitution*'s orbital trajectory took it three times over Russia and its eastern European satellites.

"The goals of my country in space have always been and shall remain peaceful," Mr. Titov said. "By its very name, however, President Eisenhower has signified the hostile nature of the U.S. Space Force, and by calling this a 'conquest,' American imperialism has been blatantly revealed."

White House spokesmen declined to respond to Mr. Titov's remarks.

THREE

In the dark hours before dawn, automobiles began moving out from the mainland communities of Titusville and Cocoa and the Orlando suburbs, their headlights forming a swift luminescent current that flowed eastward toward the Kennedy Space Center. Each bearing a NASA employee window sticker, they finally became two solid lines that drove over the Indian River on the NASA Causeway West to Merritt Island, where they passed citrus groves and wild marshes as they converged toward the distant spotlights of the launch center.

The four-lane road was wet from the brief rain shower that had passed over the Cape a couple of hours earlier; headlights cast slick reflections off the asphalt as windshield wipers beat away the last drizzle. Along the way they passed tents and RV's parked on the shoulders of the causeway: the campsites of the faithful, the relative handful of diehard space buffs who still came from near and far to witness major rocket launches. Not too many years ago, so many people used to show up for launches that the U.S. Space Force had to issue camping permits three or four months in advance, and even then many people tried to camp out in the grassy median between the road lanes. This was no longer necessary; over the last decade the crowds diminished in size and number until now only a few dozen pilgrims journeyed to Merritt Island.

As she drove past the NASA Visitors Center—itself beginning to look seedy and run-down—Cris Ryer noted that antispace protesters had once again insinuated themselves among the spectators. Six or seven cars on the right shoulder of the road surrounded a few tents that could have been mistaken for a campsite of space buffs until one spotted the signs and banners: LEAVE THE MONEY ON EARTH and ABOLISH NASA NOW! and STOP THE MADNESS! and (her personal favorite) NO ATOMS ON THE MOON! Most of the protesters were sound-asleep, curled up in sleeping bags inside tents made of light-weight materials which were spin-off products of the space program. A bearded, long-haired young man in jeans and a Mexican serape stood by the roadside, pounding metronomically against a leather Indian drum as he solemnly stared at the NASA employees reporting in for the morning shift.

"Hey, Cris! Look!" Laurell turned around in the passenger seat to point at the hippie. "It's my cousin Igor! Look, it's my cousin! Quick, pull over . . . !"

"Laur . . ." Cris began.

"No, c'mon! I swear to God, it's Igor!" Before Cris could stop her, Laurell rolled down the DeLorean's side window and stuck her head out. "Hey, look out!" she screamed from the car. "Look out! There's a gator right behind you!"

The kid jumped a few inches, nearly dropping his drum as he looked back in terror. Laurell was in convulsions; Cris had to roll up the window for her, she was laughing so hard.

"You're such an asshole," Cris murmured, grinning despite herself. Only Laurell could pull off such a gag; a theater major in college before she had entered law school, she had a knack for convincing almost anyone of the most bald-faced lie. This talent for instant persuasion had made her a good trial lawyer. It had also helped to convince a lot of conservative male colleagues in the Florida Bar Association that she was straight.

"That I am . . ."

"That you are. Now shut up and look serious for the nice man." Laurell got herself under control as Cris slowed down for the security checkpoint at Gate 3 and rolled down the driver's side window for the uniformed guard who stepped from the gatehouse to shine a flashlight inside the DeLorean.

A white-helmeted MP stood behind him at curbside, his right hand lingering near the .45 automatic holstered in his Sam Browne belt. Cris held up her plastic ID badge; Laurell found her VIP Visitor's badge and showed it through the windshield. The guard carefully examined both badges, then checked them off on his clipboard.

"Thank you, Captain Ryer," he said as he gave her a quick salute. "Good luck on your mission." He waved them through the checkpoint; the MP added his own salute as they drove past him.

Laurell glanced back at the guards. "Gee, and he didn't even ask if we were sisters."

Cris smiled again. Laurell knew she was nervous; ever since they had left their house in Titusville, Laurell had been making wisecracks, singing along with the classic rock station in Orlando and talking back to the DJ, all in a futile attempt to take the edge off the moment. It hadn't always worked, but then again Laurell had always played the irreverent cut-up next to Cris's disciplined Air Force officer.

The sisters remark was an old standby, going back to the beginning of their relationship almost three years ago when they had met at a private gym in Titusville which catered covertly to the local gay community. There weren't too many places in the area where two lesbian women could go during a long courtship without being accosted by straight single men, and fewer still where an obviously gay relationship would be tolerated. Thus the alibi of sisterhood; both Cris and Laurell were in their late thirties, and—until Laurell had dyed her hair—both were blondes, tall, and athletic-looking. Since they vaguely resembled each other, the pretense of being siblings made a good cover story.

But there were differences. Cris glanced again at her lover, still not quite used to Laurell's recent change in appearance. A few weeks ago Laurell had sprung almost ten grand for cosmetic breast reduction, a surgical operation that had left her almost as flat-chested as a prepubescent teenager. Laurell insisted that she'd done so because big tits had put her on an unequal footing—no pun intended—with her male counterparts at the law firm. It was one more yuppie fad that had emerged from California, popular among female attorneys in particular, but Cris wasn't quite certain that her companion's newfound androgyny had nothing to do with their relationship.

"You're such a guy," she murmured.

Laurell looked away from the window. "Aw, c'mon, Cris . . . you're not still pissed, are you?"

"Oh, no, no, I'm not pissed." She gripped the leather steering wheel more firmly as she shook her head. "I mean, I was married to Carl for two years, wasn't I? I should be used to a male chest by now. . . ."

"Jesus. You're still pissed." Laurell closed her eyes, putting her hand to her forehead as she sighed. "Look, I've explained to you . . . it's just something I did, all right? I always hated having boobs. I didn't like sleeping on them, I didn't like it when they started to sag, and I really didn't like guys checking me out all the time. . . ."

"I know, I know." Cris had heard it all before. "But if you could have worked out a little more, maybe . . ."

"It wouldn't have done a thing. Those mammaries were there for keeps." Laurell smiled a little. "Hey, at least I had enough money to get it done right. If I only had five grand in the bank . . ."

"Then you would have been an Amazon. Right." It was an old joke that Cris was tired of hearing.

"You're such a bitch sometimes . . ."

"You got it. I'm a bitch. That's me." The line of traffic was creeping steadily toward the cloverleaf intersection of the east-west causeways and the Kennedy Parkway, where the highways split in four directions at the center of the island. Two hours before dawn and there was already a small gridlock within KSC. At least the rain had finally let up; with any luck, the clouds would move out to sea long before the launch window closed.

Cris found herself staring in the direction of the Atlas-C launch complex, where the *Constellation* awaited her arrival. One more mission, and she would be another ex-Air Force astronaut with the abbreviation "ret" next to her name and former rank. It wasn't supposed to end this way. Crash landings, catastrophic launch aborts, Criticality One accidents—those risks she had willingly taken over the past fifteen years, well aware that any one of them could snuff out her life in a second.

It had never occurred to her that falling in love would be the finish of her career.

She felt Laurell's hand on her arm. "I'm sorry," her companion said. "I didn't mean to get on your case like that. It's just that I hate to see you . . ."

Her voice trailed off. Cris forced a smile as she grasped the back of Laurell's hand. "It's okay," she said softly. "Don't worry about it. We'll get through this. Just one more mission, then I'll be home and we can start all over again."

"If only you'd think about going public, getting those bastards to admit what they've done . . ."

Cris shook her head as she returned her hand to the steering wheel. She was past the cloverleaf; the sprawling headquarters area was coming up on the left, with Operations and Checkout just past the main office building. "We've been through this before, babe. Maybe we'd embarrass them a little, but no one would lose their jobs and we'd be eaten alive by the press. You want to hear dyke jokes about us on Letterman? That's all that would happen."

"But they'll get away with it!"

Cris turned the wheel, pulled into the wide parking lot of the O&C. "They're not getting away with anything, sweet," she said, choosing her words carefully. If things got fucked up somehow, at least Laurell could plead innocence. "Trust me . . . they're not going to get away with it."

Laurell stared at her. For a moment, Cris was afraid she was going to ask her exactly what she meant. If she did, Cris knew that she might tell Laurell something that she shouldn't know, if only because she hadn't unburdened herself to anyone thus far. Beneath the cool, professional barrier she had erected, there was a white-hot ember of anger, kept alive by contempt for the intolerant assholes who had done this to her. . . .

And a need for revenge.

But Laurell didn't ask. "Okay," she said, slumping back in her seat as Cris pulled into a reserved parking space in front of the building. "If that's what you say, I'll trust you."

"Good girl." Cris glanced at her watch. Ten minutes past

three. She had already caught flack from the mission director for insisting on spending her last night at home, and Parnell was probably pissed off about her missing his little barbecue at the Beach House. She didn't need any more shit about being late for the breakfast briefing.

Fuck it. What were they going to do . . . fire her?

She unbuckled her seat and shoulder harness, then reached into the back seat for her attaché case. "You know how to get to the commissary, right? Near the VAB. Grab a bite to eat, then get somebody to show you to the VIP viewing stands. Tell 'em . . ."

"Tell 'em I'm your sister?" A wan smile.

Cris hesitated. "No," she said flatly. "Tell 'em you're my wife." Then she returned the smile. "It doesn't matter anymore, does it?"

Before either of them could start crying, Cris pulled Laurell close and embraced her. People were walking past the car, NASA employees heading for their shifts; under the bright sodium glare of the parking lot lights, they could see into the car. She hesitated, but then realized that it no longer mattered very much.

She kissed Laurell farewell, not furtively as she had so many times before when they had been in a public place, but with all the passion she felt for the one true love of her life. Laurell's arms moved around her shoulders as her soft lips responded with equal ardor.

"Ten days," Cris whispered as she broke the kiss and gently disengaged Laurell's arms. "Ten days and I'll be home, and I promise I'll never leave you again."

Laurell reluctantly slid back into her seat. "God, I love you."

"I love you too, sweet. Be good." Cris found the door handle, popped open the gullwing and shoved it upward, then crawled out of the car, pulling her attaché case and its treasonous secret behind her. "I'll bring home a present. . . ."

Then she turned and began striding down the walkway to the entrance of Operations and Checkout, where a uniformed MP was waiting to hold the door open for her.

Captain Cristine September Ryer, USAF, NASA Astronaut Corps, reporting for her final mission.

• • •

Suit-up took only a few minutes. The blue one-piece astronaut jumpsuit over shorts and T-shirt, tucked into high-top sneakers, was preferable to the clunky old pressure suits she had worn during basic training. Cris spent several minutes stuffing her pockets with pens, notepads, penlights, food sticks, and assorted other paraphernalia—she had packed her duffel bag yesterday, and along with everyone else's it had already been loaded aboard the ferry—then went down the corridor to the infirmary, where two doctors gave her the usual pre-launch physical which told them nothing that they didn't already know.

When she was done, her next step was supposed to be joining the rest of the crew for the breakfast briefing. However, Cris had been careful to forget her mission notebook, making it necessary for her to walk back down the hall to the women's locker room. The room was empty, as she had anticipated, but she looked both ways as she reinserted her magnetic keycard into the slot of her locker and opened it.

The 3.5-inch diskette concealed within her attaché case bore the handwritten word "Tetris" on its label. Indeed, if someone booted up the disk and typed that word into a keyboard, they would find a fully functional copy of the popular Russian arcade game. Yet the other program on the disk, not listed in the directory, was a game whose stakes were much higher.

For a moment Captain Ryer hesitated. She could easily walk into the bathroom, snap the diskette in half, and shove the remains into the trash can; no one would be the wiser and she would no longer be taking this terrible risk. But all she had to do was remember her anger and the reasons for it, and it was all settled. She zipped the diskette into her left thigh cargo pocket and checked to make sure that it didn't bulge when she flexed her leg. Then she took a deep breath, pulled her notebook out of the locker, and slammed the metal door shut.

A uniformed NASA security guard checked her ID badge against his list, then saluted and held open the door of the O&C's astronaut mess. The room was long and brightly lit by fluorescent ceiling fixtures, sterile except for dozens of mission emblems painted on the beige walls. They ran the course of American manned space exploration, some dating back to the first manned orbital flights of the early fifties: the Atlas-A, B, and C test programs, the Space Station One construction missions, the various Eagle flights of Project Luna, all the way up to Project Ares. Shortly after the completion of the Mars program, though, individual patches were no longer designed for each major mission; someone in the NASA bureaucracy, in his infinite wisdom, had decreed that this custom was a quaint holdover from the old USSF days and that space had become too routine for such trivial matters as honoring crews with their own mission insignia. And it cost too much, besides.

So the practice had declined. Not long afterward, so too had the space program.

As expected, most of her crewmates had already arrived and were seated together at a long dining table, eating the traditional pre-launch breakfast of steak and eggs. Sitting next to them were the pilot and co-pilot of the *Constellation,* two anonymous ferry drivers who barely looked up as Cris put her notebook down at an empty place on the table between them and Gene Parnell. It seemed to her that their conversation faltered a bit when she made her entrance, but that was to be expected; Parnell was an old geezer who had been dragged out of semiretirement for one last hurrah, and the two rocket apes would probably drag their knuckles all the way to the launch pad.

Damn. She missed Laurell already. . . .

Cris excused herself and went up to the buffet table, where she passed up the high-cholesterol junk in favor of a cinnamon bagel and a fruit cocktail. There were butterflies in her stomach; her hand shook slightly as she poured a glass of tomato juice. She heard coarse laughter behind her, but didn't care to know what it was about. She tried to tell herself that it was just another attack of launch nerves, but she could feel the diskette in her jumpsuit pocket rubbing against her leg, and she suddenly imagined that Parnell had Superman's X-ray vision and could see right through the nylon. If that were so, the X-rays would scrub the disk's hidden program, and that would certainly take care of things, wouldn't it . . . ?

Cut it out, she told herself. Get a grip. She willed her hands to be steady and told the butterflies to get a job, and when she returned to the table she felt a little better.

"Sorry I'm late," Cris said as she sat down. "Got stuck in the morning rush."

One of the ferry pilots—his name badge read CAPT. P.A. KINGSOLVER—grunted noncommittally as he cut into his medium-rare steak. His co-pilot, LT. COMDR. H. M. TROMBLY, cast her a sullen look over his coffee mug. Neither of them said anything, but they didn't have to; it wasn't difficult to tell that they'd heard a bit about her personal life through the Cape grapevine. Although there had been no outright harassment, she knew that there were quite a few guys in the astronaut corps who didn't much care for the idea of flying with a dyke.

Don't worry, she said silently as she avoided their eyes. *You won't have to much longer. . . .*

Parnell gave her a quick smile. "Don't worry about it," he said. "You're not the only one running late. One of our passengers hasn't shown up yet either."

"Hmm? Who's that?" Gene wasn't bad. Perhaps he was over the hill for this kind of thing and had been assigned to this mission as a media overture, but they had worked well together during training and she reluctantly had come to like him, thinking of him in a patriarchal sort of way. If he had heard the buzz around the Cape about the Internal Affairs Office investigation, he hadn't said anything about it to her.

"Dooley." Parnell checked his watch. "He's staying at a motel on Satellite Beach, I think . . . must have gotten tied up in traffic coming in."

"Yeah, I hear you," Jay Lewitt said. "Route 3 was murder." *Conestoga*'s flight engineer pushed back his plate as he rubbed a napkin against his lean, brown face. He lived in Cocoa Beach off Route A1A, a few miles south of the space center. "Lisa floored the pedal, but she still couldn't get us through the mess."

"Is Elizabeth coming to the launch?" Cris asked.

"Yeah, she is." Jay and Lisa had a fifteen-year-old daughter. "It took a little bit of begging, but her principal finally let her out of classes to see her daddy go to the Moon."

"Gee," Parnell muttered, shaking his head. "Used to be that a kid whose dad was an astronaut didn't need permission to skip school."

Jay shrugged as he picked up his coffee mug. "Times have changed, Commander. I think her bus driver gets more respect." He took a sip as he added, "Better job security, that's for damn sure."

"I guess. Well, if our young hacker is running late, it gives us a chance to eat, at least." Parnell nodded toward Ray Harvey, the mission director. He was seated at the far end of the table, tapping impatiently at his leather folder as he entertained questions from the two other civilian passengers. "Speaking of food, I'm sorry you missed my barbecue, Cris. We had a good time . . . wish you could have been there."

I bet you do, she thought to herself as she spread marmalade on her bagel. *What's a good party without the token queer?*

She reflected, not for the first time, that there were probably as many closet homosexuals working at NASA as there were African-Americans with astronaut wings, but at least Jay was protected by the Civil Rights Act . . . and no one would ever call him a nigger to his face. "I'm sorry I wasn't there, Commander," she said diplomatically, "but I had some family matters to take care of before I left."

Trombly coughed loudly as he hid a smile behind his hand. "I thought you were divorced, Captain Ryer," Kingsolver said, keeping a straight face. "You mean you've found someone else?"

Cris ignored him; any reply she might make would only add fuel to the fire. She was gratified to see both Parnell and Lewitt pretending to study their notebooks. Farther down the table, however, Ray Harvey was openly glaring at her. He hadn't wanted to keep her on this mission. Given the chance, he would have yanked Cris two months ago, when the IAO presented their report to NASA's Astronaut Office. By then, however, there was little he could do about it; she had already been more than halfway through training for this mission and there was no one else qualified to take her place. The rest of the astronaut corps rated to pilot *Conestoga* had either been reassigned to other jobs or had resigned from the agency; a couple had even taken jobs in Germany for Koenig Selenen.

For this last NASA mission to Tranquillity Base, she and Parnell were the only NASA lunar astronauts available on short notice. Ray Harvey knew that. He was stuck with an old fart and a dyke, and at least one of them disturbed his shit.

Suddenly removing her from the mission, though, would have raised too many public-relations questions from the man and woman sitting next to him. Noticing the silent exchange, Berkley Rhodes and Alex Bromleigh glanced Cris's way. She smiled for their benefit; Rhodes beamed back in response and Bromleigh gave her a short, professional nod.

Cris kept smiling as she returned her attention to her breakfast. *Well, okay, so he's got five minority members on this mission. An old guy, a black, a lesbian, and two TV reporters. How politically correct . . .*

"Our media darling," Lewitt murmured out of the corner of his mouth, smiling in Rhodes's direction before he glanced back at Parnell. "Y'know, I think she actually put on makeup for this."

"I wouldn't doubt it." Parnell pulled a pair of bifocals out of his breast pocket as he studied his notebook. "Cronkite would have had a duck if he'd ever met her . . ."

"Now, don't you start with the stories again."

"It was back in sixty-four," Parnell began loftily as he turned a page, "and I was aboard the Wheel when Walter— Ol' Walt, we used to call him—came up to interview us for . . ."

He stopped as the door swung open and a plump young man strode into the mess hall. "Ah, and I see the prodigal son has finally arrived."

Cris looked up as Paul Dooley, dressed in astronaut blues and carrying a laptop computer in his right hand, walked toward the table. She hadn't seen very much of Dooley at the Cape—he had spent most of his training period at Koenig Selenen's facility in Bonn—but she noticed that he seemed to have lost a little weight.

Well, everyone did . . . but Dooley still came off as the stereotypical computer geek, despite his attempts to communicate an air of cyberpunk raffishness. He goggled at everyone from behind the round lenses of his wire-rim glasses as he stalked toward the last remaining place at the table.

"Okay, okay, so I'm late," he said impatiently. He knocked over a salt shaker with his computer case as he placed it on the table, and didn't bother to set it upright; so much for good luck, Cris thought. "Fucking traffic on the road . . . can't believe this shit . . ."

"Good morning, Mr. Dooley," Ray Harvey called out. "How nice of you to join us."

"Wouldn't have missed it for the world, Ray." Dooley nervously tossed back his thin black hair with his hand. "Look, I'm really fucking sorry for getting here so late, but . . . I dunno, where can I get some coffee?"

Parnell tipped down his bifocals, stared at Dooley, and silently pointed toward the buffet table. Bromleigh, in his dual role as ATS cameraman and network news producer, pulled an industrial Sony camcorder from beneath his seat and stood up, apparently getting ready to grab a shot of *Conestoga*'s crew eating breakfast together before their historic mission. Berkley Rhodes automatically primped for the camera as Dooley, apparently miffed that no one was catering to him, shuffled over to the buffet table in search of caffeine juice. The two ferry jockeys continued to watch Cris as if she'd lcome from another galaxy with the intent of exterminating all male life-forms on planet Earth.

"Having fun?" Parnell whispered to her.

"Loads," she replied just as quietly.

She was mildly surprised when he reached out to pat her arm. "Don't worry about it," he murmured. "A short trip up, a short trip back . . . it'll be a milk run." He removed his hand and picked up his coffee mug. "Might as well enjoy it. After this, you'll need to learn German to go to the Moon again."

"Uh-huh," she said. *And maybe the Germans won't throw me out for what I do in my private life. . . .*

Ray Harvey cleared his throat and stood up. Conversation at the table died as he opened his notebook. "Gentlemen, ladies . . . if I can have your attention, we'll start the briefing. Liftoff is currently scheduled for 0730 hours. . . ."

Cronkite: Good evening. If this doesn't look like my usual desk in New York . . . well, it isn't. Tonight, we're transmitting live from Space Station One, in orbit 1,075 miles above Earth, which was officially completed two days ago.

If we pan our television camera slightly to my left, you can see out a porthole window in the station's circular rim . . . and, yes, there it is, the planet Earth, over a thousand miles away. If you look carefully, you can make out the Florida coastline beneath a cloud formation. We won't be able to look at it for very long, because the space station is rotating on its axis and soon this window will no longer be pointing toward Earth, but it's a magnificent sight for you folks back home.

With me now, in our temporary CBS studio in the station's mess compartment, is General Chet Aldridge, the United States Space Force commander in charge of Space Station One. General Aldridge, how does it feel to have the Wheel finally operational?

Aldridge: It feels great, Walter. It's been seven years since this project was begun and four years since the first sections were launched from Cape Canaveral, so we're mighty glad to have the job done at last, and mighty proud of the men who built Space Station One.

Cronkite: When President Nixon made his televised address to the nation yesterday, he said that the purposes of the Wheel were not entirely military in nature. As a military officer yourself, can you comment on that?

Aldridge: It's not for me to dispute the words of my Commander In Chief, Walter, and so I'm not going to get into a fight with the President . . .

Cronkite *(chuckling)*: No, sir, I'm not asking you to do that . . .

Aldridge: . . . but the President is quite correct. Although Space Station One has the primary military mission of maintaining surveillance over . . . uh, countries who may pose a threat to the security of the United States, our goals are also scientific in nature. Now that the Wheel has been completed, our next major task will be the construction of the three lunar spaceships which will be sent to the Moon by the end of this decade. That's our next goal, sending men to the Moon, and we plan to accomplish it just as well as we did with the building of this station.

Cronkite: You mentioned surveillance, General. Can you tell me exactly what you're looking for down there?

Aldridge: I'm sorry, Walter, but that's classified information, and I'm also sorry that I can't show you the Earth Observation Center. However, I can tell you that, even as we speak, Space Station One is passing above Cuba. If Premier Castro happens to be watching this program right now, this should give him something to think about.

Cronkite: On the lighter side of things, the network has received some interesting mail from our viewers over the past few days, since we announced that we would be doing a live telecast from the Wheel. One letter in particular comes from a young man, Michael Walsh of Baltimore, Maryland. Mike tells that he's a fan of a science fiction TV show on one of our competing networks, and he says that everything he has seen on that program looks just like the pictures that the Space Force has sent from the Wheel. To quote him, General, he says, "How do I know this isn't just a fake?"

Aldridge *(laughing)*: Well, Mike, we watch that show up here, too, and to borrow a favorite phrase used by one of the characters, Dr. Spock, "It just ain't logical, Cap'n . . ."

Cronkite *(chuckling)*: At risk of supporting a rival network . . .

Aldridge: Didn't mean to do that, Walter. The Space Force doesn't want to play favorites. Anyway, Mike, I'll show you something they can't do in Hollywood. Here's a pitcher of water, you see, and here's a glass on the table. Now, if I were to pour water into the glass down on Earth, it would fall straight into the glass, right? But up here, we've got something the scientists call a Coriolis effect, which involves the physical properties of objects within a rotating environment, like the Wheel.

Cronkite: Bring the camera in a little closer, Bill . . .

Aldridge: That means everything inside Space Station One is spinning, but since objects close to the floor are spinning a little bit faster than objects higher up, it means nothing is moving at quite the same rate. So, if I raise the pitcher just a little bit higher above the table and pour a little bit of water toward the glass . . .

Cronkite: Whoa! Watch out there!

Aldridge: Sorry, Walter, didn't mean to splash you . . . so you see, Mike, the water goes kind of sideways and misses the glass entirely . . .

Cronkite: And lands in my lap instead. Thank you for the demonstration, General.

Aldridge: My pleasure, Walter . . . sorry to make a mess.

Cronkite: We'll return for a tour of Space Station One after station identification. . . .

FOUR

There were two men named Paul Aaron Dooley.

One of them was a young man born in Austin, Texas, in 1962, whose life coincided with the rise and fall of the Space Age and the coming of the Digital Age. Something of a prodigy, at least by his own reckoning, he was sixteen when his father gave him an Apple I as a high-school graduation present; he was twenty when he graduated from the University of Texas with a B.S. in computer science and had made a modest reputation for himself within the fledgling hacker subculture on the Internet, where he had established himself as Thor200.

Several years later, while he was working on his doctorate at MIT's artificial intelligence lab, Paul Dooley was one of a handful of darkside hackers who were investigated by the Secret Service in connection with a series of break-ins on Milnet, the Department of Defense computer network. He had only been peripherally involved with the Milnet intrusion, but Thor200 was a well-known logon in the hacker subculture and Dooley was therefore easy to trace; when the Secret Service began making raids, his was one of several doors broken down by federal agents. Although he was questioned for several hours at the agency's Boston office, he was never charged with anything—mainly because, in exchange for legal immunity, he narked on the real perpetrators of the Milnet break-in. Several self-styled cyberpunks went to jail as a result, but Paul Dooley remained free, although Thor200 maintained a much lower profile on the net after that.

Following that close shave with the law, Dooley concentrated on his true interests, the development of advanced AI programs for semiautonomous teleoperated robots. It was Dooley's contention that many of the jobs on the Moon currently performed by astronauts could be accomplished, with greater safety and at less expense, by robots guided by Earth-based operators using virtual-reality technology.

Dooley's work gained the attention of the German aerospace corporation Koenig Selenen GmbH. The Germans were interested in using lunar resources for the construction of solar-power satellites, an idea first proposed by American scientists but largely ignored by U.S. government and industry, which were backing away from space exploration in the wake of the *Challenger* disaster and the gradual dissolution of the American civil space program.

For Dooley, at least, this was just as well. By the time he was getting ready to receive his doctorate from MIT, his prospects for future employment were limited to designing computer games for consumption by a generation whose idea of adventure was booting up a new Sega cartridge . . . or, perhaps, teaching a new group of hacker wannabes the technical skills that would make them employable by a European or Japanese company. On the other hand, Koenig Selenen offered him an opportunity to develop his theories to their full advantage. The young cyberneticist was on the Koenig Selenen payroll as soon as he received his doctorate; the company allowed him to remain in the United States, working as an "independent consultant," although, in fact, he was one of its leading researchers. Several years later, when the company successfully negotiated with the U.S. government for the sale of Tranquillity Base, the person it turned to for upgrading the moon base's obsolete computer systems was Paul Dooley.

That was one Paul Dooley: an arrogant, trash-mouthed, self-proclaimed boy genius who had no known pals or girlfriends except for a few dalliances on Le Matrix, whose only hobby was collecting comic books, and who had entered astronaut training for the Tranquillity Base lunar mission with considerable reluctance.

That Paul Dooley was now being held prisoner in the cement basement of a rented house outside Orlando, Florida.

He had been stripped naked, tied to a wooden chair, and placed under hot lights by a handful of men who been methodically torturing him for several hours now. The 500 milligrams of Ketamine that had rendered him unconscious earlier that night had now produced, as anticipated, a nightmarish series of hallucinations; at times he believed he had died and was now in the depths of Hell, being tormented by demons straight out of an old EC comic. The illusion was reinforced by his captors, who were steadfastly depriving him of both water and sleep while playing, at high volume, radio sound-effects tapes of gunshots, human screams, car crashes, and wild animal noises.

A sharp tongue laden with sarcasm and bluster may be intimidating to fellow intellectuals, but it doesn't mean a thing to people who prefer to use fists, pliers, and rubber hoses, and Paul Dooley was not a strong person. It didn't take long before agony, drugs, humiliation, confusion, and outright terror took their toll. One by one, he answered their shouted questions, sometimes telling his captors far more than they needed to know in exchange for the smallest sip of water or, at the very least, temporary surcease from pain. It had taken several hours, but once he started talking, there was little he didn't tell them.

Though his face was now a bloody, swollen wreck and there were few inches of his body that were not covered with purple welts, he still held onto the dim hope that he would soon be set free, unwitting to the fact that, in the end, the only mercy he would receive from these faceless men would be the bullet one of them would eventually fire into the back of his skull.

Even as he spilled his guts about everything he knew regarding his mission, there was one final secret that he hadn't disclosed, if only because his captors had neglected to ask him. . . .

And then there was the other Paul Dooley, who, except for a surgically altered appearance, hundreds of hours in careful study of basic mannerisms and speech patterns, and vast expertise in computers, shared nothing in common with the man whose identity he had assumed.

At the same moment that one Paul Dooley howled in agony as an eight-inch length of garden hose was repeatedly slammed against his stomach, another Paul Dooley pretended to stifle a yawn behind his hand as he listened to Ray Harvey begin the final mission briefing.

The mission director stood in front of a blackboard, shuffling papers on a clipboard in his hand and trying not to look at the camcorder pointed in his direction. The blackboard was marked with a neat timetable of the main mission events; it was redundant with the printouts in everyone's notebooks, and the briefing itself was a formality that could have easily been dispensed with, were it not for the presence of the TV camera.

Dooley found himself smiling at the pretentiousness of the ceremony. How far NASA had fallen, to be catering like this to the fickle wishes of the news media.

"Following liftoff," Harvey continued, "*Constellation* will rendezvous with Space Station One, where the crew will transfer to the Wheel. At about the same time . . ."

He paused to glance at his notes. "Uh, 1300 Greenwich . . . the German shuttle *Walter Dornberger* will launch from the Kourou space center in French Guiana. The *Dornberger* will ascend to equatorial orbit and meet you at approximately the same time, pending no difficulties. The remaining members of the outbound crew, from Koenig Selenen GmbH . . ."

Harvey took another peek at his notes. "Mr. James Leamore, Mr. Uwe Aachener, and Mr. Markus Talsbach . . . uh, will join you aboard the Wheel." He consulted his clipboard. "At 2200 GMT, you are scheduled for a live TV transmission from the Wheel. Ms. Rhodes will be officiating, naturally."

The camera swung to zoom in on Berkley Rhodes, who was wearing a pair of reading glasses and pretending to look deeply interested. "The transmission will last approximately ten minutes. Commander Parnell, Captain Ryer, during this time you'll be interviewed for the ATS Evening News."

No mention of himself, Dooley noted, which was just as well; the less time he spent in front of a camera, the better.

The plastic surgery which had changed his face was good enough to get him past the security checkpoints, and so far no one in the room had voiced any doubts; still, he had been cautioned to shy away from the cameras. Dooley's mother was dead and his father was a senile old man in a Houston nursing home, yet there was always an off-chance that someone back home might detect a subtle difference.

Harvey cleared his throat. "*Conestoga* is scheduled for launch at 0800 GMT tomorrow morning, pending final check-out of the craft. It will be a two-day flight to the Moon, with touchdown at Tranquillity Base posted for Sunday, February 19, at approximately 0700 GMT. Following successful landing, the crew will enter the base, where Commander Parnell and Lieutenant Lewitt will reactivate the base's CLLSS . . . ah, closed-loop life-support systems. If no difficulties are encountered with the base's reactivation . . ."

"It wouldn't dare," Parnell murmured. Several people at the table chuckled as Harvey, caught off-guard, feigned amusement. Dooley felt a twinge of pity for the man; NASA should have put a public affairs officer in charge of the briefing.

Harvey once again consulted his clipboard. "If there are no difficulties, shortly afterward . . . uh, 1100 GMT . . . the crew will board tractors and travel to the Teal Falcon bunker, where Mr. Dooley will assist the flight team in reactivating the launch control systems."

Harvey coughed nervously. "This is, of course, the most delicate part of the mission, and although Ms. Rhodes and Mr. Bromleigh will be recording the procedure, no live TV transmissions will be allowed until the arms control inspectors from the International Atomic Energy Agency standing by at Von Braun Center are assured that Teal Falcon is under local control."

The mission director stopped and put the clipboard under his arm. "Mr. Bromleigh, turn off your camera and put it away now, please."

Alex Bromleigh reluctantly unshouldered his camcorder and placed it on a table. When Harvey was satisfied that the camera was off, he nodded to the security guard standing near the door. The guard opened the door and gave a quick, silent nod to someone standing in the corridor.

The civilian who had been waiting outside stepped into the ready room. A leather attaché case was handcuffed to his wrist. He strode across the room to Ray Harvey and held up the attaché case. Harvey carefully dialed the combination lock and opened the case; inside were two sealed manila envelopes along with a pair of small red keys, each bound by a loop of stainless-steel chain.

Withdrawing the envelopes and keys, Harvey silently walked to the table, where he gave one key and an envelope to Gene Parnell. Parnell glanced at the envelope, then tucked it into a pocket of his notebook without opening it; he then unzipped the front of his jumpsuit, looped the key chain around his neck, and dropped the key out of sight. He looked back at Harvey and nodded once.

"Thanks, Gene," Harvey said. He held out his hand, and Parnell grasped it without a word.

Cristine Ryer looked up at Harvey expectantly, but he appeared to be deliberately ignoring her. Instead, he walked around to the other side of the table, passing Dooley until he stopped behind Jay Lewitt's chair.

Lewitt raised his eyebrows in apparent surprise as the flight director extended the other envelope and key to him. "Lieutenant," Harvey said softly, "I know this is unexpected, but if you'll take possession of the second key, your country will consider it a great favor."

Dooley heard Cris Ryer's sharp intake of breath. Glancing at her from across the table, he saw her face turn bright red. She opened her mouth as if to object, but then shut up, as Dooley caught a glimpse of Parnell's hand snaking beneath the table to tightly clasp her wrist.

He carefully kept his own reaction under control. This was an unexpected turn of events. His masters would have to be informed of what had just happened.

If they didn't know about it already, of course. He was aware that he was only one card in the deck, and much of the game had yet to be revealed to him.

And yet . . .

"Thank you, sir." Lewitt accepted the second key and

looped the chain around his neck, then placed the sealed envelope inside his notebook. As Harvey turned his back to the astronauts, Lewitt looked straight at Ryer and gave a small shrug. Ryer glanced away, visibly trying to control her temper.

"Mr. Bromleigh, Ms. Rhodes, that was off the record," Harvey said as he returned to the front of the room. "In your reports, you'll note that the keys to the Teal Falcon bunker safe were assigned to two unspecified members of the *Conestoga* flight team, and their identities will not be revealed for reasons of national security. Understand?"

The two ATS correspondents traded a look. "Yes sir, we do," Bromleigh said. Rhodes hesitated, apparently wanting to ask the obvious question—*Why was the mission's second-in-command passed over?*—but she seemed to think twice and kept her mouth shut, quietly nodding instead. "Very well," Harvey said. "Mr. Bromleigh, you may continue filming."

As Bromleigh hoisted his camcorder once more, the mission director checked his clipboard. "At 1200 GMT, personnel at the Teal Falcon bunker will stand by for a televised address from the White House, when the President will deliver a speech to the American public regarding final disposal of Teal Falcon. These remarks will be relayed via NASA's Deep Space Tracking Network. Once this phase of the mission has been completed, the members of the news media will be allowed to transmit their reportage."

He took a deep breath; his eyes darted toward the camera. "By this time, authentication codes will have been transmitted from NORAD, and the keyholders will have opened the safe and removed the fire-control keys. On signal from the White House, they will then launch the Teal Falcon missiles on the solar trajectory which Mr. Dooley will have programmed into the master guidance system."

Harvey lowered the clipboard. "Following launch, the crew will return to the base, where Mr. Dooley and Mr. Leamore will continue their work in handing over control of Tranquillity Base to Koenig Selenen GmbH. If all goes well, the final phase of the mission will end at 1800 hours GMT the following day . . . um, Monday, February 20 . . . when the

American flag will be struck from the base and *Conestoga* will launch for return to Space Station One.''

He hesitated. There was a strained silence in the room, made more uncomfortable by the heat of Cristine Ryer's barely suppressed rage. ''Gentlemen, ladies,'' he said slowly, for the first time exposing some shred of unrehearsed emotion, ''I know this is a difficult mission for all of us. I've been with the lunar program for twenty years now, and no one wishes to see it end any less than I do. . . .''

''We've noticed,'' Parnell muttered from behind his hand.

If Harvey heard the remark, he didn't acknowledge it with anything more than a quick glance in Parnell's direction. ''For the record, though, I expect you to serve your country as capably on this final mission as you have throughout your careers, and on behalf of the launch team I wish you godspeed and good luck.''

If he was expecting any applause, he didn't receive it. The mission director was another NASA bureaucrat spouting patriotic homilies for public consumption; everyone knew it, including Harvey himself. He coughed uncomfortably and shuffled away from the blackboard as Bromleigh lowered his camcorder and Rhodes checked her notes. Parnell stood up and sauntered to the buffet table while Lewitt reopened his notebook, deliberately ignoring Ryer's hot gaze. The two shuttle jockeys murmured between themselves. There were a few minutes left to kill before walk-out, just enough time for another cup of coffee before they hit the road.

Watching them, the other Paul Dooley once again realized how easy it was to play traitor. Although his employers had their own agenda, he was in it strictly for the money. There was a time, in a former life, when he would have claimed revolution as his ultimate objective; now his motives were purely mercenary and apolitical. Five million dollars and a comfortable life in another country was fair exchange for wearing another man's face for ten days, and fuck the dogma he had once espoused.

And yet, he reflected, his task was made easier by the knowledge that he was taking advantage of a country that had grown apathetic toward its own achievements and former aspirations. It wasn't terrorism so much as it was mugging an old codger hobbling down a dark alley on his way to a VFW meeting. . . .

He was startled out of his reverie by a steaming mug of coffee being placed in front of him. Dooley looked up to see Gene Parnell at his elbow. "Ready for your moment of glory, son?" he asked.

Dooley forced a smile. "If you want to call it that, sure," he replied, picking up the coffee and taking a sip. "I don't think glory has much to do with it, though." And wasn't that the truth, just for once?

Parnell shrugged as he sat down next to him. "You've got a point," he mused as he sipped from his own mug. "Twenty years since Ares, and people still remember Armstrong as being the first man on Mars, but nobody remembers who was the last person to climb up the ladder." He shrugged again. "Still, last NASA mission to the Moon and all that . . . maybe we'll earn our own little place in the history books after it's over and done with."

Was this guy living in the past or what? Dooley tried to look interested, although his mind was focused mainly upon the task he was to perform a few days from now. "I don't think I'm going to be writing any memoirs about this," he said, not entirely without irony. "I'm just your basic, run-of-the-mill hacker. The company could have sent someone else, but they picked me instead."

"Hmm." Parnell looked thoughtful; he stared at Dooley over the lip of his raised coffee mug. "Well, that's not entirely true. You're the guy who believes we—or rather, your company—can replace people with robots, turn everything up there over to machines. That makes you something of a historic figure in your own right, doesn't it?"

There was the slightest hint of accusation in Parnell's voice, and Dooley couldn't ignore the hard glint in the man's eyes. He wondered how Parnell might react if he knew that the person he really intended to blame was now being subjected to slow torture less than thirty miles from here.

"Hey, dude, don't blame me," he replied. "At least we're finding some use for that base, aren't we? If my company hadn't bought it, nobody would have—"

"Mr. Dooley?"

The interruption came from a voice across the room; some NASA minion had poked his head through the door. "Right here," Dooley shouted back.

"Got a long-distance call from your sister Ruth," the young man in the blue blazer responded. "Says she wants to speak to you before you go."

He had been expecting this call. The real Paul Dooley had a sister in Austin, a fact that anyone in NASA's Astronaut Office could easily ascertain from checking his file; what they didn't know was that Ruth Weinberg wasn't on speaking terms with her younger brother and wasn't likely to call him even before he was about to board an orbital ferry.

"I'll take it, thanks." Dooley pushed back his chair and stood up. "Excuse me," he said to Parnell, glad to escape from their conversation. Parnell waved him off as Dooley sauntered across the room to the door.

The NASA flack led him down the corridor to a small office, where he helpfully punched a button on the phone to give him a private extension. When the kid was gone, Dooley picked up the receiver. "Hello, Ruth?"

"Hi, Paul?" a female voice said. "It's Ruthie." A small, nervous laugh. "Did you remember to pack your toothbrush?"

"No, Ruth," he replied, keeping his tone light. "I don't need one . . . they have plenty on the Wheel."

"But it might have germs . . ."

"I'm sure they're wrapped in plastic."

A small sigh of relief. "Well, that's good. You can't be too sure, and Mom always said you needed to have a clean toothbrush."

Passwords traded and matched. If anyone was monitoring this call, they would only hear a conversation between a brother and his doting older sister. "How's Bert doing?" he asked.

Bert Weinberg was Ruth's husband, convalescing in a Houston hospital after a minor auto accident which had injured his back. Bert Weinberg despised Paul Dooley almost more than his sister did, but there was no reason why anyone at NASA should know this. "Bert's doing okay," the voice responded, "but the doctors don't think he's going to be leaving any time very soon."

"I see . . ."

"But he says to give you his best wishes . . . oh, and he wants you to send him a photo of where you're going."

"Does he want me to write him at the hospital?"

"No," the voice said. "You can send it here . . . and we'll have a nice party when you get home."

"Are your neighbors going to be there?"

A sigh. "I'm afraid so," the voice said apologetically. "I'm sorry, but I had to invite them. They insisted on coming."

"That's okay . . ."

"But they're not bringing their kids. I told them to leave the kids at home and you'd sign an autograph for them later."

"Good." Dooley smiled. "Okay, Ruthie. I'll be there. Tell everyone I miss them."

"We miss you, too, baby brother. I've got a big kiss for you."

"Okay," he replied. "Look, I gotta go now. Everything's fine, don't worry about a thing."

"Okay . . . see you when you get back."

"Bye, Ruthie," he said. "See you later. Bye."

Dooley hung up and took a moment to settle back in the desk chair and contemplate the conversation he'd just held with his masters.

First, he had informed them that he was safely in place and that he had not been detected. That was the primary message he needed to pass them.

Everything else was news from outside. There was now only one Paul Dooley. The other one was dead and the organization would dispose of his body in an appropriate manner. The fact that the new Dooley was now a living ghost didn't bother him in the slightest; this had been anticipated from the moment the abduction took place. More importantly, though, he had been informed that the original Paul Dooley had told his kidnappers everything he needed to know in order to successfully complete the assignment. At a prearranged time, that information would be relayed to him.

And finally, his primary contact was in place.

Dooley wasn't going to the Moon alone. The organization wasn't taking any chances; there was a fail-safe option available, in the event that something got fucked up in the course of the next few days.

In short, everything was going according to plan.

Dooley rose from the chair and strode to the door. The helpful young man in the blue blazer was waiting just outside the office, eager to escort him back to the ready room. "Your sister?" he asked as they began to stride down the hallway.

"Oh yeah," he replied, tucking his hands in the pockets of his jumpsuit. "You know family . . . just can't leave you alone."

**From You Will Go to the Moon *by Mae and Ira Freeman*.
(*Beginner Books, 1959*)**

This is how you will go to the moon.
Here is the rocket that will take you up into space.
It is a tall, tall rocket.
It is as tall as ten houses.
The rocket has 3 parts.

You will go way, way up to Part 1.
The rocket men will take you up.
They will take you up in a little car.

Come on in.
Come into this little room.
This is where you will sit.
You will sit here with the rocket men.

The men will show you what to do.
The men will show you where to sit.
Hook on that belt.
Hook it tight!
Get set to go!

FIVE

"Okay, that looks good . . . Commander, move a little bit to the left, please . . . look up at the rocket now, yeah, that's good . . . no, don't look at me, look at the rocket! . . . okay, that's great, that's terrific . . ."

And now here they were: *Conestoga*'s flight crew, fresh off the vans which had transported them from the O&C Building to the Atlas launch complex, reluctantly posing for a TV camera below the base of the mobile launch platform. Egrets and sea gulls circle the tall silver-blue shaft of the rocket, their harsh cries mocking them, and a handful of pad technicians in color-coded hard hats lean against the platform railing, barely able to hide their amusement.

Alex Bromleigh stood a few feet away, peering through the eyepiece of his Sony camcorder as he sought to orchestrate Parnell, Lewitt, and Ryer. Only Paul Dooley had been spared from the photo op; he stood nearby, nervously gazing at the broad round base of the ferry rocket, while Bromleigh called out directions.

"Next thing," Lewitt murmured to Parnell, "he'll want us in swimsuits." He turned his head to spit on the tarmac. "I can't believe we're doing this."

Parnell nodded. It was a waste of precious time and everyone knew it, but it was one more photo-op which had been scheduled by the NASA Press Office for the benefit of the

ATS documentary team. There would be more like this one over the next few days, though, and they would have to get used to it.

He gazed off at the nearby beach, where pale morning sunlight dappled the receding tide. A ZV-8P Airgeep cruised low over the sands; a NASA security officer leaned out of its open cockpit, using a metal detector to sweep the perimeter of the launch pad for bombs. No one had forgotten the time an anti-space fanatic had damaged this same pad with four pounds of Semtex he'd managed to hide on the beach the night before a launch. The Airgeep moved out of sight behind the rocket, its twin horizontal blades disturbing a flock of gulls, and Parnell stole a glance from behind his sunglasses at Berkley Rhodes.

The correspondent stood behind Bromleigh's camera, checking her notes as she prepared for the interview she would soon be doing. With her perpetual smile and young Barbara Walters looks, it was tempting to write her off as just another TV bimbo, yet Parnell had slowly come to realize over the past few weeks that there was much more to Rhodes than met the eye. There has always been friction between the American space program and the press, going back before Chet Aldridge had dumped a pitcher of water in Walter Cronkite's lap on live TV. One group was committed to keeping their lips buttoned, the other to blabbing everything; little had changed in the basic nature of that relationship even after the Space Force was phased out and NASA had taken its place.

To be fair, Parnell knew that not all reporters on the space beat were bottom-feeders looking for a hot scoop. He had encountered enough good journalists—Jack Wilford of the *Times,* Ike Asimov of the *Boston Globe,* even good ol' Uncle Walter himself—to know that some were not there just to wait for the next *Challenger* disaster so they could thrust a microphone into the face of a stunned widow.

But Berkley Rhodes . . . Berkley Rhodes was another case entirely.

Parnell had been briefed on her background when she was assigned to the mission. Rhodes had been a middle-ranked Washington correspondent for ATS until a few years ago, schlepping her notebook and tape recorder from one Senate budget hearing to the next. She might have remained in obscurity, at best interviewing politicians for *First Edition* before the morning weather, were it not for a stroke of luck that turned her career around.

To this day, no one knew exactly why she had received a manila envelope stuffed with photocopies of classified documents, smuggled out of the Pentagon by a highly placed Air Force officer whose identity still remained a secret. It was understandable that Sy Hersh of the *Times* and Bob Woodward of the *Washington Post,* two of the top investigative reporters in the country, had received the same information . . . but why Rhodes instead of network power-hitters like Rather or Donaldson? There were persistent rumors that she might have slept with the mysterious Colonel X, but nothing had ever been proven. Maybe Colonel X had pulled her name out of a hat. Perhaps he liked the way she had tough-talked Jesse Helms during an interview three days before.

In the end, it was pointless to speculate on why Berkley Rhodes was one of the first reporters to break the Teal Falcon story, the scandal that had not only swept Bob Dole out of the White House, but also caused Tranquillity Base to be prematurely shut down and damaged NASA's credibility. Whatever the reason, her reputation had skyrocketed just as quickly as the agency's had plummeted, until it could now be safely argued that more people recognized her face than they did any of the *Conestoga*'s astronauts.

Which was the reason why, when she had asked—demanded, really—to cover NASA's final mission to the Moon for a network documentary about the demise of the U.S. space program, the agency had all too willingly agreed.

"Gene . . . hey, Gene, stop looking that way! Look at the rocket, the rocket . . ."

Turning around to gaze up at *Constellation* once more, Parnell recalled his meeting with NASA's Chief Administrator, a few months ago. It was a warm day in early autumn; from the window of his office in the NASA headquarters building they watched as protesters marched in circles in front of the National Air and Space Museum. *We're on the ropes, Gene,* Dan Goldin had said, his hands clasped behind his back.

Tranquillity's being sold to the Germans, and Congress is threatening to do the same with the Wheel. The deficit, the latest budget cutback . . . you know the story. Unless we can get the public back on our side, the program's dead and gone by the end of the decade. That's half the reason why we want you to go up. You're the last of the old guard, you were out of the loop during the Desert Storm thing, and . . . look, I know it's P.R. bullshit, but it's all we've got going for us right now. What do you say, Commander?

Of course, he had said yes . . . although for reasons of his own.

T-minus thirty-five minutes and counting. The stentorian voice of the Launch Control talker came over the pad's loud-speakers, interrupting Parnell's train of thought. *We are on hot countdown, observing maximum pad discipline.*

The pad rats who had been watching the astronauts turned away from the railing, heading to their last-minute jobs. It took more than three thousand men and women to get an Atlas-C off the ground, and it didn't help matters much when the passengers were loafing around instead of boarding the rocket. "Okay, let's break this up," Parnell said, clapping his hands for attention. "Ms. Rhodes, let's get this done . . . we're on a schedule here."

Rhodes looked miffed; her cameraman had just spent five minutes grabbing stock-shots, and the best thing he had gotten was Lewitt spitting on the ground. She strode past Bromleigh to stand beside Parnell and fussed with her windblown hair for a moment before she signaled Bromleigh to resume film-ing.

"Captain Parnell," she began, "this is your first trip back to the Moon in more than twenty years. How do you—?"

"It feels great," he answered shortly.

She waited for him to elaborate. When he didn't, she glanced at her notes. "You're flying with a team who are much younger than you. How—?"

"It feels great."

Again, Rhodes waited for details which were not forthcom-ing. Parnell could hear Lewitt, out of camera range, snicker-ing under his breath. He didn't look around, but from the corner of his eye he could see Cris Ryer staring off at the marshes surrounding the pad, apparently indifferent to everything going on behind her. Parnell was beginning to wonder if she should be on this mission at all; her problems were obviously getting the best of her. The bit with the key . . .

"So, Captain Parnell, which do you like better?" Rhodes asked, *sotto voce*. "Sexual intercourse with donkeys or horses?"

He looked her straight in the eye. "It feels great," he replied. "How about you?"

Lewitt broke up laughing; even Bromleigh began to chuckle from behind the lens. Rhodes turned several shades of red. "You better be glad this isn't live," she murmured as she lowered the mike.

"Ma'am, this is a live countdown, and we've wasted enough time as it is." Parnell knelt to pick up his notebook where he had placed it on the ground. "So let's cut the crap already," he added softly. "We've got a job to do here, and despite rumors to the contrary, this isn't a press junket for your benefit."

Bromleigh unjacked the microphone and let the male end drop to the ground before he quietly walked away, leaving Rhodes and Parnell alone for a moment. "I understand you've been told to cooperate with the press," Rhodes said as she began to coil the mike cable. "At this rate, I'll be having a few words with your boss before this is wrapped up."

"Fine with me," Parnell said. "But get it straight, ma'am . . . I'm in charge of this mission, not you, and I don't give a rat's ass what Goldin thinks. In fact, I could throw you and your producer off this flight right now, and you can catch a ride back to the press mound and cover the launch from there for all I care. Your boss will be real pleased if I do that, won't he?"

"You wouldn't dare."

"Give me an excuse . . . please." When Rhodes didn't respond, he went on. "Like I said, these people have a job to do and you're getting in their way. Keep this up and I'll leave you behind. It's your call."

As if on cue, the launch talker's voice came over the loudspeakers again: *T-minus thirty-two minutes and counting. All unnecessary ground personnel, please evacuate the pad and proceed to safe distance. Final hold will commence in five minutes.*

Workmen were already beginning to trot down the metal stairs from atop the launch platform, heading for the white vans parked on the crawlerway near the base of the mound. A siren blew, echoing faintly off the metalwork of the gantry, itself long-since pulled away on its rails. Cold white fumes wafted down from the first stage, curling around the mammoth supports of the launch cradle, pulled by enormous fans into the maw of the flame trench beneath the mobile platform. Parnell heard a sharp whistle from the bottom of the launch tower; a pad tech impatiently waited next to the service elevator, where Ryer, Lewitt, Bromleigh, and Dooley had already gathered.

Parnell ignored the summons. "Your call, Ms. Rhodes," he repeated. "You cooperate with me, I'll cooperate with you . . . but only on my terms. Got it?"

For a moment, he wondered if she was actually going to call his bluff . . . and it *was* a bluff, for he knew that if he left her behind, the agency would send her to the Wheel aboard another ferry, even if that meant delaying the mission's third phase by at least a week while another Atlas-C was rolled out to the pad. The ugly truth of the matter was that NASA wanted good press so badly that it was willing to hunker down on all fours and lick the boots of the Berkley Rhodeses of the world, if only to ensure that a relative handful of middle-management bureaucrats and senior officials could retain their civil-service jobs. . . .

Which, of course, was just one of the many reasons why the space program was in such sorry shape. The agency had become so used to kowtowing to a fickle press, it had forgotten that its primary purpose was to launch rockets. But, just for once, Parnell wanted to put the fear of God into one of these leeches. He could see that he had succeeded when she blinked.

"Got it," she finally whispered. "I understand."

Parnell nodded. "Good. Then let's go . . . we've got a launch window to meet." He turned and led her toward the elevator.

If the rest of the mission went so easily, he would have nothing to worry about for the next ten days.

The elevator creaks as it gradually rises through the tower's central shaft. No one in the cage says anything during the long ascent; through its wire-mesh walls, they can see the flat landscape of Merritt Island spread out before them, the giant white cube of the Vehicle Assembly Building dominating the scenery from three miles away, the Florida mainland a green line across the distant western horizon.

Constellation's sleek fuselage looms next to the launch tower. They rise past the vast wings of the first-stage booster, past the ropy coils of fuel cables, past the gently tapering second stage, where a thin skein of frozen condensation from the supercooled fuels within the rocket's fuel tanks has affixed itself to the hull like hoarfrost, until they reach the top of the tower. They catch a brief glimpse of the orbiter's vertical stabilizer before it vanishes behind its sharp delta wings as the elevator slows and comes to a clanking halt.

A technician in a white jumpsuit and helmet opens the cage door and leads them across the open platform to the crew access arm. A chill morning breeze, tinged with salt, moans through the skeletal girders and sings past the wires of the emergency cable car leading from the tower to the ground far below; their last view of Earth is from this aerie above the marshy coast, so near and yet so far.

Parnell is the first person to walk onto the access arm. He feels a gentle vibration through the soles of his shoes as he strides down the enclosed bridge, a tactile sense of restrained power that trembles against his palms as he touches the handrails. *Constellation* is a monster beginning to awaken from its slumber.

At the end of the access arm is the whiteroom. Here, there is no wind, no salt air, no sound, only a small sterile chamber nestled up against the rocket's fuselage. One technician hands Parnell his helmet, helps him fit it over his head and attach the dangling line to the communications carrier on his waist. Another technician guides him to an open circular hatch and gives him the customary backslap as he climbs into the belly of the beast.

Parnell climbs up a narrow ladder past rows of swivel-mounted acceleration couches until he reaches the top of the passenger compartment. He clambers into his couch on the starboard side and begins to fasten the lap- and shoulder-harnesses around his body. Through the open hatch above him he can see the narrow confines of the cockpit; Kingsolver and Trombly, the pilot and co-pilot, glance briefly over their shoulders as they continue running through the pre-launch checklist, repeating each item as they gaze at the myriad dials and digital indicators on their wraparound consoles, their gloved hands snapping toggles and depressing buttons.

"Primary BFS check . . ."

"BFS transferred, check. GPC on Mode Five, green light."

"Control, GPC and BFS checks complete, over."

"Select three-plus-one on screen three."

"Roger that . . ."

Sunlight lances down, as if through a narrow skylight, from the cockpit windows. Below him, Parnell can hear the rest of his crew as they climb the ladder into the cockpit. A few moments later, Cris Ryer hoists herself into the couch on the port side of the vessel, just across the aisle from him. He can barely make out her face inside the open visor of her helmet, yet she looks pensive as she snaps the worn buckles of her harness and tightens the webbed straps.

"Remember to extinguish all smoking materials," he says.

"Right," she murmurs. The joke was old and tired before she was out of diapers, and she pays no attention to it.

"I sort of meant the look in your eyes," he adds.

Ryer casts him a look which somehow manages to be both hot and cold at the same time, yet she doesn't say anything. "If there's something you want to discuss . . ." he continues.

"No, Commander, there isn't," she says, looking away again. "In fact, I'd just as soon not talk about anything right now, thank you."

The ferry pilots have paused in their metronomic recitation of the checklist. Although neither of them are looking their way, it's obvious that they're eavesdropping on the conversation. After a moment, they resume their work.

"Go for OMS pressurization."

"Third stage OMS pressurization beginning. Switch is armed, check . . ."

"We'll talk about it later," Parnell says. He hesitates, then adds, "And we *will* have a discussion, Captain."

Ryer's expression is glacial. "Yes, sir, Commander."

Parnell sighs and shuts his eyes for a moment. He feels a headache coming on; whose swell idea was it to allow women aboard spaceships in the first place, for Christ's sake? He gropes through his jumpsuit pockets for the Tylenol stashed in there somewhere as his eyes land on the digital chronometer above the cockpit hatch.

T-minus eighteen minutes, thirty-four seconds, and counting. They've come off the obligatory nine-minute hold in the countdown; unless the boys in the firing room find a reason to call another hold or even abort the launch, they'll be on their way in less than twenty minutes. That's eighteen and a half minutes too long for him.

"Mission, this is *Constellation*, conducting voice check, over . . . voice check, one, two, three."

"Load OPS-1 flight plan."

"Loading OPS-1, roger. ERR log switch set to reset. Enter Spec nine-niner, check on screens one and two."

"Roger that, Mission, we copy. Voice check over. *Constellation* out."

He finds the Tylenol tin, opens it, pulls out two tablets, and pops them into the back of his mouth, tasting their blandness on his tongue for a moment before he swallows them without the benefit of water. From somewhere behind and beneath him, he can hear muted conversation as one of the whiteroom techs struggles to help Dooley into his couch. Judging from the strident sound of the young man's voice, he seems to be having a last-minute panic attack, manifesting itself as general inability to fasten himself into his couch.

Parnell shuts his eyes again, trying to let the painkillers do their work. What did he do to deserve this? A final trip to the Moon with a hostile lesbian for a first officer and two media vultures and a computer geek for passengers. The only sane person in his crew is Lewitt; if it weren't for Jay, he'd be off this ancient tub already, taking the elevator to the nearest phone, where he'd call Goldin and tell him where he could shove this mission and exactly how. . . .

"Go for MPS pressurization."

"Initiating MPS cycle, roger."

This ancient tub. Funny how that thought just came to him. Opening his eyes again, Parnell gazes around the narrow passenger compartment. He can remember when the first Atlas-C was delivered by ocean barge from the North American Rockwell plant in Palmdale, California: brand-new, high-tech, seemingly the last word in astronautical engineering. Now, looking at it with fresh eyes, *Constellation*'s interior looks as antique as that of a B-52 bomber. The multipaned Plexiglas of the portal next to him is friction-scarred, the view of the blue sky overhead dimmed with age. The riveted seams of the beige-painted steel show the first signs of rust; the fabric of the acceleration couch is shiny with age, with a corner of his seat beginning to fray, white tufts of lining peeking out from between the stretched threads. There's a small square patch almost directly above his head, not old but not very recent either, where a nameless hangar worker once replaced a section that had suffered metal fatigue, and the bolt-holes around the service panels below the ladder are scratched and eroded from hundreds of business meetings with torqueless screwdrivers.

Parnell feels a cold shiver run down his spine. He remembers what he told Judith just last night, that *Constellation* is a reliable old bird. Now he's not quite so certain. The seats of the first Atlas-A orbiters had been equipped with evacuation capsules, much like enclosed ejection seats; if there was an emergency during launch, in theory the passengers could hit a couple of switches that would close the capsules and jettison them from the craft. But there were so many problems with the capsules—including a misfire that had killed a crewman—that they were removed from the ferries.

No one talks about it, but the Atlas-C's are flying coffins during the first three minutes of flight. If something goes during launch, the only possible recourse is for the pilot to fire the third-stage rocket and attempt an abort-to-ground landing. At least, that was the theory; he'd hate to be aboard the first spacecraft to actually attempt such a high-speed maneuver.

"Ground crew signals secure and all clear."

"Roger. Go for lock-down of main hatch . . ."

He hears the sound of the belly hatch slamming shut. Trombly unbuckles himself from his couch and quickly climbs down the ladder to dog it tight from the inside. Although he can't see the access arm from his porthole because of the starboard wing, Parnell knows that the bridge must be swinging away from the hull. The pad should be vacant now, save for a handful of technicians double-timing it to a waiting van; cabin lights flicker for a moment, a clue that *Constellation* has switched to internal power.

Placing his palms on the armrests, Parnell can feel the vibration of the ferry's fuel tanks pressurizing to maximum capacity. He doesn't have to look at the chronometer to know that the stately minuet of clocks and computers is entering its final movement.

"Abort advisory check satisfactory."

"Check, AAC is satisfactory. Channel two is clear."

"Roger, Launch Control, channel two is clear. Cabin pressurization is nominal, proceeding with hydraulic pressure check . . ."

And so it goes, on down the checklist, until in the final sixty seconds of countdown, somewhere between the closure of the first-stage vents and auxiliary power unit shutdown, Parnell finds himself murmuring a prayer under his breath. He has never considered himself a particularly religious man, especially not when it comes to leaving the ground. A bird is a bird, regardless of whether it's his Beechcraft or a three-stage rocket, and intellectually he knows that his fate rests more in the eyes, ears, and hands of the distant launch controllers and the thousands of people who prepped *Constellation* for flight than those of a mythic deity whose very existence he has always doubted.

God doesn't work for NASA, he tells himself. Yet, when he casts a stray glance in Ryer's direction, he's vaguely surprised to see that her own mouth is moving silently, and he doesn't have to be a lip-reader to know what she's saying: *Our Father, who art in heaven, hallowed be thy name . . .*

"Roger, Launch Control, we've got APU green-for-go, over."

"Main engine gimbal complete, all systems configured for launch."

"Roger that . . ."

Then Ryer's eyes move in his direction, and when she finds him looking at her, the words stop as her face blanches. Before she can look away again, though, Parnell smiles and gives her a sly wink as he silently completes the verse: *Thy kingdom come. Thy will be done in earth, as it is in heaven. . . .*

She reluctantly returns the smile.

"Main engine start on three."

"Five . . ."

"Four . . ."

The countdown reaches T-minus three seconds, and five thousand two hundred and fifty tons of hydrazine and nitric acid ignite beneath them in a deafening roar which shakes the vessel as if an earthquake had erupted directly beneath the pad. For an instant, the ferry sways back and forth within its cradle as the monster struggles against the invisible bars of its prison.

"Main engine start."

"Two . . ."

"One . . ."

And then the countdown reaches zero, the cradle opens wide, and *Constellation* slowly begins to rise.

Editorial from **The Manchester Union-Leader,** *Manchester, New Hampshire; August 28, 1968*

A "LUNATIC" IDEA

If one needs any further reason to question the fitness of Democratic Presidential candidate Robert F. Kennedy, it's his campaign promise to dismantle the U.S. Space Force and replace it with a civilian space agency.

During a campaign speech delivered last Wednesday at the McDonnell Douglas Corporation's manufacturing facility in St. Louis, Senator Kennedy told aerospace workers that as President of the United States he would phase out the USSF, and in its place, substitute a new Federal space organization which would concentrate on "peaceful and scientific" uses of outer space instead of "strictly military goals."

Unfortunately, Little Bobby the Boy Senator has considerable support for his proposal from the liberals in Congress, who have begun to question the Pentagon's oft-stated intent to use the Moon as a base for scientific research as well as in the pursuit of national security. It should also be noted that Little Bobby's cohorts in the so-called Youth International Party have seconded the notion. "If we can go to the Moon for some other reason than making war," says Jerry Rubin, "then that's fine with me."

Of course Red Jerry would agree! He and his gang of hippie radicals have already made headlines by protesting at the front gates of Cape Canaveral, including the "sit-ins" which have prevented military personnel from reporting to duty. If Kennedy got his way, he would probably appoint Abbie Hoffmann to be the director of the space program. That way they could have a "love-in" with "Hanoi Jane" Fonda on the Moon!

What the Senator and his *de facto* Communist friends don't mention is that this idea has been floated already. In 1959, Little Bobby's older brother, Little Johnny, proposed much the same thing with his Space Act, which was supported by Little Johnny's former Democratic running mate, Senator Lyndon B. "Claim-Jumpin'" Johnson of Texas. This was only one of the reasons why the Kennedy/Johnson ticket was soundly defeated in the 1960 presidential election; the American people recognized the fact that we need a strong military presence in space in order to offset the international Communist conspiracy.

Now, eight years later, we've got old whine poured into new bottles. It's clear that Little Bobby wants to vindicate Little Johnny's political reputation, although Boston's mayor could care less since he's busy destroying the city's schools with his desegregation program. It doesn't seem to matter to Senator Kennedy and his running mate, Senator Eugene "Pothead" McCarthy, that the very reason why America has Space Station One in the first place, and will be sending the first reconnaissance mission to the Moon next December, is its commitment to preserving the ideals of liberty and freedom.

During this past decade, President Nixon has held the public trust by insisting upon a military space program. Conducting scientific research on the Moon is a great idea, but a civilian space agency cannot possibly fulfill the objectives of the U.S. Space Force. As a ranking member of the Senate Armed Forces Committee, Little Bobby must know this . . . which makes us question why he would propose something as ludicrous as a civilian space program.

Could it be that Senator Kennedy's fellow travelers have received instructions from the Kremlin to stop Project Luna?

—William F. Loeb,
editor and publisher

SIX

Constellation left Earth atop a dense column of fire, the twenty-nine motors in its first-stage booster consuming more than a thousand tons of liquid propellant in less than ninety seconds.

The rocket's ascent could be seen from hundreds of miles away. On Florida's Gulf Coast, the vessel was a tapering contrail rising at a sharp angle from the eastern horizon, while on Cocoa Beach the sand itself seemed to vibrate as early-morning beachcombers paused in collecting shells to watch as the enormous rocket ripped upward into the deep blue sky. Within a minute and a half, *Constellation* had climbed almost twenty-five miles into the sky and was a little more than thirty-one miles downrange from the Cape. Traveling 5,256 miles per hour, it left in its wake a sonic boom that rattled the windows of houses far behind.

At this point, the pilots throttled the engines back to 70 percent. *Constellation* began to gradually fall, its nose dipping slightly toward the horizon. Left on its own, the rocket would have continued its shallow dive until it finally crashed at hypersonic speed into the Atlantic Ocean, but the throttle-back was only the prelude to its primary staging maneuver.

The first-stage engines expired, its fuel tanks drained, and a couple of moments later explosive bolts at the juncture of the first and second stages ignited. The winged booster cleaved away from the second stage; as it began to fall toward the ocean, a ring-shaped parafoil made of whisker-fine mesh steel blossomed out from beneath the wings, braking its descent until it splashed-down in the Atlantic nearly two hundred miles from the Cape, where it would be recovered by a NASA freighter and towed back to Merritt Island.

Long before this occurred, though, eight engines in the second stage fired at full-throttle as 155 tons of fuel kicked *Constellation* farther into the upper atmosphere. For two more minutes, the ferry fought its way up the gravity well, penetrating the topmost regions of the atmosphere until, at an altitude of nearly forty miles and more than 330 miles downrange, the second stage was jettisoned, whereupon it followed its mate on a parafoiled glide into the drink.

By now *Constellation* had lost most of its take-off mass and was accelerating at more than fourteen thousand miles per hour. Behind the orbiter's delta wings and vertical stabilizer, its single engine throttled up as the spacecraft accelerated to nearly 18,500 miles per hour . . . until, sixty-three miles above the Atlantic and a little more than seven hundred miles downrange from the Cape, the third-stage engine shut down and the winged craft coasted into low orbit.

Within the ferry, everyone took a deep breath.

Parnell thought he still remembered what it was like to ride a fireball into the heavens; as he raised a trembling hand to lift the visor of his helmet, though, he realized that his memory wasn't quite as sharp as he'd once believed. If there were four minutes in anyone's life that were as terrifying or traumatic as being inside an Atlas-C during launch, then it had to be birth itself . . . and nobody remembers what that's like.

"Jesus," he murmured as he stuck his fingers inside his helmet's foam padding to wipe away the sweat. "I'm too old for this crap."

He shifted his buttocks against the upholstery of his couch, only to discover that his ass barely rested against the seat. Indeed, it felt as if he were now floating a half-inch above the couch, restrained only by his harness. There was a moment of disorientation until he realized what had happened.

Weightlessness.

Free-fall.

There was a low, mechanical groan as the acceleration couches cantilevered in vertical position; what had once been walls were now floors. He turned his head to the right, ignoring the painful crick in his neck as he peered around the edge of his helmet through the porthole next to his seat. For a few moments, he could see nothing but starless, pitch-black nothingness, as fathomless as the deepest abyss imaginable. . . .

Then the pilots ignited RCR's along the fuselage to roll the ferry over on its back, and Earth hove in view, upside-down and as vast as the eye could see. Bright sunlight sparkled across the surface of the South Atlantic, filtering through sparse white clouds which cast shadows upon the ocean. Parnell caught a glimpse of a tiny silver shape dragging faint wake-lines behind it, and then the ship—probably an oil tanker the size of a small island—was gone from sight, replaced now by the mottled brown edge of a giant landmass which, after a moment, he recognized as Africa's northwest coast.

A low chuckle began to rise in Parnell's throat as he felt tears stinging the corners of his eyes. It had been so long, so long . . .

He was in space again.

Not everyone aboard the ferry had done well during launch; someone always gets spacesick during a passenger flight. In this instance, it was Paul Dooley and Alex Bromleigh who came down with motion sickness, despite the Dramamine tablets they had taken before boarding the rocket. Berkley Rhodes had managed to keep her breakfast down, although apparently only by sheer force of will; she lay in her couch, her eyes tightly closed, not daring to look out the window.

While *Constellation* circled Earth in preparation for the periapsis burn which would boost the ferry into higher orbit, Jay Lewitt unbuckled himself and floated aft to tend to the ill passengers. Fortunately, both men had found the vomit bags tucked under their seats and had remembered to use them, so there were no free-falling messes that had to be cleaned up.

Parnell remained in his seat while the ferry completed its first orbit, contenting himself with the view from his window.

He watched Africa pass beneath him until it disappeared beneath a dense cloud bank which extended as far as Madagascar; then the ferry crossed the nightside terminator above the Indian Ocean. Australia appeared as a cluster of city lights surrounding Perth and brief flashes from a thunderstorm over the outback; the coast of New Guinea was outlined by the harbor glow of Port Moresby.

"You can never get tired of it, can you?" Cris Ryer said.

He looked across the aisle at her. She was still strapped into her couch on the port side, gazing down at the sparse constellation marking the Bismarck Archipelago. It was the first time she had spoken since they left the Cape.

"I once thought I was," he said, and she looked querulously at him. "Tired of the view, I mean," he added. "Do a couple of tours of duty on the Wheel and pretty soon you get tired of everything."

Ryer smiled a little as she shook her head. Like Parnell, she had removed her helmet; her fine blond hair had risen from her scalp until it surrounded her head like a halo. "Not me," she said, brushing the hair back from her face. "I never got tired of watching. Whenever I had a chance, I spent it in front of a porthole . . . just looking."

He raised an eyebrow. "I didn't know you were stationed on the Wheel. When was this?"

"I wasn't on the Wheel," she replied, looking out her window. "After I joined NASA, I did a three-month tour aboard the Mole. That was back in 'eighty-two, before I transferred to the Lunar Support Team."

"You were on the Mole? I'm impressed. What did you do there?"

The Mole was the nickname for Space Station Two, officially known as the U.S. Air Force Manned Orbital Laboratory. One of the last holdovers from the Space Force, the MOL had been established during the mid-sixties in polar orbit 160 miles above Earth. A small zero-g station—essentially a retrofitted upper stage of an old Atlas-B ferry—Space Station Two had served as a military reconnaissance platform, keeping tabs on the old Soviet Union until the early eighties, when unmanned spy satellites had finally rendered it obsolete. Since the station had been capable of supporting only a handful of people at any one time, there weren't too many NASA astronauts who could claim that they had spent time aboard the Mole. Most of the vets had retired from active duty, while others had taken jobs at the CIA, the National Security Agency, or the National Reconnaissance Office. Even the Mole itself was gone; a sustained period of solar activity had expanded Earth's upper atmosphere, in turn causing the station's orbit to deteriorate. By then, NASA had neither the funds nor the inclination to rescue the tiny station, and when it had plummeted to a fiery death over Antarctica in 1983, only Greenpeace had objected on grounds of the environmental hazard it posed.

Ryer glowered at him. "If I told you what I did there, Commander," she said with mock severity, "I'd have to kill you."

"Great . . ."

"I was a shuttle driver, that's all. I took spooks up from Vandenberg and I took them back down when they were through. Pretty boring work, all things considered."

"You passed over Russia several times a day. That counts for something."

"If you say so." She shrugged. "Now and then one of the spooks would let me check out the scope so I could get a good eyeful of Baikonur . . . enough to know that they were screwing up their space program only slightly worse than we were screwing up ours. Nobody aboard the Mole was taking the Russians very seriously anymore, despite all the 'evil empire' stuff coming out of Washington."

Ryer peered out her window again at the dark expanse of the Pacific Ocean. "So when the Pentagon announced that it was shutting down the Mole, I skipped over to the LST and became a moonship driver. Thought that would give me some job security and all that. . . ."

Her voice trailed off. "Great idea, huh?" she murmured. "Sometimes I'm so smart I amaze myself."

Somebody wasn't being smart, Parnell thought, that was for damn sure. If she had served on the Mole, even as a shuttle jockey, she must have had CIA clearance . . . and if she had ever posed a meaningful risk to national security, then she would have passed Top Secret info to the Russians long before now. The fact that Ryer was still on active duty more than a decade after the MOL phase-out was enough to demonstrate her loyalty.

Then why was she being drummed out of the NASA astronaut corps? Was it simply because she had been discovered carrying on a sexual relationship with another woman? Or was there another reason he didn't know about?

Stretching against his harness, Parnell leaned across the armrest. "Look, Cris," he said quietly, "about the thing with the keys . . ."

"I don't want to talk about it." Ryer gazed out her porthole again. "I've probably said too much already. No offense, Commander, but just leave me alone, okay?"

He was about to prod her when sunlight lanced through the windows. *Constellation* was coming up on the daylight terminator; looking through the window, he saw the sun rising above Baja California, describing a hazy blue line that stretched from San Diego to Mexico City.

"Okay, look sharp back there," Trombly called out from the cockpit. "We're coming up on periapsis burn, so everyone buckle in. We'll be firing at T-minus five."

Parnell heard a soft groan from someone behind him—Dooley perhaps, or maybe Bromleigh—as Lewitt pulled himself along the ladder until he reached his seat. There was no need to tighten his own harness, since the burn would last only a couple of minutes and would be nowhere near as violent as the staging maneuvers during launch. He made certain that his helmet was safely stowed beneath his couch, then watched through his porthole as the American West Coast, seen through a swirl of clouds, slowly glided into view.

As much as he wanted to ignore it, though, something about Ryer gnawed at Parnell's guts. He knew that he wouldn't be satisfied until he discovered exactly what it was.

The periapsis burn occurred as *Constellation* passed over the Gulf of Mexico. At the end of a brief countdown from the cockpit, the main engine fired and the ferry surged forward, the blue horizon rushing away beneath the vessel as it was kicked into a Hohmann transfer that would carry the orbiter on an elliptical trajectory into higher orbit.

When the burn ended, Parnell unbuckled his harness and floated out of his couch. He bent and straightened his legs to relieve the cramps he'd been feeling for the last few minutes, then grasped the ladder—which now seemed to lie horizontally along the floor—and pulled himself forward to the cockpit.

"Permission to come up, Captain?" he asked as he stuck his head and shoulders through the hatch.

"Hmm?" Captain Kingsolver glanced over his shoulder. "Oh . . . permission granted, Commander." He reattached his clipboard and pen to the console between the seats, then turned around. "Thanks for asking," he added. "Some of the VIPs we carry up don't give us the courtesy."

"Not that there's all that much room." Trombly sucked a tube of orange juice as he watched the autopilot display. For at least a little while, *Constellation* was able to fly herself, guided by the navigation computers and the laws of inertia as it glided toward its rendezvous with the Wheel. "You're welcome to make yourself at home, though, if you can, sir."

"I'll try, Commander . . . and you can call me Gene, by the way." There was very little room in the cockpit, but Parnell was able to squeeze himself into a space between the seat backs and the aft bulkhead. "Nice launch you guys pulled off."

"Thanks. We do our best." Kingsolver stolidly nodded his head, acknowledging the professional compliment. "Of course, it wasn't anything special to an old-timer like yourself. Probably like riding in a commuter jet."

If only he knew. The cockpit layout was much the same as Parnell remembered it, except that some of the analog dials had been replaced by digital instrumentation. Japanese-made, of course, he noted with some dismay, but wasn't everything these days? He noticed also that the toggle switches and computer keyboards were shiny with overuse, and the brown leather grips of the control yokes had been repaired with black friction tape. In the old days, worn-out equipment would have been long-since replaced, but there were precious few spare parts left in the NASA inventory. Budget cuts, as always— although it was debatable whether the aerospace manufacturers who had built the originals still stocked them in their warehouses.

Kingsolver seemed to read Parnell's mind. "She's a tough old bird," he said, giving the yoke a fond pat, "but she gets us where we want to go. Even if we're down to cannibalizing *Intrepid* for odds and ends every now and then."

"I heard," Parnell said. "I flew *Intrepid* on her shakedown mission. She was a brand new ship back then." He caught the apologetic look on Kingsolver's face and shook his head. "Don't worry about it, skipper. I was one of the guys who signed the papers to take her off the flight line. Broke my heart, but it had to be done."

An uncomfortable silence descended upon the cockpit, broken after a moment by tinny voices coming through Trombly's headset. The co-pilot listened for a few moments, then reached up to click the KU-band transceiver. "Ah, we copy that, Wheel. *Constellation* at angles nine-three-six, range three-five-zero. We're in the grid and preparing for OI burn. Over."

Through the angular panes of the canopy, Parnell could see the broad, blue-green curve of Earth sweeping back into view, shining against the matte-black darkness of space. The ferry was flattening out its trajectory as it began to enter the wheel's orbit. In another few minutes, the pilots would take the controls off auto and fire the main engine one more time to match its heading with Space Station One.

Holding onto the seat backs, Parnell carefully edged himself a little farther into the cockpit until he was able to crane his neck and look straight up through the ceiling window. He listened to Kingsolver and Trombly as they traded checklist instructions and spoke with the Wheel's traffic controller, the captain's fingers tapping softly upon the keyboard as he entered instructions into the orbiter's main computer.

Then he spotted it: a tiny white oval, rotating clockwise on its axis, drifting slowly into view. Looking like an old-style bicycle tire someone had left in the sky, just the way he had last seen it many years ago. He found himself grinning at the sight. Jesus, it was beautiful. . . .

"Commander? Gene?" Kingsolver's voice was apologetic as he interrupted Parnell's thoughts. "We're coming up on

OI burn, sir. I'm going to have to ask you to return to your seat. Sorry.''

Parnell forced himself away from the windows. ''That's okay, skipper. I understand.'' There would be just enough g-force during the orbital insertion burn to throw unsecured items around the cockpit, and that included a visiting passenger. ''Thanks for letting me come up front. I appreciate it.''

He was beginning to backpedal out of the cockpit when Trombly suddenly reached up to tap the back of his hand. ''Hey, Commander,'' he said quickly, ''there's one more thing you might want to see. Check out my window at ten o'clock.''

Parnell grabbed bulkhead rungs to brake himself, then gently pulled himself back into the cabin until his head and shoulders were next to the co-pilot's. For a moment, he saw nothing except the limb of the earth . . . then a new object, until now invisible except to the ship's radar, coasted into view.

It was another spacecraft, matching course with the ferry as it headed for rendezvous with the Wheel.

Almost the same size as *Constellation*, the spaceplane was a sleek, elongated bullet with narrow, wedge-shaped wings at its aft end that tilted upward above its blunt stern. The lower fuselage was perfectly flat, its landing gear bays invisible within the reentry tiles which comprised most of the vessel's outer skin. There were no portholes to be seen except a couple of windows near the front of its tapering bow.

The ESA space shuttle *Dornberger* resembled the *Constellation* about as much as a Concorde SST looks like a Douglas DC-3. The *Horus*-class orbiter had ridden into space on the back of a manned Sanger booster, which in turn had lifted from a runway in French Guiana . . . more than half an hour after *Constellation* had been launched from Cape Canaveral, if Parnell correctly remembered the mission schedule. Even now, as *Constellation*'s boosters were still being recovered from the Atlantic Ocean, the Sanger was probably touching down for landing on the same airstrip it had left barely an hour ago, its scramjets ready for refueling in a fraction of the time that it would take *Constellation* to be remated with its boosters, patched up one more time, and hauled out to the pad for its next mission.

"The hare and the tortoise," Parnell murmured as he watched the *Dornberger* glide past them.

"Pardon?" Kingsolver said. The pilot didn't look away from his controls, but Parnell noticed how tightly he clutched the control yoke.

"You heard what I said, Captain." He pushed off from the seat backs without another word and exited the cockpit, clumsily making his way down the center aisle to his seat.

Everyone was watching the German shuttle through the portholes; as Parnell floundered into his seat, he noticed that Bromleigh had recovered from spacesickness enough to hoist his camera and grab a shot of the *Dornberger*. Maybe that would impress the folks back home when they saw it on the evening news.

On the other hand, they'd probably just click over to a rerun of *Who's the Boss?*

From The New York Times; *July 21, 1969*

MEN LAND ON MOON—
10 ASTRONAUTS AVOID CRATER,
SET CRAFT ON A ROCKY PLAIN
By John Noble Wilford
(*Special to* The New York Times)

HOUSTON, July 20—Men landed on the moon today. Ten Americans, astronauts of Luna One, rode their giant spacecraft safely and smoothly to a historic landing at 4:17:40 P.M., Eastern daylight time.

Major John Harper Wilson, the 38-year-old United States Space Force expedition commander, radioed to Earth and the control room here:

"Houston, Tranquillity Base here. Eagle One has landed."

Eagle One is the code-name of the 160-foot space vessel that carried Wilson and his colleagues from Space Station One to their landing site on a level, rock-strewn plain near the southwestern shore of the arid Sea of Tranquillity. It was soon followed by the successful touchdowns of Eagle Two and Eagle Three, two unmanned yet nearly identical cargo vessels.

The astronauts reported a bleak, gray landscape covered with rocks and boulders of varying sizes, with the sun hanging low over the eastern horizon and small craters filled with shadows.

Their landing was witnessed by an audience estimated to be in the millions, who watched live television transmissions sent from Eagle One as it made its final descent. Shortly after a successful landing was confirmed by Mission Control, President Robert F. Kennedy offered his congratulations to Wilson and his crew by telephone from the White House.

"This is a great day for the entire human race, and your country is very proud of you," President Kennedy said. "God bless you."

SEVEN

Seen from a distance, the Wheel looked much the same as when Parnell last visited it twenty years before, yet as *Constellation* closed in on the station, the illusion of permanency slowly evaporated until he was faced with undeniable truth.

The space station was falling apart.

The Wheel was composed of twenty sections, each constructed of flexible fabric and nylon which had been transported into orbit in collapsed sections. Once the sections were linked together and the 250-foot torus was pressurized like an enormous inner tube, an outer hull of sheet aluminum had been built around the fabric and nylon inner wall to serve as a meteor bumper. Internal water tanks arranged evenly between the hulls served not only as internal stabilizers but also as passive radiation shields; after the interior compartments had been completed, small rocket engines along the outer hull had been fired to rotate the station clockwise at nearly three rpm's, producing one-third Earth gravity within the torus.

Parnell remembered the station when it was still new. Back then, it was the epitome of American know-how, a symbol of his country's military and technological superiority. But that had been a generation ago, and things had changed.

The meteor bumper was now a patchwork of replaced plates, the older ones rendered off-white by long-term radiation exposure, the newer plates scarred and pockmarked by micrometeorite impacts. The silver Mylar insulation protecting the electrical conduits that ran alongside the two hub spokes was torn and frayed in places; likewise, the oxygen and auxiliary water tanks on the bulb-shaped hub looked as if they had been repaired many times. The troughlike mercury boiler which ran along the top of the torus had been nonfunctional ever since the nuclear generator was installed at the hub's north turret sixteen years ago; the edges of the boiler itself were battered, and one section was missing entirely. The big high-gain antenna at the hub's south turret had a small hole in the dish; some of the portholes along the torus were permanently sealed from the outside.

Overall, the Wheel resembled an old battleship rusting in port. Its decrepitude wasn't so much the result of thirty-one years of hard service as it was of benign neglect. Space Station One had become an unwanted derelict, a giant symbol of a frontier that had been conquered, then abandoned. Keeping it operational was only slightly less costly than dismantling it altogether.

Through the cockpit hatch, Parnell could hear the pilots murmuring to each other as they eased *Constellation* into a parking orbit a half-mile from the station. Watching through his porthole, he could see the *Dornberger* as it closed upon the station's hub. Motors rotated the south turret counterclockwise to produce a stable target at the docking bays, but unlike *Constellation*, the German shuttle was equipped with a universal docking adaptor which enabled it to link up directly with the Wheel. *Constellation*, on the other hand, would have to await the arrival of a taxi that would ferry her crew and cargo to the station.

Dornberger's advantage lay in having shorter wings, and thus the ability to maneuver close to the station, although Parnell wondered if its designers didn't have a hidden agenda when they added that docking adaptor. Had the Horus shuttles been built for the day when the Europeans would own Space Station One? ESA maintained that it intended to place its own space station in low orbit and that it had no desire to acquire the Wheel. On the other hand, Parnell remembered when the Europeans had said nearly the same thing about establishing their own lunar base.

"Okay, folks, we're here." Kingsolver had unbuckled his harness and was floating through the cockpit hatch into the passenger compartment. "Main-Ops says that a taxi's on its way and should be with us in a few minutes, so y'all better shake a leg." He paused next to Parnell's seat. "Commander, if you'd like to give me a hand in back . . ."

"Sure thing, skipper." Parnell slipped out of his harness and followed the pilot toward the aft end of the compartment. Ryer and Lewitt were both taking this in stride, but two of the civilians were having problems. Dooley was still green-faced and looked as if he was ready to blow his guts again any moment, while Bromleigh was struggling to unfasten his buckles and at the same time keep his camcorder from wandering away.

Berkley Rhodes, on the other hand, was completely fascinated by everything going on around her. Already unbuckled from her couch, she floated in the center aisle, almost doing somersaults as she savored her first taste of unfettered weightlessness. Not much of a surprise; some people adapt to microgravity faster than others, and physicians had long ago noticed how women usually get over spacesickness faster than men. Still, she should have paid closer attention to the training films; her euphoria was almost out of control, and she came dangerously close to kicking Kingsolver in the teeth as he tried to squeeze past her.

The captain impatiently grabbed her ankles and pushed her out of the way. Rhodes cried out, more in surprise than in pain, as her shoulders banged against the ceiling. "Dammit," she snapped, "just ask next time!"

"Whoa. Take it easy." Parnell grasped her forearms and hauled her back toward her seat. "It's fun, but don't go nuts. Equal and opposite reaction, remember?"

"Uh, yeah . . . right." Her happy grin faded; she hadn't forgotten their encounter on the launch pad. "Sorry, Commander," she said stiffly. "I'll try to remember."

"Don't worry about it," he told her. "You've just got to be a little careful, that's all."

Her expression softened a bit; for the first time, he noticed her gray-green eyes and the lovely way her long hair billowed out like a blond cloud around her head. She really was an attractive woman, Parnell reflected, once she turned off the hard-nosed journalist routine. On impulse, he reached over the back of Lewitt's seat and snagged the NASA flight cap from the flight engineer's head. Jay looked around and started to complain until Parnell gave him a wink.

"Put this on," he said as he handed the cap to Rhodes, "and don't forget to return it to the lieutenant. Someone should have told you to wear a barrette."

"Thanks, Commander." She caught her loose hair under the cap and pulled the scrambled-eggs bill over her forehead. "Sorry to be such a jerk."

"There's a first time for everyone, Ms. Rhodes."

Her grin returned; this time, there was a hint of sly sexuality to it. "Call me Berkley," she said in a low voice, clasping his shoulders. "Most guys do."

Lewitt gave a low, smart-aleck whistle at this; glancing over his shoulder, Parnell caught the shit-eating grin on his face. Ryer appeared to be studying the rivets along the ceiling. "My name's Gene," he replied as he gently disengaged himself. "That's what my wife calls me."

She was still giving him a 100-watt smile as he pulled himself down the aisle. All in the name of good press relations, he told himself . . . although he now had a clue as to why Berkley Rhodes was such a successful journalist.

The airlock was located midships, on the opposite side of the compartment from the belly hatch. Kingsolver had already attached his headset prong to the intercom next to the hatch and was talking to the incoming taxi: "Okay, you're looking good . . . turn twenty degrees starboard, keep that inclination . . . there you go, looking good."

Through a small window in the airlock hatch, Parnell could see the taxi as it cautiously approached *Constellation*'s hull, carefully avoiding the leading edge of the vertical stabilizer. The taxi was a long white cylinder with open cone-shaped cages at its bow and stern. Small liquid-fuel engines, mounted on swivels, were located inside each cage; a hardsuited astronaut occupied the forward cage, clinging to the lateral struts with one hand as he manually controlled the bow rocket. Aft of the forward cage, above the taxi's fuselage and just behind the rubber docking ring, rose the pressurized pilot turret; Parnell could make out the pilot's head and shoulders through its circular windows as he followed the cargo grunt's hand signals. Two more hardsuited astronauts on EVA tethers clung to grommets on the port side as they prepared to open the cargo hatch and unload the duffel bags belonging to the ferry's passengers.

As the taxi swung around for final docking, Parnell caught sight of the old USSF insignia above the cargo hatch. Painted above the insignia was the spacecraft's name: *Harpers Ferry*. A name with a double meaning: the taxi was christened not only in honor of John Harper Wilson, the first man to set foot on the Moon, but also for a Civil War battle.

"Must be a Southerner running that boat," he commented.

"Not anymore." Kingsolver didn't look away from the window. "Used to be Dan Caldwell's boat, but he went groundside last year. Drives a warehouse forklift now. Says it's better money."

There was an audible thump as *Harpers Ferry* hard-docked with *Constellation*; the rubber ring slid neatly into the round groove surrounding the hatch and instantly pressurized, forming an airtight seal between the two vessels. "Okay, you're in," Kingsolver said. "Resetting for fourteen PSI, over." He let out his breath as he touched buttons on the control panel to equalize the atmospheres between the orbiter and the taxi, then cupped a hand over his headset mike.

"Now they've got some kid running Dan's boat," he murmured with obvious disdain as he glanced over his shoulder at Parnell. "Every time we do this, I'm scared he's going to ram my ship."

"Why? He's a bad pilot?"

Kingsolver stared at him. "Ever heard of Dr. Z?" Parnell shook his head and the captain looked away. "You'll love him," he muttered. "He's a load of laughs."

A couple of minutes later Parnell felt his ears pop as the atmospheres between the two vessels equalized. The passengers were shaking their heads and swallowing spit by the time Kingsolver undogged the airlock hatch and hauled it open. At least Dooley and Bromleigh had gotten over their panic attacks, although both men still gripped vomit bags in their free hands. Parnell led the way through the airlock; the lock-lever of the taxi's bow hatch was covered with frost, freezing against the palms of his hands as he shoved it upward.

"Right this way. Step lively now." The voice from within the chilly, cramped confines of the passenger cell was fairly young. "Just cram in and grab hold of something."

The pilot could only be seen from his waist down to his feet, which were strapped into stirrups on top of a short platform. The feet were wearing scuffed black Doc Martens; above them were long, thin legs wearing faded Levis, and through a hole in the right knee peeped a pair of woolen long johns. The rest of him was invisible within the turret.

Parnell pushed himself to the far side of the passenger cell, where he grabbed a leather ceiling strap next to a small porthole. Through the tiny window, he could see the two astronauts outside *Harpers Ferry*; they had opened the hatch to the unpressurized bay behind the cell and were unloading cargo containers from the *Constellation*. His breath fogged the porthole; it had to be thirty-five degrees at most inside the taxi.

"It's cold in here!" Rhodes found a strap next to Parnell and clumsily fell against him, hugging herself for warmth. "Can you turn up the heat a little, please?" she called to the legs. "I can't believe how cold it is!"

"Cold? You think this is cold? Try being outside with those guys. This is a lovely spring day in Minneapolis, compared to out there."

The legs bent at the knees as the pilot lowered himself on his haunches from the turret. First came an old "Lollapalooza '92" sweatshirt, then a head that was shaved almost bald, with a gold ring in its right ear. The pilot had to squat low; in his mid-twenties he was at least 6'3", almost too tall to be working in space.

"Hey, we've got a celebrity aboard!" His lantern-jawed mouth arched into a wide grin as his gaze settled on Rhodes. He stretched out a wool-gloved hand. "The name's Curtis. Curtis Zimm. My friends call me Dr. Z. Welcome aboard."

"Berkley Rhodes. ATS News." She gave him an uncomfortable smile as she reluctantly extended her own hand.

"I know. Watch your show all the time." Dr. Z grasped her hand palm-up in a formal handshake. "Always a pleasure to have a member of the fourth estate aboard. Perhaps we could do an interview sometime while you're . . ."

"Hey, man! Turn up the heat or something! It's fuckin' freezing in here!"

Dr. Z turned to face Dooley, whose nasal whine had interrupted the little chat. "What's it to you, boomer?" he asked, dropping Rhodes's hand. "And watch your language . . . there's a lady present."

Before Dooley could do more than glare at him, Dr. Z smiled again. "Oh, you must be the right honorable Paul Dooley. I've got a message for you, passed along from a mutual friend."

Confusion crept into Dooley's face as he nestled in beside Rhodes. "A message?" he asked uncertainly. "What sort of message?"

Curtis Zimm peered at him long and hard before his smile reappeared. "From our mutual friend Mr. Grid, of course," he said. "Says he wants you to call him tonight."

Rhodes looked at Dooley. "Mr. Grid . . . ?"

Before Dooley could answer, Dr. Z touched the earphone of his headset, listening intently to inaudible voices on the comlink. "Sorry to be short," he said apologetically, "but we're running a little behind schedule. Your stuff's aboard, so dog that hatch tight and we'll be off."

His head and shoulders disappeared back into the turret as though he'd gone through a wormhole into another dimension. Which, from what little Parnell had witnessed, probably wasn't so far off the mark.

"Who's Mr. Grid?" Lewitt asked. He was the last person through the airlock, sliding in just behind Cris Ryer. The passenger cell was crowded now, with everyone jammed together in the center of the compartment, jostling one another's elbows, knees, and feet. Kingsolver slammed the airlock hatch shut; Ryer leaned past Lewitt to close the taxi hatch and spin the lockwheel.

"Friend of mine," Dooley said reluctantly. He glanced at Dr. Z's legs as if afraid that the pilot was eavesdropping. "Umm . . . just someone back home I keep in touch with on Le Matrix. I told him I'd send some e-mail from here." He shrugged noncommittally and pretended to look out a porthole, now fogged over from the combined respiration of the taxi's passengers.

Mr. Dooley, Parnell thought, *you are one weird son of a bitch.*

"Okay now," Dr. Z called down from the turret, "everyone comfy?" He laughed, knowing they weren't. "You'd better be, 'cause we're casting off."

Another *thump!* and a shudder as *Harpers Ferry* disengaged from *Constellation*. Parnell wiped off the porthole next to him just in time to see the winged space plane drifting away. Earth was a blue-green hemisphere in the background that, along with the ferry, quickly vanished from sight as the taxi turned around and headed for the Wheel.

Welcome home . . .

Excerpt from "Lost In Space" by Lucas Trilling; New Times, *May 1972*

It doesn't seem possible, upon observing American astronauts and Russian cosmonauts training together in the massive centrifuge at the Von Braun Space Center, to believe even for a moment that their joint mission a few years from now may be the last hurrah for either country's manned space program.

I stood in the observation cupola above the giant room and watched the mockup of the Ares lander swinging round and round, hearing the Slavic-accented voice of Alexei Leonov calmly reporting the gradual buildup of g-force within the capsule, interrupted by Neil Armstrong—"We're fine, let's go for another spin"—and thought, *that's the way it should be, the way it should have always been, Americans and Russians working together for a mission to Mars.*

And so it will be. The International Mars Exploration Treaty is two years old and both countries are committed to the project, if only for the sake of preserving *detente* between the United States and the Soviet Union. Bobby Kennedy's ghost haunts Ares as well; no one can forget that the treaty was his brainstorm and that NASA, also his baby, was given its first major goal as a Federal agency by the Mars program. His next stop in Texas after Dallas would have been to deliver a speech here in Houston. It is not enough that the NASA launch center at Cape Canaveral was renamed in his memory; an American flag on Mars, standing alongside the hammer and sickle of the U.S.S.R., is the only way this country can pay tribute to its fallen president.

Yet, like a ferry coasting into orbit, the only thing that seems to be keeping the American space program going is mass and inertia; the boosters have been exhausted and dropped off, and all that remains is free-fall. President McCarthy's inability to set a long-term agenda for NASA is only one more indication that his administration has been a failure, and the only thing George McGovern and George Wallace agree upon is that the hatchet will fall on the space budget, regardless of who wins the November election.

Without leadership from the top, the American space program cannot prosper for very long. Roosevelt, Truman, Eisenhower, Nixon, Kennedy—an unbroken chain of presidencies have supported the Final Frontier, from World War II through the Cold War, all in the name of defeating The Enemy, whether it be Nazi Germany or Communist Russia. But after we beat the Russians to the Moon, only to then discover that the Soviet space program had been so badly mismanaged that they were barely in the running, the impetus fell off. What glory and honor is to be gained from a race when the opponent crosses the finish line in a wheelchair?

By then, the Space Force was so thoroughly affiliated with America's role in Vietnam that it was difficult for many to disassociate Space Station One and Project Luna from the secret bombing of Cambodia and the My Lai massacre. Orbital reconnaissance from the Wheel didn't stop American casualties from mounting south of the DMZ, and a USSF uniform looks just like a USAF uniform to an antiwar demonstrator with fire in his belly and spit in his mouth.

Even after Kennedy phased out the Space Force and replaced it with NASA, public sentiment continued to shift against space exploration. Perhaps the first indicator was the Nielsen ratings; someone in the White House should have paid attention when *Star Trek,* once the number two show on television, was canceled because of bad ratings. Or they should have noticed the "Fuck the Moon" buttons college students were wearing. It hardly matters now. One by one, the American public has been turning against the space program, long before the politicians got hip.

We'll go to Mars, if only because the funds have already been appropriated and because no one wants to back out on the Russians. Yet, like Archie Bunker and his family, stranded together on a forgotten lunar outpost where Edith serves up endless slices of green algae pie and Meathead always forgets to shut the airlock, America is clearly lost in space. . . .

EIGHT

Climbing the ladder through the Wheel's western spoke from the hub, Ryer felt the tug of gravity gradually increase with each rung she passed.

She had been virtually weightless when she left the hub, and at first the spoke seemed to be a horizontal tunnel, its ladder a nigh-useless handrail running along its ceiling. A third of the way down the spoke, she found a sign painted in large red letters on the walls: USE LADDER NOW. By then the tunnel had become a vertical shaft, the ladder a necessity. For the first time in a couple of hours, Cris could feel the objects in her pockets, and her duffel bag hung like a dead weight from its shoulder strap. Her hair settled back down around her neck, her breasts no longer seemed to bob an inch above her chest, and her arm and leg muscles had to exert themselves once again.

It was almost a shame; she had forgotten how much fun zero-g could be. Experiencing a moment of vertiginous nausea as her guts resettled, she paused on the ladder to briefly close her eyes and reorient herself to the up-and-down perspective. Breathe deeply, she told herself. Take it easy . . .

A foot clanged on the rung next to her left hand, barely missing her head: "Oops! Sorry."

Glancing up, she saw Parnell holding onto the ladder just above her, his duffel bag suspended a few inches over her

shoulder. He gazed down at her with concern. "You okay?"
he asked.

"I'm okay. Just resting a sec." She noticed that his face
was ashen. "How are you doing?"

Parnell nodded. "Fine . . . fine." He looked around the
shaft, pretending not to be unsettled by the gravity gradient.
"Last time I was here, this thing was lined with rope nets.
Made the climb a little easier." He took a deep breath. "And
the elevator still worked."

"The elevator hasn't been used in years," Cris said. "The
cables wore out and—"

"Nobody wanted to spend money to replace 'em." Parnell
shook his head. "Made it easier for the Geritol bunch. You
sure you're okay?"

"Sure," she replied, and recommenced the long climb
down to the torus.

Two young NASA officers had met the lunar team when
Harpers Ferry docked at the south turret. Once everyone had
reclaimed their bags, one lieutenant led Rhodes, Bromleigh,
and Dooley down the eastern spoke to their quarters on one
side of the wheel, while the other officer escorted Parnell,
Lewitt, and Ryer to operations center on the opposite end of
the station. It had been almost four years since Cris's last
visit to Space Station One, and it was a relief to cycle through
the main airlock; at least she was off the *Constellation* and
no longer had to deal with Kingsolver and Trombly. There
were probably homophobes among the station crew, but if so,
they wisely kept their prejudices to themselves. The unwritten
code among Wheel personnel was that if you disliked someone because of race, politics, religion, or what they did in the
privacy of their bunks during off-hours, you either kept your
opinions to yourself or transferred to a ground job. Put up,
shut up, or get-off: that was the rule.

Not that there was a shortage of privacy inside Space Station One anymore. Signs of the cutbacks which had trimmed
the crew by two-thirds were obvious the moment Cris floated
from the docking node into the suit-up compartment. The
walls of the spherical chamber had once been crammed with
spacesuits and racks of helmets: one for each crew member,
in the unlikely event of an emergency which would force a

mass evacuation of the station. Now only thirty-odd suits remained; the rest had been taken back to the Cape and warehoused as surplus.

Lewitt and the j.g. were waiting for Ryer and Parnell at the bottom of the ladder. "Right this way, please," Lieutenant Frierson said, holding open a hatch that led onto Deck One. "The commander's waiting for you in Main-Ops."

The Wheel had never been made for comfort or aesthetic appeal. Its bare metal walls were studded with rivets and painted a utilitarian shade of gray; small blue plastic door signs affixed to hatches and the occasional red fire extinguisher or intercom were the only colors. The torus had about as much charm and homeyness as an old Polaris sub, yet it occurred to Cris that it had always been full of life. The last time she'd been here, one couldn't walk ten feet down an upward-curving corridor without having to stand aside and allow another crew member to squeeze by. One heard voices constantly: conversations through half-open hatches and airducts, general announcements from ceiling speakers, people talking to each other in the corridors. If you remained standing in one place for a short amount of time, you would probably see half of the crew walk past, heading for duty-shifts or taking care of roster details or just getting a little exercise by jogging the decks. What life aboard the Wheel had lacked in style, it made up for in round-the-clock human activity.

Now, there was not even that. Most of the hatches they passed were shut, some sealed and locked, and they didn't need to stand aside for anyone as they marched toward Main-Ops. No voices. No intercom messages. No light jazz or country music coming from the officers' wardroom. Just the tread of their shoes on the threadbare carpet of the corridor, the hollow sound of air circulating through wall vents, the faint gurgle of water running through ceiling pipes from one ballast tank to the next.

"I think everyone's gone AWOL," Parnell said quietly.

Cris nodded. "That or the biggest furlough you've ever seen."

"Hey, look!" Lewitt said, pointing somewhere just ahead. "I saw a tumbleweed!"

"Maybe they all got abducted by UFO's . . ."

"Your congressman, more likely."

Dismal laughter, humorless and flat. Space Station One was a cold ghost town, spent and used up. If there was a museum big enough to hold a 250-foot bicycle tire, then the Wheel belonged there.

They were walking through an historical relic, and even history didn't seem to give a damn anymore.

Main-Ops was the only place where there seemed to be any life remaining aboard the Wheel, if only because it was the station's nerve center and, as such, was manned on a twenty-four-hour basis.

The operations center was the largest single compartment within Space Station One. While the rest of the torus was divided into three concentric decks, Main-Ops was a double-decker comprising half of one of the station's twenty torus sections. They stood on a catwalk overlooking the central floor, which was lined with carrels much like Launch Control at the Cape. An electronic Mercator projection of the globe, traced with parabolic curves depicting the Wheel's footprint as it orbited Earth, took up one entire wall, and above the map was a set of dial clocks displaying the various time zones.

Main-Ops was dimly lit. Most of the illumination came from computer screens that cast a pale blue glow across the faces of the duty officers who were seated at the carrels conversing quietly with one another via headset mikes. A laser printer chattered as it churned out the endless scroll of the station's logbook; the air held a vague odor of coffee from the enamel mugs nearly everyone had on their desks.

A hatch opened on a balcony at the far end of the catwalk; a young man in jeans and a flannel shirt stepped through and trotted down the spiral staircase to the main deck, carelessly allowing the hatch to remain ajar. Through the hatchway could be seen a smaller, single-deck compartment, its walls lined with television monitors.

The Earth Observation Center. There was a time, Ryer recalled, when she would have had to show Top Secret security clearance to an armed guard posted just outside the hatch before she was allowed to enter the EOC, and leaving its hatch open would have been unthinkable. That was back in the days when Space Station One's role had been almost exclusively military and the screens would be displaying any number of scenes relayed to the Wheel by ISPY, the space telescope positioned in polar orbit 1,075 miles above Earth: Soviet submarines surfacing off the coast of Cuba, troop movements in the Angolan desert, suspicious-looking freighters gliding between China and North Vietnam, U.S. Navy carrier convoys heading toward the Philippines, NATO exercises in the North Atlantic.

In its time, the Wheel had helped keep the Cold War nice and chilly. Indeed, a former Space Force officer named John Walker had been sent to prison for life for selling ISPY's orbital parameters to the Russians; most of his information had been stolen during duty tours aboard the Wheel. That time was over. Long before the Soviet Union had crumbled, unmanned spy satellites in low orbit had rendered ISPY, and by extension Space Station One itself, obsolete. While ISPY could only pick out the vague shape of a Soviet boomer as it entered Havana Harbor, the cameras aboard a KH-11 had superior resolution, making it possible for a CIA analyst in McLean, Virginia, to tell if it was an *Oscar, Delta,* or *Typhoon*-class sub . . . and the Keyholes' orbits could be repositioned far more easily than ISPY, making them flexible in ways never possible for either the Wheel or the Mole.

Now the Wheel served other purposes. ISPY monitored environmental degradation in South America and Africa, charting the recession of Brazilian rain forests and the growth of deserts in the Sudan, while the station itself kept track of the low-orbit Global Positioning Satellites, occasionally dispatching repair teams to overhaul them. Every now and then, DEA or Coast Guard intelligence experts would come aboard and try to ferret out the location of secret coca plantations in Colombia and Mexico, but that was the closest affiliation the Wheel still had with national security. In terms of day-to-day military application, the Wheel was now as useless as the filled-in Minuteman ICBM silos scattered across the Midwest.

And it showed. Leaning against the catwalk rail, Ryer couldn't help but notice how antiquated Main-Ops had become. The workstation computers were clunky old Digitals whose CRTs flickered with snow, their keyboards first-generation AT-clones that audibly clacked with each keystroke. Vintage 1985 hardware, she guessed, and her observation was confirmed when she spotted an operator carefully sliding a 5.25-inch floppy into a disk drive. Some of the other equipment made the computers look brand-new in comparison; the master console of the attitude-control bay beneath the stairwell resembled a prop from some fifties science fiction movie, and much of the equipment in Main-Ops, with its dials and meters, looked as if it had been installed when Cris was in kindergarten. Even the round air-conditioning vent in the ceiling vaguely reminded her of a hubcap from a 1963 Oldsmobile.

A junkyard owner would love this place.

"Gene! How the hell are you?"

Cris looked around as several pairs of soft-soled shoes trod up the spiral staircase. A tall, skinny man with a horsy-looking face and a gray mustache appeared on the catwalk. He was followed by three other men who seemed to be an entourage.

Gene Parnell turned away from a wall plaque he had been studying. "Hello, Joe," he said as he formally extended his right hand. "Nice to see you again."

"Aw, don't gimme that crap!" The man ignored Parnell's hand as he rushed down the catwalk and gave him a bear-hug instead.

Parnell gasped slightly, the surprise on his face evident, before he wrapped his arms around the tall man's narrow shoulders and returned the hug. "Nice to see you, too, Commodore."

"Commodore . . . Jesus, you're such an asshole." Joe Laughlin broke the hug and stood back, his hands lingering on Parnell's shoulders. "Eleven years since I last saw you . . . what do you want to do, salute me or something?"

Ryer traded looks with Lewitt; he grinned and gave a small shrug. As junior officers, they had never known Laughlin as anything except Old Joe, the NASA commander of Space Station One; although formally he wore the U.S. Navy commodore's stripe-and-star insignia on his shoulders, he seldom demanded that anyone salute him.

Joe Laughlin didn't try to hide the fact that he was the last of the original Project Luna astronauts who was still on active duty. He had retired from the Space Force when it was phased out in 1972, although he retained his rank by serving in the naval reserve. During the next twelve years he worked as a civilian consultant for Lockheed and, as a sideline, wrote and published a few science fiction stories under the pseudonym of Hal Robinson. For a time, that had been all right with him, but when he received the Nebula Award for best SF short story of 1984 two weeks after he lost his wife to cancer, something snapped deep inside that he still wouldn't discuss.

He resigned from Lockheed, stopped writing, rejoined NASA, and retrained for astronaut duty; anyone who thought he was over the hill quickly reconsidered after they watched him master a flight simulator at Von Braun. Five years ago, NASA had given him command of Space Station One—rumor had it that he finally resolved the age question by trouncing former NASA administrator James Fletcher and Senator Albert Gore on the golf course—and he had been here ever since. Save for an occasional vacation groundside to visit his grown-up son in Alaska, he seldom left the Wheel, contenting himself with the role of gruff Dutch uncle to a crew who, by and large, were young enough to be his kids. A framed photo of his wife hung above the desk in his quarters; his acrylic Nebula cube, scratched and cracked, was used as a paperweight.

"Jesus, that beard looks terrible." Old Joe scowled at his former Luna Two crewmate as he stood back to inspect him. "You could do something about the gut, too. What's Judy doing, feeding you barbecue all the time?"

"Barbecue, pork rinds, and a six-pack of beer every day. Breakfast of champions."

"For the love of . . ." Laughlin's voice trailed off in disgust. He caught sight of Ryer and edged around Parnell to graciously extend his hand to her. "Hey, I'm sorry, Cristine. I almost missed seeing you back there. Welcome back, Captain."

"Thanks, Commodore . . . Joe." Laughlin's hand grasped her palm for a moment longer than necessary, his humorous eyes searching hers for some reaction; she gave him a polite smile before gently pulling her hand free. Old Joe was notorious for coming on to female astronauts; although he had never done anything that could be misinterpreted as sexual harassment, it was clear that he was not a believer in political correctness either.

Parnell coughed politely and nodded toward the three men standing behind Laughlin. "I take it these are our people," he said.

"Hmm?" Old Joe managed to tear his attention away from Cris. "Oh, yeah . . . sorry for my lack of manners. Permit me to introduce you to—"

"Leamore," the first man said, stepping past Laughlin to extend his hand. "James Patrick Leamore, Commander Parnell. Executive vice-president of lunar operations, Koenig Selenen. Delighted to meet you."

As Parnell grasped his hand, Leamore gestured to one of his companions, then the other. "And this is Uwe Aachener and Markus Talsbach. They're astronaut-candidates, currently completing their training period."

Another round of handshakes as *Conestoga*'s flight team introduced themselves to the mission's remaining passengers. With the exception of Paul Dooley, it was the first time the NASA astronauts had met the contingent from Koenig Selenen GmbH. The German company had insisted upon training its crew members independently, as an acid test of how well European methods of selecting and educating its astronauts stacked up against NASA's. The agency had balked at this, of course, until Koenig Selenen made it clear that although its astronauts would have already passed muster in basic space-survival techniques, they were not expecting to pilot *Conestoga* and would act instead as passive observers. NASA finally caved in. After all, once this mission was completed, Koenig Selenen would be the sole owners of Tranquillity Base; how well or how poorly they prepared their space crews was up to them.

The agency in turn had insisted on training Dooley at the Von Braun Space Center; since the hacker would be expected to help reactivate Tranquillity Base and assist with the disposal of the Teal Falcon missiles, he needed to know a little more about the lunar base than the German astronauts.

Leamore was much what Ryer had expected from reading his dossier during earlier briefings. Although in his mid-forties, he looked considerably younger, his build slender and athletic, his brown hair only slightly speckled with gray. A former RAF fighter pilot who had moved to Berlin after earning a post-graduate degree in international business from Oxford, he had worked his way up through the European aerospace community until he joined Koenig in the early eighties, just as it was beginning to seriously invest in commercial space enterprise. When the company formed its Selenen division, Leamore was the person they'd chosen to head up the lunar operations program; in fact, he had been the company's chief negotiator when it opened discussions with the Dole administration over acquiring Tranquillity Base from NASA.

"Captain Ryer, delighted."

"Likewise, Mr. Leamore."

"James, please . . ."

"You can call me Cris."

Not bad for a British expatriate working in Germany. If Koenig Selenen GmbH came out a winner with its lunar program, Leamore stood to earn quite a few deutsche marks for his efforts. Euro-yuppie or not, Ryer thought, she was probably shaking hands with the first millionaire to make his fortune from the Moon. If only the American business community had been so foresighted. Had that been so, of course, then most American computers wouldn't have Japanese microchips, most American cars wouldn't be constructed of materials made in Europe and Asia, most American airliners wouldn't be built in France, and most Americans wouldn't have their paychecks drawn on banks owned by God knows who, but it sure as hell wasn't other Americans.

Leamore had a nice, firm handshake.

He helped her remember the computer diskette in her pocket.

Aachener and Talsbach were stiff and overly formal; they stumbled over their English as, one at a time, they shook hands with Ryer. In their mid-twenties, both were almost young enough to be her children; however, if she'd ever been inclined to become pregnant during the time when she pretended to be heterosexual, she would have been appalled to produce sons as colorless as these two. Aachener had light brown hair and Talsbach's hair was jet black, and Talsbach was slightly shorter than Aachener: beyond that, there was little to distinguish one from the other. Finely chiseled features, good looks, Teutonic demeanor: the last time she'd seen guys this perfect, it was in a New York gay bar, and at least the Village queens had more life to them than these two Aryans. . . .

"Glad to meet you," she said to Talsbach, hoping that neither of them could guess what she'd been thinking. "So . . . uh, you're astronaut-candidates, right? How far along in training are you?"

"Ah . . . yes, we're astronaut-candidates," Talsbach replied haltingly. "We have almost completed our . . . ah, training program. The final phase, this is."

He looked nervously at his colleague. "Yes, Captain, this is the final phase of our training program," Aachener said. His English was a little better. "We have been in orbit before, in our shuttles, but this is the first time we will be going to the Moon."

"To the Moon, yes, the first time," Talsbach said.

"And we are looking forward to the voyage . . . the trip, how you say?" Aachener's gaze was unwavering; although his mouth was stretched in a smile, the corners of his eyes didn't crinkle. A cold, false grin. "And how many times to the Moon have you been there?"

"This is my eighth trip . . . uh, voyage." Cris hesitated. "But I haven't been back in four years, so it's been a long time."

"A long time, yes." Aachener nodded his head.

"Yes, a long time." Talsbach also nodded his head.

Oh, my God, she thought, it's Hans and Franz. . . .

Cris stepped back from them, trying to find a way out of the conversation. She spotted Jay Lewitt standing alone on the catwalk behind her; catching his eye, she smiled at him, then turned back to the two astronauts. "Well, it's nice to meet you guys," she said. "We'll have to get together again sometime before the flight, okay?"

American colloquialisms seemed to confuse Talsbach.

Again he cast an uncertain glance at Aachener, who once more responded with that humorless smile. "Yes, Captain," he replied. "We'll get together again soon. Pleasant to meet you."

Ryer kept a straight face until her back was turned to the Germans, then allowed herself a wry grin as she walked over to Lewitt. The flight engineer stood next to the wall plaque Parnell had been inspecting before Laughlin and the Koenig Selenen team had arrived.

"How did you like the Germans?" he asked.

"They're great," she whispered. "They're here to . . . *pomp* . . . you *op!*"

"Jesus, Cris . . ." Lewitt hid a smile behind his hand as he caught the old *Saturday Night Live* gag. "Better not let Gene hear you say that."

"Who gives a shit?" She sagged against him for a moment, quivering with barely suppressed laughter. "I mean, these are the guys who are taking over Tranquillity?"

"Cris . . ."

" 'I'm a Choiyman astronaut in training, yah . . . to the Moon the first time, I am. Want some schnitzel, yah?' "

"C'mon, Cris . . . it's not that funny."

No, it wasn't funny, but it was the first good laugh she'd had all day. If Laurell were here, she would understand. But Laurell was probably at work by now, dealing with a dozen lawsuits before she went home to curl up on the couch, devour the rest of the Ben & Jerry's in the fridge, and watch *Seinfeld* on TV, while she was stuck up here with guys so straight they couldn't . . .

Her eyes rose to the plaque on the wall, and the laughter died in her throat. She had seen it many times before, during previous visits to the Wheel, so it was nothing new. Nonetheless, she felt shame wash over her as she saw the long list of names carved into the slab of lunar aluminum.

Twenty-three men and women, their lives lost during the construction of Space Station One and the establishment of Tranquillity Base. Victims of random EVA accidents, for the most part, although a few had been killed while rescuing other astronauts. One had died during the installation of the Wheel's nuclear reactor, and three on the list had been incinerated during an uncontrolled Atlas-A reentry through Earth's atmosphere back in 1961.

She had never met any one of them, but it didn't matter. Their names were inscribed here, and this was a sacred place; laughing at stupid Kraut jokes was as appropriate as goofing off in Arlington National Cemetery. But for the grace of God, her own name could be on this list. . . .

And it was never too late, because whoever had engraved the names on this plaque had been careful to leave several blank spaces at the bottom.

"Let's go find something to eat," she said softly, turning away from the plaque. "I think I need some ice cream."

It was hard to say why, because she felt very cold just now.

Don Garrett, anchor: Among the items included in the McGovern Administration's proposed "Big Freeze" federal budget is the gradual reduction of spending for the nation's space program. Science correspondent Clyde Fuller reports from NASA's Von Braun Manned Space Center.

(File footage: Neil Armstrong and Alexei Leonov stepping off the ladder of Ares One to plant U.S. and Soviet flags on the surface of Mars; the exterior of the Wernher von Braun Manned Space Center in Texas.)

Fuller (VO): Barely a month after the successful landing of the international mission to Mars, White House sources have told ATS News that President McGovern will soon propose cutting NASA's budget by ten to twenty percent over the next four fiscal years. Although the President hasn't yet officially made this announcement, it has been supported by key members of Congress.

(On-screen: Senator Walter F. Mondale, D., MN.)

Mondale: The fact of the matter is that taxpayers are sick and tired of throwing away their money in space. If NASA had their way, they'd be building permanent bases on Mars. What about building permanent houses for poor people in America? We've got too many problems right here at home that need to be taken care of first. . . .

(Shot of Senator William Proxmire, D., WI, addressing the Senate. Vice-President Jimmy Carter watches from his seat behind the podium.)

Proxmire: We've got runaway inflation in this country, government spending is out of control . . . and NASA wants us to shell out five billion dollars next year to send a space probe to Jupiter! I've got a better idea . . . let's send a rocket to NASA with a note inside: "Forget it, pal! Show's over!"

(File footage: Space Station One, Tranquillity Base, the launch of Ares One from low orbit above Earth.)

Fuller (VO): Critics of the space program point to the fact that total costs of the American space effort have exceeded two hundred billion dollars over the last twenty years. This includes the maintenance of the Wheel, the Tranquillity Base lunar outpost, and the American half of the Ares program. They also cite recent Gallup polls showing that fifty-five percent of the American public believes NASA receives too much money. However, NASA supporters disagree with this assessment. . . .

(On-screen: Sidney Brown, president of the National Space Institute.)

Brown: For each tax dollar spent on space over the last two decades, every American has earned two dollars a year from technological spinoffs. Microelectronics, weather and communications satellites, advanced medical technology, even digital watches and household appliances . . . all are possible because of scientific developments made while we were sending people into space. We can't just shut off the tap now and pretend that the country will continue to be a world leader in high technology . . .

(File footage: President McGovern stepping off Air Force One; the Ares astronauts working on the surface of Mars; Republican presidential candidate Gerald R. Ford shaking hands during a campaign stop.)

Fuller (VO): Several sources at NASA, who declined to be interviewed for this story, charge that the President is trying to win reelection next November by roping NASA into his Big Freeze program. They also claim that the White House leak was timed to correspond with the last few days of the Ares expedition, which so far has failed to find any evidence of life on Mars. This itself is a major embarrassment to the space agency, since it had all but promised discovering extraterrestrial life on the red planet in return for funding the mission. Likewise, the Ford campaign's support for the space program has been lukewarm at best . . .

(Shot of Republican candidate Gerald R. Ford, speaking to a reporter's mike in the middle of a small crowd of supporters.)

Ford: Well, uh . . . I like space. I think space is good . . . and, uh, I think the astronauts are doing a swell job, and . . . uh, I look forward to seeing them come home . . . excuse me . . .

(Shot of Clyde Fuller standing in front of the entrance of the Von Braun Space Center.)

Fuller: Although the administration's proposal is hardly seen as a major issue in this campaign, it is one more sign that neither Democrats nor Republicans are willing to embrace space exploration as much as they did in years past. This can only be seen as an omen for NASA in years to come. Clyde Fuller, ATS science correspondent, reporting from NASA's Von Braun Space Center in Houston.

NINE

The quarters he had been assigned were not much larger than the Amtrak sleeper compartment it closely resembled: a narrow metal bed with a thin mattress that folded down from the bulkhead; a small chair, a fold-down desk, a wall phone; a small round porthole in the curved wall. When the lieutenant slid open the door and showed it to him, Dooley's first impulse had been to ask if anything more spacious was available.

"Not unless you're the commander, sir." Lieutenant Hollis was politely amused. "This is one of the VIP cabins . . . everyone from senators to movie stars has slept here. Come over to the next section, and I'll show you the bunk I've been living in for the last two months."

"The bunk?"

"Yes, sir. Six and a half feet by two and a half feet, with a locker and a curtain, and it's all mine." The lieutenant pointed to the porthole on the far side of the compartment. "Count your blessings, Mr. Dooley. I'd kill to have a window by my bed."

If Dooley could have given it to him, he would have; as soon as Hollis was gone, he hastily lowered the porthole's louvered blinds, shutting out the ever-spiraling Earth which threatened to make him spacesick all over again. Then he folded down the bunk, shoved his laptop computer beneath

it, took off his sneakers, switched off the overhead light, and
did his best to get a little sleep.

As it turned out, he didn't have to try very hard. It had
been nearly twenty hours since he had last slept, and the
launch had left him more exhausted than he thought. At some
point, he was briefly awakened by Hollis knocking at the
cabin door, telling him that it was time for dinner mess.
Dooley ignored him, the j.g. went away, and he went back to
sleep.

When he finally woke up, he had no idea how much time
had passed; with the light switched off and the porthole
closed, the cabin was as dark as a tomb. He raised his Timex
close to his face and pressed the stud: only five P.M., which
confused him until he remembered that he had neglected to
reset his watch to Greenwich time. What do you call jet-lag
when you've been traveling on a spaceship?

The corridor was vacant when he slid open the door and
peered out. So far as he could tell, no one else was in the
VIP section. It took him another minute to recall the schedule;
the ATS reporters were supposed to be doing a live interview
with the flight crew at 2200 hours. Naturally, that would be
in another part of the Wheel, and since he had already skipped
mess, they must have decided that it wasn't important to wake
him up. Just as well; despite almost eight hours of sleep, he
was still a little queasy, and he wasn't quite ready to discover
the pleasure of VIP cuisine aboard this tub.

Dooley found towels, a bar of soap, a sponge, a toothbrush,
and a small tube of toothpaste in the locker. That was normal
enough, but the men's bathroom just down the corridor was
something else altogether. Although its tiny shower stall resembled one in a cheap motel on Earth, there was no show-
erhead on the plastic-tiled wall; instead, there were a couple
of spigots which only allowed water from the waist-level tap
to flow when he twisted them and shut off as soon as he let
go. A small bubble-meter between the spigots regulated the
water supply; just testing the system dipped the meter by almost 10 percent.

A sponge bath for the VIP suites. Of course. Water wasn't
something that was wasted up here; although water tanks
lined the station's inner hull, the liquid they contained was

irradiated and unsuitable for either drinking or bathing. The real Dooley would have known this from his training at the Cape and the Von Braun Space Center; once again, the other Dooley was uncomfortably reminded of just how shallow his own preparations had been. His masters had invested countless hours in changing his face and making sure that he looked and talked just like a dead man, but they had neglected to tell him a few simple things, such as that he would likely blow his breakfast within five minutes of leaving Earth or that an evening bath aboard the Wheel amounted to swabbing himself with a wet rubber sponge. . . .

At least the water was warm.

He considered that as he mentally counted the dollars that would soon be deposited in a numbered bank account in Geneva. Gold-plated taps in his bathroom in Argentina: that's what he would have when it was all over and done with. Gold-plated taps, and a woman to scrub his back for him.

The shower woke him up. He returned to his cabin and zipped into the blue cotton jumpsuit he found in the locker. He was hungry by now, and he briefly considered wandering through the station to find the mess deck, until he realized that dinner was long over by now and the crew chefs probably didn't keep leftovers for VIPs who had missed their chance.

So be it. There were more important things that needed to be done.

Examining the wall phone above his desk, he was pleased to see that it had a modem port. The last time the station's electronic infrastructure had been retrofitted, someone had apparently decided that visitors should be able to plug in laptop computers. After folding the bunk against the wall, he lowered the desk, placed his Tandy/IBM on it, and used a slender cable to hardwire its internal modem to the phone.

A slip of paper concealed inside his right shoe contained the instructions he needed to connect directly with the ATT system. Although it sounded complicated on paper, it was mainly a matter of using the Wheel's communications system to interface with the Iridium cellular Comsat network, which in turn linked him with Bellcore. The numbers he needed to use to make the connection were already written down; the calls he planned to make would be billed to the real Dooley's Citibank account.

He picked up the receiver and placed a call to a motel room outside Brunswick, Georgia.

"Hello?" a voice answered.

"First race at nine o'clock," he said. "Fifty dollars on Jake's Leg."

"First race, nine o'clock, fifty bucks on Jake's Leg," the voice repeated. "Your name is Good Sex."

"Good Sex. Got it." Dooley scribbled the words on a slip of paper. "Thanks."

The person at the other end of the line hung up without replying. If anyone at Main-Ops had monitored the call, it would seem as if he had placed a bet on a horse race with a bookie in Georgia and, in return, had received a code name by which he could later confirm the bet.

He switched on the laptop computer, typed LEM, and waited until the opening image of the Le Matrix communications program appeared on the screen. He then selected the Orlando, Florida, node of the computer network and dialed into it. There was a long pause as Iridium opened a line between the Wheel and Le Matrix; then the net flashed a key-shaped icon on the screen.

Dooley's Le Matrix password was a vital bit of information that had to be tortured out of him; the imposter hadn't been able to access it after he'd taken possession of this laptop computer the night before, since it was not stored within the program itself. It was a small but essential detail, since it was the only way his employers could reliably pass key information to him.

GOODSEX, he typed. How sophomoric . . .

After a moment the computer responded, PASSWORD VERIFIED, and the icon disappeared. So far, so good.

Almost immediately, there was a double beep and the e-mail icon appeared on the screen. Using the trackball, Dooley moved the cursor to the envelope-shaped symbol and toggled it. The system told him that he had two new messages waiting. He selected the first one and double-tapped the track ball. An instant later, a brief message appeared on the screen:

FROM: RaceTrak
TO: Thor200
DATE: 1/16/95 4:00 a.m. EST
Copy code sequences as follows:
1-6-9-5-9-7
3-8-3-9-7-0
GIF attached.

Dooley carefully wrote down the two sets of numbers, then moved the cursor to another icon, this one a paper clip attached to a file folder. He toggled it, then waited while the system decrypted a graphic-image file which had been sent to him.

A few moments later, a scanned photo of his contact was painted on the screen. Dooley smiled; he recognized the face immediately.

He closed the file and the message, then moved to the second message in the e-mail queue and toggled it.

FROM: Mr. Grid
TO: Thor200
DATE: 1/16/95 8:00 a.m. EST
Watched the launch this morning on TV. Looked great!
I'll be waiting for you tonight in the Castle. :)

"Damn," he said under his breath. Whoever this Mr. Grid person was, he was beginning to get under Dooley's skin; first the unfinished conversation last night, then the unsubtle reminder from the taxi pilot that he was expected to call Mr. Grid this evening. As if he didn't have more important things to worry about right now . . .

Dooley sighed as he tapped nervously at his teeth with his fingertips. Like it or not, he needed to do everything possible to keep his cover intact, even if that meant talking to some keyboard jockey back on Earth. Otherwise, someone might get suspicious.

But what the hell did Mr. Grid mean by "meeting him in the Castle"? Obviously it was a prearranged rendezvous point somewhere in Le Matrix. He thought hard, trying to remember all that he had been told about Paul Dooley, until he remembered that Dooley's hobby was collecting comic books.

What the hell. It was worth a shot . . .

He paged through Le Matrix's main directory until he located the "Comics" area and entered it. At the bottom of a

long list of headings—DC, TIMELY-ATLAS, DARK HORSE, CON-
VENTIONS, BUY, SELL & TRADE, MESSAGE BOARD—he located
an icon of a talking face marked "Chat."

That would be real-time conversations. Dooley toggled it,
only to be confronted by another long list. Some of the headings were innocent enough (COMIX CLUB, WHO KILLED SUPER-
MAN?, CEREBUS FANS ONLY), while others hinted at seedier
interests (LONELY HOUSEWIVES, MAN 2 MAN, SWINGERS BAR).
Like any computer network, Le Matrix catered to all tastes,
even if some of them gravitated to the sort of thing scrawled
above the urinals in a bus station restroom. The imposter had
seldom wired into the commercial nets; so far as he was concerned, net surfing was much the same as being addicted to
TV, and he had long since learned to parlay his hacking skills
into more lucrative pursuits.

There was nothing on the comics board marked "Castle"
per se. Dooley was about to give up, when he noticed a set
of buttons beside the list, the top one marked "Private
Rooms."

Of course. The Castle would be a secret subroutine within
Le Matrix, inaccessible to any user who didn't know its name.
He toggled "Private Rooms" and, at the prompt, typed: **The
Castle.**

The screen changed, displaying a blank gray slate. For a
moment he thought he was alone; only his own logon,
THOR200, appeared at the top of the screen.

Then another user-name appeared beside his own: LADYG.
Hello? he typed.

There was a pause, then: **Welcome, m'lord. Enter freely
and of your own will.**

He stared at the screen. What the hell . . . ?

A second later, another line appeared: **You must be exhausted after your long journey to the north country.
Come in, please . . . rest comfortably by the hearth.**

He hesitated, then typed: **Mr. Grid?**

A longer pause, then: **((C'mon! ;p You're not making
this any fun! Was the launch *that* rough?))**

He was still confused. **Sorry,** he typed. **It's been a long
day. How are you doing?**

Waiting with great anticipation for your arrival. (Pat-

ting the sofa cushion.) Please, sit down . . . you must be cold and tired.

Dooley frowned. Obviously, this was Mr. Grid, albeit under another logon; the allusion to the launch attested to that. But what kind of crazy shit was the rest of this?

He typed: **Liftoff was rough. Vomited on the way up. Still feeling a little queasy.**

Another pause, then: **I understand, m'lord. They say passage to the north country can be strenuous. Come sit by the fire and relax.**

Come sit by the fire? What did that mean? Dooley wondered if he had stumbled into the wrong private room by mistake. He recalled the message that Dr. Z, the taxi pilot, had passed to him. Was it possible that this could be Dr. Z pretending to be Mr. Grid?

He typed: **Mr. Grid, is that really you?**

The reply was instantaneous: **((YES, it's me, stupid! : (Now get your ass over here NOW!))**

Before he could react, another line appeared: **M'lord must not be feeling well. Have some nectar . . . it will soothe your stomach and make you feel better.**

And yet another line: **Then come sit beside me, and warm thy feet by the fire.**

At a loss, Dooley shrugged. **OK, it's you. Sorry. Yes, I'll have some nectar.**

He waited for a reply, which was not forthcoming. This was some sort of role-playing game; he was expected to respond to Mr. Grid's clues as if they were real-life stimuli.

He typed: **Thanks. That's good nectar. Feel better. Now I'll come over and sit down by the fire.**

A couple of seconds passed, then: **I'm pleased, m'lord. (Her hand slips to the front of her blouse and opens the first button.) So your journey was long and . . . trying?**

Dooley abruptly realized that, whoever Mr. Grid was, he was not male. Or perhaps he was a male pretending to be a female in cyberspace. The gender switch made him uneasy, but there was no backing out now; he had to play along as best he could.

Yes, milady, he typed hesitantly. **Long and arduous in-**

deed, but it's good to linger by the hearth and sip nectar with you.

The reply was immediate: **It's good to hear this (extending her long legs until her toes almost touch his feet). And you like the nectar?**

Nectar's good. What the hell was he supposed to say now? **Your feet tickle,** he added.

Another pause, a little longer now, then: **I thought you might like the nectar. The young boy who contributed it is . . . exquisite.**

Baffled, he stared at the screen. **Pardon me?** he typed.

A virgin, I think (unbuttoning her blouse a little more, exposing her pale breast). You will like him . . . he's in the dungeon, awaiting your pleasure once we've sated ourselves.

His breath whistled through his teeth as he read this. Whoever Mr. Grid/LadyG was, Dooley had obviously been indulging in some sort of weird cybersex fantasy with him/her, with a bit of pedophilia on the side. Was there yet another player involved, taking the part of this so-called young boy?

Dooley didn't care to find out. **Interesting idea,** he typed, **but I prefer your company instead. (Reaches out to caress her breast.)**

Next line: **And you don't find this repulsive? (shifting slightly to allow his hand further into her blouse).**

The very thought was enough to make him puke. He typed: **Not at all (she moans with pleasure as his fingers encircle a nipple). I'd rather have you instead.**

A moment passed, then: **Where is the Duke?**

The Duke? Who the hell was the Duke? Probably a third player in this game. **I haven't seen the Duke lately,** he typed. **Probably somewhere else.**

For almost a minute, there was no answer. He tried to scroll upward to read what he had written a couple of minutes earlier, but the system wouldn't allow him to do this. He was beginning to wonder if he had said something wrong, when a new line appeared on the screen:

I must be gone (sitting up and rebuttoning her blouse). I hear the Dane calling for me from the upstairs bedroom. He will be suspicious if I tarry here much longer.

He sighed with relief. More than likely, the Dane was another user, waiting to role-play this same masturbatory fantasy. Whoever he was, he would probably enjoy this sort of thing much more than he did; masquerading as Paul Dooley was hard enough without also having to indulge his on-line wet dreams.

Very well, he typed. **I will come again soon, after I have returned from the north country.** As an afterthought, he added, **Don't let the Dane know I was here.**

A long pause. **I shan't. Fare-thee-well . . .**

Fare-thee-well, he responded. **Good night.**

LadyG's logon vanished from the top of the screen, leaving Dooley alone in cyberspace. He took a deep breath as he fell back into his chair. That had been almost as tough as plastic surgery, but it was over and done with.

He reached out to toggle the buttons that would ease him out of the private room, but he hadn't exited from Le Matrix before the computer double-beeped once more and a small rectangle appeared on the screen.

INSTANT MESSAGE
From: Mr. Grid
Are you on the Wheel?

Christ. He couldn't get rid of her. He shook his head and typed: **Yeah, I'm here.**

He waited for a response. After a moment it came:
Good. Bye.

And that was that. He signed off Le Matrix, then stood up, wincing at the crick in the small of his back. The real Dooley must have been one repressed son of a bitch; it was just as well the little bastard was dead.

"Mr. Grid," he murmured at the hard drive's blinking C-prompt on the screen, "you're going to have to find someone else to squeeze your tits from now on."

Time to get back to business. He sat down again, typed **DIR** and watched as a long list of files scrolled up the screen. The particular file he needed was right where he had located it last night, listed under **TF111.BAT.** When he typed **read TF111.BAT** next to the C-prompt, it flashed: **Encrypted file. Password?**

He carefully typed in the first six-digit string he had received from RaceTrak. The computer repeated the same prompt, and he entered the second string. The screen went blank for a moment and he held his breath.

As he'd done with his Le Matrix password, the real Paul Dooley had safeguarded this file behind two sets of double-key encryptions, the numeric passwords of which he had committed to memory. It had taken hours to drag all that information out of him; if either of the keys was wrong, even by one digit, then the imposter's mission was shot. He would no longer be in a position to tell his masters the real code-numbers, and no one else in the world knew those numbers.

The denouement came a moment later as a subdirectory appeared on the screen: a short list of file servers, each easily accessible at the stroke of his fingertips.

"Yes!" he whispered. "Gotcha!"

Ten queues, containing half of the computer program needed to access the c-cube system of Teal Falcon. The other half of the program was safeguarded within the Teal Falcon launch bunker on the Moon. Once both halves of the program were linked together, the complete command, control, and communications of the missiles would literally be at his fingertips.

All too easy . . .

The imposter spent a few minutes scanning the algorithms, making certain that there were no gaps or hidden passwords. Satisfied at last, he saved the file and folded the slip of paper containing the encryption codes into his breast pocket. Then he switched off the computer, folded the screen, and stood up.

After a moment, he walked over to the porthole and raised the blinds. The distant view of Earth no longer bothered him. Tomorrow morning, he and his accomplice were on their way to the Moon.

Just then, there was a double knock on the door. He started, then hastily checked his watch. A moment later, there was a third knock.

Speak of the devil, and right on time. He turned around and slid open the door.

(File footage: Tranquillity Base as seen from the surface, where two astronauts fire rocket mortars to simulate moonquakes; this is followed by shots from within the habitat: men working in laboratories, eating breakfast in the mess compartment, sleeping or reading magazines in their bunks.)

Harry Reasoner (VO): This is Tranquillity Base, the United States moonbase, as the public knows it . . . a civilian installation devoted to peaceful scientific research, permanently manned by a rotating crew of twenty men and women. America's "Beachhead in Space," as NASA's public relations office likes to describe it. And this . . .

(A series of still photos: the Teal Falcon silos, as seen from the wall of Sabine Crater; a close-up shot of a silo hatch; the entrance to the launch bunker; a blurred shot of an open silo, exposing the nose cone of a Minuteman II missile.)

Reasoner (VO): . . . is a part of Tranquillity Base the government would rather not have you know about . . . six missile silos located at the bottom of Sabine Crater, about eight miles northwest of the base itself. Each silo contains a modified Minuteman II rocket, nearly identical to ICBM's found in SAC missile silos scattered across the United States, and each rocket is tipped with a one-megaton nuclear warhead. The installation is code-named Teal Falcon, and until these pictures were given to *Sixty Minutes* by a NASA civilian astronaut, who shot them with a hidden camera while visiting the site several months ago, it was the most carefully guarded of American military secrets . . . one which both the Pentagon and the White House flatly refuse to discuss.

(Medium shot of an unidentified man, sitting in a darkened room with his face carefully shadowed, his voice electronically altered.)

Source: The missiles have been on the Moon since September 1, 1969, when they were brought there by the Space Force during the Luna Two expedition. During that same expedition, the silos were excavated by high explosives and the missiles were put in place. Three months later, the Luna Three team completed the second phase of the operation by excavating the control bunker, and when they were done, the missiles were activated and the first two men were placed in the bunker.

Reasoner *(off-camera)*: And when was this?

Source: December 25, 1969 . . . Christmas Day.

Reasoner: That was over seven years ago. Are the missiles still there?

Source: Yeah, they're still there. I saw them myself a few months ago, when I took the pictures.

(File footage: President Richard Nixon waving to supporters during a public appearance; President Robert Kennedy walking into the Oval Office with two U.S. Space Force officers; moonships leaving Earth orbit; a May Day parade in Moscow's Red Square; President Eugene McCarthy being sworn into office aboard Air Force One in Dallas, Texas.)

Reasoner *(VO)*: According to a classified Pentagon document code named SR-192, secret plans to base nuclear missiles on the Moon had been in the works since 1958. President Nixon formally authorized the plan as a so-called "black budget" item during his second term in office, meaning that it was not made known to the public or even most members of Congress. Although President Kennedy was publicly opposed to the Space Force's predominant role in the American space effort, sources tell us that he allowed Luna Two to carry the Minuteman II to the Moon before he phased-out the Space Force and replaced it with the civilian National Aeronautics and Space Administration. Both leaders saw Teal Falcon as an "ace in the hole" against the Soviet Union's rapid escalation of its strategic nuclear capability, and it wasn't until President McCarthy's short-lived term in the White House that the twenty-four-hour doomsday watch at Teal Falcon was terminated. The men were taken out of the hole and the missiles were deactivated . . . but they were never removed.

Source: The missiles are still in the crater, and the bombs are still on them. The bunkers are sealed, but not permanently. They can be reactivated, targeted to virtually any place on

Earth, and launched within a few hours' notice. All President McGovern has to do is send a handful of Air Force officers back to the Moon with orders to enter the bunker and do what needs to be done, and the birds will fly.

(More film clips and still shots of Teal Falcon: a lunar tractor slowly moving down a steep roadway into the crater; a high chain-link fence surrounding the crater; a distant shot from atop the crater wall of the silos; Earth rising above the barren moonscape.)

Reasoner *(VO):* If a similar Minuteman were launched from a silo in Nebraska toward Moscow, the missile would be there in less than twenty minutes. However, it's estimated that the same sort of missile would take at least two days to reach its target if launched from the Moon. So why place missiles nearly a quarter of a million miles away? It's because Teal Falcon is intended as a second-strike weapon . . . If the U.S.S.R. were to attempt a sneak attack on the United States, the lunar missiles would remain untouched and, therefore, be used to retaliate against the Soviet Union. Likewise, the Soviets could not take out Teal Falcon as a preamble to war against NATO without tipping their hand, and in turn the U.S. could attack the U.S.S.R. On the surface, it appears to be sound logic . . . or is it?

(On-camera: Lex Klass, Professor of International Affairs, George Washington University.)

Klass: If Teal Falcon is indeed a lunar-based ICBM installation, then we're once again confronted with questions of basic morality regarding strategic nuclear forces. By the time those missiles reach their targets, both the U.S. and the U.S.S.R. will have used their triad of land, air, and sea-based ICBM's to pound each other into the ground . . . which means the Teal Falcon missiles are redundant at best.

Reasoner *(on-camera):* But aren't they supposed to be a deterrent to nuclear war?

Klass: It's tempting to call them a deterrent, but let's face it . . . nuclear weapons have never been used during wartime. They arrived a little too late for World War II, and they weren't used during Korea or Vietnam. They've never been detonated elsewhere than in the desert and in the South Pacific. No one knows exactly how much damage they would cause to a city . . . and as a result, it's easy for generals and politicians to think of them in abstract terms. Do you feel any safer knowing that there are nukes on the Moon? I don't.

(Shot of the Moon as seen in lunar orbit; the camera slowly pans across black, empty space until it focuses on distant Earth.)

Reasoner *(VO):* The official policy of the United States under the McGovern Administration prohibits first-use of nuclear weapons. At the same time, though, the White House will neither confirm nor deny the existence of Teal Falcon. No one can say when the bombs at Tranquillity Base will be removed . . . if ever.

(Shot of a ticking stopwatch.)

TEN

His second interview with Berkley Rhodes went much better than the first, although there was no reason why it shouldn't have.

The first time around, he had been tense about the launch, and Rhodes had rubbed him the wrong way; by that evening, though, things were different. Although his attention had been occupied for most of the day with the last-minute details of the mission, Parnell managed to get a quick nap in his quarters before catching dinner on the mess deck. Mindful that *Conestoga*'s crew would have to endure freeze-dried food for the next few days, the Wheel's chefs had served up fresh green salad, London broil with new potatoes and steamed asparagus, and strawberry rhubarb pie for dessert. It was a feast, compared to the station's usually spartan fare; together with rest and the peace of mind that comes from knowing that everything that could be done *had* been done, it put Parnell in a much better mood than he'd been in that morning.

The only person who missed the send-off dinner was Paul Dooley. The lieutenant who had gone to summon the programmer had come back to report that Dooley was sound asleep in his cabin. Gene didn't mind his absence; the less he had to put up with Dooley's cynicism, the better. Although Ryer was still being bitchy and it was difficult to understand what the Germans were saying half the time, the pressure was off, at least a little bit, for the first time in several days. By the time he was polishing off dessert, Parnell was beginning to wonder if he actually might *enjoy* this mission after all.

All this made him relaxed and ready for the TV interview which followed dinner. Bromleigh set up his equipment on Main-Ops' main deck, where the big map made a perfect backdrop and his camera could be easily interfaced with the Wheel's communications system. A couple of duty officers surrendered their seats to Parnell and Rhodes, and after the lapel mikes were tested and Laughlin raised the overhead ceiling lights to unaccustomed brightness, Rhodes conducted a six-minute live interview which was fitted into the second slot of the half-hour *ATS Evening News* broadcast.

Much to Parnell's relief, she avoided the sort of touchy-feeley questions which had spoiled their earlier interview, focusing instead on specific technical aspects of the mission. Parnell had no trouble answering her questions; he crossed his legs and rattled off the usual facts and figures that any bright junior-high-school kid with an interest in space could have supplied. At the end, though, Rhodes threw him a hardball that caught him by surprise.

"Commander," she said, glancing up from her notes to look him straight in the eye, "doesn't it seem ironic that the last American mission to the Moon is for the purpose of undoing one of the mistakes of the past . . . the placement of nuclear missiles at Tranquillity Base?"

Parnell blinked and almost stammered when he heard that. She knew damned well that as commander of Luna Two it had been his assignment to bring those Minutemen to the Moon in the first place; now she wanted him to admit that it was all a terrible mistake and, in effect, recant his past sins. In other words, was he still beating his wife?

"It may seem like a mistake now, Ms. Rhodes," he replied, "but you have to remember that the world was a different place back in 1969. Right or wrong, many people thought the Teal Falcon missiles were a necessary deterrent to Soviet aggression."

She opened her mouth to interrupt, but he didn't give her a chance. "Now, as commander of the second lunar expedition, it was my duty as a Space Force officer to follow a

Presidential directive. It wasn't my job to set policy . . . that role belonged to the White House and the Joint Chiefs of Staff, and at the time it seemed to be the right thing to do. However, I'm glad that times have changed and we're going to finally destroy the missiles.''

''And you don't see any irony in this?'' she asked.

He allowed himself a faint smile. ''Not really,'' he said. ''I know how those missiles can be fired, so it's only appropriate that I launch them myself.'' He shrugged. ''I'm just happy that we're going to aim them at the Sun, not Earth.''

And that was that.

When the interview was over, the camera shut down, and he was unclipping his lapel mike, she walked over to him. ''Sorry if I made you nervous with that last question . . .'' she began.

''Nervous?'' He gave her a blank stare.. ''No. Didn't make me nervous at all.'' *You just tried to make me look like a jerk again,* he added silently. ''That was a good interview,'' he said diplomatically, handing her the tiny mike.

''Thanks. I thought it went well, too.'' Rhodes glanced over her shoulder as she wound up the mike cable. The duty officers had already retaken their seats, and Bromleigh was dismantling his camera and tripod and returning them to their cases. ''I heard there's a rec room over in Section 14,'' she said, favoring Parnell with a smile. ''Perhaps we could go over there and continue this discussion over a couple of beers.''

Jeez, did this lady ever turn it off? He had no problems about socializing with the press, so long as everyone understood that it was time to put away the notebooks and recorders. He had done so on many occasions, in fact, with journalists whom he trusted, either through past experience or by gut instinct. Rhodes didn't meet those criteria; one look in her eyes told him that she was still on the job, and that having a beer with her was tantamount to submitting to an off-the-record interview.

''Not unless they've changed the rules around here,'' he said. ''If there's any beer in the rec room, then it's the non-alcoholic variety. Booze and one-third gravity don't mix.''

She shrugged. "Fine with me. I'm not a heavy drinker anyway."

"Well . . ."

"Gene, are you through here?"

Unnoticed, Joe Laughlin had slipped up behind them to clap a hand on Parnell's shoulder. "All done, Joe," Gene said, looking around at his old friend. "Did you watch the interview?"

"Caught it off the Comsat feed in the next room." He looked at Berkley. "Nice job, Ms. Rhodes. You actually got Gene to tell the truth for once in his life."

Rhodes fixed him with a venomous gaze. "Thank you, Commodore," she said stiffly, clearly irritated by his intrusion. "I was just about to . . ."

"You're welcome, ma'am," Joe said before he turned a shoulder to her. "Gene, we need to review the pre-launch checklist before you retire. Can you give me a few minutes?"

Parnell could have hugged Joe. He had already gone over the checklist earlier in the day; Laughlin knew it, because he had been in the room with him, Lewitt, and the three engineers in charge of making certain *Conestoga* was flightworthy. "Sure, Joe. Berkley wanted me to show her the rec room, but . . ."

"That's all right, Commander." Rhodes's smile was frigid; she had already figured things out. "I think I can find it myself."

"Thank you, ma'am. It's down on Deck 2, about halfway around on the other side of the station, adjacent to the crew quarters. Just follow the noise." The commodore pointed to the hatch leading to the Deck 2 corridor. "We'll see you bright and early at 0600 tomorrow. Good night."

Before she could reply, Laughlin led Gene away by the arm, guiding him toward a hatch on the other side of Main-Ops. Parnell caught a last glimpse of Rhodes walking over to Bromleigh and saying something quietly to him; then Laughlin opened the hatch and guided him inside.

They entered the lower deck of the observation center. Like the compartment above, its walls were lined with TV monitors, but these displayed close-up views from the ISPY. The room was empty, its round center table covered with maps and logbooks.

"Thanks for rescuing me," Parnell said, once Laughlin had slammed the hatch shut. "She had me cornered back there."

"So I noticed. Besides, if anyone gets to buy you a bon voyage drink on this relic, it's me." Old Joe walked over to a wall cabinet and unlocked it with one of the keys on a ring dangling from his belt. "Anyway, I sort of thought you might like to see something."

Parnell eyed the fifth of Maker's Mark the station commander produced from the cabinet. "That? And I just got through telling Ms. Rhodes that booze was *verboten* up here."

"Oh, hell, Gene . . . I did away with that rule a year ago. So long as no one shows up drunk for duty, I don't care if they get crocked once in a while." He shook his head as he poured whiskey into two shot glasses and passed one to Parnell. "This isn't the old days, brother. Cheers."

"Cheers." It had been a while since Gene had knocked back a shot of good whiskey; it burned its way down his throat and made him hiss with pleasure. So much for the twelve-hours-from-bottle-to-throttle rule. Nevertheless, knowing he had to fly *Conestoga* tomorrow, one more drink was all he could have before hitting the sack. "So what is it you wanted to show me?"

Old Joe glanced up at the chronometers above the wall, then walked to the control console beneath the screens. "Thought you might want to take a look at the future," he said softly as he tapped instructions into the keyboard and coaxed a couple of pots by a few millimeters. "You're going to love this."

Studying the screens and chronometers, Parnell could see that the space telescope was at 129 degrees east, sweeping down across China on its way to the equator. It was already tomorrow in that part of the world; on the screens, he could see dawn shadows thrown by the mountains of Manchuria.

"We're coming up on the North Korean coast, just a few miles south of Pukchong. About 41 degrees north." Joe's voice was very soft as he continued to fine-tune ISPY's tracking system. "Watch the screen on the left . . . look sharp, because you're only going to see it for a couple of seconds.''

Parnell moved to the screen Laughlin indicated, the one displaying the telescope's highest resolution. At 1,500 feet, it was nothing compared to what a KH-11, let alone one of the new radar-mapping Lacrosse spysats, could view from orbit. Nonetheless the view looked much as it would if he were flying over the North Korean countryside in his Beechcraft, if such a feat were possible.

Mountains, rivers, small villages connected by meandering roads . . . then suddenly, as ISPY began to approach the coast of the Sea of Japan, a small cluster of off-white buildings surrounding a wide concrete circle. From the middle of the circle rose a tower; from one side of the tower there was a short, dark line . . . a cement roadway. Close to it were a couple of small ponds, their still waters reflecting sunlight like an oasis; nearby was a row of squat, cylindrical tanks. The entire area was encompassed by a circular roadway.

At first glance, Parnell thought it was a factory, but the layout was much too familiar. In fact, it looked like . . .

"I'll be damned," he murmured. "It's a launch complex.''

"Yep. That it is.'' Laughlin walked over to stand beside him. With the hand holding the shot glass, he pointed at the screen. "There's the vehicle assembly building . . . there's the gantry tower, with the access ramp below it . . . there's the acoustic suppression pools, and here's the fuel tanks. Everything's there.''

Parnell stared as the satellite view crept from the top of the screen to the bottom. "I don't see a rocket," he said after a moment, "but it's not an ICBM silo. Everything would be underground in that case . . .''

"Oh, no. It's nothing like that.'' Laughlin took a sip of his whiskey. "They'd put it further inland if it was an ICBM site. Coastal location like this . . . it's gotta be a polar launch site. And, no, we haven't seen the rocket yet.'' He pointed to the largest structure on the screen. "Whatever it is, my guess is that they've got it hangared in the VAB, but they still haven't rolled it out yet. Could be anything, I suppose . . . but it sure as hell isn't an ICBM.''

Parnell nodded. An ICBM would have been hidden in an underground silo, which in turn could have been concealed with a camouflage tent. A facility of this size indicated a much larger rocket. "A satellite launcher?"

Laughlin shrugged. "Probably . . . but it could be anything. Even a spaceplane, for that matter."

Parnell opened his mouth to object, then thought better of it. Space technology was no longer the private domain of the superpowers. In fact, it was probably easier to build a man-rated rocket than it was to construct an atomic bomb. Even before the Soviet Union had collapsed, their rocket scientists had been quietly defecting both East and West, following the demise of the Russian space program after the Ares expedition. If the European Space Agency could benefit from the influx of disgruntled Russians, why not North Korea?

"I take it our guys know about this already," he said.

"CIA? Sure. How could they miss it?" Laughlin had already picked up the whiskey bottle and poured himself another shot; he silently offered it to his friend, but Parnell shook his head. "We've been watching this day after day for five months now," he continued, carrying his glass back to the screen. "At first we thought we had stumbled upon something, so we opened a secure line to McLean and blew the whistle. Pretty soon, someone from NPIC phoned back and told us to put a zipper on it. Turns out they'd known about it a month before we did."

Parnell nodded. NPIC was the National Photographic Interpretation Center, the section of the CIA's Science and Technology Directorate responsible for analyzing data received from the agency's reconnaissance satellites. "But, of course, they wouldn't tell you exactly what it is," he surmised.

"Of course not." Laughlin leaned against the console. "And nobody else is going to know, I reckon, until the State Department figures out exactly how to handle this mess."

The image was already drifting off the top edge of the screen, disappearing from sight as the telescope passed over the Sea of Japan. Laughlin continued to gaze thoughtfully at the screen. "Remember the Treaty of Versailles, and how the Germans got out from under it by starting the V-2 program, and later the *Amerika Bomber*? Well, it looks like history's repeating itself. We finally got Kim Jong to agree to U.N.

inspections of his nuclear facilities, but we forgot to rule out the possibility of—quote unquote—peaceful space research. So now North Korea's in the process of launching their own weather satellite, or whatever the hell they want to call it.''

"And nobody can touch them.''

Laughlin smiled grimly and nodded his head. ''I don't think anyone wants to go public with this. A launch site seven hundred miles from Japan . . . no, we're going to keep this quiet for a while longer. At least until someone finds out what the weather satellite looks like.''

Parnell continued to gaze at the screen long after the telescope began to pass over South Korea. The Russians might be long out of the space race and the Americans quickly following suit, but this wasn't preventing the rest of the world from edging into the game. It was bad enough that the Europeans were taking the lead in space, with the Japanese not far behind; at least they were trading partners and military allies, and as such, their objectives could be anticipated as genuinely benign, although hardly beneficial to America's technological and economic future. Germany wasn't going to restart World War II because it was purchasing Tranquillity Base. In ten to fifteen years, Koenig Selenen GmbH stood to make billions by selling electrical power to the United States, generated by the solar power satellites it intended to construct in high orbit from lunar materials, just as France had already captured more than half of the commercial launch-services market by sending communications satellites into orbit less expensively than NASA.

But even if North Korea's first orbital rocket contained nothing more sinister than a cheap knockoff of an obsolete American weather sat, it would have proved they were capable of lofting a payload into low orbit. And if North Korea had their hands on space technology, South Korea would have to get it, too. In turn, China would accelerate development of their Long March missiles; when that happened, the Middle East nations would get into the game.

Libya, Egypt, Iran, Iraq, Israel . . . and so on down the line, until the night sky was filled with real or bogus weather and communications satellites.

And meanwhile the United States—one-time world leader

now suffering from premature senescence, mumbling to itself as it played one endless Sega game after another while pretending that its undisputed position as the *numero uno* global exporter of exercise videos actually meant something—fell headlong toward the inevitable rude awakening.

Whether or not this was the future Laughlin had intended to show him, the glimpse Parnell had caught was enough to chill him to the bone.

He picked up his glass and turned to Old Joe. "I think I need that drink now," he said.

Uwe Aachener and Markus Talsbach sat next to each other on the bunk in Aachener's cabin, assembling the tools of their trade.

When they returned to the VIP section after dinner, Talsbach had gone straight to his cabin and retrieved his equipment from its hiding place inside his duffel bag. Tucking it inside a folded towel, he had undressed, pulled on a robe from the locker, gathered his toiletry kit and waited exactly five minutes by the door, carefully listening for sounds from the corridor. When he was certain the corridor was empty, he switched off the light, slipped out the door, and quickly walked the seven paces it took to reach Aachener's cabin. If anyone had seen him, he would have once again pretended not to understand English quite as well as he actually did, and claimed that he was taking a late-night bath.

No one had observed him, though, and Aachener was waiting for him. Once Markus was safely inside the cabin, Uwe had thrust a pillow against the bottom of the door to block the light; then, without saying more than was absolutely necessary, the two men went to work.

The guns they had smuggled aboard the *Dornberger* were both lightweight Glock 17s, all-plastic automatics which had been purchased on the European black market and shipped to French Guiana through a series of cutouts supplied by one of the South American drug cartels. The guns had been taken into space disassembled, the parts hidden within various articles of clothing in the astronauts' duffel bags so that they were not likely to be discovered in a casual search; even so, they had not been required to pass through either a metal detector or fluoroscope at the Kourou spaceport. After all, the Sanger spaceplanes weren't airliners; no one had ever given much credence to the idea that someone might actually try to hijack a shuttle. Still, the organization for which the two men were working didn't want to take any unnecessary chances.

Now they sat, side by side, methodically cleaning, assembling, and inspecting the two Glocks. Between them lay two cans of shaving cream from their kit bags; their false bottoms had been unscrewed, revealing the 9mm Teflon-nosed rounds stored within. The bullets were perfectly suited for their assignment; although they could stop a man cold, they would fragment if they hit something less yielding than flesh and bone.

As they carefully fitted the bullets into their clips, neither man said anything. They listened intently to every sound in the corridor outside, pausing whenever someone passed by. Yet they were both professional soldiers, albeit in a war of a more covert sort than that which was now being waged by their comrades a thousand miles away; although they were in enemy territory, they knew that the odds of their mission being detected at this last stage of the game were quite slender.

For a time, they had worried about the man who'd assumed the role of Paul Dooley. It wasn't just that he didn't belong in their class; the organization had recruited him for talents which they simply didn't possess, and they accepted that as a matter of course. Yet the fact that he had undergone facial surgery to change his appearance, however necessary that might have been, was the potentially weak link in their plan. He had also been ill-trained for this mission, and although he had been able to disguise this as general incompetence so far, Talsbach and Aachener had barely been able to keep from looking at each other every time Dooley stumbled against a bulkhead or was unable to climb through a hatch without assistance.

Fortunately, Dooley wasn't their leader. That was someone else entirely. Talsbach took some comfort in that fact as he glanced at his watch. It was almost 2300 hours, and the person they awaited was scheduled to arrive at any minute. . . .

Footsteps approached from down the corridor. Markus and

Uwe glanced at one another, then laid their guns on the bed, dropping towels and pillows over them.

The footsteps stopped outside their door. There was a double-rap on the door, a short pause, then a single knock. Markus looked at Uwe and nodded his head; Aachener stood up, unlocked the door, and opened it.

Without saying a word, their contact stepped inside.

(Music fades; studio applause)

Boone: Thank you, thank you . . . double rations of cheese dip for the audience, Moose! They deserve it!

Moose: Hah hah hah hah . . . yes!

Boone: Fresh cheese dip, an American favorite . . . that's right. Can't get enough of our official dairy product. . . . Anyway, later in the show we'll have on that lovely and talented actress, Miss Pia Zadora . . .

(Wild studio applause)

Moose: Hah hah hah hah . . . they love her! Yes!

Boone: Right . . . but first, please give a warm welcome to our next guest, all the way from West Germany, astronaut Karl Schiller!

(Polite applause as Schiller enters and shakes hands with Boone and Moose. Studio band plays an off-key Bavarian drinking song.)

Boone: Thanks for being on the show, Karl . . .

Schiller: Yes, yes . . . thank you. Good to be here today.

Boone: So, Karl . . . or maybe we should call you Colonel Schiller . . . ?

Schiller: No, no . . . it is okay to call me Karl, thank you . . .

Boone: How about Colonel Karl?

(Laughter)

Schiller: Karl is okay, thank you . . .

Boone: Anyway, Karl, I understand you're soon going to be flying West Germany's first privately developed spaceship into orbit, the . . . uh . . .

Schiller: The Sanger XS-1, yes, Roy. It's an experimental . . .

Boone: The XS-1? Does that mean it's going to be excessive in one way?

Moose: Yo! Everything in excess! Hunga-hunga!

(Laughter)

Schiller: No, no, it's really . . . it's a prototype of a new spaceplane my country is developing to . . . uh, how should I say it? . . . explore outer space.

Boone: But it's not excessive?

(Laughter)

Schiller: Ummm . . . I don't know. How do you mean, excessive . . . ?

Boone: Well, here's a picture of it . . . show the folks back home that picture, Mike . . . yeah, there it is . . . and, gee, it looks kind of puny to me, Karl. Not much compared to an Atlas. Kind of a shrimp-ship, if you ask me.

(Laughter)

Moose: A shrimp-ship! Yes!

Schiller: Yes, it is rather small, if you should compare it to an Atlas-C, but that is the point, correct? A smaller spacecraft, we believe, can achieve much the same goals as an Atlas-C, but with less time to prepare on the ground . . .

Boone: Uh-huh, right. But it can only take one person.

Schiller: This is correct, yes. But it is only the experimental prototype for a much larger—

Boone: And you're going to fly this thing?

Schiller: That is correct, yes . . . I will be the test pilot.

Boone: There's just one seat aboard, right?

Schiller: No, no . . . there are three seats, but I'll be . . .

Boone: Three seats? Maybe you could take Pia Zadora and Moose along with you, then?

Moose: Yo! I'd do that for a dollar!

(Laughter)

Schiller: I don't think so, no. It will be very dangerous, this mission, and this is why I will be the sole occupant.

Boone: I see. Taking any cheese dip?

(Laughter)

Schiller: No. I will not be taking any cheese dip. We will be conducting experiments in . . . ah, how do you say? . . . new theories of aerobraking maneuvers, so . . .

Boone: How about beer? Maybe some schnitzel?

(Laughter)

Schiller: No, I think not. The XS-1 is configured to take advantage of newly developed . . .

Boone: Yeah, I see. Very interesting. So what does your country intend to do with this schnitzel-ship . . . excuse me, spaceship?

Schiller: Ah! I'm pleased you asked! The European Space Agency believes we can open new commercial opportunities in space . . . umm, building solar power satellites, perhaps, or mining the Moon for valuable substances . . . if we can lower the costs of launching spacecraft into orbit. The XS-1, therefore, is a way of proving that we can . . .

Boone: Such as going to the Moon? Or building space stations?

Schiller: Yes, to begin with, but—

Boone: We've done that already. Read the papers sometime.

(Laughter)

Moose: Yes! We've done that already!

Boone: Ten seconds left, Karl. So tell us . . . are you going to put any German babes on your space station?

Moose: Yo! The man has a point! Hunga-hunga!

Audience (*in unison*): Hunga-hunga!

Schiller: I cannot . . . I don't see what is the point in discussing European space objectives if you will not seriously consider . . .

Boone: Well, time's up. Thanks for coming by, Karl. Hang around, folks, Pia Zadora's up next . . .

(Applause as the studio band strikes up the Star Wars *theme; screen fades to a still-shot of Moose wearing a space helmet painted with the* Late Show *logo.)*

ELEVEN

Joe Laughlin had told her to follow the noise to the rec room; it turned out he wasn't joking. As she climbed down a ladder to the second deck of Section 14, Berkley Rhodes heard music reverberating through the narrow corridors: ''Concerto for Guitar and Orchestra,'' by Jimi Hendrix, as performed by the Los Angeles Symphony Orchestra. Just under it was the unmistakable porcelain clack of billiard balls striking one another, and voices:

''Oh, f'r chrissakes!''

''I told you I could make that shot.''

''Coriolis effect . . .''

''I'm telling you, spin doesn't have anything to do with it. Rack 'em up again and I'll prove it.''

''Okay, but put something else on the deck. This classical stuff's distracting me.''

The concerto stopped in mid-movement as Rhodes walked down the narrow corridor toward a half-open hatch at the end; the opening bars of ''Stairway to Heaven'' were greeted by a disgusted howl until the music abruptly stopped in mid-chord.

''Goddamn, Billy! Anything but that!''

Someone else laughed. ''Just kidding . . . okay, hold on.''

Rhodes hesitated, then gently pushed open the hatch and peered inside. Several crewmen were hanging out in a narrow compartment which looked as if someone had made a conscientious attempt to furnish it like a comfortable den, but were doomed to failure by the metal walls and the pipes that ran across its low ceiling: a TV showing a video of an old Bruce Willis movie; an unpainted Revell model of the Wheel, suspended by a string from the ceiling; a small refrigerator, above which was taped a poster of Lou Reed's "Satellite of Love" World Tour.

One man sprawled across a sagging couch, drinking beer as he watched two other crewmen playing eight-ball on the battered pool table that dominated the center of the room. Another crewman was sorting through an enormous rack of CDs next to an old Sony stereo system; someone else had his legs propped up on a table next to a computer terminal, typing into the keyboard in his lap.

Everyone stopped what they were doing to stare at her.

The white cue ball slowly rolled across the scratched felt to gently tap a striped ball out of place; the two men playing pool barely noticed. The uncomfortable silence was broken only by a static hum from the stereo speakers.

Rhodes swallowed. "Hi," she said brightly. "I'm Berkley Rhodes."

"So what?" said one of the men at the pool table.

"Berkley Rhodes," she repeated. "ATS News."

The other pool player sighed as he picked up the triangle and placed it on the table. "Great. It's one of the TV reporters."

His companion began digging balls out of the pockets. "You're not going to find a story here, miss," he said as he rolled the balls across the table. "Maybe you ought to hunt down one of the uniforms and interview them instead."

It dawned on Rhodes that there were only a handful of women aboard the Wheel, and none of them were in the rec room. She tried to bring Alex with her, but he had wanted to get some sleep before the flight tomorrow, so she'd let him go. Now she wished she had insisted . . .

She was about to back out of the compartment when the crewman sitting at the computer spoke up. "Chill out, guys," he said. "I picked her up from the ferry this afternoon."

It was only then that she recognized him as Dr. Z, the pilot of *Harpers Ferry*. He didn't seem much friendlier than the others, but neither was he openly hostile; at any rate, it was a small relief to spot a familiar face.

"Doesn't mean shit, Doc." The man racking the balls took a beer out of the fridge and opened it. "She's press. She wants a story, she can go interview Old Joe. This is our place."

"C'mon, Fred, you don't have to be an asshole all the time. You don't see her carrying a camera right now, do you?" Dr. Z waved her into the room. "Want a beer, Ms. Rhodes?"

Rhodes took a tentative step through the hatch. "Thanks. Yeah, I'd love a beer . . . but I was told that wasn't allowed here."

Quiet laughter from the group, except for the two men at the pool table. "Whoever told you that was a liar," the man on the couch said. He was the oldest one in the room; with wire-rimmed glasses, a potbelly, iron-gray hair that nearly reached his shoulders, and a four-day beard, he looked like an aging hippie who had somehow panhandled his way into orbit. "You're looking at the last of the great space drinkers."

"Speak for yourself, Poppa . . ."

"Hey, guys," Rhodes insisted, "I'm not here to do a story about you. I'm off the clock. I just came to—"

"Bullshit. Open your mouth in front of a reporter, tomorrow you read it in the paper." Fred stopped racking the balls, picked up his stick, and dropped it in a stand near the TV. "C'mon, Lou, let's get out of here. I gotta fifth of tequila my wife sent me back at my bunk."

"I hear ya." Lou placed his stick on the table and walked toward the hatch. "Who needs this shit?"

Each of them cast cold glares at Berkley as they passed her on their way out of the rec room. "Media slut," Fred muttered to her back before he slammed the hatch shut behind him.

An uncomfortable silence descended upon the room. "Sorry about that, ma'am," Poppa said softly. "They've just been up here too long and have forgotten their manners, that's all." He looked at the kid who had been sorting through the CDs. "Billy, give the lady a beer, please. And put something on that won't peel the paint off the walls."

"I think it's peeling already," Billy murmured, but he slid a CD into the stereo. The first low-key riffs of "Black-Eyed Man" by the Cowboy Junkies filtered from the beat-up speakers, as raw and mellow as a winter morning in eastern Kentucky. Billy looked as if he might have come from coal-mining country himself; mid-twenties, tough and stringy-looking, greasy black hair, and narrow sideburns stretching down his jaw. He reached into the fridge, pulled out an ice-cold can of Budweiser and silently handed it to her before slumping into a chair to watch Bruce Willis kill some bad guys.

"I'm sorry I caused a problem," Rhodes said as she sat down next to Poppa and cracked open the beer. "I was told I could get a drink here, and . . . well . . ."

"Let me guess. You wanted to meet some people here, maybe see what we're like off-duty." The old man crushed the empty can in his hand and lobbed it toward a nearby waste can; it bounced off the wall and hit the floor, but he made no move to pick it up. "Your arrival wasn't exactly a surprise, ma'am. In fact, we sort of thought you'd show up sooner or later."

"I wasn't . . ."

"Horseshit," he said slowly, smiling a little. "You're not the first journalist who's come calling, and you ain't gonna be the last."

Rhodes took a nervous sip from her beer. There was no point in denying it; Poppa had caught her in the middle of a lie. "Don't take it personal, miss," he continued, "but there's not a whole lot of sympathy for reporters among the people who work here. Ain't that right, Curtis?"

Dr. Z didn't reply; he had already returned his attention to the computer screen. "Of course," Poppa went on, "Dr. Z and Billy are young turks, so they don't remember the old days. Now, take Bill here, f'rinstance . . ."

"Shut up, Poppa." Billy's right foot tapped the floor in time with the music; he didn't look away from the tube. "I've got enough trouble as is."

Poppa ignored him. "Billy's my co-pilot. We fly a satellite retriever, when we're not hanging out here. Now, Billy here . . . he spends six years in the Navy, flying air-sea rescue choppers out of Jacksonville while getting some astronaut training on the side, all 'cause he wants to be an astronaut when he grows up.''

"Shut up, Poppa."

Poppa paused to belch into his fist. " 'Scuse me . . . only problem is, the program's going down the tubes by the time he gets out. Kid wants to go to Mars, but he's lucky to be picking up busted American Comsats with me so we can sell 'em to the Japs.''

"You're salvaging dead satellites for NASA?'' Rhodes asked.

"No,'' Billy replied. "We're salvaging dead satellites for us.''

"McGraw Orbital Services,'' the old man explained. "Edmund McGraw, president and chief executive officer, at your service.'' He winked at her. "NASA keeps us up here to get rid of the low-orbit junk, and we make a few extra bucks by selling it to the Wogs and Krauts as scrap and spare parts.''

He groaned as he heaved himself out of the couch to fetch another beer out of the fridge. It wasn't hard to tell that he was already drunk. "At any rate, it's a living. Sucks, but it's a living.''

"Gravity sucks,'' Billy said, "but only by one-third . . .''

"Old joke, Bill, and watch your mouth.'' Poppa McGraw fell back into the couch as he opened his beer. He stretched out his legs and motioned with his can toward Curtis Zimm. "And as for the right honorable Dr. Z over there . . .''

Zimm only half-listened as Poppa McGraw droned on, telling Rhodes more than she probably cared to know of his life story.

Not that he particularly minded. Ed McGraw was an old-timer whose service record aboard the Wheel went back to the old Space Force days, and he always welcomed the opportunity to rehash his stories when anyone gave him half a chance. Everyone aboard the Wheel had already heard them a dozen times; pretty soon, Poppa would start telling Rhodes about his glory days as the pilot of the retriever ship that had rendezvoused with Ares One when it returned to Earth back in '77. Rhodes, of course, would believe every word; so had

Zimm, when he first came aboard Space Station One a year ago.

Over a year ago, he reminded himself; fourteen months, two weeks, and three days, to be exact.

Curtis Zimm had wanted to be an astronomer ever since his father had given him a small hobby telescope for Christmas when he was eleven years old. Although his family didn't have the money to send him through college, Zimm had partially solved the problem by enlisting in Air Force ROTC. The decision had caused him to lose a few friends among the Minneapolis hard-rock crowd he'd been hanging out with, but it enabled him to go to CalTech to study radio astronomy. Given a choice between searching for black holes or watching another Prince-wannabe at a downtown club and pumping gas for the rest of his life, he chose black holes.

Zimm had completed the requirements for his B.S. and M.S. in record time, but in his sixth year of college the federal tuition money began to run out. As a career prospect, radio astronomy is practically worthless unless one has earned a Ph.D., but since his ROTC funds had dried up and the National Science Foundation had turned down his grant application, it looked as if Zimm's academic term at CalTech would come to an end before he could complete his doctoral thesis on quantum singularities.

As it turned out, his faculty advisor at CalTech had once been a major in the old U.S. Space Force and still had some connections at NASA. On behalf of his student, Professor Beason managed to swing a deal with the space agency: in exchange for spending a year aboard the Wheel, during which time he would learn to fly *Harpers Ferry,* NASA would pay Zimm's tuition, as well as giving him preferred access to its low-orbit Advanced X-ray Astrophysics Facility. The last part of the arrangement was particularly sweet; although it was difficult for students to book time with the AXAF satellite, it was controlled from the Wheel, and therefore Zimm would be pushed to the head of the line every time he wanted to log an hour or two with the observatory. And in return, NASA had a new taxi pilot, just when the last one was quitting and going back to Earth.

Zimm had jumped at the chance; if everything worked out,

he'd come out of the twelve months with a doctorate and enough real-world experience to land him a nice professional job at one of the better radio observatories. But everything didn't work out. Ten months after he joined the Wheel's crew, AXAF had gone on the fritz before he could complete his studies of the Cygnus X-1 pulsar. The satellite's starboard solar array had been nailed by a micrometeorite, causing the telescope to lose half of its internal electrical power.

NASA didn't have the necessary funds to purchase a replacement wing from Martin Marietta, and wouldn't have until half a dozen congressional subcommittees decided whether the cost of maintaining AXAF was worth sacrificing some senator's favorite pork barrel. The last he had heard, the satellite was competing against a proposal to build a railroad museum in Scranton, Pennsylvania.

So here he was: stranded aboard a broken-down space station, his doctoral thesis in limbo, his future prospects uncertain. At this point, it was beginning to look as if his next job would be teaching Astronomy 101 at a junior college in Duluth. . . .

"Now, back in '77, things were different," Poppa was saying. *Tell me about it,* Zimm thought. "I was running MR-13 . . . Mars Retriever One-Three, and she's still my ship . . . and we had gone out to lunar orbit to pick up Ares when it came back, and ol' Neil . . . that's Neil Armstrong, y'know . . . Neil radioed in to say that he had lost power to the port engines and he was . . ."

Poppa would soon get to the part in which he would claim that if it weren't for him, Ares One would have shot past the rendezvous point and its crew would have been lost in the cold, fathomless reaches of outer space. It was the same bullshit story Curtis had heard a dozen times over.

If it wasn't for on-line pals like Mr. Grid, he would have gone nuts by now.

OK, so let me get this straight, he typed as he tried to focus on keeping up his end of the conversation. **The Duke came to the Castle, but he wasn't interested in sex. Right?**

He had begun using Le Matrix shortly after he arrived on the Wheel, first as a way of communicating with the rest of the astronomy community, but later as simple escapism. He had first met Mr. Grid on the *Lost In Space* fan board, and since then she had become one of his closest friends on the net. She had some kinky interests, to be sure, but at least she didn't flame like many of the teenagers he had encountered on Le Matrix, nor did she sign off at the mention of an event horizon.

When it turned out that her on-line boyfriend was supposed to be visiting the Wheel—indeed, that Thor200 was Paul Dooley, a crew member on the upcoming *Conestoga* mission to Tranquillity Base—he promised to meet Dooley when he got off the ferry from the Cape and pass a sly word that she was waiting for him this evening on Le Matrix. His private impression of Dooley was that he was as weird as a three-dollar bill. However, judging by the way she was talking to-night, he wasn't entirely certain Mr. Grid hadn't gone off the deep end herself.

A long pause. The system was running slow, but that was to be expected. His downlink was being bounced across any number of Iridium Comsats, so it sometimes took more than a few seconds for their messages to be transceived between the Wheel's rec room and her small apartment in Phoenix, Arizona.

Finally, the reply came: **It wasn't just THAT, damn it! He didn't ID himself as the Duke either! He signed on as Thor and he thought the Duke was someone else!**

He shrugged. **So he forgot he was supposed to be the Duke & signed on as Thor200 instead. Where's the beef?**

"So why do they call you Poppa?" Rhodes asked.

" 'Cause I'm the poppa dog, Miss Rhodes. Like a retriever . . . *Fido's Pride,* that's my ship, the MR-13. You'll see it tomorrow when Dr. Z runs you out to *Conestoga.* It's parked next to the garage. Gimme another beer, Billy."

That's not all, Mr. Grid replied. **I don't think he knew I was a woman. When I started to come on to him, he didn't know what to do at first, then he started to tell ME what I was supposed to be feeling!:(**

Curtis picked up the Coke he'd been drinking, found it empty, and tossed it in the waste can. **He looked a little shaken when I picked him up at the ferry, Gaby. Shuttle flights can be rough sometimes.**

"In fact," Poppa continued, "we're going to be flying the ol' boat out tomorrow, right behind you guys . . ."

"Really?"

"That's the fact. We have to pick up *Conestoga*'s departure tanks after y'all drop them. They usually let them go, but after *Conestoga* comes home, the Smithsonian wants to dismantle the whole thing and bring it back to Earth for storage at the Air and Space Museum annex in Maryland. So they want the whole ship, drop-tanks 'n all."

That's not all, Mr. Grid replied. **He drank the nectar without realizing that it was blood. When I told him that it had come from a young boy I had captured and placed in the dungeon, he thought I was talking about having SEX with him!**

Curtis blinked as he read that. **Well, OK, that's a little weird, all right . . . but he could have still been shaken up!**

"The entire ship?" Rhodes asked. "That's going to cost a lot to bring back to Earth."

"Sure it is. Kind of a bitch, ain't it . . . 'scuse my language. We've got enough money to dismantle the last moonship and make it a tourist attraction, but we can't pay to keep it operational. I mean, what's this country coming to?"

I got suspicious, so I told him the Dane was calling for me from upstairs and I had to leave . . . and he reacted as if the Dane was still alive!! BUT HE MURDERED THE DANE 6 MOS. AGO! :0

Dr. Z nervously rubbed his hand across his shaved scalp. There was a lot about cybersex that he still didn't understand. How two adults could achieve erotic satisfaction from indulging in on-line fantasies was still beyond his comprehension; for him, it was like trying to masturbate with a copy of *PC World*. Nonetheless, his friendship with Mr. Grid was as intimate as if they were brother and sister sharing stories about a real-world rendezvous with a secret lover; because of that, he knew a lot about the romance between Thor200 and Mr. Grid . . . or rather, under different screen-names, DukePaul and LadyG.

At least once a week the Duke and LadyG had rendezvoused in a private room on Le Matrix, where they gradually collaborated in a romantic liaison that combined elements of various gothic horror novels they had both read. A bit of Bram Stoker, a dash of Anne Rice, some cable-TV reruns of *Dark Shadows* . . . soon they had created a scenario in which Lady Gabrielle, a vampire of noble blood, had seduced Duke Paul and, after biting his neck and transforming him into her undead consort, had coerced him into murdering the Dane, her husband. Now they got together on Le Matrix to grope each other in the Castle. They traditionally began each session by drinking the blood of fictional teenage boys LadyG had lured from the nearby village . . . the "nectar," as she preferred to call it.

All in all, it was safe sex, albeit taken to a cybernetic extreme. Neither Mr. Grid/LadyG nor Thor200/DukePaul had ever met face to face, which was probably just as well. If Paul Dooley was nobody's dashing duke by real-world standards, it was only because Curtis had recently laid eyes upon him. Dooley likewise was innocent of the fact that his secret lover of the net was one Gabrielle Blumfield, a former computer engineer in Phoenix, Arizona, whose multiple sclerosis had confined her to a wheelchair. She used the Mr. Grid pseudonym as a way of hiding the fact that she was female; only Curtis was aware that she was sick . . . and neither Thor200 nor Dr. Z had the slightest idea what she looked like in real life.

So what are you getting at? he asked. **Are you trying to say that someone else was posing as the Duke tonight?**

The reply came as quickly as cyberspace would permit. **No. I think someone on the Wheel is posing as Paul Dooley.**

He frowned as he read that. True, she knew who Thor200/ DukePaul really was, even if Dooley didn't know her true identity; Dooley had let her know about himself a few months ago, including many of the details of his upcoming mission to Tranquillity Base. However, Zimm had no idea what sort of side-effects her medication might give her; he couldn't discount drug-induced paranoia.

Do you realize how hard it would be for someone to pretend to be Paul Dooley? he typed. **You can't just waltz into KSC, claim to be someone else, and climb aboard the next rocket. Maybe someone managed to hack into Le Matrix and get DukePaul's password.**

Billy switched CDs, changing the music from the Cowboy
Junkies to Midnight Oil, while Poppa Dog continued to tell
tall tales about the old days aboard the Wheel.

I thought of that, Mr. Grid replied. **I asked him if he was
aboard the Wheel, and he said yes. Also, there was a
LONG pause last night while we were talking, when he
was still in Florida . . . and he was really short with me
when he came back. ;/**

That doesn't mean anything, Zimm typed, although he
was beginning to have his doubts.

Le Matrix's double-key encryption system was virtually
foolproof when it came to foiling the so-called cypherpunks
who specialized in such activity, to the point that it was nearly
impossible to gain access to another user's password. Unless
Dooley had unwisely blabbed his Le Matrix password to
someone—which was unlikely, considering his own reputation among hackers—then the only way someone could have
signed on as either Thor200 or DukePaul was for someone
to . . .

No. That was too weird.

But was it? He recalled introducing himself to Dooley,
when *Constellation*'s passengers had climbed aboard *Harpers
Ferry*. Dooley had seemed confused, almost evasive, when
he had mentioned Mr. Grid. And ever since his arrival aboard
the Wheel, Dooley had holed up in his cabin in the VIP section.

There's something fishy going on, Mr. Grid said. **I don't
know how . . . but that's NOT Paul Dooley.**

Prove it, he typed.

A short pause, then: **I'll get back to you. Until then,
KEEP AN EYE ON HIM!!**

OK, OK, I will. Zimm grinned, then added, **If you're
wrong, then you pay my bill next month!**

Deal! BRB! Nite!!

A moment later, her logon disappeared from the top of the
screen, leaving him alone in the private room where they had
held their conversation.

Dr. Z signed off Le Matrix, then stood up and stretched
his aching back. Turning around, he noticed for the first time
that Berkley Rhodes had left the rec room. Apparently she

had decided to call it a night. No wonder; tomorrow morning, she would be heading for the Moon.

"Have fun with your friends?" Poppa asked. He was cracking open another beer and settling into a frayed armchair next to Billy. *Die Hard* had ended, and they were watching the opening credits of some Jean-Claude Van Damme kick-boxer flick.

Zimm picked up the pool cue that lay on the table and slid the white ball into position. "Same as usual."

From The Washington Post; *January 12, 1981*

**Reagan Set to Launch New
Military Space Program**
News Analysis
by Maureen McCoy

WASHINGTON—Only a week before his inauguration, part of President-elect Ronald Reagan's transition team is already planning a new American space initiative. Although members of the group refuse to disclose its details at this time, insiders among Reagan's so-called California kitchen cabinet say that the plans call for a revival of the long-dormant military space program.

Formally known as the Strategic Defense Working Group, its members include former NASA administrator James Fletcher, physicist Edward R. Teller, and former Air Force General Omar Bliss, who led the Blue Horizon project during World War II. The group is headed by William J. Casey, widely considered to be Reagan's choice for Director of Central Intelligence.

Although the group will not propose reinstatement of the U.S. Space Force, which was phased out in the early 1970s during the Kennedy Administration, they will recommend that the White House pursue defense-related objectives as the nation's first priority in space, with the U.S. Air Force being the lead agency instead of NASA. Possible suggestions include:

De-emphasis of basic scientific research, and shifting technological resources to space-based national defense, including development of a new generation of surveillance satellites;

Final authorization of a new "space shuttle" which will eventually replace NASA's aging fleet of Atlas-C space ferries;

Downscaling operations at Tranquillity Base, and eventual curtailment of NASA lunar operations;

Opening the civilian space program to participation by American business, allowing U.S. private enterprise to compete on a "free market" basis with the burgeoning European space industry.

It is also possible that the Strategic Defense Working Group will recommend to the President-elect that the Air Force develop an orbital "space shield" of laser satellites, which would protect the United States against nuclear attack. Dr. Teller is known to be a leading advocate of this plan, and General Bliss made several public speeches urging the outgoing McGovern Administration to fund research in this area. Fletcher is regarded as an advocate of the space shuttle, an advanced spaceplane which was shelved during the McGovern Administration.

Teller and Bliss apparently have Governor Reagan's ear. During the presidential campaign, Reagan made several references to the declining state of the American space program, which hinted at his interest in renewed military involvement. In his acceptance speech at the Republican National Convention last July, he spoke of NASA's "liberal agenda" which placed "higher priority on studying moon rocks than on looking for ways to protect Americans." Reagan also cited the $52 billion spent in the last decade on Project Ares, claiming that it was "money the Democrats invested in the Russian propaganda machine" which could have been better used for military space objectives.

Space was not a major topic in the 1980 campaign, compared to the economy and the Iran hostage crisis, yet it seems as if Reagan was able to play upon widespread disenchantment with NASA as a minor theme. President McGovern was never able to successfully answer Republican charges that the past three Democratic administrations turned NASA into a cash cow for special interests, although McGovern trimmed NASA's budget by 15 percent during the past eight years.

The prospect of Reagan's turning the ailing American space program into a defense program hasn't been embraced by many people within NASA.

"This 'space-shield' business is pure sky-blue malarkey on Teller's part," says an unnamed senior NASA official. "Livermore labs has conducted some promising experiments in that area, but nothing that could result in a reliable strategic defense system within the next twenty years. Teller is selling Reagan a bill of goods his people can't deliver."

As for the space shuttle, the same source is dubious about the idea of using throwaway solid-rocket boosters. "We need a new generation of ferries, yes," he says, "but using SRB's for a manned spacecraft is a risky business. If we dive headlong into something like that, especially as a crash program, then we may pay for it down the road."

Wendell Haynes, president of the American Institute of Astronautics, is also skeptical of a renewed military space program. "Under the current budget environment, the only way Reagan is going to be able to fund this effort is by cutting civilian space efforts to the bone," he says. "If he does that, there goes interplanetary science, research into solar power satellites, lunar operations . . . the whole works. NASA will be emasculated, and Europe will continue to take the lead."

Will American industry be able to take up the slack, as the working group believes it will? "I rather doubt it," Haynes says. "More than likely, commercial users will just hitch a ride aboard German rockets rather than developing new domestic launch systems. In the long run, we'll be handing the space industry to the Europeans."

Transition press secretary Larry Speakes refused to comment on this issue. . . .

TWELVE

Okay, kids, Dr. Z said, *hang on back there. I'm opening the hatch now.*

Darkness clutched *Harpers Ferry*'s cargo bay for a few more seconds, then pure white light sliced across one bulkhead, gradually widening into a chasm as the hatch silently cranked open. The raw glare of the naked sun caused everyone to wince and hastily reach for the reflective gold visors on their helmets.

And there it was: the U.S.S. *Conestoga,* berthed inside its enormous orbital hangar. Spotlights along the hangar walls cast complex shadows from the skeletal framework across the dull-gray globes and cylinders of its fuel tanks, which separated the massive array of engines at the stern from the giant personnel sphere at the bow. Its landing gear and the outrigger antennas were still folded up against the tanks, lending the moonship the vague appearance of a humongous insect slumbering within a cocoon.

Whatever sleep this bug had enjoyed for the last three years, though, was now at an end. As *Harpers Ferry* glided into a parking orbit several hundred feet from the hangar, another taxi began to haul *Conestoga* out of the hangar at the end of a short, thick cable. The taxi was assisted by two astronauts in EVA bottlesuits which functioned as miniature one-man tugboats, their operators holding onto the moonship's slender girders. A fuel tender, itself a modified taxi outfitted with rows of propellant cylinders, approached the large craft as it prepared to pump lox and hydrazine into the fuel tanks. Working together, the taxi and the bottlesuits gently coaxed the moonship from the hangar which had protected it against micrometeorites during its long dormancy, the pilots making sure that no part of its superstructure banged against the hangar walls.

It was the first time Parnell had laid eyes on *Conestoga* in two decades; despite the humid warmth of his hardsuit, he felt a chill run down his back. He had forgotten how bloody huge this machine really was. Simply saying that it was 160 feet long—taller than the Statue of Liberty, as the old USSF fact-sheets once proudly proclaimed—wasn't sufficient, nor was the fact that it had taken almost two dozen flights of Atlas-C cargo ferries to loft its unassembled parts into space.

The *Conestoga* was, succinctly put, a monster.

That's a big ship, Dooley said.

Parnell glanced across the narrow compartment at the programmer. "If I didn't know better, Mr. Dooley," he said, "I'd swear you were impressed."

He heard the others laugh through the comlink. *Conestoga*'s flight team and passengers were huddled together in the taxi's unpressurized bay, hanging onto the cargo net with their gauntleted hands. Because the taxi couldn't directly dock with the moonship's main airlock, they had all donned their lunar hardsuits before they left the Wheel; having done so, however, it was impossible for them to ride in the taxi's forward passenger compartment.

Is that the retriever ship? Berkley Rhodes asked, pointing through the hatch.

Parnell turned to look. Tethered to the side of the hangar was a much smaller, yet no less ungainly spacecraft. The MR-13 was a mutt of a ship; a third-stage *Atlas*-class orbiter, its wings and vertical stabilizer cut off and replaced by a ring of seven barrel-like fuel tanks. A saucer-shaped docking probe protruded from a long boom at its bow; a high-gain dish antenna rose from behind the pilot canopy, while the stem of a bottlesuit stuck out from beneath the hull. Someone had painted a picture of a golden retriever on the fuselage; the dog held a rocket in its smiling mouth, and below it were inscribed the words *Fido's Pride.*

"That it is," Parnell said. "How did you recognize it?"

I talked to the pilot last night in the rec room. Rhodes paused, then added somewhat reproachfully, *You should have come down, Commander. We had a good time.*

"You met Poppa McGraw?" Parnell chuckled and shook his head. "Ma'am, I hope you didn't do an interview with him. Half of what he says is—"

Total bullshit, according to Dr. Z.

Parnell smiled. "I'm not going to call him a liar, but he does tend to embellish the truth."

Did he tell you about the time he saved Neil Armstrong's life? Lewitt asked Rhodes. *No offense, but I'd get Neil's side of the story first before you run with it.*

I didn't say I believed it! she retorted. *I just said I . . .*

Parnell ignored the rest of the conversation. Now that *Conestoga* was free of the hangar, Dr. Z gently maneuvered *Harpers Ferry* as close as possible to the moonship. One of his crewmates had already crawled out of the forward cage and was using his MRU pack to jet over to *Conestoga,* dragging one end of a long tether cable behind him. In a few minutes he would attach the cable to a circular catwalk surrounding the main airlock, which was beneath the personnel sphere. Once this job was completed, the crew would be able to traverse the cable, hand over hand, from the taxi to the moonship.

The close approach gave Parnell a good opportunity to look over *Conestoga.* It was the fifth moonship the USSF had commissioned, and also the last. Constructed in the early seventies as a lunar shuttle, it had followed the same general plans as the *Eagle*-class vessels the Space Force had used during Project Luna; after the four earlier vessels were decommissioned and cannibalized on the Moon, *Conestoga* had remained in service, flying bi-monthly supply missions to Tranquillity Base.

This made the ship more than twenty years old and its design almost thirty. Although it was true that a moonship escaped the weathering that caused Atlas ferries to age before their time, countless landings and liftoffs had gradually taken their toll on *Conestoga*. The fuel tanks had been patched many times, the broad shoes of the landing gear were eroded by moondust, and the engine exhaust nozzles were blackened and scarred. Even the American flags painted across either side of the personnel sphere were faded and streaked from coarse lunar regolith.

It was an old vessel, worn-out and tired, just capable of making one more voyage before it was dismantled and retired to the Smithsonian. As mighty as it was, the *Constellation* would soon be rendered obsolete by the spacecraft that Koenig Selenen GmbH already had in production: smaller, more cost-effective nuclear-powered ships that could make the trip straight from French Guiana to Tranquillity Base.

He glanced at Leamore, who had remained silent during the trip. If Koenig Selenen's vice-president had any comments, he kept them to himself, nor could Parnell perceive his expression behind the gold visor of his helmet. Uwe Aachener, though, murmured something in his native tongue to Markus Talsbach, to which Talsbach responded with a short, derisive laugh and an unintelligible comment.

"You've got something to say, Mr. Talsbach?" Parnell asked.

A short pause. The two Germans pivoted slightly as they turned toward him. *I said only that it is a beautiful ship, Commander,* Talsbach replied. *It has . . . um, much history behind it, and it shows.*

"How old are you, Mr. Talsbach?"

Talsbach hesitated. *I am twenty-eight years old,* he said.

"Twenty-eight. That means you were six when this ship was built, and the men who built it were old enough to be your fathers and grandfathers. Try to keep that in mind, please."

Talsbach said nothing. *We intend no disrespect, Commander,* Aachener said after a moment.

"I'm sure you don't," Parnell replied. He looked out the hatch again. The taxi crewman had secured the transfer cable to *Conestoga*'s catwalk and opened the airlock hatch; his right arm was raised, signaling that it was time to come aboard. "Just wanted to make sure you knew."

Parnell heard Lewitt and Dr. Z chuckle as he hauled his

duffel bag out of the net. Pulling the strap over his left shoulder, he gently pushed himself toward the cargo hatch. The other crewman grabbed his arm and brought him to the cable; for a moment, their helmets touched.

You tell 'em, skipper! he heard the crewman yell. *Have a good trip!*

"Thanks for the ride!" he shouted back. He grabbed the taut line with both hands and took a deep breath. The crewman slapped his forearm, then pushed him out of the hatch.

Fifty minutes later, Parnell pushed shut the interior hatch of *Conestoga*'s main airlock and spun the lockwheel. A faint hiss told him that the astronauts inside were depressurizing the compartment; one of them looked up through the airlock window and gave him the thumbs-up. Parnell returned the gesture, then grasped the ladder and pulled himself through a narrow crawl space onto Deck D.

The circular deck was lined with lockers, most of them containing the crew's hardsuits. Jay Lewitt floated in front of the master electrical board at one end of the deck, making a last-minute check of the circuit breakers.

"Found that fuse yet?" Parnell asked.

Jay nodded. "Found it and replaced it." While they were running through a general systems test on the command deck, the main computer had informed them of a blown fuse in the primary electrical backup circuit. Nothing critical, but it had halted the countdown by ten minutes while Lewitt located the problem and dealt with it. "Go on up," he said. "I'll be there in five minutes."

"Okey-doke." Parnell pulled himself along the ceiling handrails until he reached the gangway ladder next to the head, then glided up the ladder to Deck C, where he paused to check on the passengers.

As the ship's living quarters, C-deck was the largest compartment in the personnel sphere. Near the gangway was a round mess table and small galley, with a small TV and VCR mounted above the table. On the other side of the room were fold-down acceleration couches, only half of which were occupied. As usual, Paul Dooley seemed to be having trouble strapping himself in; he was being assisted by Berkley

Rhodes, who seemed to be getting more accustomed to space travel with every passing hour. On the other hand, Alex Bromleigh looked as if he was beginning to regret making this trip; he stared out the porthole next to his couch, his hands nervously gripping the padded armrests.

"When are you going to be leaving, Commander?" James Leamore called from his couch. The two Koenig Selenen astronauts appeared to be taking everything in stride, although Uwe Aachener seemed to be secretly amused by Dooley's battle with his harness. Markus Talsbach was reading a paperback; Parnell earnestly hoped it was an English-German dictionary.

"Very soon," Parnell replied. "I'm sorry for the delay, but Jay's got it under control." Leamore nodded, and Parnell continued his ascent up the ladder.

Next stop was the logistics area on B-deck, where the ship's computer mainframes surrounded the navigation plotting table. When the first *Eagle*-class moonships were built, this deck had been jammed with clunky IBM System/360s programmed by big spools of magnetic tape. Those big machines were long gone, replaced by smaller Japanese computers, with only the empty bolt-holes in the deck plates to mark their passing. Even so, the new computers were obsolete by at least ten years, and the plotting table was a seldom-used holdover from the old days.

Still, all that empty space was useful for something; before Tranquillity Base was shut down, it had served as a cargo hold. As well, there were five extra couches folded against the bulkhead on the far end of the compartment, next to the tiny shower stall which could only be used once *Conestoga* was on the Moon. The women could benefit from the privacy, if they didn't mind sharing the showers with seven men. Parnell grinned at the memory of the Luna Two mission, when the ship had been filled to maximum passenger capacity and the Eagle had the ambiance of a college frat house. Back then, the only females aboard ship had been a few pregnant lab rats and a Raquel Welch pinup on C-deck.

He checked the row of CRTs above the plotting table to make certain that all the computers were operational, then pulled himself up the ladder to Deck A. Located at the top of the ship, the command center was *Conestoga*'s most crowded compartment. Banks of dials, switches, and gauges surrounded the astrogator's station, a swivel-mounted telescope and armchair positioned directly beneath a large transparent dome in the ceiling, leaving just enough room for three couches. Like B-deck's plotting table, many of the dials and gauges lining the sloping walls were now redundant at best, their once-essential functions replaced by retrofitted LCDs and keyboards; they remained wired only because, like the astrogator's station, removing them was more trouble than it was worth.

A generation ago, five men were required to fly *Conestoga* to the moon. Now only three people could do the same job . . . and, in a pinch, one guy could do it himself, if he or she knew how to reprogram all the computers.

Cristine Ryer lay in the pilot's couch at the opposite end of the deck, a clipboard propped in her lap as she ran through the launch checklist. "Jay says he's replaced the fuse," she said, barely looking up as Parnell floated to his own couch. "He says he'll be up in . . ."

"Five minutes. I know, he told me." Parnell hoisted himself into his couch and began to buckle the straps. "I just checked below and everything's tight. How's the countdown going?"

"Everything's green and A-OK. All tanks loaded and pressurized, no leakage detected." Ryer stowed the clipboard in the net beneath her couch, then reached up to flip a couple of switches. "Just completed telemetry check with the Wheel. We've got permission to fire engines when ready."

"Sounds good to me." *Conestoga*'s launch timetable wasn't quite as strict as those held to by ferries sent up from the Cape; if he fudged it by a couple of minutes, it wouldn't be too much. Parnell pulled his headset over his ears, and adjusted the mike. He lowered the master control board from the low ceiling until it was just above his lap, then tapped a few commands into the keyboard. The tiny LCD screen lit to show him a status rundown of the ship's primary systems. "Okay," he said, "if you're ready for final sequence . . ."

"Ready."

"Arm engines, starting with cluster one."

She reached up to unlock a panel above her head and snap a set of toggles. "Cluster one, engines one through three, armed and ready . . ."

"Check. Cluster two, arm."

"Cluster two, engines four through nine, check . . ."

Parnell glanced at the gangway ladder. No sign of Lewitt yet, although the board showed no more warning lights on the backup electrical loop. The engineer was probably double-checking things on his own. For a moment, they had some privacy. "Cluster three, arm . . . you know, we never had a chance to have that little discussion."

"Cluster three, engines ten through fifteen, check . . . don't remember what you're talking about, Commander."

He cast a glance across the compartment at her. "Call it an attitude check, Captain," he said softly.

Ryer didn't look his way. "Attitude's fine, Commander," she said stiffly. "Ready to arm next engine cluster."

"Hang on a sec." He pushed aside the board and sat up as far as the straps would permit. "The Moon's not going anywhere. I want to know what the hell's bothering you."

She continued to stare fixedly at her board. "Nothing is bothering me, Commander, and this isn't a good time to be asking." Before he could reply, Ryer looked straight at him. "Does the Commander wish to hold countdown so he can have the pilot replaced?"

It was a tempting notion, one which would possibly save the mission a lot of grief. A mission commander had to have absolute faith in his first officer; otherwise, he would be put in the position of having to second-guess him or her. If this exchange had occurred only twenty-four hours ago, while they were still at the Cape, then Parnell might have scrubbed the launch and waited for someone at NASA to find a replacement for Ryer.

On the other hand, he reminded himself, he wasn't at liberty to do that, then or now. Ryer was on this mission because she was the last flight-rated moonship pilot in the astronaut corps; everyone else had retired three years ago. It was much too late for her to be replaced, and she damn well knew it.

"No," he said, "I don't . . . but I want to know what's bugging you."

Ryer let out her breath. For a moment, he thought she was about to open up to him. Then the implacable hostility came back in her eyes as she returned her gaze to the console in front of her.

"Awaiting arm command for cluster four," she said.

At that moment, he heard Lewitt climbing the ladder up from B-deck. He sighed and sank back into the coach's cracked leather upholstery. "Resume countdown," he said. "Cluster four, arm and check."

There was the snap of toggles being thrown. "Cluster four, engines sixteen through twenty, armed and ready . . . sir."

Lewitt's head and shoulders appeared in the hatchway. "Okay, folks, we're ready to roll," he said as he pushed off a bulkhead and glided toward the engineering station midway between the pilot couches. When neither Parnell nor Ryer said anything, his expression changed to mild confusion. "What, did I miss something?"

"Never mind," Parnell replied. "Just a minor disagreement. Cluster five, arm and check."

Ryer flipped another set of switches. "Cluster five, engines twenty-one through twenty-five, armed and ready, Commander."

Lewitt looked back and forth between his crewmates, but chose to remain silent. Instead, he strapped himself into his couch and swiveled around to face the enormous bank of gauges. "Okaaay . . . primary electrical backup is now green. Master hydraulics . . ."

They ran through the remainder of the checklist without any further snags.

Despite the countdown hold, the launch window was not seriously impaired. By this time, *Conestoga* had been towed to a safe distance from its hangar and the Wheel. The taxis and fuel tender were long gone, leaving the moonship alone in high orbit. On a TV monitor above his head, Parnell could see Space Station One rotating fifty miles away, perpetually falling toward the limb of the earth. The screen next to it displayed a forward view from the main antenna boom; dead ahead was the Moon, as bright and full as the first time he had sat in a commander's chair twenty-six years ago.

Yet despite the similarity between that moment and this,

he felt none of the anticipation or excitement that had preceded the Luna Two launch. Instead, for some reason he couldn't put his finger on, there was a sense of foreboding.

He put it out of his mind as he switched on the S-band transceiver. "Wheel command, this is *Conestoga*," he murmured into his headset mike. "Checklist is complete and we're go for launch."

We copy, Conestoga, Joe Laughlin's voice said over the comlink. *You're green for go. Anytime you're ready. Good luck.*

"Roger that, Wheel command, and thank you." Parnell's eyes swept his panel one last time; then he flicked back the tiger-striped guard above the main engine ignition switch and let his finger hover in place over it. "Captain, are you ready? On the count of zero."

Ryer had pulled the pilot's T-yoke up between her legs; her right hand gripped the yoke while her left hand rested on the throttle bar. "Roger that, Commander," she said, her eyes fastened to the screens above her head. "On your mark."

Parnell nodded and lay back in his couch. "Five . . . four . . . three . . . two . . . one . . . zero and mark."

He pushed the button, and felt the massive vessel tremble as twenty-five engines simultaneously ignited, producing a combined thrust of over four hundred tons. There was no roar, yet he heard a dull moan from somewhere beneath him, combined with the strained creak of the fuselage and the faint rattle of loose objects within the bulkheads and fuselage. His couch shuddered as the unaccustomed force of gravity gently shoved him back into the foam upholstery, as if an invisible hand were pushing against him, a hand that grew more insistent as Ryer eased the throttle forward, pumping nearly three thousand pounds of fuel per second from the departure tanks into the engines.

"We have ignition!" he called out.

Roger that, Conestoga, *looking good.* Vaya con Dios . . .

He looked up at the monitors. The Moon seemed no closer, yet the Wheel had disappeared from view, and so had Earth's broad, blue-green curve. He raised his hand against the mounting g-force and pushed a button that changed the view on his monitor; the aft camera, mounted just above the bow, showed a bright orange-yellow nimbus of light surrounding the engines. Beyond it, Earth was falling away, slowly at first, more quickly now, as if it were a giant sphere plummeting into an infinite black well.

For better or worse, they were on their way.

A SOVIET SPACE SECRET
COMES TO LIGHT
After 11 Years, A Mystery Is Solved . . .
And With It, New Doubts About
"Star Wars"

For more than a decade, it's been one of the most daunting mysteries of the Cold War: why did the Soviet space program, which once rivaled the United States for superiority on the high frontier, suddenly collapse?

At one time, Russian space scientists seemed to be gaining on their American counterparts. They launched the first two-man space station in 1961, then soft-landed an unmanned probe on Mars in 1969, only 11 days after John Harper Wilson walked on the Moon. Shortly afterward, the Kremlin announced that the U.S.S.R.'s primary space objective would be to establish a permanent colony on the red planet by 1980 . . . and few people doubted that the Soviets were capable of doing this.

Yet by 1976, when Ares One carried the first—and last—American-Russian expedition to Mars, it was already clear that the Soviet Union was abandoning its manned space efforts. Indeed, many observers noted that Ares was largely an American effort, with a few Soviet cosmonauts hitching a ride for the sake of *detente.* The Soviets have claimed that they shifted their technological priorities to solving domestic problems, but this week the truth was finally revealed: a catastrophic disaster, rather than a central policy change, was responsible for the Russian retreat from space.

The revelation came from no less than dissident Russian physicist Andrei Sakharov, who was released from internal exile in Siberia and allowed to return to Soviet Georgia. Unrepentant and outspoken as ever, Sakharov told visiting Western correspondents last week about a 1972 launch pad explosion at the Baikonur cosmodrome at Tyuratam which killed at least two dozen people, including three cosmonauts and several leading Russian space scientists, just as the Soviets were on the verge of achieving a goal which had previously eluded the U.S. Space Force: the development of a man-rated nuclear spacecraft.

According to Sakharov, the Russian spacecraft was designated the G-1, code-named Zenith. Unlike the Atlas-B spacecraft briefly used by the USSF in the sixties, which was composed of a liquid-fuel booster and a nuclear-powered upper stage, Zenith was a single-stage rocket with a nuclear engine. Somewhat resembling a streamlined spaceship from a 1950's sci-fi movie, Zenith was capable of both vertical lift-offs and landings, alighting on tripodal landing gear which extended from its aft fuselage. Eighty feet tall and capable of carrying a six-person crew, the sleek vessel's nuclear engine was rated at 900 ips (impulse per second). This is comparable to the Atlas-B's 950 ips, and far outstrips the performance of NASA's new *Challenger* space shuttle, which is rated at 450 ips.

The top-secret project was initiated in the late fifties, when the Kremlin hoped to use Zenith to beat the USSF's Project Luna to the Moon. But development of a reliable nuclear rocket proved to be more complex than originally envisioned; it also soaked up most of the resources of the Russian space program. By 1972, though, two prototypes had been built, and in the early morning hours of September 3, Zenith-1 was rolled out to its Baikonur launch pad, where a three-man test crew climbed aboard and awaited final countdown for its maiden flight.

The launch never took place. Sakharov is uncertain about what happened, since he himself was not present at the time, and exact details of the disaster are still a closely guarded secret. Nonetheless, Sakharov believes that the main fuel tank ruptured during fueling and its hydrogen fuel ignited. The result was a massive non-nuclear explosion which not only destroyed Zenith-1 and killed its crew, but also snuffed out the lives of scientists, engineers, and workers who were on the launch pad at the time. It was only luck that prevented the rocket's uranium-core reactor from being breached; otherwise, a nuclear fire might have destroyed the entire Baikonur complex.

The disaster was successfully hidden by GRU, the Soviet military intelligence agency. The wreckage was masked from American satellites by massive camouflage tarps hastily thrown over the pad after the fires were extinguished, and the fatalities were ascribed to a fictional airplane crash in the Urals. The remaining Zenith rocket was never tested; it was transported by rail to a Red Army warehouse somewhere in Siberia, where it presumably remains mothballed to this day.

As crude as this cover-up may seem, it apparently worked; Western intelligence agencies never learned about the launch pad explosion, much less the existence of the G-1 program. Yet the Soviet space program was delivered a blow from which it never recovered. Indeed, says Sakharov, the reason why Soviet leader Leonid Brezhnev so readily agreed to Russian participation in Project Ares was not diplomatic so much as it was to save face.

The new Kremlin government of Yuri Andropov has categorically denied Sakharov's allegations, but a number of Western space experts say that it seems to fit previously available information . . . including the mysterious crash of a Tupolev transport jet on September 4, 1972, in which it was claimed no bodies were recovered. They also say that it casts new doubt upon the validity of the Reagan Administration's proposed "Star Wars" strategic defense initiative.

The first stage of the program is already underway as *Challenger* nears completion at North American Rockwell's plant in Sunnyvale, California. SDI was dealt a setback last April by the death of one of its major proponents, nuclear physicist Edward R. Teller, and now many space experts are beginning to doubt whether the Soviet Union's "secret space superiority," previously claimed by the White House as justification for an orbital defense system, is a paper tiger . . . a tiger born in the predawn fires of a Baikonur launch pad, 11 years ago.

THIRTEEN

Conestoga did not leave Earth for the Moon by itself. For the first 6,525 miles of its journey, it had an escort.

A few minutes after the moonship commenced its upward climb through Earth's gravity well, *Fido's Pride* ignited its main engine and began to follow its lunar trajectory. The retriever ship couldn't hope to keep up with the massive vessel in front of it; even if it had attempted to do so, the fuel in its seven strap-on tanks would have been long exhausted before it got halfway to the Moon.

Yet that wasn't its mission; *Fido's Pride*'s small role in the greater scheme of things was to shadow *Conestoga* only until it reached the first checkpoint. So, for the next half-hour, the retriever chased the moonship like a greyhound pursuing a mechanical rabbit down a racetrack six thousand miles long.

Through the canopy windows, Ed McGraw could see the brilliant flare of *Conestoga*'s engines against the dense blackness of cislunar space as it gradually outraced his small, aged ship. The computer and radar screens showed that they were both right on course, following a shallow semielliptical arc which would eventually take *Conestoga* into lunar orbit. By then, of course, McGraw's job would be done; he would have long since returned to the Wheel, bringing with him fragments of history.

In the aft cabin behind the cockpit, an R.E.M. tape blared

from a small Sony deck which dangled on its strap from an equipment rack, swaying backward with the force of constant acceleration. Poppa was getting just familiar enough with recent rock 'n' roll to recognize "Orange Crush" when he heard it; either that, or Billy had played it so many times that he could practically mime Michael Stipe's voice.

" 'Follow me, don't fall on me . . .' " Poppa sang under his breath until he forgot the rest of the words. Sort of appropriate, although he would have preferred Beethoven's Fourth just now. Maybe a little Elvis, if he had to listen to rock, although he knew he was dating himself with that thought; the last time he had caught up with the King, he was touring with U2. Leave it to the younger generation to make you feel so goddamn old. . . .

"How's it coming back there?" he shouted over his shoulder, careful not to take his eyes off the screens.

"Almost ready," Billy called back. "Go ahead and pressurize the bottle."

Billy had pulled on a pressure suit and was fitting a bubble helmet over his head; the suit was just sufficient to protect him if the ship's bottlesuit suffered decompression, although that had never occurred while he was a pilot. Poppa pumped air into the bottlesuit; when the gauges told him the pressures had equalized, he hit a switch which popped the round hatch in the floor of the aft compartment. Billy climbed down into the bottlesuit's cocoon and shut the hatch above him.

By now, thirty-three minutes had passed since *Conestoga* had left Earth orbit. McGraw didn't need the computer to prompt him on the next event; he whispered the countdown under his breath. "MECO in five . . . four . . . three . . . two . . . one . . ."

Right on time, the distant flare of the moonship's engines abruptly disappeared as the giant vehicle began its long glide to the Moon. Keeping a sharp eye on the radar screen, McGraw throttled the engine back by 50 percent.

"Okay, Gene," he murmured, "don't keep me waiting. Get rid of your baggage now . . ."

Sure enough, the blip on the radar screen split into three smaller parts; the one in the center remained on its original heading while its two other parts cleaved away.

"Okay," McGraw said aloud, "we've got departure tank separation."

Got it, Billy said through the comlink. *Are they staying in range?*

Poppa watched the radar display for another few seconds. Although the two blips were drifting in opposite directions, they remained within a few hundred feet of each other. "Ayup, they're in the ballpark," he replied. "Let's go get 'em."

Conestoga no longer needed the four spherical tanks that had contained the lox and hydrazine necessary for departure, so they had been jettisoned, in racks of two apiece, from the moonship's frame. Under normal circumstances they would have been ejected with small explosive charges which would have sent them tumbling into deep space, never to be seen again, but because it was desirable to retrieve the tanks so that they could later be remated with the rest of the moonship as a museum exhibit, the pyros had been removed from the strutwork. Instead, *Conestoga*'s flight had rolled the ship on its axis, causing the departure tanks to gently disengage from the frame and drift away so that they could be retrieved by *Fido's Pride.*

"Nice job, Gene." Poppa Dog grinned as he turned his ship toward the closer of the two braces. "Fido to Wheel Command," he said, toggling the KU-band radio, "this is Mars Retriever One-Three. We've got a lock on the DTs at angles six-two-fiver and going to collect."

It took a few moments to get a response; the Wheel was now of the far side of Earth, so McGraw's signal had to bounce across a series of low-orbit Comsats. *We copy, Mars Retriever One-Three,* a voice replied through his headset. *Keep us posted, over.*

"Will do, Wheel," Poppa replied as he throttled back the main engine another ten points. "Poppa over and out."

Most of the time, Wheel Command couldn't care less what he and Billy were doing out here, so long as they didn't interfere with other space traffic. On the other hand, this time they weren't hauling in a dead weather satellite or somesuch piece of orbital flotsam. Today, they were bringing home a piece of history. . . .

Yeah. And when he was a doddering old fool, he could take the grandkids to the Smithsonian and show it to them. McGraw's grin faded as he considered the prospect. *See those fuel tanks? They're from the last American spaceship to visit the Moon, and your grandpappy brought 'em home for you to look at. Doesn't that make you feel proud?*

"Hell of a note," he muttered to himself.

What's that? Billy asked.

"Never mind, son. Just thinking aloud."

Still, it wasn't often that he got to take *Fido's Pride* out this far. Besides the occasional run out to geosynchronous orbit, most of the salvage missions he and Billy performed were in lower orbit; if they'd had enough fuel and oxygen aboard, he would have liked to chase *Conestoga* all the way to the Moon. Almost twenty years in the saddle and he had never walked on the Moon, and unless he cared to learn how to speak German and handle a new type of vessel, he probably never would.

Fuck it. Glancing through the canopy windows, he could see stars beginning to appear around him as the Sun set behind Earth. It was always a pretty sight, one of the few things that still made it worthwhile to be an astronaut. The mission was going well enough for him to sneak a peek.

Carefully keeping one hand steady on the yoke, McGraw loosened his shoulder straps so he could turn slightly to his left and look out the portside windows. Earth was a vast, dark shape behind him, its curve described by a thin blue-yellow line of light. A smile reappeared on his face as he savored the view. Damn, it sure was pretty. He should remember to bring a camera out here sometime, snap a few pictures for the grandkids back home. Maybe they would . . .

All at once, something caught his eye: a tiny spot of light within the darkness, like a fireball lancing across Earth's atmosphere.

"Whoa!" he yelled. "You see that?"

For a moment, he thought it was a large meteorite entering the atmosphere. He had seen that a few times over the years: pieces of a passing Apollo asteroid, meeting its final fate as it disintegrated within the upper reaches of the stratosphere. Yet this miniature comet didn't quickly burst and fade from view. And it was going in the wrong direction, heading out instead of in . . .

See what? Billy asked.

Of course, he couldn't see anything. Sealed inside the bottlesuit, Billy couldn't see jackshit until he had disengaged from the belly of the retriever ship.

As abruptly as it appeared, the fireball vanished. Poppa watched as it disappeared among the stars. In another moment, it was indistinguishable from any one of dozens of satellites in low orbit.

"Uh . . . naw, never mind." McGraw turned back around, blinking rapidly as he put his eyes back on the radar display. The first brace of tanks was coming up fast; he couldn't afford to screw around with UFO sightings right now. "Thought I saw something, that's all."

What did you see?

"Forget it," McGraw replied. "Just get ready for the drop."

Damned if it didn't look like an orbital rocket being launched from somewhere on Earth. Yet, when he glanced at the Zulu-time chronometer and did a little mental figuring, the likely point of origin didn't make much sense. Given the time of day, the rocket must have been launched from somewhere in Southeast Asia. With the exception of Japan's launch sites at Kagoshima and Tanegashima Island, there weren't any there, and the Japanese weren't scheduled for any night launches the last time he had checked.

His right hand drifted uncertainly toward the communications panel; then he stopped himself. He could see the departure tanks through his front window now, and *Fido's Pride* was going a bit too fast for an effective capture rendezvous. McGraw hastily throttled back to zero and fired the ship's forward RCR's; the harness dug into his chest and shoulders as the mutt put on the brakes.

Poppa, what the hell . . . !

"Sorry about that, kid." McGraw returned his concentration to the tricky maneuver he had almost botched. "Just seeing things."

And so it was. He was just seeing things.

• • •

Main-engine cutoff and separation of the departure tanks had gone as well as could be expected, and although they were to perform four course-correction burns within the next sixteen hours, the first one wasn't scheduled for another hour and a half, when they reached the second checkpoint at 21,750 nautical miles.

Nonetheless, the launch had not gone flawlessly. When Lewitt deployed the high-gain telemetry dish and the mercury-solar boiler, he reported that the long-range radar seemed to be on the fritz. Gene unstrapped and floated over to Jay's station, where he confirmed that the LR radar display was showing nothing but snow. Most likely, something outside the ship had come loose during launch. However, since the close-range radar was still operational, it wasn't an immediate source of concern; while the short-range system was vital for landing, the LRR was a secondary array which didn't need immediate attention, since it was mainly used for rendezvousing with the hangar during the return flight.

"Keep on it," he said to Jay. "If we don't get it ironed out before we get to the Moon, we'll fix it there."

Jay nodded. "Got it. Going below?"

"Yeah. Time to check on the tourists." Parnell pushed off from the bulkhead. "You've got the wheel. I'll be back in a few minutes."

He left the command deck and floated headfirst down the gangway shaft to C-deck. As he expected, most of the passengers were clinging to rungs near the portholes, watching as Earth receded behind them. Thankfully, no one had gotten spacesick; by now, even Bromleigh and Dooley had become accustomed to surges and sudden drops of g-force, and Bromleigh was aiming his Sony out one of the portholes to snag a few shots of Earth.

As he watched Dooley and Rhodes jostling for room at a porthole, like a couple of kids fighting for the best seat on a carnival ride, Parnell wondered why no one had ever taken space tourism seriously. Probably because first the Space Force, then NASA, had jealously fought off bids by various entrepreneurs to develop low-orbit spacecraft for civilians. So far, the only untrained individuals who had ever been in space were a select handful of politicians, journalists, and celebrities. Sure, NASA had let John Denver sing a couple of songs aboard the Wheel, and George Lucas had been allowed to shoot a zero-g fight scene in the hub for *Revenge of the Jedi*. But wouldn't it have been better publicity if the agency had traded one famous pop singer or film director for a couple of suburban housewives, who could have then gone home to tell their friends that spending tax money on space travel was worthwhile after all?

One more lost opportunity . . .

He had intended to brew some coffee in the galley, only to be surprised that Markus Talsbach had already found the microgravity coffee maker. "We have studied your equipment completely," Talsbach said, giving Gene a smug smile as he slipped a catheter around a squeeze bulb and handed it to him. "It is a good design . . . but it needs a little improvement, yes?"

"Yes, it . . . yeah, maybe so." Gene loosened the catheter, took a sip through the straw, and almost gagged. Talsbach had made coffee strong enough to raise the dead. "Thanks, but take it easy on the bags next time. We've got to make the supply last."

Talsbach grinned at him, then pulled himself up the gangway ladder to B-deck, where Aachener was inspecting the ship's mainframes. Gene considered following them, if only to explain the equipment, but realized that the Germans had probably studied that part of the moonship, too. In fact, their simulators probably contained computers which were more state-of-the-art than *Conestoga*'s.

He turned around to find James Leamore strapped into a seat on the other side of the mess table. The Englishman had already figured out how to cradle his squeeze bulb within one of the table's magnetic coasters. He had also discovered the gripsole sneakers in the locker beneath his couch and was now putting them on his feet.

"A nice launch, Commander," he said as he carefully adjusted the shoes for his size. "We hardly felt a thing down here."

"Thanks, Mr. Leamore . . ."

"James, please. Or you can call me Pat. Most of my friends do." Leamore laced up his left sneaker, unstrapped his seat belt, and carefully stood up, testing the cling offered by the frayed carpet. "Well . . . works rather nicely, doesn't it?"

"It should. We've had a little practice at this sort of thing." Gene nodded to his own feet, which were not shod in grip-soles. "Personally, I get along without them. Just one less thing I have to worry about."

"I imagine so." Leamore took a few tentative baby-steps around the floor. "We're still trying to decide whether to equip our ships with these things. Seems as if it's a matter of six of one and half a dozen of the other . . ."

"Something like that, yeah." Gene shrugged. "You get the illusion of gravity, but for that you give up some mobility, too." He took a seat on the far side of the table but didn't strap himself down. Instead, he crossed his legs so that his left knee pinned his right leg between the bottom of the table and the floor, anchoring him in place. "Practice is all it takes."

"Hmm. Yes." Leamore slowly walked back to his chair and sat down; he didn't try to imitate Parnell's crossed-leg trick. "Of course, our ships won't be . . . well, quite as spacious, if you know what I mean."

Gene knew what he meant. Koening Selenen's Monhunde moonships would not only make orbital hangars unnecessary, but also reduce the size of the vessels themselves. The Monhunde was to be a two-stage vehicle, the first stage of which was a retrievable liquid-fuel booster that would be jettisoned once the vehicle reached low orbit. The second stage would utilize an advanced nuclear engine capable of sending men and cargo straight to the Moon; this engine would then be refueled on the Moon, using reactive volatiles refined from the lunar regolith. Before the first Monhunde was launched, an unmanned, teleoperated fuel-manufacturing plant would be sent to Tranquillity Base, where it would begin stocking up on fuel not only for the return flight but for subsequent missions.

In other words, Koenig Selenen intended to make Tranquillity Base self-sufficient by forcing it to live off the land instead of shipping from Earth everything needed for survival. If it worked—and there was no reason to believe that it wouldn't—the cost of space exploration would be greatly re-

duced, and large-scale space colonization would become a
real possibility. Indeed, Koenig Selenen was already discussing plans to use nuclear indigenous-fuel spacecraft to send a
return mission to Mars, the asteroid belt, and even the outer
planets of the solar system.

The sad irony of the NIF engine was that it had first been
proposed in the mid-eighties by a team of researchers from
the Martin Marietta Corporation. Unfortunately, NASA's en-
trenched bureaucracy had not paid much attention to the idea;
it was also opposed by the antispace movement, whose knees
jerked at the mere mention of the word "nuclear." Suffocated
by redundant impact studies and railed at by technophobic
newspaper columnists, the NIF engine died in the United
States. The project's key scientists quit Martin Marietta, left
the U.S., and moved to Germany, where they were quickly
hired by Koenig Selenen GmbH.

Even more ironic was the fact that once NIF moonships
entered service, one of their main jobs would be hauling high-
level nuclear waste to the Moon, where it would be stored
inside the empty Minuteman II silos. This would please en-
vironmentalists concerned about the disposal of nuclear waste
on Earth . . . but who had opposed a solution to the same
problem because it involved using space technology. Of
course, Koenig Selenen GmbH would profit handsomely from
this enterprise as well.

Now, as he sat across the galley table from Parnell, James
Leamore had the twinkle in his eyes of a patient tortoise who
has outraced a complacent, slumbering hare.

"I'm sure you'll manage somehow," Gene said. He un-
crossed his legs, swiveled the chair around, and pushed off
from the table, taking his coffee with him. "If you'll excuse
me, I need to return upstairs."

On his way up the ladder, Gene paused on B-deck. The
two German astronaut-trainees were bent over the plotting
table, their feet restrained by floor stirrups as they closely
studied the highlighted map of the lunar farside. He was about
to join them, when he noticed Cris Ryer on the far side of
the deck.

She had lowered one of the cots from the bulkhead and
was sitting on it as she changed into gripshoes from her duffel

bag. She looked up warily as Gene pulled himself along the ceiling rail until he grabbed a support stanchion.

"If I had known you were coming below," he said, "I would have offered to buy you coffee."

"That's all right, Commander," she replied. "I just needed to change shoes. I'll get some coffee myself before I go back up."

"You sure? I could run down and grab another bulb."

Ryer shook her head; the sudden motion caused her short blond hair to drift across her face. "No, sir, that's fine. I can manage by myself."

Her eyes darted to the open privacy curtain, as if she were wishing she'd thought to draw it around her bunk. She was clearly uncomfortable in his presence, and Parnell suddenly felt a twinge of guilt. After all, he had been prodding her in a sore spot ever since they left the Cape; they didn't have to be friends, but neither her job nor his would be made any easier if they couldn't tolerate each other for a few days.

"Look, Cris . . ." he began, then glanced over his shoulder to see if either Aachener or Talsbach were paying attention. They were engrossed in the map, murmuring to each other in German. He lowered his voice. "Look, let's just drop it, okay?"

"Drop what, Commander?"

"Drop the hostility, that's what I mean." He took a deep breath. "I know you're upset about . . . y'know, what's happening with you and the agency. Believe me, I understand . . ."

"Oh. You understand." Ryer angrily shoved the discarded boots into her duffel bag, then raised her left foot and thrust it into a gripsole sneaker. "So how's the wife, Commander? How's the kids?"

"I don't see what my family's got to do with . . ."

"No? Of course you don't." Her eyes were cold when she glanced at him. "I hear your son's got a dope problem and you've spent a lot of time trying to keep him out of jail. That right? Funny how nobody questions your patriotism or calls you a security risk."

Parnell felt his face grow warm. "That's not the same thing, Captain . . ."

"It isn't?" Ryer impatiently swept the hair out of her face. She laced up the sneaker and reached for its mate. "It's your private business, something that stays at home. Right? Well, what I do stays at home, too. In fact, it had for almost ten years, until someone saw me kiss my wife in a bar. Then I became a security risk . . ."

"Cris . . ."

"Yeah, okay . . . you're right. Maybe we should just drop it." She nodded toward a nearby bunk while she laced the other sneaker. "The TV queen is supposed to sleep over there. You think she'll mind? I mean, she's really not my type, but you never know about us queers . . ."

"Cut it out!" he snapped.

He heard Aachener and Talsbach abruptly go silent. He didn't have to look behind him to know that they were staring in his direction. Parnell forced himself to calm down; it wouldn't do any good for him to blow up at Ryer now.

"Look," he said, "let's go back to square one. We've got our jobs to do. Regardless of everything else, that's the first priority. We can't go to the Moon and back snarling at each other . . . we're the guys in charge here. Got it?"

Ryer was about to retort, then apparently reconsidered. She sighed, nervously flicking her hair away again; she didn't look his way. "Yeah. Okay. Got it."

"Good. So let's make a deal. You do your job, and I'll stay off your case."

"Yeah, okay, Commander." She pulled the duffel bag closer and began to dig into it. "Whatever you say . . . Christ, where's that cap?"

Parnell felt his temper rising once more. She was avoiding him again, and the silly-ass game was beginning to piss him off. He reached forward to grab the duffel bag, intending to yank it aside so that she couldn't use it to escape the conversation.

"And another thing," he said as his fist grasped the bag's nylon cord. "Cut the 'Commander' crap. My name's . . ."

What happened next was the sort of accident that can only occur in free-fall. He didn't intend to spill the duffel's contents, but she wasn't holding it firmly enough; in the next instant, boots, rolled socks, a sweatshirt, underwear, a spare jumpsuit, a toilet kit, a computer diskette . . . all practically exploded in midair, pulled outward by the force of his tug.

"Goddammit!" she yelled, but she was redfaced and laughing in spite of her anger as her personal belongings were made public. "Oh, shit, Parnell! Look what you've done!"

"Jeez . . . Cris, I'm sorry!" He heard the Germans laughing as he let go of his squeeze bulb and began grabbing for anything within reach.

He managed to snag one of the boots, a pair of white silk undies—he tried not to look at them too hard—and a sweatshirt before he spotted the computer diskette tumbling past his shoulder. He snatched it up and, out of curiosity, glanced at the handwritten label.

"Tetris?" he said. "Hey, I love this. My daughter got me into it . . ."

"Gimme that!"

Before he could react, Ryer dropped the clothes she'd retrieved, flung herself across the six feet of space separating them, and grabbed the diskette out of his hand. "That's not for you!"

For an instant, he saw terror in her eyes. "Hey, whoa," he said, surprised by her expression. "Easy does it. I'm just surprised you brought a game with you, that's all." He cocked his head toward the nearby computers. "If you've got a minute, let's load it up and . . ."

"No," Ryer said. "Let's not."

She unzipped a hip pocket of her jumpsuit, shoved the diskette inside, and zipped the pocket closed again before she forced a smile on her face. "C'mon, Gene," she said. "Help me get all this stuff. We've got the second-post burn to do in a few minutes."

"Uh . . . yeah. Sure." Parnell handed her the armful of clothing he had already collected, then went to retrieve the toilet kit which was spiraling end-over-end toward the other side of the deck. No problem with him getting a good, close look at her panties, but let him touch a knock-off copy of an arcade game . . .

Damn, but she was a strange woman.

From The Associated Press (national wire); January 25, 1985

WASHINGTON—President Ronald Reagan today ordered that the remaining NASA space shuttle, *Discovery,* be temporarily grounded, following last Tuesday's explosion of the shuttle *Challenger.*

The order was made public by White House spokesman Larry Speaks, in a brief statement issued to the press. "Until we know exactly what destroyed *Challenger,* we cannot allow *Discovery* to remain in service," Speaks said.

The Executive Order follows preliminary reports by NASA accident investigators which indicate that *Challenger* was destroyed by a malfunctioning solid-rocket booster. Although Navy divers are still probing the wreckage of the shuttle off the Florida coast, analysis of film footage of its launch shows that flames erupted from part of the right SRB seconds before the explosion occurred.

The investigators theorize that the fire from the SRB might have burned through the shuttle's external fuel tank, thereby igniting its volatile hydrogen-oxygen fuel.

Seven astronauts were killed in the disaster, which occurred during *Challenger*'s third test-flight. *Challenger* was the first vehicle in NASA's new shuttle fleet. They were intended to eventually replace the Atlas-C space ferries, which have been in continuous use since 1965.

NASA spokesman Hugh MacDonald said that the Atlas ferries will continue to be launched from Cape Canaveral. "It's an older class of vessel, but it has a superb safety record," MacDonald said. "For the time being, we will be using the Atlases as the main workhorse for manned orbital operations, until *Discovery* is judged to be completely reliable."

However, Speaks left little room for *Discovery* to be returned to service any time soon. "Until key safety issues are resolved, the President believes that we must act prudently to prevent a recurrence of this tragedy," he said.

FOURTEEN

There were a fleeting few seconds after he pushed open the outer airlock hatch and before he attached the tether of his suit's lifeline to the catwalk railing, when Parnell felt an old, atavistic fear.

Oh my God, I'm falling . . .

And indeed, so he was. But so was *Conestoga* itself, and even if by some strange accident he was cast away from the moonship, he would fall with the vessel. If such a thing were to occur, it would be embarrassing, because someone might have to suit up and come outside to haul him back in, but hardly fatal . . . so long as the lifeline held.

Yet, in those few seconds, common sense and experience did little to ease his nerves. Even though it had been half a lifetime since he'd taken his first spacewalk, and only a few hours since he made the short jaunt between *Harpers Ferry* and the moonship, this was different, because back there he was still in Earth orbit, while here . . .

Blackness. Utter starless void. A pit as deep as the universe itself, vast as all eternity.

And he still hadn't attached the tether . . .

Parnell remembered when he had taken Gene Jr. on a camping trip to Canyonlands National Park, one of the last times he and the boy had been close enough to share a holiday. For three days they hiked through the Utah desert, sleep-

ing in canyons and atop mesas, following trail markers and
his map until they reached their destination, the confluence
of the Colorado and Green Rivers. For three days they
walked, sang Boy Scout campfire songs and Creedence Clear-
water Revival hits, took snapshots of the Needles and Druid
Arch, complained about boot blisters, sipped canteen water
and dined on trail mix, and walked some more until, almost
unexpectedly, they reached a place where the ground fell
away and they found themselves staring into a primitive can-
yon with rock walls like the prows of enormous petrified bat-
tleships and the Y-shaped confluence so far below, it seemed
as if they were in an airplane.

They had stood there, the toes of their hiking boots at the
verge of the drop-off, soaking in the scenery, listening to the
wind as it whispered through the enormous gorge . . . and then
Gene Jr. did something only a goddamn fifteen-year-old
would think of.

He grabbed his father's shoulders and shouted, "Hey, don't
jump!"

In that instant, Gene's knees had turned to butter, his arms
flailed helplessly at the dry air, and a soundless scream threatened to emerge from his parched throat, because he imagined
his feet losing contact with the dry crumbling soil, falling
forward, plummeting thousands of feet down, down, down
into the gaping abyss below.

It was one of the scariest moments of his life.

It had also been the first, last, and only time he had ever
struck one of his kids. He lost his temper and gave the boy
a slap. A glancing swat off the top of the head, not a solid
punch to be sure . . . but Gene Jr. had never forgotten it, nor
completely forgiven him. The following day they trudged out
of the desert without saying much to each other, and it was
only a few months later when Judith found a couple of joints
hidden underneath a *Captain America* comic book in the
boy's bedside table drawer.

Hey, Gene? You copy? Lewitt's voice was crisp and clear
within his helmet.

Hell with it. "I'm here. Just taking in the view." Parnell
reached forward, clamped the tether to the railing and gave

the line a swift, hard tug to make sure it was secure. "Okay, I'm on the catwalk," he added.

We gotcha. Lewitt chuckled. *Don't fall off now.*

Coincidence. Jay was only joking. Gene had never told anyone, not even Judith, about the incident in Canyonlands.

He swallowed, gave the line another perfunctory tug, then pushed himself off the catwalk. "I won't," he murmured. "Going out to check the antenna now."

He had originally intended to let the failure of the long-range radar system go unattended until they reached the Moon. It was nonessential equipment, after all, at least as far as their mission was concerned; it was there mainly to track other vessels in cislunar space. *Conestoga* could easily make touchdown at Tranquillity Base without it, using the short-range dish alone for the approach and final descent. Yet his conscience had continued to bother him until, sometime during lunch, he announced his intent to go EVA and fix the damn thing once and for all.

Both Jay and Cris had argued with him, each maintaining that a spacewalk wasn't necessary and that they could handle the landing maneuvers without the LRR. Perhaps they could, but the fact of the matter was that Gene wanted a reason to leave the vessel for a few minutes. The tortured syntax of the Germans, Leamore's remarks about obsolete American space technology, Dooley's inability to eat without throwing food all over the place, Rhodes and Bromleigh wanting to video-tape everything short of his visit to the head . . . altogether, his passengers made him need to escape the ship for a few minutes. Get a breath of fresh air, as it were, although he reckoned that if someone had so much as farted, he would have taken it as a good excuse to check the oxygen tanks.

So now he was alone, and what good had it done him? Just given him the time to confront old memories, and bad ones at that.

Parnell pushed it all to the back of his mind. Letting the lifeline trail behind him, he pulled himself hand over hand along the railing until he reached the outrigger spar leading to the radar mast. His helmet lamp traced the long I-beam until it ended at the pair of silver dish-shaped radar antennas at its end.

"Going out on the starboard mast now," he said.

We copy, Lewitt replied. *Good luck.*

Easy now. One hand over the other. A rookie in the water tanks at Houston could do this. The LRR dish was the closer one of the pair, only fifteen feet away.

Once he was out from under the hemispherical bulge of the personnel sphere, he could have looked straight up and seen the Moon, but he didn't allow himself that privilege. It was too distracting. Instead, he concentrated on the beam, absently humming to himself until he realized that he was doing the refrain from "Susie Q," one of the CCR songs he and Gene Jr. had sung during the Utah trip. He stopped himself. Now was no time to be woolgathering, for chrissakes . . .

When he reached the dish, he checked it first. It was still intact, so he moved to the silver Mylar-wrapped instrument module mounted behind it. "Nothing seems to be wrong here," he said, gently jostling both the antenna and module. "No sign of micrometeor impact. Looks good as new."

Ummm . . . copy that, Gene. Lewitt's voice sounded distracted. *I'm still not getting anything here, though.*

"Nothing?"

Not even a twitch. Flatline all the way. Jay paused. *Maybe the module connection is bad. Try it again.*

The instrument module was about the size of a shoebox, attached to the antenna by a single long bolt through its center. Parnell slipped a torqueless screwdriver from his utility belt and used it to unfasten the bolt. He caught the bolt with his right hand before it could drift away, then gently pulled off the module and turned it over in his thick gloves. The eight-prong connection appeared to be undamaged, and he told Lewitt so.

Might be a hardware failure, Lewitt said. *Why don't you bring it in for a test? If it's screwed up, maybe I can run a bypass.*

"Yeah. Sounds like a good idea." Parnell opened a cargo pocket on his thigh and slipped both the module and the retaining bolt into it. "Okay, I'm coming back in. Have some hot chocolate waiting for me."

Roger that. We'll keep the porch light on.

Clumsily turning around, Parnell began to make his way

back down the spar, his hands gripping the I-beam for support.

Halfway down the beam, though, his extended left leg became tangled in a dangling loop of the lifeline. Cursing under his breath, he reached down with his right hand to pull the line free. This caused his left hand to slip from the girder, and for a few moments he was drifting free of the spar.

He almost called out, but caught himself. He wasn't in trouble, and he didn't want to sound like a panicky rookie on his first EVA. Just the type of thing Rhodes would love to put in her next dispatch. He could almost hear it now: "A moment of peril today aboard the U.S.S. *Conestoga,* when mission commander Eugene Parnell, during a routine spacewalk to fix a radar dish, was nearly lost when he . . ." and so forth.

Instead, he quickly reached up with his right hand to grab the beam again. As he did, his fingers happened to slip within a slender electrical cable attached to the beam itself.

To his surprise, the cable was loose; the slightest pull of his forefinger yanked it several inches from the brackets that held it to the beam.

He managed to catch the beam itself with his left hand, while he stared at the loose cable. Twisting his body until he could clearly look through his helmet faceplate, he saw that the cable led straight to the LRR antenna.

This was the electrical conduit leading to the radar antenna, and it should have been snugly fitted against the spar.

Having some problems out there? Lewitt asked.

Parnell glanced up at the personnel sphere looming above him. A few people were watching him through the portholes, more than likely, while listening to the exchange through headsets or intercom speakers. On the other hand, they wouldn't be able to see him clearly, because the spar itself was in their way.

"Nothing to worry about," he replied, keeping his voice even. "Just checking on something."

Hand over hand, he moved the rest of the way back down the spar, following the slender tapeworm with his helmet lamp as it snaked its way to the hull of the personnel sphere. Once he was on the catwalk again, he continued to trace the cable as it led beneath the catwalk, then up again to a small service panel about five feet from the airlock hatch. When he reached its end, he involuntarily sucked in his breath.

The cable was dangling free of the panel, its end floating a few inches from the junction box.

Certainly this would have been noticed by someone at the hangar while *Conestoga* was being prepared for launch. If an astronaut had accidentally pulled the cable loose, then either he would have fixed it on the spot, or a last-minute inspection of the moonship would have uncovered the problem.

No. It looked as if someone had deliberately pulled the cable loose from the junction box just prior to launch.

Yet, save for a couple of Wheel technicians who had briefly been inside *Conestoga,* the last people to come aboard the moonship had been its own crew and passengers.

It would have been easy for any one of them to reach over and give the cable a good, hard yank . . .

Gene? You copy? What's going on out there?

Parnell almost said something, but once again he checked himself. Too many people could be listening to this conversation. Besides, what he was thinking was absurd . . .

Why would anyone want to knock out the LRR? It didn't make sense.

"Nothing, Jay," he said. "Just looking at the Moon, that's all."

Nonetheless, as he spoke, he pulled the screwdriver from his belt again and opened the service panel. "Nice night for a spacewalk," he continued, trying to sound breezy as he quickly stretched the cable back to the panel and used the screwdriver to carefully reattach its bare end to the junction pole. "Moon sort of looks like . . . y'know . . . the way I saw it from the Beach House the other night."

Just a lot closer, right?

"Right." With the conduit now firmly back in place, he closed the panel and slipped the screwdriver back in his belt. "Okay, I'm coming back in now. Hope you've got that hot chocolate ready for me."

What, is it cold out there on the beach?

Parnell pushed himself toward the open airlock hatch. "You could say that, yeah."

• • •

As he expected, there was nothing wrong with the LRR module.

Lewitt taped it down to the old map table on B-deck, opened its case, and hooked it up to a computer diagnostics kit. Most of the crew members and passengers hovered or sat around and watched as he and Parnell pushed and prodded at it with electrodes and tweezers while consulting a loose-leaf service manual. Bromleigh caught the whole thing on videotape, of course; Rhodes said it looked like a scene from some old B movie Roger Corman once did, and when Dooley asked her if it was the same one where the spaceship computer goes insane and starts killing the crew, everyone laughed except for the Germans, who apparently weren't into film trivia.

The unit came up aces, which was just as well, since there were no spares aboard. In the old days there might have been one, but these weren't the old days. So the next, obvious step was to put the module back in place and see what happened.

Gene didn't tell anyone about the loose electrical cable. He tried to convince himself that he was keeping his mouth shut because he didn't want Rhodes and Bromleigh to get wind of what he'd found, that he didn't want NASA to suffer embarrassment for avoidable hardware failure during the last American mission to the Moon. But the truth of the matter was, he harbored suspicions that he didn't want to admit to himself, let alone to anyone else.

So he sipped at his hot chocolate and waited for the next shoe to drop.

He had gone EVA twice already that day, counting the spacewalk he had made from the ferry to the moonship. Therefore it was someone else's turn to go out on the spar and put the LRR unit back in place.

Jay volunteered for the job, and so did Uwe Aachener, but Cris insisted on doing the dirty work, pointing out that as flight engineer, Lewitt needed to remain on A-deck to monitor the systems in case there was another failure, and Aachener didn't know quite enough about *Conestoga* to be qualified for the assignment.

Her reasoning was inarguable. Within a couple of hours she was on D-deck, suiting up for EVA with the assistance of Hans and Franz. Leamore floated nearby, watching the procedure and clucking about the ''terrible shape of American technology.'' Parnell personally carried the LRR module down from the logistics deck, having already made sure that no one else placed their hands on the unit after he and Jay had completed their inspection. Only when Ryer was completely suited up and had climbed into the airlock did he hand the module to her.

Aachener shut the inner hatch above her. Through the airlock window, Parnell watched her carefully store the module and its retaining bolt in the same leg pocket he had used only three hours ago. She gave the thumbs-up; then Jay decompressed the chamber and opened the outer hatch.

It should be a cinch. If the unit was successfully put back in place, then the long-range radar would be operational once again, since Parnell had secretly repaired the real cause of the problem. It was that easy, and no one had to be any the wiser.

A few minutes later, Parnell sat in his couch on A-deck, silently listening while Ryer repeated his journey across the catwalk and down the radar spar. When she'd made it all the way out to the LRR antenna, she unsealed the pocket and pulled out the module. She was withdrawing the restraining bolt when her voice suddenly rose.

Oh, shit!

Lewitt leaned forward in his seat. ''What's going on?''

It's . . . goddammit!

Parnell clicked the VOX switch. ''What's happening, Cris?''

Fuck! It just slipped, I . . .

''Just tell me what's going on,'' he said.

A deep sigh came over the comlink, then: *I lost the module, Gene. I was trying to get the bolt out of my pocket and I . . .*

''You lost the unit?'' Lewitt snapped.

Hell, yes! I let it go for just a second while I was pulling this . . . aw, damn!

''Can you still grab it?'' Parnell asked. ''Can you retrieve the module?''

A longer pause. Static over the comlink. *No can do. It's gone, out of reach . . . Christ, Gene, I was just trying to get the bolt out of my pocket when it slipped from my hand and . . .*

"You lost the unit?" Lewitt repeated. He let out his breath. "Is it out of reach?"

What did I just tell you? Her voice was harsh, then instantly apologetic. *I'm sorry, Jay. Can't help it.* Another pause. *Sorry, guys, but I screwed up big-time. That thing's on its way to Mars.*

Gene closed his eyes for a moment. "Don't sweat it, Cris. It's not that important. Just reel yourself back in. First cup of hot chocolate is on me."

Yeah, I copy. Another pause. *Hell with hot chocolate. Anyone smuggle any booze aboard this boat?*

"I'll try to find some," Parnell said, then clicked off.

It could have been an accident that the electrical cable had been pulled free in the first place. It certainly sounded as if another accident had just occurred as Ryer lost the LRR unit during spacewalk. And it wasn't as if the long-range radar system was vital hardware to *Conestoga*'s mission. If someone wanted to deliberately sabotage this flight, there were plenty of Criticality One components from which to choose.

Still . . .

Parnell unbuckled his seat belt, and pushed out of his couch. The lady would want a squeeze bulb of hot chocolate after spending an hour in an ice-cold spacesuit, her desire for something stiffer notwithstanding.

Yet, even as he pulled himself toward the ladder, he remembered Gene Jr.'s voice as he grabbed his old man's shoulders when he was standing at the edge of a bottomless pit.

Hey, don't jump . . .

From **TV Guide;** *October 30, 1987*

Critic's Notebook:
It Still Ain't Logical, Cap'n
By Oral Fletcher

Star Trek: The New Generation (Syndicated).

Although it was a top-rated show for eight seasons between 1958 and 1966, not many people today recall the original *Star Trek*. In its time, Irwin Allen's NBC adventure series inspired great loyalty among its viewers, mainly because of its heroic (if somewhat melodramatic) depiction of near-future space exploration just when the public was fascinated with the real-life exploits of the U.S. Space Force. Legions of children came of age following the orbital derring-do of USSF Capt. Jimmy Kirk (William Shatner) and his wise-cracking scientist sidekick, Dr. Arnold Spock (Leonard Nimoy, now better known as the Oscar-winning director of *The Good Mother*).

But that was a generation ago, and today the only devotees of *Star Trek* are the tiny cadre of sci-fi fans who have memorized Dr. Spock's favorite line, "It just ain't logical, Cap'n." So it comes as a surprise that a spin-off series, *Star Trek: The New Generation,* is being syndicated in the U.S. and Canada, particularly in an era when the American public has become disenchanted with space travel.

The creator and producer of the new series, Gene Roddenberry (*The Lieutenant*) seems mindful of this. Instead of doing a remake of the original show, the new *Star Trek* takes place three centuries in the future; instead of a USSF space station above Earth, its all-new cast travels the galaxy in a giant starship, the U.S.S. *Enterprise.* They include Capt. Jean-Luc Picard (Anthony Quinn), first officer Ryker (Steven Seagal), an emotionless android (Rob Morrow), and a telepathic counselor (Susan Sarandon), all of whom wear futuristic one-piece Spandex jumpsuits.

Their allies and adversaries include a mixed bag of aliens in heavy makeup. These include benign Klingons, treacherous Vulcans, comic-relief Romulans, and in the two-hour pilot episode, a mysterious, omniscient entity called "Q" (Robin Williams) who puts humanity on trial for real or imagined crimes until finally outwitted by Picard and his teammates.

It's an ambitious start, particularly since very few sci-fi TV shows have attempted to depict life so far in the future, let alone realistically. The press kit proudly claims that scripts are checked by NASA scientists in order to ensure scientific accuracy, and several of these teleplays have been written by leading science fiction authors, including Harlan Ellison, David Gerrold, Norman Spinrad, and Salman Rushdie. The result is refreshingly adult scenarios; most notable is the third episode, "The Satanic Verses," in which Picard confronts religious fanatics on a colony world who are bent on stamping out the last vestiges of creativity among its inhabitants.

Despite such careful attention to details, the new *Star Trek* is hampered by its low-budget special effects. The sets are obviously made of papier-mâché and wood; props are repainted kitchen utensils, and even the *Enterprise* itself is suspended against a painted backdrop by half-visible fishing line. Compared to the sophisticated computer FX work pioneered by Japan's Toho Studios for its Godzilla movies, *Star Trek: The New Generation* is primitive indeed.

Less obvious, but nonetheless more indicting, is the show's naiveté. *Star Trek: The New Generation* portrays a future in which humankind has left Earth and gone to the stars, coexisting in one way or another with all forms of alien life. It's a sweet bit of sentimentality that will doubtless be applauded by diehard "trekkies," but hardly realistic; the *Enterprise* is little more than Aladdin's magic carpet with "dilithium warp drive." At least the old *Star Trek* had enough sense to confine its adventures to the Moon and Mars, and the events of the last two decades have shown them to be false, not final, frontiers. A few years after cancellation of the original series, its gung-ho attitude was effectively lampooned by *Lost In Space,* the Emmy-winning sitcom that more viewers will probably remember than the series it satirized.

However, if you enjoy this sort of thing, *Star Trek: The New Generation* is uplifting fantasy, whose thought-provoking scripts more than compensate for the cheesy effects. Seen as such, the show is a winner, worth watching if your local independent station happens to carry it.

Catch it while you can, though. It's dragging the bottom of the Nielsen ratings, and probably won't last more than a season. And that ain't logical, Cap'n.

FIFTEEN

It's nearly midnight by the ship's chronometer and all is quiet. Down in C- and B-decks, the passengers and most of the flight crew are strapped into their bunks, sleeping until the wake-up call at 0500. The decks are darkened, but moonlight shines through the portholes, eerily illuminating the long shadows of the slumbering forms; unencumbered by gravity, their hands drift above their chests, making them look like sleepwalkers who have been pinned down against their will.

Aside from the occasional digital beep from the computers on B-deck, the only sound is soft music that filters down the gangway shaft from A-deck: cool jazz, Miles Davis's "Kind of Blue," a perfect sonata for fire watch.

Gene Parnell lies in the astrogator's couch, peering at the stars through the telescope's binocular eyepiece. The shutters of the ceiling dome are irised open, allowing moonlight to illumine the command deck; he has clicked the lunar filters in place so he can spend a few hours studying the constellations before Jay Lewitt relieves him at 0200 Zulu. Two days out from Earth, *Conestoga* is nearly at the end of its long journey; tomorrow morning it will roll over, fire main engines to brake its outbound velocity and commence the direct descent to the lunar surface. For the first time since the mission began, Parnell is completely alone, and he relishes the peace and quiet while he can still get it.

Enjoying the moonlight, music, and rare solitude, he pans the telescope across the starscape, playing a solitary game of identifying constellations without consulting the star chart on the clipboard strapped to his leg. There, just to the right of Jupiter, is Libra; below it is Lupus. Scorpius is easy to find, but he has to cheat by checking the chart before he can name Ara.

However, when he looks at the chart, he notices that Pluto should be in sight, not far from Ophiuchus. Now there's a challenge; Pluto is a dim object, difficult to locate even under the best of conditions. He reaches down to grasp the wheel which will turn the couch on its pedestal, when his headset buzzes.

Startled by the sudden sound, for a moment he thinks it's someone down below trying to get his attention. Then he hears a faint voice:

Conestoga, this is Space Station One . . . Conestoga, this is Station One, Wheel Command. Do you copy? Over.

He fumbles at the communications carrier on his belt until he finds the VOX switch. "Um, roger that, Wheel Command, this is *Conestoga*, Parnell speaking. We copy, over."

Conestoga is now over 200,000 miles from Earth, so there's a four-second transmission lag: time enough for Parnell to wonder why the Wheel would be calling during a scheduled sleep period. Of course, they would know he'd be on duty at this hour—it's customary for the mission commander to take the fire watch—but the practice of hourly status checks between en route moonships and the Wheel was retired years ago.

Gene, this is Joe . . . ah, we need you to switch to the KU-4 band if you can, please, and prepare for a Code One transmission. Do you copy? Over.

Recognizing Joe Laughlin's voice, Parnell frowns. The KU-4 band is a secure channel which can't be monitored outside A-deck, reserved only for emergency transmissions. Code One means that the RF scrambler is to be used, further safeguarding the privacy of the comlink; not only that, but if anyone else is on A-deck, he is supposed to get rid of them.

He flips the switch again. "Okay, Joe, I copy that. Next transmission will be on KU-4, Code One. Over."

He unbuckles himself from the astrogator's station and pulls himself along the ceiling handrails until he reaches the pilot's couch on the far side of the deck. He considers shutting the gangway hatch, but decides against it; the noise might awaken someone below and raise uncomfortable questions he couldn't answer. Besides, the music should mask his side of the conversation.

Parnell slides into Ryer's couch and hastily knots the seat belt around his stomach. He replugs his headset into the console, then types the appropriate commands into the computer keyboard. A subaudible buzz through the headset tells him that he's on the right frequency and the scrambler is activated. "Wheel Command, this is *Conestoga*, Parnell on Code One. Do you copy, over?"

Laughlin's voice comes back on line: *Gotcha, Gene. Are you alone?*

"All by my lonesome. A little paranoid tonight, aren't we?"

It's meant as a joke, but Laughlin isn't in the mood. *Look, Gene, I'm patching through one of my boys here. You met him a couple of days ago . . . Curtis Zimm, the taxi driver who brought you guys over from* Constellation *and took you to* Conestoga. *He's got something to discuss with you.*

Parnell only vaguely remembers Zimm; it takes a moment before he matches the name with the skinhead kid he had encountered briefly aboard *Harpers Ferry.* Kind of a smart-ass, as he recalls. "Dr. Z, right," he says. "Jeez, Joe, is this important? I've got a ship to run here."

A few seconds later, Dr. Z himself comes on-line. *Commander? This is Curtis Zimm.* His voice is hesitant, uncertain. *Umm . . . I'm sorry to bother you like this, but I've learned something I think you should know about, and . . . well, I know this is going to sound crazy, but when I told Joe about it he said I should talk to you at once and . . .*

"Yeah, okay, son." Parnell rubs his closed eyelids with his fingertips. "Let's just hear it, okay?"

He hears Zimm take a deep breath. *I think someone on your ship is an imposter.*

•   •   •

It took a while to get the entire story out of Zimm. Initially everything came out as a rushed, disjointed babble of names, places, dates, and coincidences; Parnell had to stop him several times and get him to repeat something more slowly.

At first, Parnell was incredulous. The idea that Paul Dooley wasn't who he claimed to be was a bit hard to swallow; he almost laughed out loud when he heard about Mr. Grid and the kinky computer-sex games she had been playing with Dooley for several months. Yet Joe Laughlin seemed to be taking this seriously, and Joe wasn't the type to be gulled into believing nonsense. If Joe said that there might be something to Zimm's story, then Parnell had to give the kid the benefit of the doubt.

It wasn't until Dr. Z started giving him a blow-by-blow account of the Le Matrix dialogue between Mr. Grid and Thor200—or rather, between Dooley and a lonely young woman in Phoenix named Gabrielle Blumfield—and listed all the missed cues in their on-line conversation, that Parnell began to have misgivings of his own about Dooley. As Zimm spoke, Parnell recalled Dooley's erratic behavior over the past three days; from the moment they had climbed aboard *Constellation,* when he couldn't fasten his couch harness without assistance from the whiteroom techs, to dinner earlier this evening, when he had been unable to eat a simple meal without making a floating mess, Dooley had demonstrated clumsiness at every turn. More than once, Parnell had wondered if Dooley had slept through his training sessions at Von Braun; he couldn't even visit the head down on D-deck without someone giving him instructions on how to properly use the zero-g toilet. If Parnell hadn't known better, he could have sworn that Dooley hadn't been trained at all, but instead had tried to get by with reading old instruction manuals.

And then there was the fact that Dooley had been keeping to himself during the entire mission. Parnell had chosen to overlook the young hacker's absence from the going-away dinner on the Wheel three nights ago, just as he had dismissed Dooley's tardy arrival at the Cape before the ferry launch. Yet ever since *Conestoga* had left Earth orbit, Dooley had confined himself to his bunk on C-deck, where he either slept or watched an endless parade of videos on the VCR. He seldom went anywhere else in the personnel sphere; seemingly, there was no impulse to explore the mammoth spaceship. Not once had he visited A-deck, not even to send a personal message to someone on Earth.

On reflection, Parnell realized that the overbearing young man he had briefly encountered at the Cape during mission rehearsals had subtly changed. Dooley had been a pain in the ass, to be sure; a few NASA trainers had wanted to smack the little son of a bitch just on general principles. But he had never been aloof, never been so repetitively clumsy . . . and despite his arrogant dismissal of obsolete American space technology, he had nonetheless displayed curiosity about the mock-ups of the machines he would soon be riding into space.

To be sure, this Paul Dooley had the same face, the same strident voice, the same tendency to accentuate everything he said with four-letter words. Nonetheless, now that it was pointed out to Parnell by a third party, there was a mile of difference between *this* Paul Dooley and *that* Paul Dooley.

It was almost as if they were two different people entirely.

And there's one more thing, Zimm said as he finished re-iterating the dialogue between LadyG and DukePaul. *It may be nothing, but it really began to make us wonder, y'know, if . . .*

"Spell it out, son," Parnell said impatiently. The Miles Davis tape had long since ended, leaving a cold silence on the command deck. He glanced at the gangway ladder; no one had entered A-deck, but he wished he had closed the hatch. "Let's hear everything," he added, lowering his voice so that it wouldn't carry.

Gaby . . . Mr. Grid, that is . . . got curious about the long time-delay she had with Paul when they were on the net, the night before the launch, when he was staying at the motel. Remember how I told you about the pizza delivery, and how he seemed to take a while to get back on-line after he said the pizza boy had come?"

There was a short pause. *Well, sort of on impulse, today she signed onto CompuNet. That's another computer network, see, and it carries the on-line edition of the* Orlando Sentinel. *That's the major daily paper in . . .*

He knows the paper, Curtis, Joe interrupted. *He lives in Florida, remember?*

Uh . . . right. Sorry. Anyway, she scanned all the recent stories in the regional edition . . . just a shot in the dark, y'know . . . and she found a small item on page ten.

Parnell heard him take another deep breath. *The story said that the body of a local kid, name of Jeff Norton, had been found yesterday in an orange grove on Indian River. He was shot in the back of the head. This kid had been reported missing by his parents after he didn't come home from work last Wednesday night.*

Another pause. *The paper said that he worked as a delivery boy at a pizza place on Satellite Beach. He hadn't been seen since he left to make a delivery at six-fifteen, and he never returned to the restaurant.*

Parnell felt his heart skip a beat.

"Dooley was staying at a motel on Satellite Beach," he said, remembering small talk at the breakfast table in the Operations and Checkout ready-room, the morning of the launch. "Does this lady remember when Dooley said his pizza was delivered?"

The response came a few seconds later. *Le Matrix logged the time of her last chat with Dooley before the launch,* Zimm said. *She looked it up on her billing record. He talked to her between six-thirty and six-forty-one that evening, Eastern time. That's about the same time the Norton kid disappeared . . . and she says Dooley was real short with her when he came back on-line.*

They were both quiet for a minute. There were a lot of coincidences, to be sure . . . yet somehow, Parnell didn't hear his bullshit detector ringing.

His mind churned over the facts. A teenager disappears from the same area where Dooley is staying the night before the ferry launch, on his way to deliver a pizza to Dooley. The pizza is delivered, but the kid's body later turns up in a grove in the general vicinity. A few hours later, Dooley appears at the Cape . . . but he doesn't act quite the same way, either to professional acquaintances or to his secret on-line lover.

And this is the same person who has a pivotal role in the final disposal of six nuclear missiles on the Moon.

Gene? You copy?

Laughlin's voice broke his train of thought. "Roger that, Joe," he replied. "I'm just trying to pull it together."

By the way, I don't know if it means anything, but remember that . . . y'know, the thing I showed you the other night?

It took him a moment to recall the secret launch site in North Korea. "Yeah, Joe, I remember. What about it?"

Another four-second delay. *I checked it out again today, when ISPY made another pass over the same area. No rocket, but there's a lot of scorch marks on the pad. Looks like something might have lifted off while we weren't looking. And if it means anything to you, Poppa McGraw of MR One-Three reported spotting something that looked like a liftoff from that hemisphere, about the same time you jettisoned the DTs. We were at perigee when the event happened, so we couldn't see anything. Have you?*

"No, we haven't." On the other hand, Parnell reminded himself, they hadn't been looking. The long-range radar system was still down. "Who else knows about this?"

There was a long delay. Parnell wondered whether Dr. Z was still in Main-Ops or if he had been dismissed from the deck. Probably the latter; Joe was nothing if not cautious about keeping military secrets.

I've reported the launch and sighting to our friends in Virginia, Laughlin said after a few seconds, *but they haven't said boo about it. Your guess is as good as mine.*

Okay. So the Koreans had launched their first satellite. "It's probably nothing that you won't see in the papers tomorrow," Parnell said. "What about the Dooley thing? Who knows about that?"

No one else yet, Laughlin replied. *We wanted to take it up with you first before anyone went screaming to the feds. I mean, it's all pretty goddamn bizarre, when you think about it. I wouldn't want the FBI to think we've lost our shit up here, know what I mean?*

Parnell nodded his head, forgetting for the moment that his friend couldn't see him. "Roger that, but I think you better take it up with Washington anyway. It looks pretty weird, all things considered. You copy?"

A few more seconds of delay. The connection was getting

scratchy as the Wheel traveled around the far side of Earth, its signal once again fuzzed despite satellite relays. *Roger that, Gene. Look . . . it may be nothing, but keep an eye on that guy of yours, okay? Let us know if anything's fishy. Over.*

"We copy, Wheel," Parnell said. "I'll take it under advisement. *Conestoga* over."

Okay, pal. We'll keep you posted. Wheel Command over and out.

Then Parnell was left with nothing but white noise. He switched off the radio, lay back in the couch, and reflected upon everything he had just been told.

He was still thinking some two hours later when he heard someone coming up the ladder from belowdecks. Looking around, he saw Jay Lewitt float up the gangway shaft, bleary-eyed and clutching a squeeze bulb in his free hand.

"Morning, skipper. Why's it so dark in here?" Lewitt found the dimmer switch next to the ladder and turned up the ceiling lights a few degrees. Parnell blinked in the sudden glare, and the flight engineer grinned at him. "You haven't been sleeping on watch, have you?"

"Naw. Uh-uh." Parnell shook his head. "I was on the telescope for a while; then I got off and came over here." He didn't want to mention the conversation he'd just had with the Wheel. Not yet, at least. "How's everything below? Everyone still asleep?"

"Like babies." Lewitt signed himself into the logbook next to the command couch, then glided over to the engineering station. " 'Cept for the Germans, of course . . . man, Hans and Franz sure snore loud."

Parnell smiled despite his worries. The nicknames Ryer had given Aachener and Talsbach had stuck but good, even if they were known only among the command crew. And the Germans *were* loud; Parnell's bunk was below Aachener's, and last night he had to shake him several times before the astronaut-trainee finally shut up. "I hope the jazz I put on didn't keep you up," he said.

"Hmm?" Lewitt glanced away from his console for a moment. "Naw, it didn't keep me awake. Didn't even hear it." He swore under his breath as he studied one of the meters.

"Hey, you bastard! You forgot to realign the solar array. Battery's down three percent."

"I did? Sorry about that." He watched as Lewitt carefully adjusted a knob which turned the outrigger mercury-solar mirror toward the Sun. Still, he was relieved to find that Lewitt hadn't overheard his end of the conversation with the Wheel; if Jay hadn't heard it, then the chances were good that no one else had either.

Nonetheless, Parnell knew that he couldn't handle this by himself. He had to confide in someone he could trust, and Lewitt was the best prospect. As the flight engineer settled into his couch, Parnell unbuckled himself from the pilot's seat and pushed over to his friend.

"Hey, Jay," he said softly, grabbing hold of a ceiling rail and looking down at the engineer, "there's something I've got to tell you. While you were asleep, I received a call from the station . . ."

It took just a few minutes for Parnell to relate the gist of the emergency transmission from Laughlin and Zimm. He left out many of the details, if only because it would have taken too long to explain the exact nature of the relationship between Thor200 and Mr. Grid. He was surprised to see that Lewitt took it so calmly; his only outward display of emotion was a raised eyebrow and a slight pursing of his lips as he listened to his commander's suspicions.

"And you believe this?" Jay asked when Parnell was finished.

Parnell shrugged. "I don't know. It sounds kind of far-fetched, but . . ."

"But it came from Old Joe, and Hal Robinson doesn't write science fiction anymore." Jay took a sip from his luke-warm coffee, grimaced, and tucked the squeeze bulb between his knees so it wouldn't drift away. "I dunno. I gotta admit, Dooley's been acting sort of flaky ever since we got started. But that's no real reason to start thinking he's . . ."

"An imposter?"

"An imposter, whatever you want to call him." Lewitt grinned. "Did you ever see that movie . . . what was it, *The Manchurian Candidate?* The one where John Lennon is supposed to be brainwashed into killing a presidential candidate?'' He shrugged. ''Good movie, but I thought it was kind of a crock.''

''Maybe so.'' Gene had been pursuing the same line of thought for the last two hours. ''This isn't a movie, though . . . and Dooley's the guy who's supposed to reactivate the bunker computers at Teal Falcon.''

''We've got the keys . . .''

''We've got the keys, sure, but he's the man carrying the football.''

''The computer codes?'' Jay's eyes narrowed. ''What are you getting at?''

''Think about it.'' Parnell gripped the bar above his head and performed a clumsy chin-up. ''He's carrying half of the program that activates the bunker's c-cube system. Once he plugs it in, he's got complete control of the Minutemen. That means he doesn't have to fire them toward the Sun. If he wants, he can aim them at any point on Earth . . .''

''Yeah, but what does that do?'' Lewitt looked at him askance. ''C'mon. So he decides to fire them at . . . I dunno, Washington, D.C., or New York, whatever. It would still take two days for the rockets to reach ground zero. NORAD would see them coming long before then and do something about it.''

''Like what? Evacuate Washington or New York? You have any idea what that would take?''

''Maybe it doesn't have to be a city. It could be Crystal Palace itself.'' Crystal Palace was the code name for NORAD's strategic defense complex beneath Cheyenne Mountain in Colorado. ''Maybe it would be Owl Hoot, Minnesota. Point is, they'd have two days to scramble an a-sat system and blow 'em out of space.''

Parnell had to admit that Lewitt had a point. If nuclear terrorism was the objective, then taking over Teal Falcon was a poor way of going about it. The six Minutemen at Sabine Crater were intended to be second-strike weapons; they were useless when it came to launching a sneak attack against anyone but the lowliest third-world nation, and even Somalia or Bangladesh would be able to find some patron superpower with the technological capability to protect them within two days. International ABM treaties notwithstanding, it wasn't

impossible to intercept an incoming nuke from the Moon;
everyone knew that antisatellite systems had been devised in
the eighties which could knock down a low-orbit target.

Gene absently rubbed his beard. "I don't know how it
would work, either . . . but that doesn't mean we can ignore
this." He stifled a yawn as he checked his watch. It was
almost 0230 Zulu. With luck, he could manage a couple of
hours of shut-eye before he had to get up again and prepare
for the landing at Tranquillity Base. "I'm just saying we
should keep a close eye on Dooley. Call it paranoid, but . . ."

"I hear you." Lewitt nodded, although skepticism was
written across his face. "Anything else?"

Parnell hesitated. "Yeah. One more thing . . . if this isn't a
snark hunt, then he may not be acting alone. If I was a ter-
rorist group or whatever, I wouldn't send Dooley out here
without some sort of backup."

"Ah, c'mon!" Jay's credulity had clearly been stretched
as far as it would go. "Who else do you think is involved?
Leamore? Hans and Franz?"

For the first time since he had brought up the subject, Gene
wondered if he wasn't indeed jumping at shadows. He realized how all this must sound to Lewitt: an old Cold War
astronaut, brought back into service for one last mission, still
searching for commies beneath the bed. Now more than ever,
he was feeling his age. . . .

But he had gone this far already, so he might as well spell
out everything that had crossed his mind.

"Keep a sharp watch on Ryer," he said quietly. "Dooley's
not the only one who's been acting a little weird lately. Know
what I mean?"

Jay slowly nodded, his expression suddenly very somber.
"Yeah," he murmured. "I've noticed that." He frowned.
"But why would she . . . ?"

"She's got a grudge. Let's just put it that way."

A corner of Lewitt's mouth lifted. "So I've heard." He
shrugged. "Okay. Maybe you got a point, skipper. I'll watch
'em both."

"Do that." Gene's eyelids were beginning to feel heavy.
The human body needs less rest in free-fall than it does on
Earth; on the other hand, he had been on duty for the last

sixteen hours. For some reason, though, he didn't feel like going down to C-deck.

"If you don't mind," he said, pushing off from the bulkhead, "I'm just going to catch a few winks at my station. Mind if I turn down the lights a bit?"

Lewitt looked a little surprised. "What, too tired to go below?"

"Just don't want to deal with the snoring, that's all." Parnell pulled himself along the handrails until he reached the command couch, pausing by the astrogator's station to hit the switch that irised the ceiling dome shut. He didn't want to admit it to Lewitt, but he was also reluctant to leave his post on A-deck just now.

Nor did he relish the idea of going to sleep in a dark room so close to Dooley.

From the transcript of a hearing before the Ways and Means Committee, United States Senate; March 14, 1988.

Sen. Warren P. Rudman (R., NH): The chair recognizes Senator Hollings.

Sen. Ernest F. Hollings (D., SC): Thank you, Senator. First off, I wish to compliment Mr. Ballou and his staff for being so candid in their review of NASA's current status. This committee hasn't always received straight answers from the space agency, but I'm pleased to see that the current NASA administrator has broken from the past and supplied us with such a comprehensive report.

Hamilton Ballou, Chief Administrator, NASA: You're welcome, Senator. I don't agree with your assessment of my agency's honesty in dealing with Ways and Means before now, but I'll accept even a left-handed compliment.

Hollings: In an election year, Mr. Ballou, any compliment is a good one. I'm particularly impressed with the sheer size of the report NASA has prepared—1,125 pages in all, almost as long as Tom Clancy's new novel—and the presentation you've just given us, but there are still quite a few questions I have about its summation.

If I may quote from . . . ah, page 12, paragraph 3—you say, "We strongly believe that unless the United States acts now to preserve the technological infrastructure of its civil space program, this country will continue to lose ground to competing foreign space programs, until NASA becomes an agency without any clear purpose or objective." Can you clarify that statement for the committee, please?

Ballou: Certainly, Senator. Last September, the European Space Agency successfully tested its new Sanger spaceplane. A private German aerospace corporation, GmbH Koenig, has already expressed interest in purchasing three Sangers for the purpose of commercial space activities. This follows the success of the French-German firm Arianespace in capturing over fifty percent of the global commercial satellite launch industry with its expendable Ariane boosters. Koenig has also declared its interest in constructing solar power satellites in geosynchronous Earth orbit.

Once the Sanger becomes fully operational, Germany will have a reusable manned spacecraft which can outperform our Atlas-C ferries. After the President permanently grounded *Discovery* and Congress voted down NASA's request to build either a replacement for *Challenger* or a new generation of single-stage-to-orbit spacecraft, this country has been left with a fleet of spacecraft which is over twenty-five years old.

Not only that, but the last time Space Station One was retrofitted was three years ago. As grateful as NASA is for the appropriations which made this possible, the new computers are already a generation behind state-of-the-art cybernetic technology, and in five more years they will be hopelessly obsolete. Because the Reagan Administration also downscaled operations on the Wheel and at Tranquillity Base, we're left with a space station and a moonbase which are critically undermanned as well as underfinanced. We believe . . .

Hollings: Okay, hold it right there. You just hit the key word—"underfinanced." Of course, it shouldn't be seen as coincidental that your report comes at the same time as the NASA budget for the next fiscal year is being considered by both the House and Senate, but this report seems to state that unless this country continues to spend as much money as it already does on space, if not increase appropriations, then the space program will fall apart tomorrow.

Ballou: Not tomorrow morning, Senator, or perhaps not even by next Tuesday . . . but it will continue to deteriorate over the coming decade until it becomes next to negligible. In the meantime, Europe will continue to develop its spacefaring capability. In all likelihood, so will Japan. When this occurs, the United States will be left with a space station and a lunar base that will be unable to compete in the global marketplace for space-based services.

Hollings: Such as these . . . um, solar-powered satellites? Mr. Ballou, may I remind you that this country already has an energy surplus? Even without building new nuclear power plants, the U.S. is able to furnish ample electrical power to all its citizens.

Ballou: Senator, may I remind the committee that our energy lifeline is largely dependent upon foreign oil? For now, yes, we enjoy the advantage of having the OPEC nations in disagreement over production and shipping, but we can't depend on that forever. Europe and Japan have already learned that lesson, which is why they're working on developing long-range forms of energy supply. If we . . .

Hollings: And I should remind the chief administrator that we are facing a budget deficit which requires all sectors of the government to make cutbacks in spending . . .

Ballou: Yes, sir. I've noted the salary increase the Senate just voted itself . . .

Rudman: Mr. Ballou, please keep to the matter at hand.

Ballou: I apologize, Mr. Chairman. Please ignore that outburst. It was uncalled-for.

Rudman: I quite agree. Senator Hollings?

Hollings: As I was saying, under the Deficit Reduction Act we've required all federal agencies to trim their fiscal outlays to reduce the national deficit by half over the next five years. NASA is no exception to the rule, Mr. Ballou, and I don't see any reason why we should make an exception. NASA may want to explore the stars and galaxies, but we've got many pressing matters on Earth which need to be taken care of first. If our European allies and Japan want to squander their money on sky-high projects, they can do so.

But down at the Air and Space Museum there's a rock in a display case that looks no different than a rock from South Carolina, and it took almost three hundred billion dollars to get it here from Mars. Your study says we should spend more tax money to go back and get another rock to keep it company. Now, how do you justify that sort of expenditure, Mr. Ballou?

Ballou: Senator, a follow-up to Project Ares was suggested as a long-term proposal, with another manned mission occurring sometime in the early twenty-first century if all other objectives in our proposal were first achieved. We're not seriously suggesting that we go straight back to Mars. We're simply saying that NASA's operating budget cannot be trimmed much further without cutting into muscle and bone. We . . .

Rudman: Thank you, Mr. Ballou. The chair calls for a recess. We'll continue this discussion on Friday, April 2.

SIXTEEN

"Altitude seventy-five hundred feet, manual attitude control is good."

We copy, Conestoga. *You're now in final approach phase.*

"Landing gear lowered, landing shoe deployed. Passing high gate at angles seven-three and all systems are nominal."

You're go for landing.

His palms were sticky with sweat; Parnell wiped them off on his trousers, then took a second to glance around A-deck. On the opposite side of the flight deck Ryer had her hands locked on the control yoke, her eyes flickering across the myriad dials and digital displays at her station, while Lewitt carefully watched the engine status board at his console.

Conestoga had passed "high gate," the point of no return. At this juncture, it was a captive of lunar gravity and was committed to touchdown except in the most dire emergency, in which case firing engines to achieve escape velocity meant using the fuel reserves. If that happened, they would have no recourse except to limp home.

That wasn't going to happen, though. So far, the descent had been smooth. One of the CRTs on Parnell's console displayed a map of the landing site, with a series of concentric circles expanding outward from the ground-zero mark. He tapped a command into his keyboard and the computer responded by pinging twice; the tiny crosshatch designating *Con-*

estoga's position was slightly to the left of the circles.

"Altitude two thousand feet and closing," he said. "Landing beacon is acquired, thirty-five degrees from mark. Over."

"Correcting altitude," Ryer said. "Closing in on landing beacon."

Parnell felt the ship tremble as Ryer fired thrusters to compensate for *Conestoga*'s drift. The crosshatch moved closer to the bull's-eye as the moonship homed in on the automatic radio beacon at Tranquillity Base.

Roger that, Conestoga. *You're looking good. Over.* Main-Ops was monitoring radar telemetry sent from the base, playing backseat driver.

"Fuel reserves nominal," Lewitt said. "The shoe is down, gear is locked." The shoe was a vertical probe which extended straight down from the center of the engine array, designed to absorb most of the landing shock and stabilize *Conestoga* once it was on the ground.

"Altitude one thousand two hundred feet, seven degrees off the zero and closing." Parnell glanced away from his board, looking across the compartment at Ryer. "Need to goose it a little there, Cris. There's a boulder field you need to . . ."

"I know, I know. I've been here before." Ryer was fighting the yoke with one hand as she worked the thrusters with the other. Landing four hundred tons of flying skyscraper on a dime was not a job Parnell envied. Ryer had the skill and guts needed to pull it off, but he had done this once himself, and he didn't recall being so goddamned nervous back in '69. . . .

Forget it, he told himself. Let her do her job.

Conestoga was now only a thousand feet above the base's cleared landing area. Although Ryer had managed to compensate for engine drift, the ship's terminal velocity was sixty-five mph above touchdown speed. "Angles one and we're on the beam," he said. "Coming in a little fast . . ."

As he spoke, he felt the entire fuselage shudder as Ryer throttled up the engines. She was braking *Conestoga* just in time; the ship listed one degree starboard, but she gimbaled the port thrusters and quickly brought the mammoth vessel back in line.

We copy, Conestoga, *you're on the mark. We check you at altitude seven hundred fifty feet and closing. Over.*

"Roger that, Main-Ops. Altitude seven-two-five, all systems a-okay for touchdown." For the first time since they had commenced final approach, Gene looked up at the TV monitors. The lunar horizon was no longer curved, but instead lay as flat as a Kansas prairie, gray volcanic maria with short rounded hills in the far distance. Dust was already being kicked up by the engines, but through the dirty haze he could make out boulders and small impact craters, and glimpses of unnatural man-made shapes reflecting sunlight. . . .

No time for sightseeing. He pulled his eyes away from the screens and back to the console where they belonged. "Altitude four hundred, altitude three-five-oh . . ."

We copy, Conestoga . . .

"Reserves down by point two percent," Lewitt said.

"Throttling back five percent," Ryer responded.

"Staying on the beam, zero drift. Altitude one-fifty, one twenty-five. Throttle up a notch there . . ."

"Engines up one percent . . ."

"Altitude seven-fiver, attitude nominal . . ."

We copy, Conestoga. *Looking good.*

"Altitude fifty, engines down two percent." The entire vessel shook as if it were caught in a minor earthquake. Nothing could be seen on the screens now except dust and dense shadows. Parnell licked his dry lips. "Altitude twenty-five, altitude twenty . . ."

"Engines back two percent . . ."

"Shoe contact light!" Lewitt shouted.

"Altitude fifteen . . . twelve . . . ten . . ."

Now he could hear an almost impossible roar as *Conestoga*'s engines baked the hard volcanic floor. "Eight . . . six . . . five . . . cut main engines."

"Roger. Cutting main engines. Engine arm off."

The trembling stopped, and for an eternal half-second there was the sensation of falling . . . then the landing gear slammed into the regolith.

"Touchdown!" Ryer yelled.

Conestoga teetered on its legs like a drunk fighting for balance. For an instant it seemed as if the towering vessel would keel over and crash on its side, but then the gyros told the hydraulics which end was supposed to be up, and the moonship remained erect. The fuselage creaked as gravity settled old bulkheads and deck plates into unfamiliar positions, but after a moment that, too, passed.

And then there was nothing but silence.

Parnell took a deep, shuddering breath. "Wheel Command, this is *Conestoga*. We have landed. Over."

We copy, Conestoga. *Good job.*

"Engines safed," Lewitt said, his fingers quickly moving across his console to click switches. "Internal pressure okay, landing gear intact, main computer reset on standby mode. All systems green."

"Sounds right to me." Parnell unbuckled his harness, then swung his legs off the couch and stood up, stretching his back and arms. His muscles ached slightly from the unaccustomed effort, but it was nice to feel gravity again, even if it was only one-sixth Earth-normal. "Nice flying there, Cris."

"Thank you, Commander." She had pulled out her logbook, and didn't look up to acknowledge the compliment. "Couldn't have done it without you."

He couldn't tell if she was being sarcastic or not, but decided to let it pass. He had other things to worry about just now. He sat down in the couch again and tabbed the radio key. "Wheel Command, this is Parnell. We're down and all systems are copacetic. Joe, you there?"

Joe Laughlin's voice came over the comlink five seconds later. *Right here, Gene. Looks like a good landing.*

"You can credit Captain Ryer for that. All I did was ride shotgun." Ryer smiled a little and nodded her head, but continued to write in her logbook.

Let's see if I can shake you up a little, he thought.

"Listen, Joe," Parnell continued. "I want to alter the mission plan a bit, if you don't mind. I want to hold off entering the base and proceed straight to Teal Falcon instead. You copy? Over."

Ryer looked up sharply as he said this. Lewitt swiveled his couch around, his right eyebrow raised querulously. "Hey, Gene," he began, "what are you . . . ?"

Parnell slightly held up his hand and shook his head. *Fine with me, Gene,* Laughlin said, *but Mission is going to want a reason. In fact, we've got Ray on the line. Hold on.*

A few seconds later Ray Harvey's voice came over the S-band, relayed from the control room at Von Braun Space Center. *Hi, Gene. Nice to see you guys made it safely. What's the deal with wanting to head over to Sabine? Over.*

Damn. Parnell hadn't expected this, although he should have. Harvey was mission director, after all; any major change in the schedule would have to be approved by him. Joe Laughlin would have seconded the motion with no questions asked, but Harvey was a stickler for details.

"Thanks, Ray," he replied. "Look, on the way down, I got to wondering about the status of the missiles. They've been mothballed for a long time now, y'know, and we're probably going to want to give them an inspection before we ready them for launch. There might have also been some system decay in the bunker mainframes, so we may want to give them a good shakedown."

These were the best excuses he could concoct on the spur of the moment. "Anyway," he went on, "it might be a good idea if we hold off on entering the base until after we've fired the birds, and use the time instead to go over everything at Sabine. You copy? Over."

Parnell held his breath as he waited for the reply. Right now, he could imagine Harvey conferring with the Mission Control team at Von Braun. In the old days, no one would have asked permission; they would have just gone ahead and done whatever needed to be done, and let the suits scream about it later. But if his plan was going to work, he had to give the appearance that he suspected nothing sinister of anyone.

A minute passed before Ray Harvey came back on the air. *Ah, we copy that, Gene, but our people here say both the missiles and the mainframes were thoroughly checked out before the last team left Teal Falcon and everything was working fine then. I'm not sure what another inspection is going to accomplish. Over.*

Ryer was watching him intently; her headset was still plugged into her board, so she could hear both sides of the conversation. Gene rolled his eyes for her benefit and mouthed the word *dummy.* "That's great, Ray, but that was three years ago. We've had some solar activity between now and then, though, and I'm just concerned that something might have gotten fried in the meantime."

Parnell shrugged offhandedly as he played his trump card. "Hey, if your guys think everything's okay, that's fine with me. But if the President tries to launch those missiles at 1200 and they don't go up on time . . . well, y'know, don't say I didn't warn you. Over."

A longer pause this time. Although he didn't believe in ESP, Parnell almost felt as if he had established telepathic contact with Ray Harvey across a quarter of a million miles of space. No one at NASA had forgotten what happened when *Challenger* was rushed into launch despite dire warnings from Morton Thiokol engineers about the effects of extreme cold upon the shuttle's solid-rocket boosters; several senior NASA bureaucrats had decided to take the gamble because Reagan was going to mention the shuttle during his State of the Union Address that night. If Clinton came on live TV and pushed an ornamental button to launch the Teal Falcon missiles, only to have the Minutemen fail to fly . . .

Ah, Gene, we copy. Harvey's voice was stiffly formal, as if he was prepared to summon up this exchange later before a blue-ribbon board of inquiry. *We concur with your decision to deviate from mission profile. You have permission to proceed directly to Teal Falcon for purposes of inspecting the missiles. Do you copy? Over.*

Parnell tried hard not to look relieved. "Roger that. Thanks, Ray. We'll be in touch. *Conestoga* over and out."

He switched off the radio, pulled the headset down around his neck and unplugged the cord, then took a deep breath. Nothing like arguing with a pen-pusher . . .

"What was that all about?" Ryer asked.

Parnell stood up again. "Just what I said. I want a couple of extra hours to make sure Teal Falcon is shipshape. After we get done there, we've got plenty of time to go inside the base and play around before we go home. Any objections?"

Lewitt unbuckled his harness, stood up, and arched his back. "None here. I've never been to Sabine before . . . gives me a chance for a last look-see before we give it to Hans and Franz.''

Ryer looked skeptical, but she said nothing. ''Sounds like a unanimous decision.'' Gene pulled off the headset and tossed it on the couch, then stepped toward the gangway ladder. ''Go ahead and lower the crane, Jay. I'll go below and tell everyone about the schedule change. I'm sure Ms. Rhodes and Mr. Bromleigh will be happy, at least.''

Then he started down the ladder to C-deck. He could already hear the mixed buzz of conversation from the passengers as they gazed through the portholes at the primitive landscape.

So far, so good . . .

Conestoga's elevator was little more than an open bucket with a hinged door on one side, lowered from the catwalk by a retractable bridge crane. Parnell and Ryer brought the ATS news team down with them; when the elevator touched ground, Rhodes tried to step off first, but Parnell stopped her with a raised arm.

''Sorry, ma'am,'' he said. ''Command privilege. Sort of a traditional thing.''

Actually, there was no such ritual; he just didn't want to allow Rhodes the dubious honor of being the first person from the last American lunar expedition to set foot on the Moon. The press had done enough for the space program already. She harrumphed a bit as Parnell swung the door open, but didn't say anything as he stepped onto the cold gray dust of *Mare Tranquillitatis*.

Tranquillity Base looked much the same as the last time he had laid eyes on it. Sunlight cast long, skeletal shadows across the gray, pockmarked basalt and reflected off the rectangular black arrays of the solar power station. Just beyond it lay three long humps, like oversize Quonset huts buried beneath the regolith: the base habitats, along with the unpressurized garage. A few spotlights around the camp perimeter were still operating, but most were dark, their filaments either long-since eroded or their globes shattered by micrometeorite impacts.

Countless footprints lay upon the dusty ground, crisscrossed by tracks left by lunar tractors. Parnell added a few more prints as he slowly walked toward the habitat, feeling again the strange dry-yet-slippery sensation of the regolith with each step he took.

At the farthest perimeter of the camp, the cannibalized carcasses of three abandoned moonships rose above the flat terrain. One of them was Eagle Four, the freighter from the Luna Two expedition that had brought the Teal Falcon missiles to the Moon a generation ago; it and the two other freighters parked nearby had been stripped of all usable parts once their one-way missions had been completed. They stood like mute sentries above a ghost town.

Everything was still and silent.

A few dozen yards away, Parnell spotted the American flag that John Harper Wilson had raised here almost twenty-six years ago, its bunting stiffened by fine wires laced through the fabric so that it appeared to be waving in a nonexistent breeze. A small bronze plaque had been laid on the ground beneath the staff; Parnell bunny-hopped over to it, raising the gold visor of his helmet so he could read the words more clearly.

**HERE MEN FROM THE PLANET EARTH
FIRST SET FOOT UPON THE MOON
JULY 1969 A.D.
WE CAME IN PEACE FOR ALL MANKIND**

"Liar," he whispered.

Excuse me, Commander? Berkley Rhodes's voice was sharp in his helmet earphones. *What did you just say?*

He turned around to see her and Bromleigh coming toward him, shepherded by Ryer. The two correspondents seemed to be having a difficult time mastering the fine art of moonwalking. The white fabric outer covering of their hardsuits was caked with dust, showing that they had already fallen a few times. Fortunately, Bromleigh's camcorder was still aboard *Conestoga;* it was not designed to operate in hard vacuum, and the last company to manufacture lunar-grade TV equipment had lost the design specs when it had been bought out by a Japanese conglomerate five years ago.

Just as well. Parnell didn't want a picture of this. "Never mind, Ms. Rhodes," he said. "Just thinking to myself."

Looks strange, Bromleigh commented. He stood hump-backed, still trying to get accustomed to the mass of the life-support unit on his back. *You kinda think someone else should be here, y'know? Like someone should be coming out to meet us.*

"You're right." Parnell looked away from the plaque and cast his eyes around the abandoned moonbase. "Someone should."

Did someone come out to greet ships when they landed, Commander? Rhodes asked. *I mean, was there a welcoming committee, or . . . well, did they . . . ?*

"Oh, sure." The flag was a little crooked, probably bent over from *Conestoga*'s landing exhaust. Parnell reached out to straighten it. "We had flaxen-haired maiden girls in grass skirts, walking timidly out to offer us baskets of fruit. And then we went inside where there was a feast awaiting us. . . ."

Seriously.

"Seriously?" He managed to get the staff to stay straight. Not that it mattered; by this time tomorrow, he would be pulling down the flag, folding it and taking it home to a glass case at the Visitors' Center at the Cape, where tourists could stare at it with bleak stupidity. "Seriously, I think you should—"

He stopped himself. What he was about to suggest was anatomically impossible, especially in a spacesuit. "Never mind. Cris, if you'll escort Ms. Rhodes and Mr. Bromleigh back to the ship, they can help you bring down the rest of the passengers."

Okay, Gene. He was rather surprised to hear her use his first name for a change; he couldn't make out her expression through her visor. *You're going over to the base?*

"Yeah. I'm going to check out the tractors, make sure they're still operational. Jay, are you there?"

Loud and clear, Gene. Lewitt was still on A-deck aboard *Conestoga*, checking out the ship before he left her. *What's the word?*

''Tell the Wheel we're all going EVA,'' he said, ''then shut her down and suit up. When you get down, c'mon over to the garage and help me get the tracs rolling. Okay?''

Will do. Over and out.

''Thanks, pal. See you in a few minutes.'' He looked back at Ryer. ''When everyone is down, bring 'em over to the garage. Try to make sure no one else falls down, okay?''

Got it. She turned around and began treading back to the ship, keeping Rhodes and Bromleigh in front of her. *Now remember what I told you . . . small steps at first, big steps when you've got your balance.*

Parnell watched them go—and sure enough, Rhodes hadn't taken ten steps before she went sprawling in a cloud of dust. He turned around and headed for the base, taking bunny-hops which covered a lot of ground in a hurry. He was alone for a few minutes; he could make it count.

The garage was an open shell, unpressurized and vaguely resembling an immense coffee can half-buried in the silt of a country river. Two lunar tractors were parked side by side within its shelter. Great steel tanks with caterpillar treads and bubble cockpits, they were designed for long-range expeditions, capable of transporting five men apiece across the harsh terrain.

After he flicked on the ceiling lamps, Parnell made certain that the electric charge cables were still in place; with luck, the tractors' nickel-cadmium storage batteries would still be functional. They should be; the General Motors Corporation had built the tanks to be the best vehicles that 500 million dollars could buy, cost overruns notwithstanding.

But the tractors were not his top priority. He went to the far wall of the garage and opened the hatch leading to Habitat One's airlock. He checked the gauges on the wall; as he had been briefed, the last crew to leave Tranquillity had depressurized both habitats before abandoning the base. They had done so in order to prevent anything inside rusting from disuse; right now, though, this meant that he didn't have to wait for the entire habitat to be repressurized before he could enter the airlock.

He opened the inner hatch, then switched on his helmet lamp and climbed into the base. He had to move fast now;

although he was counting on the ineptitude of the ATS reporters and the inexperience of the Koenig Selenen astronauts to slow things down, he didn't want to be caught inside the base.

The oval glow of the lamp cast weird shadows across the empty racks of the suit-up room. Another set of hatches led into the wardroom, where a long mess bench faced a wall-size projection TV screen. He stepped on something that slid beneath his boot; looking down, he saw an old issue of *People* magazine with Mick Jagger on the cover.

"Talkin' 'bout the midnight rambler," he whispered under his breath, careful not to let anyone overhear him on the comlink.

He found the ladder leading to the habitat's upper deck. It wasn't made to be climbed by someone in a hardsuit, so he wasted a couple of precious minutes trying to gain good hand-and foot-holds on the rungs, but when he finally squeezed through the small round hatch, he found himself in the base commander's quarters, an attic-sized space barely large enough to hold a desk, a chair, and a set of metal file cabinets.

Breathing hard now, he went straight for the desk, praying that it wasn't locked. He tugged at the bottom drawer and was relieved when it easily slid open. Fine dust sprayed against his faceplate as he pushed empty file folders out of the way.

When the USSF had established the base, someone had decided that the base commander should be issued a pistol, just in case someone among the crew lost his mind during the long lunar night and tried to blow out the airlock. That had never happened, but so far as Parnell knew the weapon had remained at the base.

For a few anxious moments, he thought that the gun has been removed. Then the bright glare of the helmet lamp glinted against something resting at the bottom of the drawer. Parnell sucked in a deep breath, then shoved aside some old paperwork until he found the Colt .45 Officer's ACP automatic.

"Gotcha," he whispered.

From The New York Times; *July 11, 1991*

WHITE HOUSE CONSIDERED USING
MOON NUKES DURING
DESERT STORM
By Arthur M. Erikson
(*Special to* The New York Times)

WASHINGTON, July 10—According to classified Pentagon documents, President Bob Dole issued a secret directive to the National Aeronautics and Space Administration and the Department of Defense during the Desert Storm military campaign that called for first-use of lunar-based nuclear missiles against Iraq in the event that U.S. ground forces in Saudi Arabia were overwhelmed by Iraqi soldiers.

The six-page memorandum, which was released to *The New York Times, The Washington Post,* and ATS News by a high-ranking Pentagon official, was signed by President Dole and dated September 14, 1990. The memo states that the U.S. Air Force should "immediately place SAC officers in the Teal Falcon bunker" and have them ready to "target vital military sites within Iraq" in the event that conventional forces were defeated in combat by Iraq's army.

According to the Pentagon source, one of the sites which would have been targeted by the lunar missiles was Baghdad, Iraq's capital city. Other sites would have included Iraq's oil fields and key military installations surrounding Baghdad.

The Teal Falcon base, located near Tranquillity Base on the Moon, holds six modified Minuteman II missiles, each containing a single nuclear warhead. Teal Falcon's existence was made public in 1983; it has not been officially operational since 1972, although the missiles were never removed from their silos. It was intended to be a second-strike nuclear alternative in the event of a preemptive strategic attack by the former Soviet Union (*see sidebar, page 10*).

The Dole Administration has denied the existence of the memo, claiming that it is a fraud. However, White House chief of staff John Sununu says that if the memo indeed exists, it would only prove that President Dole was willing to "do whatever it takes to protect the lives of American servicemen."

Congressional critics of the Dole Administration were quick to condemn the White House for its willingness to use Teal Falcon in the Desert Storm conflict. "If the President had decided to use nuclear weapons against Iraq," said Senator Edward M. Kennedy on the Senate floor, "then the Middle East would have been engulfed in a nuclear war which could have cost millions of lives, both civilian and military. The decision might have ignited World War III . . . it's rash and inexcusable."

SEVENTEEN

A large aluminum sign, inscribed in three languages, was posted a hundred feet from the entrance to Sabine Crater. In English, it read:

> **WARNING!!**
> **U.S. GOVERNMENT PROPERTY—NO**
> **TRESPASSING DO NOT PASS THIS POINT!**
> **This Area Is A Protected Military Area And**
> **Is Off-Limits To Unauthorized Civilians.**
> **Injury Or Fatality May Result.**
> **Intruders May Be Subject To Fines And/Or**
> **Prison Terms.**

The warning was reiterated in Russian and German. Just beyond the sign lay the ten-foot chain-link fence that completely encircled the low walls of the impact crater; the hard-packed dirt road which led straight across the maria from Tranquillity Base to Teal Falcon stopped at the gate.

Isn't that a little redundant? James Leamore commented. He was gazing at the sign through a window slot in the cabin of Tractor One. *After all, if we're killed trying to break in, how can we be fined or sent to jail?*

It was written by the government, Paul Dooley replied. *They'll find a way.* He looked up at Parnell, who was sitting in the driver's seat beneath the Plexiglas bubble dome. *Hey, what the fuck do they mean by that, anyway? Is the place mined or what?*

Gene didn't immediately respond. Instead, he looked over his shoulder to make sure that Tractor Two had halted behind him. The second vehicle was being driven by Cris Ryer; she was carrying Rhodes, Bromleigh, Aachener, and Talsbach, while he had Dooley, Leamore, and Lewitt. They could have pressurized the tractors, but since the nine-mile journey was so short, everyone was still wearing their hardsuits.

Through her dome, Ryer gave him a silent thumbs-up; she was waiting for him to clear the way through the defense perimeter. Wisely, she wasn't using her radio. "No, not mines," he told Dooley. "See those things on top of the crater wall?"

Everyone in the passenger compartment peered through the windows. Every twenty feet or so, the wall was ringed with small, swivel-mounted pairs of tubes, each vaguely resembling a double-barreled shotgun. "Those are automatic gyrojet guns," he explained. "They fire self-propelled thirteen-millimeter rounds with explosive charges in their noses. They can punch right through these tanks . . . and you don't want to know what they can do to your hardsuit."

Nasty, Lewitt murmured, shaking his head inside his helmet. *Don't mess with them.*

Leamore looked worriedly at the thin aluminum shell of the tractor, but Dooley still wasn't impressed. *But nobody's inside to fire them,* he said, his voice once again assuming an irritating whine. *I mean, if they can't . . .*

"Watch and learn," Parnell said, although he made certain that Dooley didn't watch too closely.

He switched the tractor's radio transmitter to a different frequency that only he knew, then tapped a six-digit code number into the keypad beneath the transmitter. There was a short pause, then the digital readout above the radio displayed six zeros. At the same moment, electric motors opened the fence gates, allowing them entry into the compound.

Okay, Dooley said. *You sent a radio password. I'm im-*

pressed. He leaned back in his seat as much as his life-support pack would allow. *Real impressed.*

Parnell smiled to himself as he grasped the oversized knob of the stick-shift and moved the tractor into gear. Dooley didn't know the half of it. The regolith between the fence and the crater wall was crisscrossed with tiny wires, a motion detector that would set off the guns if the proper code wasn't received by the bunker on this particular frequency. Moreover, only the tractors contained radios capable of transmitting on this wavelength; none of their hardsuit radios could do the same. This meant that the only way into Sabine Crater was inside a tractor; an individual on foot would be shredded by the gyrojet guns if he attempted to gain entrance. Mines could be dodged, if one knew the exact pattern in which they had been laid out or if an intruder had a metal detector. This way, only someone driving a tractor from Tranquillity Base who knew the correct code sequence could enter the crater.

Yet there was no sense in letting Dooley know this. So far as Parnell was concerned, this man wasn't really Paul Dooley. Even if Cris Ryer was working with him, she didn't know the code . . . and neither of them knew that the defense perimeter worked both ways, coming *and* going.

Welcome to my little rattrap, he thought.

Their caterpillar treads bumping over small stones and spewing little plumes of dust, the two tractors moved through the gate and down the access road to the lip of the crater, following the arrows on signs posted along the way. The road led up the crater wall and through a narrow passage which had been excavated in the crater lip. As he drove into the pass, Parnell downshifted to accommodate the steeper grade inside the crater and switched on the headlights.

For a few moments he could see little but the dense shadows thrown by the walls on either side of his vehicle. Then he was through the pass; Sabine Crater opened up before him, and there at the bottom lay Teal Falcon.

At first glimpse it seemed as if nothing man-made existed inside the crater. Everything was the same dull-gray color; not until the tractors moved slowly down the access road that wound around the interior wall did one realize that this was the result of camouflage paint. The small, squat dome of the

control bunker, the short masts of the telemetry array, even
the hatches of the six missile silos on the far side of the
crater—all had been disguised to fool Earth-based telescopes,
LEO spysats, even orbiting lunar probes.

Parnell only half-listened to the exclamations of his passengers as he maneuvered the tractor down the roadway. If
Laughlin and Dr. Z were right, he was leading a saboteur—
possibly two saboteurs—straight to the heart of one of America's most lethal defense systems. He was taking a terrible
risk; his only hope of thwarting him, her, or them was the
fact that he was forewarned, and that he probably knew a
little bit more about this system than they did.

He glanced down at the passenger compartment. As if he
were reading his mind, Jay Lewitt looked up at him. Their
eyes met for a moment; Lewitt nodded his head, then point-
edly fixed his gaze upon Dooley, who was studying the complex through the windows.

Parnell almost sighed with relief. At least he wasn't going
into this alone. Dooley might have an accomplice, but Gene
also had his own backup. That, and the pistol hidden in the
thigh pocket of his suit, gave him some reassurance.

The road leveled out as the tractor reached the bottom of
the crater. Hauling its wheel to the right, Parnell drove directly to the launch bunker's dome, putting on the brakes
when he was a dozen yards away. Glancing back over his
shoulder, he saw that Cris Ryer had brought Tractor Two to
a stop just behind him.

"Okay," he said. "We're here."

The dome was only the most visible part of the Teal Falcon
bunker complex, an anteroom containing a couple of oxygen
tanks for replenishing life-support packs and a few maintenance tools. In the center of the floor was a large round hatch,
which Parnell unlocked by tapping another six-digit code into
a keypad on the wall. The hatch popped open; Lewitt raised
it, exposing the top of a ladder leading down a sixty-foot shaft
into the lunar crust. Fluorescent light fixtures along the mooncrete walls automatically flickered to life as Parnell led the
way down into the bunker.

The bunker was composed of two underground spheres,

both containing three levels, connected to each other by a single passageway between the second level of each sphere. They had been excavated by U.S. Space Force crews using small nuclear charges, similar to the methods used for subsurface bomb tests in the Nevada desert. After the chambers had been formed and decontaminated, polystyrene balloons had been inflated within each sphere, forming airtight inner walls which were later protected by aluminum outer walls. Once floors, ladders, bulkheads, furnishings, and equipment had been installed and an airlock built on Level 1A of Unit A, the shaft leading down to Unit B was filled and permanently sealed; the shaft in Unit A was the only way in or out of the bunker.

Teal Falcon was self-sustaining, its electrical power coming from a small nuclear generator placed in another underground sphere within the crater, its water and oxygen drawn from subsurface tanks near Unit B. It contained living quarters for four men, and was designed to sustain them for up to four weeks. It was capable of surviving all but a direct hit from a one-megaton nuclear warhead, but that hardly mattered; an incoming missile from Earth would be detected long before it reached ground zero, by which time the launch crew would have fired its own birds in retaliation and retreated from the bunker.

In a word, Teal Falcon was a fortress.

Or better yet, a doomsday machine.

Fitting nine people into the airlock was a tight squeeze, but fortunately it had been designed to accommodate the USSF military engineers who had built the complex. Once the ceiling hatch was shut, Parnell flipped open a wall panel near the inner hatch and activated the pressurization controls.

As air rushed into the compartment, electromagnetic scrubbers kicked in, cleansing their suits of all the dust they had collected. A small dust storm swirled around them as the grime was swept down through the metal grids in the floor. Even here, Parnell recalled, there was a fail-safe method of protecting the base: a candy-striped toggle switch inside the airlock control panel, labeled VOID, would blow out the airlock and render it unusable to forces attacking the base from within the crater.

In the old days processing through the airlock would have taken a couple of hours, while their bodies absorbed enough nitrogen to prevent a mass-attack of the bends. Fortunately, NASA had managed to invent zero-prebreath suits before its life-sciences budget got slashed. As a result, they only had to endure each other's company for about thirty minutes before the indicator chimed, signaling that it was safe to exit the airlock.

Unlike Tranquillity Base, the Teal Falcon bunker had been pressurized by the last crew to depart, so that the base could be used quickly in the event of war. The hatch opened into a larger chamber surrounding the airlock. Its cold metal walls were lined with racks and lockers.

"We'll stow your suits here," Parnell told the others once he had removed his helmet. "You'll find jumpsuits in the lockers . . . sorry, but you'll have to look around until you find something that fits."

As Berkley Rhodes took off her helmet, she gasped at the sudden rush of frigid air. She wisely didn't complain, but went wide-eyed at the thought of undressing in front of seven men. "Uhh . . . Gene, isn't there a place where a lady can change in privacy?"

Parnell shook his head as he disconnected the feedlines from his backpack. "Sorry, ma'am, but the people who built this place didn't think women would ever be allowed down here." He cast a glance at Dooley and Leamore, who were standing on either side of her. "I'm sure these gentlemen will turn their backs, though. Right, guys?"

Leamore nodded distractedly; he was too busy disconnecting his air and electrical cables to wonder what Rhodes looked like in her skivvies. Aachener and Talsbach were ahead of him; they had already pulled off their life-support packs and were helping each other out of their suits, murmuring to each other in German. Bromleigh was, as usual, keeping his customary silence as he patiently went through the de-suiting routine. Ryer apparently didn't care one way or another; she was taking the usual shortcuts known to professional astronauts.

Dooley, as always, was utterly lost. He had finally managed to wrench his helmet off the ring collar; he, too, gasped at the first rush of frigid air. "Why's it so goddamn cold?" he yelped, then he wrinkled his nose. "Jesus, it smells like gunpowder in here!"

"That's moondust you smell," Lewitt told him. He turned around to help Dooley out of his suit. "The place hasn't been used in three years . . . what else would you expect?"

Parnell saw the break for which he had been searching. "You're right," he said, exhaling a plume of steamy air. "It's pretty cold. No telling how the CLLSS is operating, either." His backpack and helmet off and stowed on a rack, he detached the thick gloves from the wrist cuffs and shoved them into the locker he had just opened. "I'll go below and check the system, make sure everything's up to par."

"Need help?" Ryer asked.

"No thanks. I can manage." Without bothering to remove the rest of his suit, Parnell trudged over to the floor hatch, hauled it open, and climbed down the ladder to Level 2A.

The logistics deck was slightly wider than the one above it. It was packed with consoles and IBM computer mainframes, their lights glimmering in the darkness until he found the switch that turned on the ceiling fluorescents. It didn't take him long to find the master panel of the closed-loop life-support system. He spent a few minutes reactivating the base's oxygen supply and adjusting the thermostat until it was reset at a relatively comfortable 55 degrees Fahrenheit.

The ceiling ducts creaked as dusty warm air began to seep through the vents. He could hear muted conversation from the suit-up room above, along with a little bit of dry laughter. Once again, Parnell was alone for a few minutes.

He reached into his thigh pocket and pulled out the automatic he had taken from the base commander's office. Now he had to find a place to hide it: somewhere he could grab it in a hurry.

The narrow passageway leading to Unit Two was open, its hatch slightly ajar; beyond that were the bunker's living quarters. That was secure—he could always stash the gun beneath a mattress or in a galley drawer—but it was also too far away. He needed a spot close to the ladder leading down to the bottom level of Unit A.

There. A small, narrow space between one of the IBM

mainframes and the bulkhead, close to the hatch leading down
to level 3A. He knelt as low as the cumbersome hardsuit
would allow and shoved the gun into the darkness. When he
withdrew his hand, the Colt remained in place, squeezed between the back of the computer and the wall. It couldn't be
seen, yet it was near enough to the hatch that he could snatch
it in a second.

He stood up and walked across the deck back to the ladder.
Perhaps he had a chance after all. . . .

Ryer was removing the diskette from a pocket of her hardsuit
when she heard Parnell climbing back up the ladder. Her back
was turned to the floor hatch, but she didn't want to risk
letting him spot the diskette again. Once had been enough to
arouse his suspicions; if he saw it again, especially here and
now, its presence would raise too many questions.

The jumpsuit Cris had found in the locker where she had
stowed her helmet and gloves was one size too small for her,
and she had intended to search through the other lockers until
she located a larger one. She didn't have a choice now,
though; she hastily picked up the one-piece garment and
shoved the diskette into a breast pocket.

She was beginning to step into its legs just as Parnell
reached the top of the ladder. She glanced over her shoulder
at him; their eyes met for a moment, then his face reddened
and he quickly looked away, obviously embarrassed at catching a glimpse of his second-in-command in her undies. She
hid her smile by turning her head; pretending that nothing
had happened, he walked over to help Rhodes hang her hardsuit on a rack.

The chivalry of Southern gentlemen. There were times,
Cris had to admit, when heterosexuality had its advantages.

The others were nearly finished getting dressed. Zipping up
the front of the suit—it *was* a little small, although she reckoned Laurell would have enjoyed the way it clung to her
body—Cris looked over at Dooley to see how he was doing.
With Lewitt's help, he had finally managed to struggle out of
his hardsuit. The jumpsuit he'd found was not his size, either,
and the tight fit did little to flatter his body, but at least he

had stopped bitching about it. He caught her gaze for a fleeting second, then looked away.

Uwe Aachener and Markus Talsbach had the benefit of experience and training. They had long since traded their hardsuits for jumpsuits and were now leaning idly against the outer airlock wall, murmuring to each other in German as they studied the Americans with ill-disguised contempt. Talsbach checked his wristwatch, but Aachener didn't look away when Cris's eyes met his; judging from the leer on his face, he must have been watching her the entire time she had been wearing nothing but bra and panties.

He gave her a salacious wink, and it was Ryer's turn to blush and avoid eye-contact. There were also times, she reflected, when she was goddamned glad to be gay.

As she bent to try on the pair of high-top sneakers she found in the locker—at least these were too large rather than too small—she noticed that the diskette made a slight bulge against her left breast. If she could see it, someone else might, too. Maybe if she turned around, she might be able to switch it from her breast pocket to . . .

Her train of thought was broken as Parnell clapped his hands for attention. "Okay, people," he called out. "If you're ready, then we're going below."

Too late. She would just have to hope that no one took a close look at her.

There were muttered comments as everyone picked up the gear they had brought with them from *Conestoga:* Bromleigh and Rhodes their airtight camera cases, Dooley his laptop computer, Lewitt and Parnell the envelopes containing the passwords that the U.S. Government, adding insult to injury, had denied her.

Ryer finished lacing up her sneakers, then stood up, empty-handed but certainly not empty-pocketed, turned around, and fell in behind Parnell as he led the way down to the heart of the machine.

So far, so good . . .

From "The Lost Frontier" by Ellen Schaeffer; **The New Yorker,** *April 30, 1992*

The Dole Administration's announced intention to sell Tranquillity Base to Koenig Selenen GmbH has been largely dismissed by the shrinking cadre of space supporters as a wholly political decision, a blatant attempt at populism made in an election year by a Presidency which was clearly losing ground to the opposition. To be sure, there's some truth to this allegation: Dole was clearly embarrassed by the revelation that he had authorized the first-use of the Teal Falcon nuclear arsenal during Desert Storm. He attempted to soothe the public by shutting down Tranquillity Base, but by then the scandal was out of control; the only possible recourse was to sell the abandoned base to the Germans, in effect washing his hands of the entire matter.

But what space advocates neglect to mention, perhaps even purposefully, is that almost none of Dole's election opponents have come to the defense of Tranquillity Base. Arkansas governor Bill Clinton, the apparent Democratic front-runner after Super Tuesday, has actually gone on record to support the White House decision, albeit in terms of widespread military cutbacks. Senator Albert Gore, Senator Paul Simon, and Senator Tom Harkin have remained mute on the question.

Former California governor Jerry Brown alone has opposed selling Tranquillity Base. He proposes that the United States use the base for exactly the same purposes as Koenig Selenen intends: as a lunar mining colony and, in the long run, as a site for disposal of high-level radioactive wastes from the same nuclear power plants that Brown says should be shut down. The only difference between Dole's stance and Brown's is that Brown wants to keep business within the United States; however, no American corporation has any interest in pursuing high-risk space enterprise, while Koenig Selenen is clearly gearing up to accept Dole's offer.

The majority of voters aren't paying much attention to Governor Brown's counterproposal, except perhaps as another indication of how radical his campaign has become. The pro-space constituency is small, and not a particularly vocal one at that; all it takes to overwhelm their plaintive cries for the renewal of the sixties-era "High Frontier" is the mention of a single word: deficit.

That word alone is a massive, towering obstacle which none of the other candidates are willing to assault. Myopic or not, both parties agree that selling Tranquillity Base is a certain way of reducing the deficit, even though the base absorbed less than three percent of the federal budget when it was operational. It's a visible target, it's politically incorrect, and it makes for a great sound-bite on the evening news. It takes at least sixty seconds to give good reasons for keeping Tranquillity Base in American hands; a candidate's opposition to Tranquillity Base—"Let's sell the moon base, and sell it now!"—takes only two seconds before the network affiliates cut to commercials.

And this is the way we've reached the end of America's greatest dream, the conquest of space. Born out of World War II, nourished by the Cold War, matured by grand visions of permanently settling the Moon and Mars . . . now relegated to the retirement home like a doddering grandfather who thinks Eisenhower is still President and his grown-up children haven't started dating yet. And the children, entranced with the instant gratification supplied by new toys like home-computer networks, virtual reality, and fifty cable channels of reruns, are only too willing to let Gramps die so they can inherit his money and fight over the silverware.

The dream will continue. Men and women will still explore space. The frontier has been broken; like any human frontier that has ever existed, it will never be abandoned. Mankind has never turned its back on any place it has visited at least once. We have an innate urge to explore new worlds, no matter how far away they may be, or how hostile the environment. Like it or not, it's part of our genetic makeup.

However, if anyone in America still wishes to visit the Moon within the next decade, they are advised to learn another language, and get a passport.

EIGHTEEN

The launch center was located on Level 3A, a bowl-shaped room at the bottom of Unit A with fluorescent lights suspended from a low ceiling and its ladder placed between a pair of auxiliary control panels. Like the airlock on Level 1A, it was not made to hold nine people at once; getting everyone in there was a tight squeeze, made even tighter once Bromleigh began to set up his camera tripod in the back of the room.

The firing room was dominated by two identical consoles positioned fifteen feet apart, their swivel-mounted armchairs at right angles to one another. The consoles were lined with buttons and toggle switches surrounding a pair of computer screens, with six TV monitors arrayed above the consoles. On the wall between the two consoles was a small steel cabinet, sealed with two locks.

Once Parnell found the main fuse box and powered up the room, the consoles glowed like Christmas trees and the screens lit up with images relayed from TV cameras positioned in and around the crater. Like an ICBM bunker in Missouri, the firing room could be sealed off during a red alert, its only remaining contact a scrambled radio channel with Earth.

Once he was seated at the right-hand console, Parnell opened the secure KU-band channel to the Wheel. Main-Ops in turn relayed the transmission to Houston, where a group of SAC officers and inspectors from the International Atomic Energy Agency were waiting at Mission Control. When he achieved contact with the Von Braun Space Center, Gene unsealed the manila envelope Ray Harvey had given him at the Cape and read the authentication password typed across the first sheet of paper.

We copy, Teal Falcon, an anonymous voice replied from a quarter of a million miles away. *Foxtrot Nebraska Romeo, one-zero-niner, affirmative. Can you give us status of the birds, please?*

"Roger that, Mission." Parnell reached across the board and pressed a set of six buttons.

The TV monitors flickered and fuzzed, then settled into fish-eye views from within the silos on the other side of the crater. The blunt noses of six Minuteman missiles protruded from the deep mooncrete pits in which they were nestled, held in place by vertical rows of metal flanges. Electrical cables led from the silo walls to the rockets; since the silo covers had not yet been raised, the missiles were illuminated by red fluorescent lights that cast dark shadows across their sleek fuselages.

Parnell's eyes swept across the screens, his board, and the CRTs. Nothing seemed amiss. The missiles appeared to be the way he had last seen them; nothing had degraded during their long slumber. He wasn't sure if that was good or bad news.

"All missiles are intact and ready for launch," he said. "Awaiting authorization to proceed to standby."

We copy, Teal Falcon, the voice responded. *IAEA concurs with your findings. You have SAC authorization to proceed to standby status. T-minus one hour, five minutes and counting, over.*

"Roger that, Mission," Parnell said. "We're commencing final power-up and activation of launch control systems. Over."

He took off the headset and placed it on the desk in front of him, then got up from the chair. "Mr. Dooley?" he said, looking over his shoulder. "It's your turn."

"About time," Dooley murmured as he traded places with

Parnell. "I was beginning to feel like a tourist."

Parnell said nothing. He leaned over the back of the chair, studying Dooley as he placed his laptop computer on the desk and unfolded its screen. While Dooley pried open the back of the CPU and pulled a rolled cable out of his equipment case, Parnell glanced around, surreptitiously noting everyone's position in the firing room.

Jay Lewitt was seated at the left-hand console, watching Dooley as he interfaced his Tandy/IBM to the master fire-control system through the right console's serial port. Cris Ryer stood directly behind Lewitt, observing everything that was going on. In the back of the room, Alex Bromleigh had set up his camera and was fiddling with the lens; Berkley Rhodes was helping out by running a coaxial cable to the main communications panel on Lewitt's board. According to their agreement with NASA, the ATS news team would not transmit live pictures until after the missiles were fired; before then, they could only record the launch procedure.

Markus Talsbach lingered near the ladder, his arms folded across his chest. Curiously, there was no sign of either Uwe Aachener or James Leamore.

"Mr. Talsbach?" Parnell asked, and the German astronaut looked up. "Where are your friends?"

"Eh?" Talsbach raised his eyebrows and cocked his head. "Ah! Oh, they have gone elsewhere, I think."

"You think?" He was beginning to wonder if Talsbach was twice the idiot he seemed to be. "There's not too many places they could have gone, Markus. Where did they go?"

"Oh! Ahh . . . James needed to find the . . ." He seemed to be searching for the correct word. "The levorotary, I believe. Uwe decided to go with him, in order to look at the rest of the base." He frowned. "Is this wrong? Should I go in search of them?"

Parnell shook his head. "No . . . I just wish they had told me where they were headed, that's all."

In fact, he didn't care to have anyone out of sight just now. The head was located in Unit B, on the other side of the bunker; that was a long way from the firing room. Parnell's first impulse was to go looking for Leamore and Aachener, but when he glanced down at Dooley again, he saw that the hacker had already linked up with the main computer system.

"Okay, here we go." Dooley rapidly typed a set of commands into his computer. As he did, the CRTs on his console and Lewitt's simultaneously began to scroll long lists of program code. "Yeah, baby," he whispered to himself as he eagerly watched the screen in front of him, his fingers periodically stabbing at the keys. "Go, mama, go . . ."

"What's happening?" Parnell asked.

"I'm reintroducing my buddy to his long-lost brother." Dooley blinked from behind his glasses as he looked up at Parnell. "I'm matching my half of the c-cube codes with the ones Teal Falcon has in memory. When they've finished shaking hands, we'll be ready to go ahead with the rest of the sequence."

"I see." It was a simplistic explanation, but it matched what Parnell had been told during his briefings. Once the two sets of programs were matched and final authentication was received from Houston, he and Lewitt would be able to proceed with electrical check-out and the arming and targeting of the Minutemen.

So far, everything was going according to plan. In only an hour, the President would go on live network television, make his carefully scripted statement to the nation and the world, then push a button on the Oval Office desk. A few seconds later, Parnell and Lewitt would receive the green light from Houston. A final twist of a pair of keys, and the birds would leave their nests.

The only thing stopping him were a few suspicions cast by a couple of civilians, and who were they? A college kid on the Wheel and an ill woman somewhere in Arizona: All they had for proof were a couple of strange conversations on a private computer network and the coincidental murder of a pizza delivery boy.

Insane . . .

Sure, Joe Laughlin thought there was something amiss, but Joe could be wrong. Just as Parnell himself could be wrong by believing any one of them. Did he really want to end his career by screwing up to this magnitude?

"Okay!" Dooley's shout interrupted his thoughts. "We're

in!" He looked up at Parnell. "All systems are nominal, Commander. It's all yours."

Parnell sucked in his breath as he stood erect. "Well done, Paul. My compliments."

Lewitt dipped his head and pulled the key from around his neck. "Anytime you're ready, Commander," he said, jingling the key in his hand. "Let's get it on the road."

"Sure, Jay." Parnell checked the digital chronometer between the two launch stations. The clock stood at 1110 Zulu.

Just enough time for him to take a reality check . . .

"I'm going topside for a sec," he said to no one in particular as he stepped away from the chair. "Nature's calling."

Rhodes looked up from her work. "You're going to worry about that now?"

"Jesus, I don't believe it . . ." Dooley irritably rubbed his mouth. "You picked a fine time to take a whizz, man."

Lewitt seemed equally baffled, but he gave his commander an amused grin. "Hell of a time for a pee-break."

"We're running ahead of schedule." Parnell managed a sheepish shrug and grin as he headed for the hatch. Talsbach said nothing as he stepped aside. "Might as well take care of business. Excuse me . . ."

Then he began to climb up the ladder to Level 2A.

The logistics compartment was vacant. This shouldn't have troubled Parnell, but it did.

He walked softly past the computers to the lateral hatch leading to Unit B. The hatch cover was still open; light glowed from the opposite end of the fifteen-foot connecting tunnel. When he bent over and listened carefully, though, he could hear no sound from the crew quarters on the other side of the bunker.

"Hello?" he called. "Anyone there?"

No one answered. Of course, that could mean nothing. The head was located on Level 1B, one deck up in the second sphere. They might not have heard him. For all he knew, Leamore and Aachener could be raiding the galley fridge.

His first impulse was to enter the tunnel and go investigate their prolonged absence. He bent low, raised his right foot and set it in the tunnel . . . then stopped himself. His first priority should be to return to the firing room, where he could keep a close eye on Dooley and Ryer.

He reminded himself that he had left the unsealed launch codes on the desk in front of the right-hand firing console. That was stupid; although the missiles couldn't be armed or launched without the key which still hung around his neck, someone could nevertheless make use of the authenticators.

He couldn't be in two places at once.

He hoped he was only being paranoid.

Parnell reluctantly turned away from the tunnel and went back to the ladder. Before he set foot on the first rung, though, he reached behind the adjacent mainframe and retrieved the Colt from its hiding place.

He chambered a round and flipped off the safety, then carefully slipped the pistol into the right pocket of his jumpsuit. It made a slight bulge and the handle stuck out a little; he would have to be careful to conceal it.

He took a deep breath, then climbed back down the ladder into the control room.

Dooley was still sitting at the right-hand console, slouched over the keyboard of his computer, which was still connected to the console. Parnell noted that Ryer had left Lewitt's side; she was now standing above Dooley, intently watching what he was doing. She looked up as Parnell reentered the compartment, but Dooley either didn't notice his return or ignored it.

Ryer started to step away from the chair, but Gene waved her off, mindful to use his left hand while keeping his right hand close to his pocket, hiding the butt of the gun. "Never mind," he said, walking past her toward Lewitt's seat. "I think I'll run the left seat instead. Can you hand me the envelope, please?"

Cris blinked, but said nothing; she merely picked up the envelope—which had apparently gone undisturbed during his absence—and passed it to him.

Jay looked bewildered as Parnell approached his console, but he didn't protest. "Any particular reason, Commander?" he asked as he surrendered his chair to Parnell.

"Kind of drafty over there, that's all." Gene pointed to an air duct above the right console. "I was getting chills sitting there. Hope you don't mind switching, but . . ."

"Naw, that's okay. I don't think it matters much anyway."
And it didn't; in terms of function, the consoles mirrored one
another. However, Parnell wanted to be able to keep an eye
on Dooley and Ryer without turning his head . . . and from
the left console he would be able to get a clean shot at either
or both of them, if push came to shove.

"Don't forget this." Parnell picked up Lewitt's envelope
and handed it to him as he slid past. As Lewitt took the
envelope, Parnell leaned a little closer to him.

"Watch 'em," he whispered.

Jay nodded very slightly, then strode over to the right console. Dooley had already vacated the chair; he pushed aside
his laptop computer to make room for Lewitt, but he remained
close to the console. It was a little crowded at that end of the
room, but, Parnell noted, Ryer didn't stray from the console,
either.

The chronometer now stood at 1131 Zulu. Less than a half-
hour remained before launch.

Sitting down, Parnell glanced over his shoulder toward the
back of the control room. Bromleigh stood behind his camera,
ready to begin filming the operation; Rhodes was next to him,
absently fiddling with the lapel mike on her jumpsuit collar.
Talsbach stood near the ladder, seemingly bored with the
whole procedure.

Still no sign of either Leamore or Aachener. There was
nothing Parnell could do about that now.

"Ready to go, Commander?" Jay asked.

"Yup. Let's get to it." Parnell clamped the headset around
the back of his neck and adjusted the mike, then switched the
comlink to the secure frequency he had used earlier. "Houston, this is Teal Falcon. All systems nominal. We're ready to
begin pre-launch sequence."

The usual five-second delay, then the same anonymous
voice he had heard before came on-line. *Roger that, Teal
Falcon. Stand by to receive authentication code, over.*

Parnell picked up the manila envelope, opened it again, and
pulled out a red letter-sized envelope printed with official
threats regarding stiff prison sentences if opened without
proper authorization. As Lewitt did the same, he tore off one

end of the envelope and withdrew a short slip of paper.
"Houston, we're ready to receive authenticator," he said.

Teal Falcon, this is Houston. The authenticator is . . .

Parnell stole a sidelong glance at Dooley. He was bent over
his computer, resting his hands on the edge of the desk. His
right hand wasn't touching the keyboard, but it was uncomfortably close.

Rattrap, Parnell reminded himself. This is a rattrap . . .

*Bravo . . . Zulu . . . Tango . . . six . . . three . . . seven . . . Al-
pha . . . Romeo . . . Nebraska. Do you copy? Over.*

The authenticator matched the large red code-sign printed
on Parnell's slip: BZT 637 ARN. He held the paper up for
Lewitt to read and Jay reciprocated. The codes were identical.

"We copy, Houston," Parnell said. "Authentication received and confirmed by Lieutenant Lewitt and myself. Proceeding with pre-launch sequence. Over."

He pulled off the headset and stood, then reached up to
pull the long key chain from around his neck. Lewitt did the
same; they leaned across their desks until they were both able
to fit their keys into the locks of the steel cabinet between
their consoles.

A quick twist of each key opened the locks; the lid swung
down, revealing another pair of keys, these oversized and
painted red.

"Do you concur with launch?" Parnell asked.

"Yes, sir," Lewitt said formally. "I concur with launch."

It was all part of the apocalyptic waltz of nuclear warfare.
Neither man could launch the missiles on his own; both had
to receive and match the authenticator codes, both had to open
the cabinet and take the launch control keys; once inserted in
the consoles, both keys had to be turned within five seconds
of each other for the missiles to be fired. The two master
consoles had been deliberately positioned far enough apart to
guarantee that one man in the bunker couldn't go crazy and
launch the missiles on his own.

Parnell sat down again. He flipped open a small zebra-
striped panel on his console and inserted his key. The switch
had three positions: OFF, STANDBY, and LAUNCH. He waited
until Lewitt had done the same; then he said, "On my mark
. . . three . . . two . . . one . . . mark."

"Mark," Lewitt said, and simultaneously twisted his key clockwise to STANDBY.

Orange lamps on their consoles switched to amber. The CRTs began to display line columns of type, showing the status of each missile in its silo. A red-bordered warning across the bottom of their screens told them that the Minutemen were ready to be armed.

Curtsy and bow. The *danse macabre* had begun.

"Go with pre-launch ignition," Parnell says. His hands move quickly across his console, flicking toggle switches in succession.

"Roger that," Lewitt says. "Commencing pre-launch ignition sequence."

Vertical bars rise on their screens, telling them that the Minutemen's solid rocket engines are being armed. "Primary electrical check," Parnell says, flipping another set of switches.

"Roger on primary electrical." Lewitt carefully watches another screen as the missiles are powered up. "All missiles on external power. Umbilical source nominal, internal batteries on storage mode, green for go."

"Roger that. Standby for primary gyro check."

Reviving the missiles doesn't take very long; the last crew to visit Teal Falcon, three years ago, left the missiles in prelaunch status, just in case the CINC changed his mind about Baghdad's fate. As he and Lewitt run through the checklist, though, Parnell watches Dooley out of the corner of his eye.

The younger man has stood behind Lewitt the entire time, never moving far from his laptop computer. Ryer, on the other hand, has silently moved to stand directly behind Parnell; he can see her reflection in the glass of the computer screen in front of him.

"Gyros green," Lewitt replies. "All onboard systems check out and we're green for go. Ready to load targeting instructions."

"Roger that." Now comes the tricky part: inserting the flight parameters and trajectories into the onboard guidance computers of the six missiles. Parnell types a set of commands on his keyboard; the screen changes to display the empty grid for the targeting system. He turns the pages of his notebook until he finds the list of numbers which, once entered into the computer, will send the Minutemen straight toward the Sun.

As he begins to carefully type the figures into the computer, he notices that Dooley's right hand has innocuously moved to the keyboard of his laptop. Trying not to appear as if he's doing anything, Dooley is quietly entering his own commands into the computer.

The rat has sniffed the bait.

Parnell doesn't say anything. Lewitt hasn't noticed what's going on behind his back; he is too busy making certain that the missiles are ready for launch.

Parnell glances at the chronometer. T-minus nine minutes, thirty-two seconds and counting.

He finishes entering the codes into the computer, but before he transmits them to the missiles, he sneaks another glance at Dooley. The other man's right hand is lingering near the ENTER button on his own computer; he appears to be waiting for Parnell to finish the job, so he can . . .

"Gene? Are you ready?"

Lewitt's waiting for him. Everyone is waiting for him. Especially Dooley, who is prepared to secretly alter the trajectory of one or more of the missiles with a touch of a button.

"Sure." Parnell tries to sound relaxed. He raises his hand to his keyboard. "Targeting instructions entered and loaded . . ."

He pretends to hit his own ENTER key. At that instant, Dooley taps his keyboard.

The numbers on Parnell's screen subtly change of their own accord.

The trap has been sprung.

Parnell leaps to his feet, his right hand diving into the pocket of his jumpsuit. He whips the gun out of the pocket; kicking the chair aside, he brings the Colt into two-handed firing position, aiming straight at Dooley.

"Freeze!" he shouts.

Startled, Dooley jumps back from his computer, his eyes wide with astonishment. Lewitt's mouth falls open as he sees the weapon in Parnell's hand.

Behind him, he hears Ryer moving. Pivoting on his hips,

Parnell points the automatic at her; the barrel is only a couple of feet from her face.

"You too!" he shouts. "Back off! Keep your hands in sight!"

She can't say anything, although her face has gone pale. She stands still, her hands half-raised above her waist.

Behind her, Bromleigh is just beginning to react. He points the camera in their direction, trying to get everything on film.

Rhodes is the first to say anything. "What the hell is going . . . ?"

"Shut up!" Parnell takes a deep breath. "I'll tell you in a minute. Ryer, move back . . . way back." He jerks the gun back toward Dooley. "You, too. Keep your hands where I can see 'em . . ."

Dooley slowly raises his hands to shoulder level. "What the fuck is going on here?" he demands, his voice high and quavering. "I haven't . . ."

"Just keep your hands in sight." Parnell carefully steps away from the console. Blood jackhammers in his ears; he quickly points the gun at Ryer again. "Over there, kiddo. Next to your buddy."

Hands still half-raised, Ryer begins to slowly move backward on leaden feet. "Gene . . ."

"Shut up."

"Gene." Her voice is soft; she's trying to reason with him. "I don't know what you're talking about, but this is . . ."

"Shut up. Put your hands on top of your head. Both of you." He inches past the camera tripod, careful not to stumble over its legs. Out of the corner of his eye, he can see Talsbach standing frozen against the wall.

Lewitt rises from his chair. "What did he do, Gene?" he asks, his eyes darting toward Dooley. "I'm sorry, but I couldn't keep my eye on him."

Ryer is almost next to Dooley now; both of them have their hands clasped on top of their heads. "Just what I thought he was going to do," Parnell murmurs, keeping the gun trained on the pair. "He entered new coordinates in the targeting system. I caught him doing it a second ago."

Dooley's entire body seems to tremble. "That's . . . that's a bunch of shit!" he stammers. "I didn't do a goddamn thing!'' He glances helplessly at Lewitt. ''He's out of his fucking mind, man!''

''Gene,'' Ryer says, ''I've got nothing to do with this, I swear . . .''

''Shut up.'' Parnell keeps walking toward Dooley and Ryer, marching them backward at gunpoint. He's past the camera now, but there's some cold comfort to be had in the fact that Bromleigh has captured the entire scene on film. ''You're in it with him. I didn't figure it out until . . .''

He stops, taking another breath. The situation is under control. ''We'll get it straightened out later. Right now, I want both of you on the floor, facedown.''

''Commander, what the . . . ?'' Rhodes gets hold of herself. ''What's going on here? What are these people being charged with?''

Ryer is already clumsily bending to her knees, hands still laced together above her head. ''Commander, this is nuts . . .''

Dooley is on the verge of panic; his Adam's apple bobs as his eyes shift left and right. ''Holy fuckin' Jesus . . . he's gone crazy!'' He glances at Bromleigh. ''Are you getting this, for chrissakes?''

''We've got everything,'' Bromleigh says from behind the camera. ''Oh my God, Berk . . .''

''Keep shooting, Alex.'' Rhodes has regained her professional composure. ''Commander Parnell, why have you stopped the countdown? Why are you holding these people at gunpoint?''

Calm down, calm down. Everything's under control. You're on camera; when this tape is transmitted back to Mission Control, you can't afford to look like a lunatic.

''Mr. Dooley and Captain Rhodes are part of a conspiracy to take control of the missiles,'' he begins. ''They're—''

At that instant, he feels the hard muzzle of a gun press against the back of his head.

''Drop your weapon,'' Talsbach says from behind him, ''or I shall shoot.''

Parnell feels his blood turn to ice water.

His finger involuntarily relaxes inside the trigger guard. Even then, the cold sensation of the gun at his head isn't half as bad as what he feels a moment later when Lewitt steps forward, lays his hand atop the Colt, and removes it from his grasp.

"Actually," Jay says without a trace of irony, "you're only half-right."

From The Associated Press (Le Matrix on-line news service); February 19, 1995, 6:00 A.M. EST

WASHINGTON D.C.—President Bill Clinton will give a live tele-vised address today from the Oval Office at the White House, scheduled for 7:00 A.M. Eastern time, during which he will is-sue the final launch-and-destruct order for the six Minuteman II nuclear missiles stored inside a crater in the Sea of Tran-quillity on the Moon.

The six missiles were placed on the Moon in 1969, prior to the United States signing of the United Nations Space Treaty of 1992, which outlawed the use of such weapons. All six mis-siles will be launched on a trajectory that will send them into the Sun.

An eight-member international expedition, comprising American, German, and English astronauts, landed on the Moon earlier today at 2:01 A.M. Eastern time. A spokesman at NASA's Von Braun Space Center in Houston, Texas, reports that the astronauts have already entered the once-secret launch bunker, code-named Teal Falcon, inside Sabine Crater nine miles from the closed-down United States moonbase.

The expedition is being led by Commander Eugene Parnell, who was in charge of the U.S. Space Force's Luna Two mis-sion which placed the missiles on the Moon in 1969.

After the missiles are launched, the astronauts will journey back to Tranquillity Base, where they will prepare to hand over the base to the German space corporation Koenig Selenen GmbH. The corporation intends to use the site for industrial operations; the abandoned Teal Falcon silos are expected to be turned into a disposal site for high-level nuclear wastes.

"This marks the final end of the Cold War," says Presidential advisor George Stepenopolous. "When the Minutemen have been destroyed, our friends in the global community will have certain proof that the United States does not intend to wage nuclear war without provocation."

President Clinton's remarks will be carried live on CNN and ATS. Following the successful launch of the missiles, ATS will broadcast a live report from the Teal Falcon launch bunker.

NINETEEN

"Mind if I ask why?" Parnell asked.

Lewitt calmly nodded. Unlike Talsbach, who had a smug grin on his face, at least he refrained from gloating. While the German astronaut kept everyone in the firing room at gunpoint, Lewitt quickly checked the Colt's six-round clip; satisfied that it was fully loaded, he looked past Parnell at Bromleigh and Rhodes.

"Turn off your camera," he said. "In fact, unplug it from the communications board . . . carefully, please." As Bromleigh switched off the Sony, Rhodes walked to the communications panel and, under Talsbach's watchful eye, yanked the cable free.

"Thanks," Lewitt said. He stepped away from Parnell, still keeping the gun leveled at him. He looked at Dooley and silently cocked his head toward the left console; Dooley slipped around Parnell and sat down in the chair the commander had just vacated. "Now everyone just stay calm," Lewitt continued. "If you cooperate, no one gets hurt and everything's going to be okay."

Parnell sincerely doubted he was telling the truth, but it wouldn't do anyone much good to raise the issue. "You haven't answered my question," he said, ignoring Dooley as he kept his eye on Lewitt.

Lewitt looked at him askance. "C'mon, Gene. You don't

really expect me to tell you, do you?'' He smiled and shook his head. ''We're after the nukes. That's all you need to know right now.''

Which was exactly the reason why Parnell didn't believe Lewitt's assertion that no one would be hurt if they cooperated. The stakes were much too high for witnesses to be left alive. For the moment, though, he wanted to keep Lewitt talking, if only to buy them a little more time.

''That's not what I meant,'' he said. ''What I want to know is why you're involved.'' He nodded toward Ryer, who was still crouched on her knees, her hands on her head. ''After all, I thought Cris here was the mole. You're a surprise.''

''That explains a lot,'' Ryer murmured. It was difficult to tell who angered her more, Lewitt or Parnell.

''Oh, I see.'' Lewitt shrugged slightly. ''Well, let's put it this way . . . if you hadn't screwed things up just now, I'd be several million dollars richer and no one would have been the wiser. Now I'll just have to settle for a million bucks. Put your hands on top of your head.''

Despite fear, Parnell managed a smile of his own. ''Gosh, Jay,'' he said as he slowly raised his hands and folded them atop his head, ''that's disappointing. If you're going to be a traitor, you might as well be a good traitor and do it for political reasons. Selling out for cash is pretty lame, don't you think?''

The smile disappeared from Lewitt's face, replaced by a dark scowl. ''Don't push your luck, Gene,'' he said softly.

''What's going on here?'' Rhodes demanded. She was standing next to Bromleigh again; although Talsbach hadn't ordered the reporters to do so, they had also placed their hands on top of their heads. Talsbach stood in front of them, his back to Dooley. ''If you're going to issue some sort of ultimatum, we'll need to reconnect the camera and . . .''

''There's not going to be any ultimatum,'' Lewitt said, his eyes darting toward Rhodes. ''That's not what's going on here . . . and don't even think about turning on the camera.''

''But . . .''

''Just shut up, okay? All of you.'' Parnell and Ryer fell silent, both avoiding each other's eyes, as Lewitt glanced toward Dooley. ''Cecil? Time?''

"T-minus six minutes, twenty-three seconds." Dooley, or whoever he really was, had pulled on the headset and was watching the screens. "The new trajectory for number six is loaded. We're ready to . . ."

He stopped, raising his right hand to cup the headset more firmly against his ear. He listened intently for a moment, then looked up at Lewitt. "Houston's back on the line. They want a status check."

"Shit . . ."

"Plan beginning to unravel a little, huh, Jay?" Parnell shrugged offhandedly. "Put me on, old buddy. I'll tell 'em everything's okay."

"Fuck off." For the first time since he had taken the gun away from him, Lewitt was beginning to sweat. He carefully stepped sideways to the right-hand console, his left hand feeling for his headset. "Hang on, I'll take . . ."

At that moment, the lights went out.

As the control room was plunged into darkness, it seemed as if everyone shouted mindlessly at once. Parnell instinctively froze for a moment . . . then he ducked and simultaneously dived through the blackness straight for where Lewitt had been standing a moment earlier.

A gun fired somewhere just above his head; the muzzle flash dazzled him. For an instant, he thought he'd been hit . . .

A woman screamed, then Parnell slammed headfirst into a body that cushioned his impact with the hard mooncrete floor.

Ryer gasped beneath him, the breath punched out of her lungs. Parnell rolled off her at the same moment Lewitt fired again, his second shot ricocheting with a *spang!* off something metallic.

In the second flash, Parnell caught the briefest glimpse of Rhodes sagging against the far wall . . .

Talsbach howled something in German and fired his own gun in some wild direction. Parnell couldn't see where it hit, but from somewhere close to his left he heard Lewitt:

"Goddammit, stop . . . !"

Parnell lashed out with his right leg, kicking blindly in the direction of Lewitt's voice. His foot connected with soft flesh; he heard a harsh grunt, but as he pulled his leg back for another kick, Lewitt fired once more, again at close range.

Miraculously, the bullet missed him; it whizzed as it split the air somewhere just past his right ear. Dooley was yelling incoherently at the top of his lungs; there was a loud crash as the TV camera toppled over.

"There!" Talsbach shouted. "He's there, in front of—!"

Another gunshot, then a loud crash which sprayed glass across the room: a TV monitor had been shot out. At that same instant, a hand grabbed Parnell's arm and wrested him aside.

His head slammed against the bottom of a chair; without thinking, he grabbed it with both hands and hurled it as hard as he could in Lewitt's direction.

He heard a grunt as the chair connected with someone; something metallic clattered to the floor about six feet away. Thinking it was the pistol, Parnell clawed for it . . .

"Fuck, stop shooting!" Dooley shouted.

A gun roared, this time from the other side of the room. Parnell reflexively ducked; as he did, he felt Ryer's hands grabbing at his shoulders.

"The hatch!" she gasped in his ear. "Get to the hatch!"

The hatch? What the hell was she . . . ?

Right. The ceiling hatch. The ladder was only a few feet away. Forgetting about the dropped gun, Parnell struggled to his hands and knees and began scrambling across the cold floor toward a dim oval of light. Ryer was directly in front of him, making for the same target.

"Goddammit!" Dooley yelled. "Fuck! Fuck, shit, fuck. I've got somebody bleeding on—!"

"Shut up!" Talsbach shouted. "Uwe! Where are you?"

Ryer reached the bottom of the ladder, but instead of grabbing the rungs, she crouched and leaped straight up. For a moment, it seemed to Parnell that she had learned how to fly; the last thing he saw of her was her legs and feet disappearing through the hatch.

"Fuck him!" Lewitt hollered from somewhere back in the darkness. "They're getting away—!"

"Don't shoot!" Dooley yelled. "Don't shoot! You'll hit—!"

Parnell didn't wait for them to make up their minds. He

grasped the ladder, crouched low, then sprang upwards as fast as he could, letting the lunar one-sixth gravity do the rest. There was another gunshot as he soared upwards, bypassing the ladder as he hurtled out of the control room.

The sudden glare of the overhead lights made him wince, but he barely had time to raise his hands to his eyes before someone grabbed his arms and yanked him the rest of the way out of the hatch . . .

"C'mon, goddammit! Move your silly arse!"

Then he was shoved away from the hatch by a pair of strong arms. As he sprawled painfully across the floor, a gun was fired from somewhere above him.

Blinking furiously, he managed to clear his vision enough to see James Leamore crouched above the hatch, firing a Glock 17 down into the control room. As Parnell fought to get up, Leamore kicked the hatch cover into place.

"You?" Parnell gasped. "What the hell is—?"

"No time for that!" Leamore backed away from the hatch, reaching down to pull Ryer to her feet. "They'll have those lights back on in a second! Now up the ladder, both of you! Move!"

As Parnell got to his feet, Ryer grabbed the bottom rung of the ladder leading up to the airlock deck. Suddenly, she seemed to think better of it. "Just a sec," she said, then dropped off the ladder and dashed across the compartment to a computer terminal near the far wall.

There was a dull pounding against the bottom of the control room hatch. "We haven't got time for that, you silly bitch!" Leamore shouted, close to panic. "They're going to be up here in—!"

"Where's Aachener?" Parnell demanded.

"Out cold and trussed up like a Christmas goose." Leamore was still watching the hatch. "Where do you think I got this gun? Ryer, dammit—!"

"Shut up!" Ryer unzipped a breast pocket of her jumpsuit and pulled out a diskette. Parnell had just enough time to recognize it as the same 3.5-inch diskette he had briefly glimpsed aboard *Conestoga,* then she slapped it into the terminal's floppy drive. She tapped several keys on the computer, waited a few seconds until a line of type appeared on the monitor, then yanked it back out of the computer.

"Okay, let's get out of here!" she snapped, turning around and running back to the ladder.

Parnell didn't ask what she had done; there wasn't enough time. As Leamore covered them, he scurried up the ladder behind Ryer. He had just entered the top deck when he heard a shout from below, followed by a gunshot.

"Leamore!" he shouted.

A few moments passed, then Leamore clambered up the ladder, the Glock still gripped in his right hand. "That'll hold 'em for a few more minutes," he said as he slammed the second hatch shut, "but they'll figure out things soon enough. Now suit up, both of you . . . I'll hold down the fort."

"Will someone please explain what's going on?" Ryer was already hauling her hardsuit out of the locker where she had stowed it.

Out of breath, Leamore squatted on his haunches next to the hatch. "Certainly, ma'am," he said, his voice a dry rasp. "I'm working for SIS, and your dimwit commander here just managed to botch an intelligence operation."

Parnell's jaw dropped. "I—?"

"Yes, you flaming idiot," Leamore said, glowering at him. "You."

Talsbach was still holding onto the ladder, his gun gripped in his right hand as he pressed his ear against the closed hatch. "I cannot hear anything," he said as he glanced down at Lewitt. "They've left the second deck, perhaps?"

"Maybe," Lewitt answered, "but don't try going up again until we're sure." Just now, Lewitt had more important things on his mind. Talsbach had located the light switch Leamore had managed to throw; Lewitt was surveying the scene in the firing room. "Shit," he breathed. "Things sure got fucked up in a hurry, didn't they?"

The compartment was a mess. The TV monitor that had been shot out by a stray bullet had strewn glass across the consoles. Notebook pages were scattered everywhere, top secret codes and procedures lying on the floor like so much trash. A chair was overturned; pulling it upright, Lewitt discovered the gun Parnell had managed to dislodge from his hands.

Worst of all, though, were the two bodies in the far corner of the room. Berkley Rhodes was slumped in a sitting position against the wall, her legs sprawled out before her, her head draping blond hair over the wet red blotch in the middle of her chest. In his dying moments, Alex Bromleigh seemed to have curled protectively around the ruined camcorder on the floor; the bullet that had punctured his left lung had left him staring sightlessly at the firefight that had ended his career and his life.

"Christ," Lewitt whispered. He stared down at the gun in his numb hand, then carefully placed it on the desk. Although he couldn't be certain, it was possible that it was he himself who had killed Rhodes and Bromleigh. "Sorry, guys," he muttered, as much to himself as to the dead man and woman. "You were supposed to stay alive . . ."

"Jay! Snap out of it!"

Lewitt tore his eyes away from the bodies. Paul Dooley—Cecil Orvitz, actually, if one cared to use the name on his birth certificate—had resumed his seat in front of the left-hand firing console.

"We've got T-minus three minutes and counting," he said, as matter-of-fact as if he were discussing a ferry launch from the Cape. "Houston wants to know what's going on up here."

Lewitt took a deep breath. "Did they hear anything?" he asked, trying to gather his wits.

Dooley shook his head, and Lewitt turned to the console behind him and picked up the headset, just as he had been about to do before all hell broke loose. He held the headset to his ear and adjusted the mike, then pushed the vox button.

"Mission, this is Teal Falcon," he said. "Sorry for the delay, but we experienced a small difficulty in the master fire control system. Commander Parnell has gone up to the logistics deck to correct the problem. Over."

There was a brief pause, enough time for him to wonder whether they had bought the lie; then a voice came over the comlink. *We copy, Teal Falcon. What's the nature of the problem? Over.*

He shot a glance at Dooley; the hacker mouthed something, pointing at the CRT in front of him. "It's just a software glitch," he replied. "Nothing to be concerned about. We've corrected it and are proceeding with countdown as planned."

Dooley nodded, circling his thumb and index finger. Lewitt waited another few seconds before the voice of the Von Braun controller responded: *We copy, Teal Falcon. Is Commander Parnell available?*

"No, Houston, not at this moment," Lewitt said quickly. "He's still on the upper deck, making sure that the glitch doesn't reoccur." He glanced at the chronometer. "We're at T-minus two minutes, twenty seconds. All systems are go for launch, and we're not requesting a hold. Repeat, we're go for launch, no hold requested. Over."

He looked back at Dooley, expecting affirmation of his message. Dooley, however, was staring intently at his screen; as Lewitt watched, the hacker's fingers raced across the keyboard, entering commands Lewitt couldn't make out from across the room.

Roger that, Teal Falcon. We confirm. You're go for launch at T-minus two minutes, ten seconds and counting. Final launch authentication as follows . . .

"Shit!"

Dooley's eyes were wide with amazement. Lewitt ignored the last set of code-numbers transmitted over the comlink; it wasn't necessary for him to enter the authentication in order to launch the missiles. "What's going on?" he said, cupping his hand over the mike.

"I dunno!" Dooley was becoming frantic; he bent closer to the screen as he stabbed urgently at the keyboard, anxiously watching the display. "Everything's freezing up . . . I can't get anything to work!"

"Nothing?" Lewitt glanced up at the remaining TV monitors. The silo covers had slid open, allowing pale earthlight to bathe the five Minutemen he could see on the remaining monitors; the missiles were poised for launch, but the work platforms were still in place within the silos and the umbilicals hadn't detached. "What about the primary ignition system?"

"I'm telling you, nothing works!" Dooley was almost

pounding the keyboard in frustration. "Fucking computer is ignoring everything I send to it! I can't—!"

His head jerked up, mouth gaping as he stared at Lewitt. "Goddamn," he whispered. "I'll be goddamned . . ."

"What?"

"A fucking virus." Dooley shook his head incredulously as his eyes moved back to the console. "I don't know how they did it, but they've put a fucking virus in this thing. There's no other explanation." A weird grin appeared on his face. "I don't . . . fuck, how did they . . . ?"

Lewitt was about to say something when Mission Control came back on line. *Teal Falcon, do you confirm final launch authentication?*

Lewitt quickly uncupped the mike. "Ah, we copy, Houston. We're go for launch at . . ."

The chronometer told him that seventy seconds remained until launch. "T-minus one minute, ten seconds," he finished. "Standby, over."

He reached across the board and switched off the radio. "Fuck that," he murmured, then looked back at Dooley. "Do you have time to reboot the program?"

Dooley laughed out loud. "Are you kidding? This is a mainframe crash! I can't get anything up and running without dumping everything and starting over from scratch . . . and that's only if I can locate the virus and rub it out of the system."

"What about Uwe?" Talsbach was still standing on the ladder, apparently oblivious to everything that was going on behind him. "He could be injured, or . . ."

"Fuck Uwe." Lewitt ran a hand through his hair; it came back slick with sweat. Right now, the President would be wrapping up his pithy speech from behind the Oval Office desk. It was Sunday, so he would be wearing a blue cardigan and a golf shirt. A picture of his wife and daughter would be visible on the table behind him, and on the antique desk would be the ceremonial button he would press that would supposedly send the Minutemen into solar oblivion. When Houston saw that the missiles didn't leave their silos . . .

"Okay," he said softly, trying to get a grip. "Maybe the computer's feeding you wrong info or something . . ."

"Wrong info?" Dooley's laugh was a nerve-racking bray. "Hey, dude, take a reality check! This isn't a Nintendo game. This is—"

"Shut up and grab that other key!" Lewitt controlled a sudden urge to twist the obnoxious little twit's head off his shoulders. "Just do it!"

Dooley seemed as if he were about to add another slacker-generation sarcasm; one look at Lewitt's face, though, made him reconsider. Without a word, he grasped the metal key in the slot on his console.

Lewitt grabbed his own key. "Okay," he said quietly, peering at the flashing numbers on the chronometer. It was now T-minus twelve seconds and counting. "When I say 'mark,' turn it to the right. Got it?"

"Got it," Dooley said. "But I'm telling you, this isn't going to—"

"Just do as I say." Lewitt's heart was thudding against his chest as he watched the last few digits flash by. "Three . . . two . . . one . . . mark!"

In the same instant, both men twisted their keys from STANDBY to LAUNCH.

Nothing happened.

On the TV monitors, the Minutemen remained dormant in their silos. No flash of engine ignition, no billowing exhaust fumes, no graceful rise of sleek missiles from their berths. The rockets were frozen in place.

As Dooley let out his breath and sank back in his chair, Lewitt reached out to stab buttons which killed all telemetry to the Wheel and Earth. If there was any grim satisfaction to be had in the fact that the President of the United States had just pushed a buttom which was absolutely useless even as a formality, he didn't feel it.

"Okay." Lewitt settled back in the chair and fitted the headset over his ears. "Time to go to the backup plan."

He turned a dial on the communications panel before him, readjusting it to a seldom-used S-band frequency. "Ghost Rider, this is Blue Falcon. Code red. I repeat, code red. Do you copy? Over."

Fortunately, the radio still worked. While he waited for a

reply, Lewitt glanced over his shoulder at Talsbach, who was still hovering beneath the closed hatch. He jerked his head upward.

"Get 'em," he said.

"My fellow Americans . . .

"Twenty-six years ago, a previous Administration determined that, for reasons of national security, it was vital to protect American interests at home and abroad by placing weapons of mass destruction on the Moon. This plan was carried out in secret, without prior knowledge or approval of the American public or most of its elected officials. Although the existence of this small arsenal was eventually made known, to this day these weapons—six Minuteman II missiles, each containing a one-megaton nuclear warhead—have remained on the Moon.

"A generation has passed since then, and the world has become a different place. I will not apologize for the actions taken by another President, or for the willingness of his successors to continue his policies, since they were done in the spirit of defending the United States. However, this Administration believes that it is no longer necessary, or desirable, for this country to maintain a nuclear deterrent in outer space at a time when we're actively dismantling our land-based strategic nuclear arsenal.

"Three years ago, President Dole signed the United Nations Space Treaty which outlawed the deployment of weapons of mass destruction in Earth orbit or on any heavenly body. In accordance with this international treaty, I am today issuing the final order for the destruction of all six missiles stored at the Teal Falcon installation at the Sea of Tranquillity on the Moon. This order will be carried out at twelve o'clock P.M. Greenwich meridian time, seven o'clock A.M. Eastern Standard Time, under the remote supervision of the International Atomic Energy Agency.

"On the desk before me is a button which, once pressed, will signal our astronauts on the Moon to launch the missiles. Instead of heading for Earth, as they were designed to do, the missiles will be sent into the Sun, where they will be harmlessly consumed by its vast energy. This action is as symbolic as it is practical: just as the Sun gives us life, so it will aid in the destruction of our engines of death.

"After the missiles are launched, the base where they were stored will be turned over to a private German corporation, which intends to eventually use it for the safe disposal of high-level nuclear waste from Earth. In this way, what was once a secret military site will be used to enhance the quality of the global environment.

"As I said earlier, I will not apologize for the decisions made by my predecessors in the White House. However, as President of the United States, I beg forgiveness for the fear and anxiety which those actions may have caused the people of the world.

"And now, I will press the button . . ."

TWENTY

"What does SIS have to do with all this?" Parnell demanded. "And why didn't you tell me you're spying for them?"

They were taking turns holding the pistol while they climbed into their suits. Parnell was wearing everything except his helmet, and Ryer had half-completed her suit-up process. Leamore was just getting started; he barely looked up from the heavy boots he was struggling to pull on.

"For starters," he said, grunting as he shoved his left foot into the matching boot and attached its ring to the cuff, "I'm not a spy, but an agent. There's a difference, you know . . ."

"I don't care if you're a circus clown." Parnell's eyes never left the closed hatch leading up from the lower levels. If it budged so much as an inch, he'd fire a bullet down the ladder. He glanced at Ryer; her suit was sealed, and she was now shouldering her life-support pack. "When you get done," he said to her, "help him."

Ryer nodded as Leamore heaved his right foot into the other boot. "What I really meant to say," Leamore went on, "is that I'm not fully aware of all the details because I'm not a full-time operative. The fellows at Century House recruited me when they first learned about this entire business, because I had already been assigned to this mission, but they didn't take me completely into their confidence."

He cast a quick grin at Parnell. "So you're not talking to

James Bond here. I'm just fortunate that I got the drop on Herr Aachener before he took me out instead.''

"So tell us what you do know," Parnell said. "Who are those guys working for?"

Leamore fastened the right ankle ring, then stood up and hastily pulled the heavy suit up over his chest and shoulders. "Ever heard of a gent named Wolff-Dieter Rautmann?" he asked. Parnell shook his head. "Not many people have," he went on. "He's a freelance arms dealer working out of Germany, the same party who has been supplying secondhand Russian munitions to various Middle Eastern countries for several years. All perfectly legal, but SIS has suspected for a while now that he's also been trading in nastier stuff—nuclear components, chemical and biological agents, and so forth and so on—to whoever will buy them."

"Can we skip the life history, please?"

"Quite. At any rate, early last year Germany's State Security Ministry raided a Baader-Meinhof safe house in Bonn and arrested a number of suspected terrorists. When they interrogated one of the prisoners, they learned about Markus and Uwe."

"Talsbach and Aachener are terrorists?" Ryer snapped shut the buckles of her backpack and began connecting its oxygen hoses to the chest valves. "I've heard about Baader-Meinhof. This is kind of a big operation for those guys, isn't it?"

Leamore nodded. "Markus and Uwe were once with the Red Army Faction a long time ago, but this isn't a Baader-Meinhof operation." He shoved his right arm down a sleeve. "If they've got ideological reasons, it's secondary to whatever they're being paid. They were recruited for this job because they were about to enter astronaut training. Seems that these characters had decided to get straight jobs, even if they themselves weren't quite straight. Like your man Lewitt intimated, money speaks louder than ideology, particularly when it comes to treason."

He paused to pull the suit the rest of the way on, then ducked his head to stick it through the collar ring. "Anyway," he gasped when he came up for air, "the Germans tipped off SIS, and Century House investigated on its own.

To make a long story short, its informants discovered that Rautmann went to the trouble of finding and recruiting these gents for the purpose of getting hold of your nukes here.''

"For Baader-Meinhof?'' Ryer asked, sounding slightly confused.

"Them?'' Leamore blew out his cheeks. "Not bloody likely. Nothing so small. This whole thing is being done at the behest of the People's Democratic Government of North Korea.''

"North Korea?'' Surprised, Parnell looked away from the hatch. "What would it gain from firing missiles from . . . ?''

"No, you idiot.'' Leamore was becoming inpatient. "Not firing missiles . . . acquiring missiles. Or rather, the warhead from one of those Minutemen.''

He paused in his labors at suiting up. "Look. Missiles they've got—they've already built their Nodong-1, in case you haven't heard—but when the U.N. clamped down on their bomb factory last year, they had to look elsewhere. They knew that was coming, so a couple of years ago they hired our friend Herr Rautmann, who in turn set up this entire operation. SIS also learned that Cecil Orvitz—or rather, Paul Dooley, as you know him—was recruited by . . .''

"Hold on.'' Parnell was still trying to absorb all this; too much was being thrown at him too fast. "Wait a minute. They're trying to hijack the missiles? How did they expect to . . .''

"Accomplish this feat?'' Leamore shrugged within the suit's cumbersome carapace. He fumbled with the seals until Ryer stepped over to assist him. "We're not quite certain— or, at least, I'm not certain, although I'm positive that SIS knows more than I. Whatever their means, though, the objective is still the same.''

"Getting the nukes from our Minutemen,'' Ryer said.

"Correct. Thank you, dear.'' Leamore's gaze turned back to Parnell. "Once Kim Jong acquires a ready-made warhead, he doesn't have to worry about U.N. inspectors. He can resell it to whoever is willing to meet his price. Or put it on one of his own rockets, if he wants to make Seoul sweat bullets.''

Something was beginning to tug at the back of Parnell's mind, but before he could voice his thoughts, Ryer cut in. "If

SIS knew about all this and sent you, then why didn't you come and tell us? It would have saved a lot of grief . . . stand up straight."

Leamore stood straighter, sucking in his gut as Ryer pulled the airtight zipper partway up the back of his suit. "Because this was supposed to be an intelligence operation, that's all. SIS knew that Dooley, Aachener, and Talsbach were involved. We also knew that Rhodes and Bromleigh were clean. Beyond that, we didn't know who among the remaining crew members might have been recruited, if any."

He looked over his shoulder at Ryer, then nodded toward Parnell. "For all we knew, you or Gene could have been part of the scheme, so I couldn't afford to trust either of you. Sorry."

Ryer and Parnell glanced at each other. Whatever quarrel they might have once had was now settled; all that mattered now was survival. "Don't worry about it," Parnell murmured. "I seem to have misplaced my trust as well."

Ryer gave him a quick smile. Another thought occurred to him. "What is it about that disk, anyway?" he asked her.

"Some private revenge, that's all," Ryer said as she fought the rear zipper the rest of the way up Leamore's back. "With any luck, it'll stop the launch, maybe buy us some time." When Gene opened his mouth to speak, she shook her head. "I'll tell you about it later."

Parnell looked at his wrist chronometer. He wasn't willing to bet on luck. It was now 1212 Zulu. The missiles should have launched twelve minutes ago. They had no idea whether the Minutemen had cleared the silos; down here, within the lunar crust, no vibration could penetrate the isolation of the bunker.

Ryer hefted Leamore's life-support pack and began to help him guide his arms through the shoulder straps. "You said this was supposed to be an intelligence operation. That means you weren't supposed to stop them?"

"Not unless it became absolutely necessary," Leamore replied. "All we wanted was evidence that two known Red Army operatives and an accomplice—Dooley, although you know better yourself by now—were involved in the theft. We intended to gain such evidence from the ATS camera footage.

Once that was accomplished, everything would be disclosed to the cousins . . .''

"The CIA."

"That's right, along with the White House and the Pentagon . . . and as a result NATO would have been able to take the matter to the U.N. Security Council, which would have attempted to resolve the matter through diplomacy and so forth. Altogether, it was supposed to be a rather low-key, hush-hush sort of affair."

Leamore picked up a gauntlet and pulled it over his left hand. "But apparently Aachener got wise to my role somehow. So far as I know, he was aware of my involvement even before we left the Wheel."

He swore under his breath. "In any event, he tried to silence me when I went to the W.C., but I managed to get the gun away from him. After that I hid out in the crew's quarters, waiting to see what would happen next."

"But by then I had wised up—" Parnell began.

"And forced the issue, which leads to our current situation." Leamore fastened the wrist link of his left glove. "I suppose I can't rightly blame you, Commander," he said as he picked up the right glove. "You had stumbled upon this bloody mess and tried to prevent it. But the whole sodding thing went to hell as soon as you pulled that gun and pointed it at the wrong fellow, and that's why . . ."

He fumbled with the gauntlet. It dropped to the floor. "Oh, damn," he murmured, and bent over to pick it up. Or at least he tried to; the bulky suit prevented him from doing so much as touch his knees.

"I'll get it." Parnell walked over to where the glove lay, his boots clunking heavily on the deck. He knelt to his right knee and retrieved the gauntlet.

He was about to hand it to Leamore when he heard the metallic rasp of hatch-cover hinges. Before he could turn around, a gun went off behind him.

Lewitt jerked at the sharp crack of a gunshot from somewhere above.

For an instant, he thought someone was firing into the control room; he grabbed the automatic from the desktop and swiveled around in his chair, staring at the open hatchway.

"Markus!" he shouted. "What's going on up there?"

No response. He yanked off the headset and started to rise from the chair, but Orvitz looked up from the left console. "Sit down," he said, almost too calmly. "Whatever it is, they'll take care of it."

Lewitt hesitated, then resumed his place at the right-hand firing console. Like it or not, Orvitz was right; this was why the Germans had been recruited, to act as backups in case something went wrong with the operation. Lewitt reluctantly put the pistol down, replaced his headset, and returned his attention to the console. Although the computers were still inoperative, Teal Falcon's radar system remained functional. A small blip had entered the scope; as he watched, it closed steadily on the bull's-eye at the center of the screen.

He reactivated the radio. "Ghost Rider, this is Blue Falcon. We have you on primary approach. Do you copy? Over."

There was a short pause, then a Russian-accented voice came over the headset. *We understand, Blue Falcon. Ghost Rider is at one hundred fifty kilometers, downrange fifteen kilometers. Landing estimated in ten minutes. Has the perimeter been secured? Over.*

Lewitt glanced at Orvitz, who was listening through his headset. Orvitz nodded his head. "Roger that, Ghost Rider," Lewitt replied. "Be advised that we're still encountering some resistance within the base, but it will be taken care of by the time you arrive. Over."

There was a long pause. After a few moments, the voice returned. *We understand, Blue Falcon. We are continuing with approach and landing. Over.*

Lewitt grimaced. Of course Ghost Rider would land; its crew had no other options.

The original plan had called for TF-6 to be launched into an elliptical cislunar orbit, where it would have been intercepted by Ghost Rider. Two Russian former cosmonauts would then have gone EVA; using special tools, and consulting schematic diagrams of the Minuteman's payload package which had been smuggled out of the West, they would have opened the missile's faring and removed the warhead. All this would have been accomplished without anyone on

Earth or the Moon being the wiser; controllers at Von Braun and the Wheel would have believed that TF-6 was on a solar trajectory along with the five other missiles, thanks to false transponder coordinates which Orvitz's program was supposed to relay to the Deep Space Tracking Network.

Ghost Rider would have returned to Earth while *Conestoga* was still at Tranquillity Base. Orvitz, Aachener, and Talsbach, and Lewitt himself, would have flown home aboard *Conestoga*. By the time anyone figured out what had happened to TF-6—if ever—he would be catching a jet to Argentina, where Lisa and their child were already waiting for him.

Lewitt sagged back in the chair, rubbing his eyes. A carefully developed plan, two years in the making, now straight down the toilet. First, Orvitz's cover had been blown because he couldn't handle some stupid gimp girlfriend Dooley had in Arizona. Then Uwe had gotten suspicious about Leamore and attempted to kill him. And even after everything had fucked up, but just when it seemed as if he could get the situation under control, this shit with a dime-store virus program . . .

"Jesus," he mumbled. "Talk about chaos theory . . ."

"What's that?" Orvitz asked.

Lewitt shook his head. "Never mind."

By now, everyone from Texas to the White House must be in a panic, trying to find out why the Minutemen hadn't launched or why they had lost contact with Teal Falcon. There was no point in trying to make up excuses; Mission Control would only want to speak with Parnell, or have Rhodes and Bromleigh transmit a TV picture from the bunker.

But they still had their backup plan.

All was not yet lost. The second plan didn't rely on subterfuge so much as brute force, but it was only a different means to the same end. Even if TF-6 was grounded, its silo doors were open, the missile itself still accessible from the surface. It meant doing the same job the hard way, but Ghost Rider's crew would still get their warheads, one way or another. . . .

Another gunshot from above. Lewitt glanced again at the hatch. What the hell was going on up there?

•   •   •

The first round had taken off the top of Leamore's head, but Parnell didn't realize he had been killed before he whipped around and got off a single, clumsy shot at the half-open hatch.

The bullet ricocheted off the inside of the hatch cover. Parnell caught the briefest glimpse of Talsbach's face before the hatch dropped shut again.

Goddamn! The son of a bitch had been listening the entire time . . . and, like an idiot, Parnell had moved away from the hatch just long enough for Talsbach to poke his head through.

"Is everyone all right?" Parnell yelled. He didn't dare take his eyes from the hatch; the Glock was cradled in both hands, aimed at the hatch in case Talsbach tried again.

"Leamore's down!"

Ryer was crouched near the wall, staring at the body sprawled across the deck at her feet. Dark red blood was pooling around Leamore's skull. "Oh, shit," she whispered. "He's dead, Gene. . . ."

Parnell stole a quick glance over his shoulder. Leamore had been lucky once, but not twice . . . and the way things stood, luck was beginning to run out for both him and Ryer.

But maybe not. They were both fully suited except for their helmets, and the airlock was just behind them. All they had to do was put on their helmets, pressurize their suits, enter the airlock, and . . .

And what? Cycle-out would take at least thirty minutes. In the meantime, they would be trapped inside the airlock chamber. Its hatch was airtight, but not bulletproof; someone could still fire through it.

Talsbach didn't even have to do that. The control panel outside the airlock could stop the depressurization cycle. If Talsbach shut off the airlock while they were inside, then he and Ryer would be cornered. The proverbial fish in a barrel had better odds of survival.

Unless . . .

"Cris!" he whispered.

She didn't respond; glancing toward her, he saw that she was staring at Leamore.

"Ryer, snap out of it!"

She blinked and slowly raised her head. She was on the verge of panic, but hadn't lost it yet.

"Put your helmet on!" he whispered. "Put on your helmet and get in the airlock!"

She blinked a few more times and shook her head; she, too, had realized that they could be trapped in the airlock. "But they can . . ."

"Shut up and do it! I'll cover you!"

Ryer nodded dully. She rose from the wall, looked around stupidly until she spotted her helmet several feet away. Parnell didn't mind the noise her boots made against the floor as she walked over to pick it up.

In fact, he was counting on Talsbach having his ear pressed against the hatch.

He waited until she had put on her helmet and sealed her suit. Then, when she opened the airlock hatch, he made his move. Carefully placing the gun on the floor so that he could grab it in an instant, he reached out for his own helmet.

Despite his caution, there were a couple of minutes when he couldn't pick up the pistol; his hands were busy, sealing his helmet ring and activating the suit's electrical and life-support systems. He left the radio off—too much chance someone in the control room might be monitoring this frequency—and he didn't allow his eyes to waver from the floor hatch until he was finished.

He retrieved the gun and straightened up, ignoring the cramp in his knees as he moved across the suit-up room to the airlock. For no real reason, he recalled a rock song his son used to play on the stereo; he whispered the refrain under his breath.

"Gimme three steps . . . gimme three steps . . . gimme three steps towards the door . . ." When he entered the airlock, he raised his left hand and jerked it down several times, palm-down, clawing his fingers as much as the heavy gloves would allow.

Ryer understood. She knelt on all fours and pushed her fingers through the open gridwork of the airlock floor. Maybe she realized what he was going to do; there wasn't enough time to ask.

The airlock's internal control panel was near the hatch.

Parnell placed the gun on the floor beneath the panel, where he could still reach it, then slammed the hatch shut as hard as he could and wrenched the lock-lever downward. If Talsbach or Aachener was listening from Level 2A, they would undoubtedly hear the noise.

If so, only a few seconds remained. He bent to one knee and grabbed a piece of the gridwork floor with his left hand; with his right hand, he flipped open the control panel. His heart was thudding as he sought for the candy-striped toggle switch at the bottom of the panel.

Glancing up at the hatch, he saw the lock-lever moving upward. They had been heard moving into the airlock, all right.

The airlock door started to open. He remembered his kids' faces, then flipped the emergency switch marked VOID.

Pyros in the ceiling hatch above their heads detonated, blowing the hatch cover off its hinges, and a miniature hurricane erupted inside the airlock as its atmosphere exploded through the manhole-size opening.

Even through his helmet, the roar was deafening; it was as if a freight train were running through the chamber. The tendons in his left hand screamed as he clung to the gridwork. His legs began to lift from the floor, and he managed to haul his right arm downward and grasp the gridwork with his right hand.

His helmet faceplate clouded, but before it completely frosted over he caught a brief glimpse of an unsuited human form flailing helplessly as it was sucked into the chamber.

He heard a scream, thinned by the escaping pressure—then Markus Talsbach was propelled through the ceiling hatch like a tree branch caught in the vortex of a tornado.

Then Parnell could see nothing as his faceplate whited over.

The noise gradually subsided; his legs sank back to the floor. Nothing remained except the soundless din of hard vacuum.

When his faceplate cleared, its moisture evaporated, he saw the airlock hatch gaping open. The ready-room beyond was wrecked; he didn't want to see what had become of James Leamore's corpse. The gun that he had laid at his feet was missing. He hoped he didn't need it any longer, but didn't expect that he would.

Parnell took a long, ragged breath, then pulled his fingers out of the floor. Turning around on his knees, he saw that Ryer was still with him. She fought her way unsteadily to her feet; her back arched slightly as she gazed up at the open ceiling hatch. When she looked back down at him again, Parnell pointed to his helmet and raised one finger. He waited until she had switched on her suit radio.

"You okay?" he asked.

Yeah, I'm okay. She gazed up again at the hatch. *You killed him.*

Parnell didn't want to think about what he had just done. He reminded himself that he might live to see his family again; that was all that mattered right now.

"Yeah, I killed him." He took another breath, then hauled himself to his feet. "We're not out of this yet. C'mon, let's get out of here."

From The Associated Press (Le Matrix on-line news service); February 19, 1995, 7:30 A.M. EST

HOUSTON—Radio contact has been lost with the multinational expedition to the Moon, say spokesmen at NASA's Von Braun Manned Space Flight Center.

Contact with the former USSF installation, code-named Teal Falcon, was lost at 6:59 A.M. Eastern time, just prior to the beginning of President Clinton's nationally televised address to the nation regarding the final disposal of the missiles.

The President delivered his speech as scheduled, which culminated with his pushing a ceremonial button that was to signal the simultaneous launch of the Minuteman rockets toward the Sun. However, NASA has been unable to confirm whether or not the lunar-based ICBM's were fired from their underground silos.

Mission controllers are unable to determine why or how communications abruptly ceased at the moment when six Minuteman II rockets were scheduled to be launched from a missile site near the lunar base.

Although a two-person ATS TV network news team accompanied the American-German expedition to the Teal Falcon bunker, no television images have yet been received. ATS correspondent Berkley Rhodes, who is credited with exposing the Dole Administration's contingency plan to use the lunar missiles during the Desert Storm war, was scheduled to transmit a live report following the launch.

NASA officials say that countdown for the missile launch proceeded according to plan until the final radio message received from Teal Falcon, when NASA astronaut Jay Lewitt reported that mission commander Eugene Parnell had left the firing room to solve unspecified problems with the installation's computer system. Contact with the expedition ceased immediately after that transmission.

NASA spokesman David Fitzhugh would not speculate on what may have caused the silence. "We're watching the situation very closely," he said.

TWENTY-ONE

Reaching the surface took longer than expected. Although neither Parnell nor Ryer had noticed it at the time, each had suffered bruises and pulled muscles in the control room fight and during the airlock blowout. Climbing the sixty-foot ladder up the entrance shaft was a painful ordeal, and by the time they reached the outer dome they had to pause to catch their breath.

It could have been much worse. Markus Talsbach hadn't needed to climb the ladder; the explosive decompression had blown him straight up the shaft. Neither of them wished to study the mangled corpse sprawled across the auxiliary oxygen tanks; one glimpse of the black, frozen blood splashed across the walls was nearly enough to make them sick.

Can we make it to the tractor okay? Ryer stared through the open door to the closer of the two vehicles. *It's only ten meters away, I think.*

Parnell pulled his gaze from Talsbach's body. "I don't see why not," he replied, swallowing hard. Thankful for the distraction, he peered through the door at the nearby tractor. "Twenty, thirty feet. Piece of cake."

That's not what I meant. What about the gyrojet guns?

"They're preset only to fire at moving objects outside the crater." Gazing at the nearest guns atop the walls, he paused to reconsider. "Unless Dooley managed to reprogram the defense perimeter to ignore the security codes, or even track anything in motion within the crater. Then we could be in trouble.''

I don't think so. Look over there. Ryer pointed to the silos on the far side of the crater. *The missiles are still in place. If they managed to get the computers working again, wouldn't they have launched them?*

Parnell peered closely at the distant silos. Through their open hatches, he could make out the nose cones of the six Minutemen. Cris had a good point; if the computers were back on-line, then firing the missiles would have been the first thing Lewitt and Dooley did. After that, they might have reprogrammed the crater guns.

"Nice little program you got there," he murmured. "Where'd you pick it up, Radio Shack?"

Ryer didn't reply, nor did she need to; Parnell could guess the rest. "Never mind," he said. "We'll work it out later." He moved closer to the door. "I think we can take the risk. Just to be on the safe side, though, we'd better run for it. You with me?"

Like we've got a choice? Ryer lowered her helmet visor. *Okay, on the count of three. One . . .*

Parnell didn't wait for the countdown. Pushing past her, he leaped through the doorway and bounded for Tractor One. His boots kicked up dusty regolith with each bunny-hop he took; on the third jump, though, his left foot found a large rock that sent him sprawling.

He instinctively rolled, taking most of the impact on his hips and shoulders, raising his arms to keep his faceplate from being fractured, until he lay chest-down on the ground. Sucking in his breath, he stared up at the crater wall, waiting for the guns to zero in on him and the first gyrojet bullet to rip through his suit.

Are you okay? Ryer asked.

She stood a few feet behind Parnell, looking down at him. Parnell clambered to his feet, dusting off his arms with his gloves. "Fine," he replied. "I guess that settles that . . . about the guns, I mean."

Ryer didn't reply. Instead, she arched her body backward, apparently to look up at something directly overhead.

I think I know why they didn't launch the missiles, she said softly.

Parnell forgot about the spill he had just taken. He copied her movements, staring past the rim of his helmet until he could see the black sky above Sabine Crater.

A bright constellation had appeared above them: four tightly grouped stars that were not fixed in the heavens. As he watched, the constellation grew closer, subtly increasing in luminosity, until he could make out a vague mass behind them that occulted the stars as it passed.

A spacecraft, descending from space for a landing inside the crater.

I think we'd better get out of here, Ryer said.

"No argument there." Parnell turned and began to run the last few yards to the tractor.

Lewitt watched Parnell and Ryer on the TV monitor as they headed for the tractor. Even if he could have reactivated the crater guns and trained them on his former crewmates, he wouldn't have done so. He wasn't about to admit it to Cecil Orvitz, but he was just as happy to let them go. Gene particularly; he had a wife and kids at home.

Pretty soon, Lewitt mused, he would be seeing his own wife and daughter. The operation had been botched, but the damage was far from irreparable. Rautmann still owed him a million bucks once a nuke was delivered; two million dollars in a numbered Swiss bank account can buy a lot of freedom, especially in South America. Lisa wouldn't understand at first, but she would get used to it. . . .

He shook it off. There would be plenty of time later to make plans. Right now, he had a job to do.

"Ghost Rider, we've got you on final approach at angles one-five," he said into his headset mike. "You're looking good for touchdown, over."

Understood, Blue Falcon. The Russian pilot's voice was distracted; he was undoubtedly focused on the task of landing his craft within the confines of the crater.

As if to underline the point, a second voice—this one American, a Southerner judging by his accent—came over the link. *Ahh . . . Blue Falcon, we see some movement within the crater. Are you sure the perimeter has been safed?*

Lewitt pursed his lips. He glanced again at the monitor. Ryer and Parnell were climbing into Tractor One; in another few minutes they would be gone.

"A couple of guys escaped," he replied. "Don't worry about them. They can't do anything."

Orvitz brayed laughter; Lewitt gave him a look which shut the younger man up immediately. There was little Parnell or Ryer could do now except return to *Conestoga*. Even when they alerted the Wheel by radio and informed them as to what had happened at Teal Falcon, there was nothing anyone could do to prevent Ghost Rider from taking as many warheads as they wanted.

Lewitt's most immediate problem was leaving the bunker. When Parnell had blown the airlock hatch, he had not only killed Markus Talsbach, he had also decompressed Level 1A. Fortunately, Aachener had slammed shut the 2A hatch and sealed it, so the blowout had been limited to the top level of Unit A. The rest of the bunker remained pressurized, and they had enough oxygen to last at least two more weeks.

However, the three of them couldn't leave the base. There were no other exits besides the airlock, and that was separated from them by the suit-up room on Level 1A, which was exposed to hard vacuum.

This was a minor detail, however. Ghost Rider's crew had been informed of the emergency; they knew that there were three men in the bunker who needed to be rescued. All someone had to do was enter the airlock, close the hatches, and repressurize the rest of the bunker.

We copy, Blue Falcon, the American replied. *We're coming in for landing.*

There was another pause. When the voice returned, it was tinted with vague humor. *By the way, Ghost Rider pilot wants to know where we should send your share of . . .*

Abruptly, the transmission was cut off.

What the hell . . . ?

"Ghost Rider, this is Blue Falcon." Lewitt stared at the radar screen as the blip entered the innermost circle of the bull's-eye. "We don't copy. Please repeat, over."

•   •   •

Parnell stopped the tractor inside the pass at the top of the crater wall. It was impossible to tell whether the guns were still operational, but to make certain, he transmitted the six-digit code which would assure their safe passage through the security buffer. At least he hoped so; he was taking Ryer's analysis of the situation entirely on faith.

That done, he turned around in his seat and peered through the driver's dome at the crater below him.

The craft that had touched down on the far side of Sabine Crater was the stuff of legend. Back in the sixties, when Parnell had been training for Project Luna, rumors had circulated within the Space Force about a nuclear spacecraft the Russians were secretly developing to beat Eagle One to the Moon. It later turned out the stories were true; however, Zenith-One had exploded on the launch pad, while Zenith-Two had apparently been dismantled for scrap metal.

Now he knew differently. Zenith-Two rested on its tripod landing gear, a streamlined, spike-nosed needle eighty feet tall, like something from an old George Pal movie. Pale lights glowed from its cockpit windows; halfway down the sleek fuselage, a red star was painted across the hull.

Good God, Ryer said from below, gazing through a window in the passenger compartment. *Where did they find that antique?*

Parnell shrugged. "Probably stashed away in a warehouse in Siberia. Purchased for a few billion dollars, shipped by freight train into North Korea, refurbished in the mountains . . . who knows? They've got it now."

A few days ago, he and Joe Laughlin had been worrying about whether North Korea had developed a reliable satellite launcher. This was better than that: a surplus nuclear spacecraft, capable of dropping nukes wherever its owners pleased. The Zenith was almost a generation old, to be sure, but who needed the latest technology if the objectives remained basic?

As they watched, a cargo hatch yawned open on the vessel's underbelly. A few moments later the slender boom of a crane began to telescope outward. Within the hatch, they could see the tiny form of a spacesuited figure.

"They'll be going for one of the missiles now," Parnell said. "All they have to do is climb down one of the silos, cut open the payload faring, and help themselves." He shook his head. "They don't even have to settle for one nuke . . . they can bring home as many as they can fit into the cargo bay."

Oh, man . . . For someone whom he had once suspected of being a turncoat, Cris sounded properly mortified. *Gene, we've got to stop them . . .*

Parnell laughed out loud. "How? We don't even have a gun anymore . . . I lost mine during the blowout. You think we stand a chance?"

We can head back to the base, she insisted. *There are mortar rockets stored in the garage, the ones they used for geological research. We can rig one up, fire it at the crater . . .*

"And probably miss," he said. "Have you ever fired one? I never did."

But we can figure out . . .

"Maybe we could. But even if we managed to hit something, what would happen? If we're lucky, we'd destroy their ship . . . and probably touch off a nuclear explosion. Do you want to be that close to a nuke when it blows? I don't."

Goddammit, Gene! Ryer crawled forward to the short ladder leading to the pilot's dome; there wasn't enough room for both of them, so she futilely grabbed the right leg of his suit, shaking it to get his attention. *We can't just let them get away with it!*

Suddenly, Parnell felt very tired. He had been fighting this battle for more than half his life. Before, it had been the Russians; now, it was with North Koreans flying secondhand Russian spaceships. In ten or twenty years, if he lived long enough and cared anymore, it would be with the Iranians or the Libyans or God knew who else managed to get their hands on cast-off technology to fulfill some cheap political ambition.

Such are the battles younger men wage, when their blood is hot with ideology and their minds are filled with unbetrayed dreams. He was an old man now, though, and he was fed up with this bullshit.

We've got to do something! Cris shouted.

In response, Parnell put his hand on the gearshift and shoved it forward, then released his foot from the brake pedal.

Ryer was pitched back as the tractor lurched forward, crawl-
ing through the excavated pass and down the far side of the
crater.

"Sure we can do something," he said. "We can go
home."

Nine miles away, *Conestoga* was waiting for them, with
enough fuel left in its tanks for the voyage back to the Wheel.
He was alive. That must count for something.

"See ya 'round, Jay," he whispered, not looking back at
the bunker. "I hope it was worth it to you."

The men in the bunker hadn't heard anything from Ghost
Rider since the Zenith touched down. Again and again, Lewitt
hailed the North Korean vessel, only to be met with dead
silence. He was beginning to harbor serious doubts when the
voice of the Russian commander abruptly came over the comlink:

Blue Falcon, this is Ghost Rider. Come in, over.

"It's about time," Orvitz murmured as Lewitt let out his
breath. He had long since given up on trying to restore the
computers to operating status. The virus had totally infiltrated
the mainframes, and even though it had been knocked out by
a system reboot, it was then that he discovered that the missile
c-cube system had been obliterated in the process. If there
were backup files, they were located a quarter of a million
miles away, in Crystal Palace's computers.

Lewitt ignored the erstwhile Paul Dooley. "We copy,
Ghost Rider. Nice landing. We were wondering about the
LOS. Over."

Behind him, he heard Uwe Aachener stand up from where
he had been sitting at the bottom of the ladder. The German
astronaut had found some stale candy bars in a food locker
in the galley. They were the only food left behind, and undoubtedly several years old; that hadn't prevented Aachener
from attempting to eat them. He crumpled a paper wrapper
and tossed it in the bloodstained corner of the firing room,
where Rhodes's and Bromleigh's bodies had lain before he
had removed them to the bunk compartment.

The Russian commander's voice resumed. *I apologize for*

the delay, Mr. Lewitt, but we have encountered some . . . ah, difficulties up here.

"I'm sorry to hear that," Lewitt replied.

It appears that some members of your landing party have managed to successfully escape, Ghost Rider continued. *We saw their vehicle leaving the crater just a few minutes ago. Do you know anything about this? Over.*

Lewitt smiled. Just as well; despite all that had happened, he bore no real animosity toward Gene or Cris. "I understand, Ghost Rider. There was nothing we could do to prevent it. We lost a member of our own team in trying to stop them."

A brief pause. *I see. And you say that the bunker airlock has been voided, is that correct? And the top level?*

"That's right, Commander. We're trapped on the lower levels." Lewitt hesitated, feeling uneasy, not quite knowing why. "Of course, when you send one of your crew down here, he should be able to repressurize the airlock and Level 1A."

Yes, that's true. Another pause, a little longer this time. *Even so, we yet have a small problem. Since you and your team members were expected to return aboard the* Conestoga, *we did not anticipate to supply . . . um, accommodations for three extra crew members.*

Cecil Orvitz went dead white. "What the fuck is he . . . ?"

Lewitt furtively motioned for him to shut up. Ignoring him, Orvitz snatched up his own headset. "You son of a bitch, that was part of—!"

"Shut up!" Lewitt snapped. He hunched over the console, cradling the headset in his hands. "Look, Ghost Rider . . . Yuri . . . the deal with Wolff-Deiter was that . . ."

I am quite sorry, Ghost Rider interrupted, *but the deal, as you say, has been changed. We shall require extra payload capacity to bring back some . . . ah, new baggage.*

"You asshole!" Orvitz screamed. "You fucking bastard! Get us out of here!"

There was a long silence from the other end of the channel. After a few moments, the Zenith's commanding officer spoke again.

I am truly sorry, he said, *but further conversation is point-*

less. Perhaps you can convince the Americans to assist you. Ghost Rider over and out.

And then there was nothing but static.

Lewitt felt a warm presence next to him. Then a hand reached past his shoulder. Before he could react, Uwe Aachener snatched up the Colt from the desktop where Lewitt had placed it. When he looked up at him, Aachener's face was impassive.

Orvitz's mouth trembled. For the first time since they had met, the man who had pretended to be Paul Dooley was absolutely speechless.

Lewitt swallowed a hard, dry lump in his throat. He toggled the vox switch. "Ghost Rider, this is Blue Falcon. Please respond, over."

Aachener studied the gun in his hand. Then he returned it to the desk and took a few steps back. He crossed his arms and stared at Lewitt.

"Ghost Rider, please come in." Lewitt stared at the TV monitor. Two astronauts were stepping off the elevator; neither of them headed toward the camera. "Please come in, over."

He waited. No reply. "This is Blue Falcon, please come in."

The static on the comlink was broken once more, for only an instant, by a sound that resembled distant laughter, as if echoing across space from a remote galaxy.

And then they heard nothing else except their own voices, until the oxygen supply finally began to run out.

By then, they had settled the question of who would use the gun first.

From The Washington Post; *February 23, 1995*

Lunar Mission Survivors Safely Return, Recount Sudden Death on the Moon
By Timothy S. Smith
Special Correspondent

SPACE STATION ONE—Three days after lifting off from Tranquillity Base, the U.S.S. *Conestoga* arrived in Earth orbit, bringing with it the two sole survivors of the American-German lunar expedition that came to a disastrous end when a freak electrical fire swept through the Teal Falcon military complex.

The two NASA astronauts, Com. Eugene M. Parnell and Capt. Cristine S. Ryer, were taken off the returning moonship in what space station doctors described as "stable and satisfactory condition." They were hurried to the Wheel's infirmary to receive treatment for extensive second-degree burns, minor sprains and contusions, prolonged effects of smoke inhalation, and acute exhaustion.

In a brief interview several hours after his arrival, commander Parnell told reporters of the blaze that swept through the underground bunker just as his team was preparing to launch six Minutemen II missiles.

"It was horrible," he said, speaking from his bed in the station infirmary. "Everything seemed to go up at once. We were lucky to get out of there alive."

Captain Ryer said, "There was no way we could get anyone else out. Gene and I were fortunate that we were able to make it to the airlock in time . . . it was terrifying, just awful."

"I'm sorry that nobody else got out alive," said Space Station One Commander Joseph K. Laughlin of the accident which killed five astronauts, as well as ATS television correspondents Berkley Rhodes and Alex Bromleigh. "It was a terrible tragedy . . . I'm just glad that two people managed to make it out, safe and sound."

NASA spokesmen were unable to give an exact reason for the cause of the fire. They said that the leading theory is that old electrical cables within the twenty-six-year-old military installation may have decayed, causing a fatal short-circuit during activation of the launch-control systems that were supposed to fire the missiles last Sunday.

Until further investigation, however, the space agency is not willing to commit itself to any specific explanation. . . .

TWENTY-TWO

After he had been interviewed by the reporters who had flown up from the Cape, the doctor ushered them out of the infirmary. Once they were gone, Parnell detached the cosmetic IV line that led beneath his bandaged right arm, pushed aside the sheets, and swung his legs over the side of the bed, demonstrating an ability to walk unassisted that ran contrary to the story that had been fed to the press.

"How much longer am I going to have to wear this stuff?" He rubbed his left hand over the bandages. "They itch like crazy."

"Not too much longer," Joe Laughlin said. He was standing at the back of the room, where he had silently watched the entire orchestrated affair. "When we fly you down to KSC tomorrow, you and Cris will be taken off the orbiter in stretchers. There'll be camera crews, of course, but neither of you have to say anything if you don't want to."

"Is she talking to them now?" Parnell nodded toward the closed door of the intensive care unit.

"Yeah. She's following the same script." Old Joe smiled at his friend's astonishment. "Don't be so shocked. She's got more to lose than you do, trying to pull that stunt with the virus program. This way at least she gets off clean . . . so long as she sticks to the official version."

As the doctor—who really wasn't a doctor, but the CIA

case officer who had debriefed Parnell and Ryer after they brought *Conestoga* back to the Wheel—fetched a plastic cup of water from the sink, Laughlin put his left foot up on a chair and tied the laces of his sneakers. "She still hasn't told us everything about that disk," he went on. "We still don't know why she was carrying it. Do you know anything about it?"

Parnell hesitated. He didn't particularly want to squeal on Cris—she had saved his life, after all—but he knew that the boys from Langley would eventually get at the truth. Better they heard it from a reliable source; this way he could vouch for her and perhaps ease the repercussions.

"Yeah, she gave me the whole story on the way home," Gene replied. "It contains a nasty little bug called Dr. Doolittle . . ."

"Because it talks to the animals?"

"Just a pun. Do little . . . get it?" Laughlin rolled his eyes and Parnell went on. "Anyway, she picked it up from some college kid at Florida State, a computer hacker she managed to track down somehow. The kid thought she was just a disgruntled employee from a local company who wanted to fuck up the in-house computer system, so he gave it to her. Your typical campus prank."

"Yeah, right." Old Joe shook his head. The CIA man, who had identified himself only as Mr. Taylor, stood quietly nearby, undoubtedly memorizing everything for his report. "Used to be that a college prank meant putting a bunch of pigs in the dean's office."

"Anyway," Parnell went on, "she was planning to install it in the computers at Teal Falcon and the base just before we left. The idea was to screw things up so that when Koenig Selenen took possession of the base, they'd find that none of the computers were operational. No one could have proved she was responsible, if they even suspected her."

Gene looked straight at Taylor. "It was supposed to be her revenge for getting dismissed from the Air Force. Nothing to do with . . . y'know, everything else that happened." Taylor nodded his head in a neutral way, but said nothing. "It was fortunate that she had that disk," Parnell asserted. "Otherwise . . ." He fell silent.

Laughlin coughed in his hand. "Anyway, to answer your question, you guys get to take off the bandages when you arrive at the Cape infirmary. As far as the media's concerned, you're going to be recovering from . . . uh . . ."

"Second-degree burns, multiple cuts and contusions, mild smoke inhalation, acute exhaustion," Taylor said, handing the water he'd fetched to Parnell. "Don't worry, Commander, we won't keep you in the hospital for long. In two or three days we'll let you go home. You'll have recovered by then."

Parnell drank the water in silence. In two or three days, Taylor's colleagues at the Cape would have also learned everything they needed to know about what really happened in the bunker, and the "accidental fire" at Teal Falcon that had claimed the lives of most of the expedition would have faded to the back pages. When it came to rigging plausible cover stories, the CIA stood second to none.

He wondered what would happen to Cris. But he'd said and done everything that he could, at least for now.

"So until then, I stay here and play sick." He shrugged and put the water aside. "Do you think I could at least have a real drink? Or am I too sick to be seen drinking whiskey?"

Taylor shook his head. "Sorry, Commander, but you've got to remain here so long as we've got the press aboard. You can't . . ."

"Naw. Don't worry about them." Laughlin sauntered over to the bed and gave Parnell a fond slap on his bare knee. "We've put them in the VIP area. Soon as they're gone from this section, Gene can stretch his legs a bit."

He winked broadly. "In fact, I think can get him to my office without being seen. A little R&R is just what the patient needs, don't you think?"

Taylor looked uncertain. He was under orders to keep Parnell and Ryer under close watch until the heat died down. Before he could protest, however, Laughlin grasped his friend's arm and helped him off the hospital bed. "C'mon, buddy . . . put on your trousers and I'll buy you a drink."

"Commander Laughlin . . ." Taylor began.

Old Joe gave him a look that shut the young man up. "He needs a drink and a walk," he said softly. "So just go empty a bedpan or something, okay?"

The CIA officer didn't like it, but he wasn't in command of the station. Besides, he needed to moderate Ryer's press appearance. There was little he could do to physically prevent Parnell from being sneaked out of the infirmary. Taylor nodded his head, then exited the room.

Once Gene was dressed, Laughlin escorted him through a hatch and down a ladder, where they followed a vacant corridor through Level B. "Nice touch," Parnell said softly as they walked through the upward-curving hallway. "Take me to your office, indeed . . ."

Laughlin grinned. "Couldn't have been done in the old days. Remember when we had resident spooks aboard?" He shook his head. "These young ones couldn't find the john without a map."

He stopped at the hatch leading to the Earth Observation Center. He laid his hand on the handle, but didn't open it. "But you've got to promise me one thing," Laughlin whispered. "When they put you under the bright lights, you don't breathe a word about what I'm going to show you. Understand?"

Mystified, Parnell nodded. No longer smiling, Laughlin opened the door and led Parnell into the dimly lit compartment.

Old Joe went straight to the bank of TV monitors. "You know where I keep the bottle. Help yourself." He checked his watch, consulted the clocks arranged above the screens, then began to work the ISPY master control panel. "We're right on time."

Parnell hesitated, then opened the locker and pulled out the Maker's Mark and a pair of shot glasses. One of the wall clocks told him that it was about 9:25 P.M. in North Korea. According to the little that Taylor had told him, the Zenith had landed just eight hours ago at the hidden rocket base in the country's northern highlands, shortly before he and Ryer had managed to guide *Conestoga* safely back to its orbital hangar. The spacecraft was probably back in its assembly building, where technicians were unloading the nukes its crew had stolen from the Teal Falcon silos.

However, ISPY wasn't over Southeast Asia. According to its ground track on the electronic map board, the orbital telescope was above the western United States, its footprint swinging down across northern California into southern Nevada. Long morning shadows stretched out across the Sierra Nevada; according to the clock, local time was 7:35 A.M. RMT.

Parnell's hand paused on the cap of the whiskey bottle. What the hell . . . ?

As if he could read his thoughts, Laughlin spoke softly from the console. "You must have heard of this place," he said, not looking up from the keyboard and dials. "Groom Lake. Area 51. Dreamland . . . whatever you want to call it, it's there. One of the best-kept secrets in the free world. At least that's what they say."

"Yeah. I've heard about it." Parnell watched the screens as ISPY's cameras swept across the high-mountain desert northwest of Las Vegas. Everything from the U-2 and the SR-71 spy planes to the F-117 and the B-2 Stealth attack craft had been flight-tested from there. Not so much of a secret now, after the press had blown the lid off a couple of years ago, with reports of odd noises coming from the secret landing strip.

"What about it?"

"Wait a second . . . okay." On the high-resolution screen, a long airstrip had appeared. The camera tracked across paved tarmac, passing rows of hangars, offices, and warehouses.

"Now," Laughlin said, pointing at the bottom of the screen. "Look there, quick."

Parnell stepped closer to the screen, peering at the spot where Laughlin was pointing. Captured for a few moments within ISPY's focal lens was a large, dartlike shape . . .

Or, rather, two shapes: a silver form similar to an F-117, mounted atop a larger, black craft which vaguely resembled an SR-71. "That's *Aurora*," Laughlin said, tapping the screen with his fingertip. "The bottom craft is the mother ship, *Senior Citizen*. It takes the bird on top up to high altitude, where it lets go. The little bastard on top is code-named Thunder Dart . . . it climbs to suborbit with scramjets."

Parnell nodded. "The new recon plane. I've heard the stories . . ."

"C'mon, Gene. You think we'd scrap the Blackbird just to

build another recon plane?'' Laughlin stepped away from the
console, picked up the whiskey bottle, and poured himself a
shot. ''It's capable of reaching low orbit in minutes, and it
can be anywhere in the world within an hour. Usually they
only fly it at night, to avoid anyone getting a good look at it.
Now, why do you think they'd haul it out of the hangar in
broad daylight?''

Parnell stared at the image on the screen. No, it didn't make
much sense to wheel *Aurora* out of its hangar at this time of
day if it was just another test flight. Dreamland's secrecy had
already been compromised by too many curious people
watching from adjacent foothills; when the Air Force wanted
to test one of its black planes, it did so under the cover of
darkness.

He looked up at the clocks again. But over in North Korea,
it was a dark, moonless night . . .

''Now let me ask you something else,'' Old Joe said. He
poured a shot of liquor into another glass and offered it to
Parnell. ''Doesn't it seem peculiar, knowing all that we do
now, that the CIA ignored everything I told them about the
North Korean launch site?''

Parnell accepted the glass. On the screen, Area 51 was
already passing from sight, lost as ISPY began to fly over
Utah. ''Maybe not,'' he said, not accepting the lie even as he
repeated it. ''They might have known about it, but just didn't
let on.''

Laughlin shrugged. ''You got a point. They didn't trust me.
But does it make sense that British and German intelligence
caught wind of this conspiracy, but didn't let the Americans
know?''

He tossed back the shot of whiskey and hissed between his
teeth. ''SIS went so far as to put Leamore on this mission.
Do you really believe, for even a second, that the Brits
wouldn't let our guys know that they thought someone
wanted to steal some American nukes?''

Laughlin picked up the bottle and poured another shot.
''When Dr. Z told me about what Gabrielle Blumfield had
told him, I went straight to the CIA. They ignored me. Poppa
Dog saw something lift off from Earth when y'all launched
from orbit. He told me about it later, and I tried to tell NASA

and the CIA, and they still ignored me. Now . . . do you really think all those sharp minds back home are that stupid?''

Parnell didn't reply. He tried to sip his own whiskey, but his hand was trembling too much. It splattered across his chin, and he wiped it off with the back of his left hand. "Maybe they were . . ."

He stumbled, unable to complete the thought that had entered his mind. It was too much, the idea that so much had been risked, so many lives had been put in danger—and ultimately lost—simply because of the same old games that had been waged and lost before.

And yet, and still . . .

The shot glass slipped from his fingers.

He barely noticed when it hit the floor, splashing liquor across the carpet.

"They knew," he murmured. "They knew about everything."

Both men were silent for a moment; then Laughlin bent down and picked up the glass. He refilled it from the bottle and passed it to his friend. "The plan was rigged from both ends," he said quietly. "The Koreans weren't the only ones carrying an ace up their sleeve. Sometime today or tomorrow, we're probably going to hear about an oil refinery in North Korea blowing up. Lots of lives lost. Very tragic . . ."

Laughlin sighed as he settled down in a chair. "Y'know, though, the real bitch isn't whether or not some third-rate country gets the bomb or not. These days, anyone can do that. That's simple stuff. But the fact that the same technology we could have used to take back the Moon, put a colony on Mars, maybe even . . ."

"I know. You don't have to lecture me." This time, Parnell managed to drink his whiskey without spilling it. Nonetheless, it took a lot of courage just to swallow past the bile which had risen in his throat.

He had just caught a glimpse of an aircraft that was capable of rendering NASA's space fleet obsolete. It remained a classified secret, tucked away in a hangar on a desert airstrip.

Games within games. Lies within lies. Meanwhile, the future is slowly lost, like one speck of sand moving past the

last one, through an hourglass that can never be set upright
again.

"Sorry. Didn't mean to get on a high horse." Laughlin
reached for the bottle. He offered it to Parnell, who shook his
head. "Still, it kind of makes you wonder," he continued,
pouring another finger of whiskey into his glass. "I mean,
what might have happened if things had gone differently."

"That's bullshit." Gene finished the half-inch of brown
liquor in his glass. He looked over his shoulder at the TV
screen, watching as Earth passed serenely beneath his feet. It
was a moot point, the type of question only a drunk old man
would raise.

History can't be changed.

EPILOGUE

Another beach, another house, another party: this time not a pre-launch barbecue at the Cape, but a small evening get-together with a couple of new friends at Gene Parnell's home on Captiva.

As the Gulf sunset tinted the waters of Pine Island Sound with color like autumn leaves, Gene grilled swordfish on the patio hibachi, watching Cris and Laurell as they stood lookout on the beach for the dolphins that sometimes played in the inlet at sundown. They had driven down from Titusville the day before, and although he and Judith had offered them the guest room, the two women had politely demurred, preferring to stay at a hotel on the mainland. They said that it was because they wanted to catch a Cardinals spring-training game in Fort Meyers on Saturday and had to leave early Monday morning in order to make their flight to Germany out of Orlando later that evening.

Still, Gene couldn't help wondering if it was because Cris felt uncomfortable about having Laurell with her, even though he and Judy had invited them both.

"Don't worry about it," Judith murmured, reading his mind. She stood nearby, tossing salad in a wooden bowl. "They're a young couple, that's all. They want their privacy."

"Helen never had any problem bringing her boyfriend here . . ."

"That's because Helen's your daughter," Judith said. "Look at it this way . . . wouldn't you have felt strange about having your girlfriend spend the night with you at the boss's house?"

"Ex-boss, you mean," he replied.

A sudden shout from the beach brought his head up. Cris and Laurell were pointing to where a dolphin had jumped. Cris glanced over her shoulder at him; she was letting her hair grow out, and in that instant when the breeze caught it and blew it in front of her smiling face, he realized what a beautiful woman she was.

"And in my case," he added, still watching her, "it would have been my boyfriend . . ."

A stifled giggle from Judy. He caught a glimpse of her grin before she covered it with her hand. "Why, Gene," she whispered. "You never told me you swung both ways."

If they didn't have guests present, he might have thrown his spatula at her.

As nervous as he had been about meeting Laurell—Judith had no reservations whatsoever—the evening went smoothly. Before dinner they sat around the patio table, sipping Scotch-and-water and watching the sun go down through the palms, chatting idly about the Cards, a minor hurricane that had hit Key West last week, the alligator that sometimes paid a visit to the Parnells' backyard from the nearby swamp. Over blackened swordfish and Italian salad they discussed Cris's upcoming job interview in Germany; if Koenig Selenen offered her the job, she and Laurell planned to temporarily relocate to Bonn for her training period, then eventually move to French Guiana, where they would live near the launch center.

That was as close as they got to talking about space, though. Cris avoided any mention of NASA or her old job, and when talk of Koenig Selenen inevitably wandered toward the Tranquillity Base mission, Judith tactfully changed the topic to the burgeoning real estate development on Captiva. Which turned out to be an unfortunate *faux pas,* since Laurell's law firm was representing a developer who wanted to buy seventy-five acres of wetland on the island's gulf shore and transform it into a condominium complex. But at least it was safer than discussing space.

Eventually, though, the subject had to come up again.

Gene had already told his wife what he meant to do, and Judy took her cue when he asked about key lime pie. When she stood up to collect the dinner dishes, Judy asked Laurell if she would like to help serve dessert, and Laurell followed her into the kitchen. That left Gene on the patio with Cris for a few minutes.

Alone for the first time since they had returned from the Moon two months ago, neither one of them knew quite what to say. Cris gazed silently across the bay at the small cluster of house lights on Pine Island while Gene searched for the right words. Although he had been mentally rehearsing a little speech for several weeks, now that it was time to deliver it, his mind had gone completely blank.

Finally, he gave up. Clearing his throat, he said, "I've got something for you."

Cris looked around as he dug into the pocket of his trousers and pulled out a small velvet box he had retrieved from his office desk a little while earlier. "It's not much," he said as he slid it across the patio table to her, "but . . . y'know, maybe it'll come in handy, next time you . . ."

He fell silent, watching as she picked up the box and opened it.

Cris's eyes widened in surprise. "Oh my God, Commander . . ."

"Gene," he said. It was the first time she had referred to him by his former rank since she'd arrived. "I keep telling you, my friends call me Gene."

The patio lights reflected the 18-karat gold of the Rolex aviator watch as she removed it from the box and turned it over in her hands. Her sharp eyes caught the tiny inscription etched on the back of the chronometer. She held the watch up closer and read it carefully, and for a fleeting moment Gene wondered if he had gone too far. The gift had been intended to heal an old wound, but it was possible that he might have ripped it open instead.

Any doubts, though, were erased when she smiled and nodded her head. "Thanks, Gene," she said, "but you know it isn't true."

"No way," he said, shaking his head. "You saved my life up there, got us both back alive. We wouldn't be here now if it wasn't for you." Another moment of uncertainty. "Maybe Uncle Sam doesn't see it that way, but . . ."

"Let's not talk about it." It seemed to him that her eyes glistened a little as she snapped off her Timex, put it in a pocket of her summer skirt, and wrapped the Rolex around her left wrist. "Uncle Sam and I have our problems, but that's not between you and me."

At least, not any longer.

He picked up his glass and jiggled half-melted ice cubes around in the tiny bit of Scotch left. No apologies had been left unspoken during the long voyage back from Tranquillity Base. If Koenig Selenen was able to forgive Cristine Ryer by offering her a job as a lunar pilot with its private space program, so Cris could forgive him for distrusting her during the *Conestoga* mission.

This was a going-away party, after all. For both of them. His NASA career was formally over, and her new life was just beginning. While he played around with his Beechcraft, worked on perfecting his stroke at the Sanibel Golf Club, and tried to keep his son out of trouble, she would be flying German spacecraft to the Moon. There was still a frontier to be settled, and giving her a watch was only another way of passing the torch.

And neither of them, either publicly or privately, would ever discuss what had really occurred in the Teal Falcon bunker. Except for Judith, Laurell, and a few people on a strictly need-to-know basis in the intelligence community, no one would ever learn the truth. Even if anyone else happened to read the inscription on the back of Cris's watch, it could easily be explained away as an expression of heartfelt appreciation from a former commander to his former first officer.

There is history, and there is truth, and the two seldom have much in common with each other. . . .

But, he thought as he gazed at the gold watch, perhaps there is still enough time for history to be changed.

"Thanks, Gene," she said.

"Thank you, Cris," he replied, tipping his glass to her. "I hope you and Laurell have a good life together."

Judith and Laurell returned with key lime pie and coffee, and not long afterward the party broke up. They made their farewells in front of the house; Cris and Gene gave each other a final hug, then she and Laurell climbed into their DeLorean and backed down the driveway to the main road. Gene and Judith waved goodbye as they watched them leave, then went inside to finish cleaning up.

Judith was still washing dishes when Gene poured himself another finger of Scotch and quietly took it out to the patio. Once the counters were scrubbed and the leftovers put away, Judith went out to see what he was doing.

She found him sprawled in a lawn chair, his eyes closed, his hands still nestling his Scotch against his belly which gently rose and fell with each slumbering breath he took. Judith considered waking him, but decided that he was content where he lay. Instead, she went inside to get a blanket and, after gently prying the glass out of his hands, she laid the blanket over him.

Then she went inside, shut the doors, and turned off the patio lights, letting him sleep in the light of the rising moon.

AFTERWORD

The Tranquillity Alternative is a continuation of two short stories I wrote several years ago: "John Harper Wilson," first published in the June 1989 issue of *Isaac Asimov's Science Fiction Magazine,* and its prequel, "Goddard's People," published in the July 1991 issue of that same magazine and in *What Might Have Been, Vol. III,* edited by Gregory Benford and Martin H. Greenberg (Bantam, 1991). An early, substantially different version of "Goddard's People," titled "Operation Blue Horizon," was published in the September 1988 issue of *Worcester Monthly,* a now-defunct city magazine.

Both "Goddard's People" and "John Harper Wilson" are included in my collection *Rude Astronauts.* This novel is independent of those stories, however; they simply relate background events behind the alternative timeline that forms the basis of this story. Many thanks to Gardner Dozois and Sheila Williams at *Asimov's,* and Michael Warshaw at *Worcester Monthly,* for publishing the original stories.

Likewise, it should be pointed out that most of the technology depicted in this novel is not entirely the product of the author's imagination. The ferry rockets, Space Station One, the MP-13 retriever rocket, the lunar base and other hardware were invented in the 1950s and detailed in some keystone nonfiction works of that bygone era: *Across the Space Frontier* (Viking, 1952) and *Conquest of the Moon*

(Viking, 1953), both edited by Cornelius Ryan; *The Exploration of Mars,* by Willy Ley and Wernher von Braun (Viking, 1956). These books were drawn from the historic *Collier's* space series which ran between 1952 and 1956. Many thanks to the staff of the St. Louis City Library for helping me locate its bound copies of these magazines.

Rockets through Space, by Lester del Rey (Fawcett/Premier, 1960) and *Rockets, Missiles, and Space Travel,* by Willy Ley (Viking, 1951) were other important contemporary sources.

Two recent books about the history of spaceflight have served as invaluable references: *Blueprint for Space,* by Frederick I. Ordway III and Randy Liebermann (Smithsonian Institution Press, 1992) and *The Dream Machines,* by Ron Miller (Krieger Publishing, 1993), both highly recommended. Many thanks to Ron for his enthusiastic support of this project and for pointing me in the right direction.

While I was researching this novel, the Glencoe Model Company reissued several plastic scale-model kits of spacecraft based upon the designs documented in those books, complete with technical specs. At about the same time, I located an out-of-production model of the "space taxi" Willy Ley proposed in 1959. Some of these models were written into this novel, although I took liberties with the internal details. Thanks to Chris Merseal and the late Dot Hill at CRM Hobbies in St. Louis for their assistance and suggestions.

During World War II, upon the proposal of Dr. Eugen Sanger of the Luftwaffe Institute, the Nazis briefly considered building a manned suborbital spacecraft called the "Amerika Bomber." Details of this spacecraft can be found in *Rockets, Missiles, and Space Travel* and "The High-Flying Legacy of Eugen Sanger" by Helmut Muller (*Air & Space,* August/September 1987). I also wish to thank my old friend and neighbor, Joe Thompson, Jr., who flew recon missions over Peenemunde during the war, for sharing his memories with me.

During the late fifties the U.S. Air Force seriously considered placing nuclear missiles on the Moon. "Securing the High Ground" by William E. Burrows (*Air & Space,* December 1993/January 1994) was one source of information; more details were obtained from articles published in *Aviation Week* during 1958 and 1959, and in *Science Digest,* May 1958.

At this writing, the Air Force's "Aurora" program is still a closely guarded military secret, although a number of articles concerning a hypersonic aerospacecraft have been published in newspapers and magazines over the last couple of years. *Aurora,* by Bill Sweetman (Motorbooks Mil-Tech Series, 1993) is recommended as a comprehensive rundown of this "black plane" project.

While filling in the fine details of the alternate history behind this novel, I opened a folder on the science fiction board formerly sponsored by *Asimov's Science Fiction* on the America Online computer network and asked for suggestions. Several AOL subscribers responded to my request, and some of their remarks made their way into this book. For their involvement in this experiment in reader participation, I wish to thank Patterner, ASterling, Spacer 9704, Surf Nut, Jimmysd and Billbeau. Keep on posting, guys.

Many thanks to Kevin J. Anderson, Lizz Caplan, Nicola Griffith, Kelly Eskridge, Frank Jacobs, Kenneth Jobe, Marilee J. Layman, Eugene Moore, George Olive, Henry Tiedemann, and Mark W. Tiedemann, for their expert knowledge and insights.

Special thanks, as always, go to my wife, Linda, my agent, Martha Millard, and Ginjer Buchanan, Susan Allison, and Carol Lowe at Ace.

One aspect of this novel that may be controversial among space aficionados is whether the United States had the technological capability to launch a manned spacecraft in 1944, thereby shortcutting almost two decades of "real" history. I'll leave it to historians, scientists, and engineers to debate this point, but this I can safely claim as fact: when Robert A. Goddard was a physics professor at Clark College in Worcester, Massachusetts, he secretly researched manned space travel. His notebooks, hidden in a file cabinet within a folder labeled "gunpowder experiments," contained detailed studies for spaceplanes, gyroscopic steering systems, radiation protection of astronauts, even a rudimentary form of atomic propulsion . . . all written during 1928, thirty years before NASA launched *Explorer 1* into orbit.

Many thanks to Dorothy Mosokowski, the curator of the Goddard Archives at Clark University, for showing me Dr. Goddard's notebooks and for telling me how to find the hilltop site on Pakachoag Hill in Auburn, Massachusetts, where he launched the world's first liquid-fuel rocket, and where the inspiration for this novel first came to me.

—October 1993–May 1994
St. Louis, Missouri